"Your medallion," the man said, gesturing with his chin toward the mandala resting on Tim Pennington's chest. "It is quite unusual. How did you acquire it?"

The manner in which the man asked his question made Pennington uncomfortable. "A friend gave it to me."

"Odd," the man said. "Such rarities are usually bequeathed only to family members."

Pennington broke eye contact and tried to sidestep the Vulcan. "You must be mistaken."

Blocking his path, the Vulcan said, "It comes from the commune at Kren'than, does it not?"

At the mention of T'Prynn's native village, a technology-free retreat populated by mystics and ascetics, Pennington froze. He suspected the man was not really interested in the medallion. Facing him, Pennington was wary as he said, "Yes, it does."

"As I thought," the man said.

The Vulcan handed him a scrap of fragile parchment that had been folded in half. As soon as Pennington took hold of it, the stranger walked away at a brisk pace and blended back into the earth-toned sea of robed Vulcans crowding the spaceport.

Pennington unfolded the note.

There were three things written on it: a set of geographic coordinates, a precise time, and a date exactly three weeks in the future.

He folded it and put it in

STAR TREK®
VANGUARD

Precipice

DAVID MACK

Based upon *Star Trek*
created by Gene Roddenberry

POCKET BOOKS

New York   London   Toronto   Sydney   Golmira

Pocket Books
A Division of Simon & Schuster, Inc.
1230 Avenue of the Americas
New York, NY 10020

This book is a work of fiction. Names, characters, places, and incidents either are products of the author's imagination or are used fictitiously. Any resemblance to actual events or locales or persons, living or dead, is entirely coincidental.

First Pocket Books paperback edition December 2009

POCKET and colophon are registered trademarks of Simon & Schuster, Inc.

For information about special discounts for bulk purchases, please contact Simon & Schuster Special Sales at 1-866-506-1949 or business@simonandschuster.com.

The Simon & Schuster Speakers Bureau can bring authors to your live event. For more information or to book an event contact the Simon & Schuster Speakers Bureau at 1-866-248-3049 or visit our website at www.simonspeakers.com.

Design by Alan Dingman
Art by Doug Drexler

Manufactured in the United States of America

10 9 8 7 6 5 4 3 2 1

ISBN 978-1-4391-3011-7
ISBN 978-1-4391-6651-2 (ebook)

For my brother:
thanks for always being on my side.

Historian's Note

This story takes place in 2267, beginning in early January and concluding at the end of December, a few weeks after the events of the second-season *Star Trek* episode "A Private Little War."

Good and bad men are each
less so than they seem.

—*Samuel Taylor Coleridge, 1830*

Precipice

PART ONE

Such Deliberate Disguises

1

Disruptor pulses thundered against the unshielded hull of the Starfleet transport *U.S.S. Nowlan*.

On the *Nowlan*'s bridge, Diego Reyes clenched his jaw and winced. The forward bulkhead blasted inward. Reyes ducked behind the command chair as shrapnel flew past and pattered to the deck around him. Fine, metallic dust rained down on his shoulders and into his thinning steel-gray hair.

He looked up from behind the chair and peered through bitter smoke to see the ship's commanding officer, Lieutenant Commander Brandon Easton, lying on the deck, his gold uniform tunic torn by jagged bits of metal and stained heavily with blood. The dull, unfixed quality of Easton's stare was one Reyes had seen far too many times: the man was dead.

Reyes looked aft for Lieutenant Ket, the Bolian security officer who had escorted him from the brig to the bridge minutes earlier. To his dismay, Ket was also gone, the victim of a wedge of duranium lodged in his left temple.

At the forward console, two figures stirred.

The first was the female human navigator and helm officer. She had been lying on the floor, apparently stunned rather than dead. *Lucky gal,* mused Reyes. *If she'd been on her feet, she'd have a faceful of shrapnel right now.* Sitting up from behind the flickering console, which housed the helm and navigator's station on the left and the sensor controls on the right, was the sensor officer, a human man with crew-cut blond hair.

The two shaken officers, both dressed in black trousers and gold command shirts with lieutenant stripes on their cuffs, looked at Reyes with desperate expressions. "Sir?" said the woman, pushing her curly brown hair from her eyes. "What do we do?"

Years of command experience snapped Reyes into action. He nodded at the two officers. "Take your posts." He brushed the grit from the seat of the command chair, then settled into it. "What're your names, lieutenants?"

"Paul Sniadach."

"Bronwen Hodgkinson."

For a moment, Reyes almost forgot that just five weeks earlier he had been convicted in a Starfleet court-martial, stripped of his rank, and sentenced to ten years in a penal colony. All it had taken was a surprise attack by an unidentified and heavily armed pirate vessel to remind him of who he'd been before being branded a criminal:

A starship captain. A flag officer. A leader.

"Hodgkinson, set an evasion course, full impulse. Sniadach, find that ship, and get the shields back up."

"Course set," Hodgkinson replied. "Engines not responding."

Sniadach coaxed his stuttering, half-shorted-out panel back into service. "Hostile vessel bearing one-three-eight-mark-seventeen, coming about at quarter impulse."

Reyes thumbed a comm switch on the armrest of his chair. "Bridge to engineering! We need aft shields! Respond!"

Static was all he heard over the open audio circuit. Engineering had been one of the first sections hit, and a coolant leak had likely forced a temporary evacuation of the deck while the crew struggled into environment suits.

"The enemy vessel is scanning us," Sniadach said. "Closing to ten thousand kilometers." Swiveling his chair to face Reyes, he added with surprise, "They're powering down their weapons."

"Are they hailing us?"

"No, sir," Sniadach said, checking his console.

"Just like pirates," Reyes said with disdain. "They don't even have the courtesy to tell us we're being boarded." He got up from his chair—and belatedly remembered it wasn't really *his* chair. "Prepare to repel boarders," he said, grateful they weren't facing the Klingons, who'd put a price on his head after the Gamma Tauri fiasco. He kneeled beside the slain Lieutenant Ket and took the security officer's phaser from his belt. "Arm yourselves. We're about to have company."

Hodgkinson got up and sprinted to a panel on the port bulkhead. She opened it, revealing four phasers. The brunette took one for herself and lobbed another to Sniadach.

Reyes adjusted the setting of his weapon. "Heavy stun," he said. "Let's not go blowing holes in our own ship."

His order received overlapping replies of "Aye, sir."

An alert tone beeped twice on the sensor console. Sniadach glanced down at the board and confirmed Reyes's suspicion. "Transporter signals," the lieutenant said. "All decks."

"Here they come," Hodgkinson said, readying her phaser. Sniadach did the same as Reyes stepped back between them to form a skirmish line.

A low, eerily musical drone emanated from the aft section of the cramped compartment. A few meters in front of the two Starfleet officers and their prisoner-turned-commander, a compact shape sparkled into view.

It was a fat cylinder about as long as Reyes's hand.

"Down!" shouted Reyes, anticipating the worst.

They ducked behind the forward console. The transporter effect faded, and silence fell upon the bridge.

Then came the soft hiss of gas spewing into the air.

Pale blue mist jetted from one end of the canister and swiftly filled the command deck.

Sprinting toward the emergency equipment, Reyes snapped, "Oxygen masks!"

Hodgkinson and Sniadach were close behind him.

Reyes felt as if he were running on rubber legs. His head spun and his stomach heaved. He pitched forward to the deck. The masks were only a meter away but behind a panel at waist height and out of his reach. He struggled to pull himself forward, but his eyes crossed against his will and left him seeing the world as if through a kaleidoscope.

All his strength ebbed at once, and he collapsed to the deck, rolling onto his back as he fell.

Once more the unearthly siren song of a transporter rang in his ears. Reyes saw several figures dressed in environment suits—or was it one figure multiplied by his blurred vision?—materialize on the bridge. No, it was more than one person; they weren't all moving the same way . . .

One of them checked a scanner and pointed at Reyes.

Another one leveled a disruptor at Sniadach and shot him in the back of the head, bathing the bridge in crimson light. Then he dispatched Hodgkinson with the same cold precision, another ruby flash illuminating an innocent woman's execution.

Two other intruders kneeled beside Reyes. One pressed a hypospray to Reyes's neck.

As his vision dimmed and his hearing dulled, Reyes reflected bitterly that he should have expected something like this. *Ten years in prison? I knew I'd never get off that easy.*

He gave up his breath and sank into darkness.

2

The situation was on the verge of spinning out of control, and Bridget McLellan was standing in the middle of it.

She was just one among dozens of nameless faces huddled around a weak fire in the middle of a ramshackle shelter. Outside, a frigid wind wailed in minor chords and pushed icy drafts through gaps in the scrap-metal walls.

Everyone's attention was on Scalzer, the grizzled, fearsome leader of this multispecies rogues' gallery. McLellan didn't know the name of Scalzer's species, but she'd seen his three-fanged, ridged-headed, black-haired kind a few times before, when she'd been closer to Federation space.

"Someone in this room has decided to go into business for himself," Scalzer said, casting an accusatory glare at the assembled smugglers. His right hand flexed on the grip of his holstered disruptor pistol. "Whoever did it, I admire your *guramba*. But when I find you, I will take your head."

Nervous looks traveled from one pirate to the next as the members of the circle sought to evade blame by averting their eyes. Scalzer pivoted slowly, his ire palpable. "I will not ask the traitor to confess." With his left hand, he reached under his jacket and pulled out a Starfleet-issue tricorder. "Your guilt will speak for itself."

McLellan's eyes widened as she saw the device in Scalzer's hand. She had no idea how he had acquired it, but she knew she couldn't leave it in his possession. *Bad enough he might use it for crime,* she reasoned, *but if it falls into the hands of the Klingons . . . .* Her hand closed around the compact phaser in her coat pocket. *Can't let that happen.*

Scalzer activated the tricorder. McLellan watched him through faint licks of orange flame that let off black wisps of smoke. He fiddled with its settings and continued his slow turn as he aimed the device around the room.

One of his cronies shouted, "What is that thing?"

"Starfleet scanning device," Scalzer said. "Very advanced. It will tell me who was the last among you to touch the missing tannot ore."

A Tiburonian henchman just a few meters from McLellan protested, "That won't prove who took it!"

Scalzer drew his disruptor, aimed at the man who had just spoken, and shot him in the knee. The hireling collapsed, writhing in agony and biting back howls of pain.

"Maybe not," Scalzer said, holstering his weapon and stalking toward his fallen retainer. "But it will give me a good place to start." The leader continued scanning, paying particular attention to the man curled up at his feet.

McLellan understood why Scalzer was in a hurry. He'd already agreed to sell to the Klingons his three hundred kilos of tannot ore—a primary ingredient in Klingon munitions that the smugglers had stolen from a Nalori mining colony several weeks earlier. The meeting was less than a day away, and there were few things more embarrassing for a thief than to admit to having been robbed of that which he'd stolen fair and square.

Looking up from the tricorder, Scalzer wrinkled his brow in confusion. "None of you shows recent traces of tannot isotope," he said. "But according to this scanner . . . one of you is *human.*"

That was McLellan's cue. Artificial skin pigment and a touch of synthetic pheromones had been enough to let her pass as an Orion and gain entry to the smugglers' cove, but her disguise wasn't going to fool a detailed scan.

She fired her phaser from inside her pocket, a blind shot. The blue beam sliced through her coat's cheap fabric and lanced through the tricorder in Scalzer's hands.

The device erupted in fire, sparks, and a plume of smoke. Scalzer fell backward, surprised but unhurt. Everyone else scattered away from him, widening the circle for a few moments until everyone logjammed at the exits.

Everyone except McLellan, who had prepared an exit strategy hours earlier. Triggering her encrypted emergency transponder, she rolled across the floor and through a wall panel she'd loosened that led to a snow-covered lane behind the building. Springing to her feet, she sprinted across a dark and narrow street and dashed into a meter-wide gap between two flimsy, jury-rigged structures.

She heard Scalzer bellowing orders. The moonless night echoed with the wet slapping footfalls of men running across muddy roads. Tinny voices squawked from two-way radios on either side of McLellan as she reached the end of the sliver-thin passageway.

Sneaking onto the surface of Amonash had been easy. Getting off it was promising to be a bit more challenging.

McLellan checked the corners ahead of her. Both directions looked clear. Brandishing her phaser, she darted into the street and straight toward the extraction point.

Bolts of charged plasma screamed past her head.

She ducked and returned fire on a wide-dispersal setting. The shots might miss their targets or not do much damage, but she hoped they would stun a few of her pursuers or blind them long enough for her to get back undercover.

A disruptor blast streaked past her, red and angry, as she somersaulted over a low stack of cargo crates. More shots flashed against the durable metal shipping containers as McLellan rolled to cover. *Too close,* she admonished herself, fleeing down another alleyway into the cold night.

One dead end after another forced McLellan to double back, risking capture—and who knew what else—with every step. Stumbling upon a downhill grade, she followed it, remembering that her ride off this miserable rock was waiting for her in a ravine near the bottom of the hill on which this abandoned town-turned-smugglers' hideout had been built.

Behind a dilapidated warehouse she skirted the edge of an industrial yard that occupied the last patch of level ground above the ravine. Inside its low-walled perimeter, a labyrinth of pipes, stairs, ladders, and catwalks filled the gaps between dozens of rusted silos, which sat several meters aboveground on corroded metal stilts. Beyond the enclosure, the ground sloped sharply downward into the end of the narrow gorge below.

Ahead of her, at the far edge of the silo field and past the corner of the warehouse, was a road that led to a hidden trail into the dry ravine where her escape vessel lay.

Flashlight beams swept back and forth across that road. Searchers with palm beacons were closing in on her.

She turned back and walked a few steps before she heard more voices drawing near, then she saw more harsh-white beams slice through the darkness, cutting off her path of retreat.

Muttering low, vile curses in a smattering of alien tongues, she steeled herself for a fight.

A hand clasped McLellan's shoulder.

She spun, lifted her phaser, and nearly shot her partner in the face.

He lifted his hands in mock surrender. "Ease up, Bridy Mac." The lean, clear-eyed scoundrel was standing in a nook along the warehouse's back wall. McLellan realized she must have walked past him moments earlier without seeing he was there. She had no idea how, when, or where he'd learned to hide himself so perfectly; for now, she added that mystery to the growing list of things she still didn't know about Cervantes Quinn.

Lowering her weapon, she shook her head and rolled her eyes at the fiftyish man. "Dammit, Quinn, I nearly killed you."

"Join the club," he said, flashing a good-ol'-boy grin.

Recalling the mission profile she'd written for this op, she snapped, "I thought I told you to stay with the ship."

"Yeah, an' we both know how good I am at followin' orders."

Nodding in the direction of her pursuers, he drawled with dead-pan calm, "Looks like you got yerself a spot o' company."

"Looks like," she replied.

"Lucky for you I poked my head out, then." He pointed at the silo field. "Here's my plan for savin' your skin. We haul ass through here, shootin' out them stilts as we go. These big-ass silos come down in a heap, coverin' our backsides. We go up that last set o' stairs, jump off that catwalk, and catch that rusty comm dish, which I reckon'll break free when we hit it. Then we ride it down the slope and over the edge into the gorge. Play it right and we should have a fair-to-medium-soft snow landing."

Despite knowing there wasn't a drop of booze anywhere on Quinn's clattertrap of a ship, she stared at him and wondered if he was drunk.

"You're out of your mind."

He smiled. "Guilty as charged."

At the far end of the warehouse someone turned the corner, aimed a flashlight beam directly at Quinn and McLellan, and started yelling for reinforcements.

Quinn drew his stun pistol and dropped the distant shouter with one shot.

"So let me get this straight," he said to McLellan. "My plan is so stupid, you'd rather take fifty-to-one odds on a stand-up fight?"

Armed men appeared at either end of the alley, on rooftops, and just about every other place in McLellan's field of vision. She gestured at the silos with her phaser and said to Quinn, "I'll take the ones on the left?"

"Deal."

They hurdled over the low concrete retaining wall and sprinted into the iron maze of the industrial yard.

A chaotic firestorm converged upon them. Ricocheted plasma bolts kicked up sparks, and disruptor blasts cut like blades through the twisted old steel around McLellan and Quinn.

There was no point returning fire. She and Quinn would need all their luck and marksmanship to pull off his crazy plan. With their weapons set to full power, they vaporized struts under each silo as they ran past.

They didn't have to hit all the struts—decay and gravity would do most of the work. Quinn and McLellan were just giving the silos a few nudges in the right direction.

Deep metallic groans preceded the whining of distressed iron, which within seconds became the screech of buckling steel. One by one the silos pitched sideways and slammed to the ground, splitting open and gushing forth their toxic contents.

McLellan and Quinn kept shooting and sprinting across the sprawl of cracked cement while looking over their shoulders at the surge of caustic acid lapping at their heels.

They reached the last staircase half a step ahead of an acid bath. A barrage of enemy fire pierced the metal avalanche they'd left in their wake and pinged off the catwalk railing and the wall behind their heads.

Running side by side, the duo leaped off the end of the catwalk toward a huge comm antenna. As Quinn had predicted, it broke free of the narrow stand on which it was mounted. Clutching the feed horn in the center of the parabolic dish, they rode it in free fall to the snowy slope below.

The convex side of the dish slammed against the ground, and they raced downhill at a perilous speed.

Plasma bolts and disruptor beams peppered the hillside around them, kicking up steam and dirt. McLellan volleyed a few shots back at the smugglers, despite there being no way for her to aim with any accuracy during the bumpy slide down to the ravine. She was rewarded by the sight of a few sizable explosions lighting up the night sky behind her.

"Here comes the fun part," Quinn said.

McLellan turned back in time to see the ground come to an end beneath their improvised sled. They were back in free fall, plummeting more than a dozen meters to a curving slope of windblown snow that filled the end of the ravine.

Their bone-jarring landing made her feel as if she were about to cough up her stomach. They spun and slid down the snowdrift, turning McLellan's world into a sickening blur.

The comm dish scraped over sand and slowed. It ceased spinning and came to a halt in front of the open aft gangway to Quinn's beat-up old Mancharan starhopper, the *Rocinante*.

"All aboard," Quinn said. He staggered to his feet and stumbled up the ramp into the mottled gray cargo ship.

It took McLellan a few seconds to regain her balance and stand up. As she climbed the aft ramp into the ship, she heard alarmed voices coming from the wooded cliff high above the ship's port side. "Quinn? Company on the left flank!"

"Copy that," Quinn called back from the cockpit.

Seconds later, a series of emerald-hued flashes lit up the woods above the ship's left wing. Thunderous explosions split the air half a second later. Then all was quiet.

"That oughtta do it," Quinn hollered over the rising whine of the *Rocinante*'s engines. "Seal the hatch. We're outta here."

McLellan closed the gangway and moved forward through the main cabin to the cockpit. As she settled into the copilot's chair, Quinn guided the ship to a swift liftoff. By the time McLellan put up her feet, they had cleared the atmosphere and were starbound.

She asked, "You mined the woods above the ship?"

"Seemed like a wise precaution." He adjusted some settings on the helm, then shot her a rakish grin. "So admit it. Not a bad bit o' rescuin', right?"

"It had its moments," she said, not wanting to puff up her partner's ego any more than he was already doing for himself.

For the past year they had worked together in the Taurus Reach as covert operatives of Starfleet Intelligence, gathering information, seeking clues to the ancient and dangerous race known as the Shedai, and disrupting the activities of criminals and Federation rivals throughout the sector.

SI had recruited McLellan shortly after the return of the *U.S.S. Sagittarius* from the now-vanished Shedai world known as Jinoteur. As the second officer of the *Sagittarius,* McLellan had experienced the transformative power of the Shedai first-hand. That, coupled with her expertise in flight ops, combat tactics, and computer science, had made her an attractive recruitment prospect for SI.

As for why SI had sought Quinn's services, she imagined it might have had something to do with the fact that he'd risked his ship and his life to save the downed *Sagittarius* by bringing a replacement antimatter fuel pod to it on Jinoteur. But sometimes she wondered if maybe he'd been hired by mistake.

She asked, "Did you get all the tannot ore?"

"Every kilo," he said. "We're gonna make a fortune selling this stuff when we get home."

"We can't sell it," she chided. "It has to be impounded."

"I don't think you appreciate the market value of—"

"If you sell it, it'll be used to kill people."

He sighed. "Right. Sorry. Old habits." Casting a sly sidelong glance in her direction, he said, "Seein' as I did kinda save your life back there, maybe tonight we could tie our hammocks togeth—"

"Just fly the ship, Quinn."

"Yes, ma'am."

3

February 18, 2267

Red desolation stretched across the horizon and filled Tim Pennington with an aching loneliness.

He stood alone in the shadow of an automated water-collection station on the edge of the desert outside ShiKahr, the capital city of Vulcan.

Behind him, the giant primary star of 40 Eridani—which, during his months-long stay on Vulcan, Pennington had learned was called Nevasa—dipped beneath the jagged peaks of the L-langon mountain range, while its binary companions trailed a few degrees above it. To the south, the monstrous orb of Vulcan's sister planet, T'Khut, dominated the sky.

His journey to this remote node in ShiKahr's municipal water-supply network had not been easy. He'd left his short-term lodging before dawn. The city, which was laid out in a circular pattern with boulevards emanating from its center-like spokes on a wheel, had a mass-transit system that was easy to navigate, and it had carried Pennington as far as the outer perimeter. There he'd hitched a ride on a hovercar that was traveling to some small settlements out on the Shival Flats. The driver had let him off approximately ten kilometers from the collection station. From there, Pennington had hiked alone up into the rocky foothills.

A nagging inner voice told him he was wasting his time. That he should not have come alone, no matter what had been asked of him. That perhaps he should have told someone where he was going before he'd left ShiKahr.

Too late now, he lamented.

An arid sirocco whipped up a frenzy of sand on the plains below his vantage point. Soon it would spawn a sandstorm that would grow as it moved east and scour the city throughout the night.

He shook his head, disappointed in himself. *Great, now I'm stuck out here. Why don't I ever learn? Always following my gut, never using my head. That's how I get into these cock-ups.*

Pennington had been scheduled to leave Vulcan weeks ago. He was beginning to wish he had done so.

Then he felt the slip of parchment in his jacket pocket and remembered the peculiar encounter in the ShiKahr Spaceport three weeks earlier that had persuaded him to stay . . .

"I've got good news and bad news, Tim," said Dr. Jabilo M'Benga as he emerged from the bustling crowd of Vulcans and assorted aliens in the ShiKahr Spaceport.

Pennington looked up from his data reader, on which he had been perusing the latest headlines from the Federation News Service. "What's the word?"

The Starfleet physician gave a small frown. "The bad news: I can't go back to Vanguard with you." A smile of elation broke through his mask of pretend gloom. "The good news is the reason why. I've been recalled to Starfleet Medical on Earth pending a transfer to starship duty."

With a fraternal slap on M'Benga's shoulder, Pennington said, "S'great news, mate! If you can find us a pub on this dustball, the first round's on me."

M'Benga shook his head. "Sorry, can't." He hooked a thumb over his shoulder. "I have less than an hour to throw my gear in a duffel and beam up to the *Tremina* before she ships out."

"Well, you'd better get movin' then," Pennington said. "I'd hate for you to miss your ride on account of me."

They shook hands. "Thanks for coming to Vulcan with me," M'Benga said.

"I didn't do anything," Pennington said with a small chuckle. "Nothing useful, anyway."

"You never know." M'Benga let go of Pennington's hand and took a step back, apparently eager to start his journey. "I'll drop you a line as soon as I hear where I'm getting posted."

Pennington nodded. "I'll be back on Vanguard in a couple of months. Might be a little hard to reach while I'm in transit."

"Sure," M'Benga said, edging back another step. "But stay in touch, right?"

"Absolutely," Pennington replied, knowing it was an empty promise. He waved to M'Benga. "Godspeed, Jabilo."

"Good-bye, Tim."

M'Benga turned and jogged away through the crowd on his way to an exit. He moved with the kind of energy that belongs to people who have something worth running to.

Heaving a tired sigh, Pennington plodded across the space-port's broad atrium. Its soaring arched ceiling made the young journalist think of red stone ribs joined by a crystal membrane the color of rosé champagne. It was shortly before noon, and all three of Vulcan's suns were visible high overhead.

The air inside the spaceport was cool by Vulcan standards but still warmer than Pennington preferred; he was grateful for its lack of humidity, however. Vulcan had made him appreciate the saying, "Yes, but it's a dry heat."

As he walked toward a row of automated travel-booking kiosks, he reflected on how he'd come to Vulcan months earlier. It had been almost a year since he had witnessed the emotional sundering of T'Prynn, the former Starfleet Intelligence liaison to Starbase 47, in the aftermath of the terrorist bombing attack on the Starfleet cargo transport *Malacca*. Moments after the cargo ship had erupted in flames, T'Prynn let out an anguished scream and collapsed.

Remanded to the medical care of Dr. M'Benga, a human physician who had specialized in Vulcan medicine, T'Prynn had languished in a coma for months. Finally, M'Benga had persuaded Starfleet to allow him to transport T'Prynn back to Vulcan, in the hope that an ancient ritual grounded in Vulcan telepathy might hold the key to her recovery.

For reasons that even he still found opaque, Pennington had asked to accompany M'Benga and T'Prynn to Vulcan. He had asked himself several times what he was really doing there, and each time the answer eluded him.

His actions weren't driven by affection—of that much he was certain. Several months before her breakdown, T'Prynn had sandbagged him; she had used phony sources to feed him a story about the Tholian ambush of the *U.S.S. Bombay* that despite being true had been seeded with enough doctored evidence to discredit it and him. Apparently not content with sabotaging his career, she'd tried to blackmail him with evidence of his extramarital affair with a female officer who had died on the *Bombay*.

He owed her no favors, no allegiance, and no forgiveness. So why in God's name had he traveled hundreds of light-years to sit by her bedside as some Vulcan mystic pulled her back from the brink of her own personal hell? He still didn't fully understand how she had become the victim of a rare form of psychic possession by her former fiancé, whom she'd slain decades earlier.

Clutching the mandala she had given him as a token of her gratitude, and that he now wore on a coarse hemp lanyard, Pennington remained at a loss for answers.

A masculine voice said, "That's an interesting medallion."

Pennington stopped and turned to face the speaker. It was a Vulcan man dressed in a hooded beige robe. His face was tanned but still had a greenish cast. He wasn't a youth but not yet middle-aged. Beyond that, Pennington found it difficult to gauge the ages of adult Vulcans based solely on appearance.

"I'm sorry," Pennington said, stalling while he got his bearings. "What'd you say?"

"Your medallion," the man said, gesturing with his chin toward the mandala resting on Pennington's chest. "It is quite unusual. How did you acquire it?"

The manner in which the man asked his question made Pennington uncomfortable. "A friend gave it to me."

"Odd," the man said. "Such rarities are usually bequeathed only to family members."

Pennington broke eye contact and tried to sidestep the Vulcan. "You must be mistaken."

Blocking his path, the Vulcan said, "It comes from the commune at Kren'than, does it not?"

At the mention of T'Prynn's native village, a technology-free retreat populated by mystics and ascetics, Pennington froze. He suspected the man was not really interested in the medallion. Facing him, Pennington was wary as he said, "Yes, it does."

"As I thought," the man said.

The Vulcan handed him a scrap of fragile parchment that had been folded in half. As soon as Pennington took hold of it, the stranger walked away at a brisk pace and blended back into the earth-toned sea of robed Vulcans crowding the spaceport.

Pennington unfolded the note.

There were three things written on it: a set of geographic co-ordinates, a precise time, and a date exactly three weeks in the future.

He folded it and put it in his pocket.

His mind was a flurry of questions. Who was this Vulcan who'd asked about the mandala? Why had the stranger given him this information? What did it mean?

It was too good a lead to pass up. Something was afoot, and Pennington had to know what it was.

His return to Vanguard would have to wait.

The shadow cast by the water-collection tower stretched eastward and vanished into the edge of the approaching night. Lightning flashed in the west, a harbinger of foul weather. Something wild roared in the darkness and sounded much closer than Pennington would have liked.

He checked his watch, which had been synchronized with ShiKahr's master clock. It was one minute before the time written on the parchment he'd received weeks earlier.

As he stood and listened to the wind, he considered for the

first time that perhaps the note was a warning of an attack—and he had foolishly placed himself in its crosshairs. The trail to the tower was shrouded in darkness now that the suns had set, but nonetheless Pennington considered making a run for it.

The alarm on his watch beeped twice.

A hand grasped his shoulder.

He yelped in surprise and spun around.

A tall, lithe figure stood before him in a brown desert robe whose cavernous hood was draped low, concealing the person's face.

"Right!" he shouted. He pulled the folded note from his pocket and waved it accusingly. "Now that you've spooked me half to death, would you mind telling me why?"

The stranger drew back the hood. It was T'Prynn.

She met Pennington's stare with a humble look.

"You're the only one I can trust. Please help me."

4

Diego Reyes hoped he was dead. He stank as if he were.

His chest expanded by reflex; he sucked in sultry air with a sound that was part yawn, part gasp. Then he gagged on a mouthful of bitter medicinal slime.

He spat it out and coughed. Bits of phlegm from someplace deep in his chest flew out of his mouth.

Feeling a rising urge to vomit, he rolled to his left but collided with a solid barrier. It was smooth and metallic. He gripped the edge and convulsed with heaves.

When the spasms in his diaphragm stopped, he opened his eyes. At first all he could discern was a shadowy red glow. Then his eyes focused, and he saw he was lying in a coffin-shaped pod inside a spartan room that had the hallmark of a compartment on a starship.

Standing around the pod and scowling down at Reyes were a trio of Klingons dressed in military uniforms. These were a different breed of Klingon from those with whom the Federation had been dealing lately. These men had prominent cranial ridges extending almost halfway to the tops of their heads. They wore their wiry black hair in thick, loose manes.

One of the Klingons pointed a small device at Reyes. The gadget buzzed and whirred for a second. The man checked its readout and muttered something guttural in the Klingons' native tongue. One of the other Klingons nodded but kept his unblinking gaze trained on Reyes.

Reyes returned the stare and asked, "Where am I?"

The one glaring at him replied in heavily accented English, "On the *I.K.S. Zin'za*. I am Captain Kutal." Lifting his chin at the other two Klingons, he barked some orders in *tlhIngan Hol*. Reyes felt at a disadvantage without a universal translator.

Kutal stood back as his two subordinates grabbed Reyes by the arms and lifted him out of the pod, naked and dripping in viscous goop. They dropped him onto the grated deck. He landed hard on his hands and knees and winced in pain.

For a moment Reyes considered standing up but thought better of it. *They might take it as a challenge,* he realized. *And I'm in no shape for a fight.* He looked up at Kutal. "What happened to my ship and crew?"

The question seemed to amuse Kutal. "You mean the *Nowlan*?" Reyes nodded in confirmation, which only broadened Kutal's jagged-toothed grin. "First of all, *Mister* Reyes, the *Nowlan* was not *your* ship. You were aboard her as a prisoner. Second, they were of no use to us, so they were destroyed."

"Not by you," Reyes replied, recalling the unusual vessel that had attacked the *Nowlan*. "Who'd you get to do your dirty work this time?"

"The same *petaQpu'* you hired to sabotage my ship in the Borzha II spaceport. Or did you think I'd forgotten?"

"I don't know what you're talking about," Reyes lied, "and you won't get away with this."

All three Klingons roared with laughter. Kutal bent down and slapped one callused hand on the back of Reyes's neck. "We already have. It's been weeks since your transport was blown to bits. As far as Starfleet's concerned, you're dead."

Reyes shook free of Kutal's hand. He glanced at the coffinlike metal cylinder in which he'd awoken and realized it was a hibernation pod. Turning his irate stare back at Kutal, he said, "So, do I have *you* to thank for my life?"

"Hardly." Kutal spat on the deck between Reyes's hands. "Had it been up to me, you would have died on the *Nowlan*." The Klingon captain snapped orders at his men, who lifted Reyes from the deck and stood him upright against a bulkhead. Then Kutal said to Reyes, "We're told you Earthers enjoy something called showers. You smell like you could use one."

Kutal nodded to his men.

One of them lifted a hose attached to the bulkhead opposite Reyes. The other turned a valve and pressed a button.

Freezing-cold water sprayed from the hose, dousing Reyes. It hit him like a blast of ice-needles, stinging his skin. He lifted his hands to guard his face and turned sideways. The frigid stream slammed against his rib cage and thighs. When he turned away from it, the hideously cold torrent scoured his back raw.

It stopped. Through the desperate rasps of his own breathing, he heard runoff water dripping through the metal deck grates to the gutter below. Chilled to his core, he shook and swayed like a weak tree in a storm.

More orders from Kutal; Reyes was given a towel. He dried himself. Kutal's men gave Reyes some clean clothes: underwear, a dark gray coverall, and shoes. He donned the drab utilitarian garb while his captors watched.

They escorted him out of the compartment at gunpoint. Moving through the tight corridors of the dimly lit vessel, they passed crewmen who eyed Reyes with contempt but said nothing. Reyes felt like a piece of prized livestock: valued up to a point but basically ignored.

They descended a series of ladders and arrived at the brig. Kutal ushered him into a cell and activated the force field as soon as Reyes stepped over its threshold. Reyes turned to face Kutal, whose parting words gave Reyes his first inkling of what was going on. "Be grateful," the captain said. "Someone high up wants you alive and unhurt."

The three Klingons departed, leaving Reyes alone in his cell. He eyed its gray-green walls, solid deck plates, and uncushioned slab of a bunk. The lavatory was just a simple seat platform that extended from the wall when called for and retracted into the bulkhead when not in use.

Cozy, he mused with weary sarcasm.

From his point of view, the attack on the *Nowlan* had lasted only a few minutes. Before the attack, he had been in a cell on the *Nowlan*'s lower deck. Now, after being conscious for less than fifteen minutes, he was back in a cell.

He was about to decide he'd broken even when he remembered the last thing he'd been doing before the *Nowlan* was ambushed. He'd been reading the interstellar bestseller *Sunrise on Zeta Minor,* and he'd just gotten to the good part.

Lying on the bunk and folding his hands behind his head, he let out a disgruntled sigh.

Crap. Now I'll never find out how that story ends.

5

February 19, 2267

The nocturnal sounds of Vulcan's desert hills had Tim Pennington on edge. From the ever-closer shrieks of a felinoid predator known as a *Le-matya* to the echoing cries of carrion birds that T'Prynn said were called *lanka-gar,* the darkness resounded with animal hungers.

"There is no need for concern," T'Prynn said, her voice almost a whisper. "That is the mating cry of the *Le-matya.* If it were hunting us, we would not hear it until it attacked."

"Hardly comforting," Pennington said.

T'Prynn detoured off the trail to an unusual-looking rock formation. "Follow me," she said.

Pennington accompanied her into the ring of tall stone slabs, which had become weathered and broken over the course of millennia. Standing in their midst, Pennington realized the slabs were menhirs, hewn by ancient Vulcan hands and arranged in a circle at the foot of the L-langon Mountains.

For a moment, he wondered if T'Prynn was indulging in some moment of mystical reverence, perhaps following some tradition of venerating elders, or meditating on the words of Surak. He watched as she reached out to a boulder, pinched its surface, and pulled away a blanket that bore a desert-camouflage pattern.

What had seemed to be a rock a moment ago now was two beige backpacks filled with gear. "Take one of these," T'Prynn said. She picked up a pack and helped him put it on. Turning away from him, she said, "Now please assist me." He hoisted the other pack onto her shoulders.

"These should have everything we need to reach the other side of the mountain range," she said, "as long as we ration our food and water." She folded the camouflage blanket and stuffed it into one of the outer pockets of Pennington's pack. "We will need this later." Then she walked out of the circle of stones and back to the trail.

"Hang on," he said. His raised voice rebounded off the rocks with alarming clarity. "We've been walking for hours. Aren't we making camp soon?"

She turned back. "We have been walking for precisely fifty-six minutes since our rendezvous at the water-collection tower. And we must continue walking for another seven hours and twenty-nine minutes. At that time, we will have exactly thirty minutes to set up camp before daybreak."

Without waiting for him to reply, she resumed walking. Not wanting to be left by himself in the middle of the desert outside ShiKahr, Pennington hurried after her. "You could've bloody warned me before I came out here that I'd be walking all night."

"If I had, would you have come?"

"At least tell me *why* we have to walk all night."

"Because the lower temperatures and absence of direct solar radiation will enable us to use less food and water than we would and walk for longer consecutive periods than we could in daylight."

As usual, there was no questioning her logic.

They trudged ahead into the mountain pass. Pennington stayed close behind the Vulcan woman.

During their first hour of hiking, he noticed she was limping slightly. As the wind-carved spires of rock seemed to grow taller on either side of them, the trail became deathly quiet. In that silence, Pennington heard T'Prynn fighting for breath.

As they clambered over small mounds of loose rocks that tumbled away beneath their feet and filled the air with faint, semimusical collisions, it became apparent to Pennington that

T'Prynn still had not fully recovered from her long coma and arduous psychic trauma. In all likelihood this journey was as physically difficult for her as it was for him.

Leading him off the rocky slope, T'Prynn veered wide around one of the few patches of smooth ground he had seen since leaving ShiKahr. She pointed at the path's sandy stretch. "Avoid that. There is a sinkhole beneath it."

"Noted," Pennington said. He resolved to step where she stepped and not question why until they were out of the desert.

Hours passed as they followed the narrow, winding road through majestic towers of rock. Lightning forked between far-off peaks and was followed by a crash of thunder.

Eventually, Pennington lost track of time and was aware only of the gnawing emptiness in his stomach, the parched feeling in his mouth, and the dull aches in his feet and lower back. Despite a few brief respites during which they sipped water and devoured small pieces of dried fruit from their packs, the lean young journalist felt as if he were growing heavier with each step.

Plodding forward in a trancelike state, he was startled when T'Prynn stopped, turned, and declared, "It is time to make camp." She doffed her pack and started to pull out fabric. "I need your help. There are additional pieces in your pack."

He set down his burden, opened its top flap, and began pulling out stakes, rope, and anything that looked like a tent component. Looking around, he asked, "Where are we setting up?"

T'Prynn pointed to a spot in the shadow of a long slab of rock lying on a diagonal against some boulders, creating a large gap underneath. "In there. We will first have to check it for *aylakim* and *k'karee*."

"I'm sorry—for what?"

"The *aylakim* is a hand-size scavenging arthropod with two stinging tails. The *k'karee* is a venomous serpent."

"Brilliant."

Pennington focused on assembling the tent while T'Prynn checked their daytime shelter to ensure it was free of other occupants. When she returned, the sky showed the first traces of predawn gray. "Suns are coming up," he said.

"We should make haste," T'Prynn said. "Minerals in these rock formations will mask our life signs from scanners, but we must still evade visual scans."

As he continued putting together their tent, which he noted had an outer skin made from the same camouflage-printed fabric that had concealed their packs, he remained fixated on the implications of what T'Prynn had just said. "Why are we evading sensors and search parties?" When she didn't answer him, he filled in the blanks for himself. "Because you left Kren'than without permission. You're AWOL from Starfleet, aren't you? A fugitive."

She met his accusatory look with an untroubled gaze. "Yes, I am." Acting as if there were nothing else to be said on the matter, she finished assembling the tent's frame and began stretching the fabric over it.

"Why would you flee custody?" Pennington asked. "Won't that just make things worse when they catch you?"

Dragging the tent under the rocks, T'Prynn said, "That is a risk. However, it is a necessary step if I am to continue my career as a Starfleet officer."

Pennington planted the first stake to secure the tent. "Sorry, 'fraid you've lost me. Why is it necessary?"

As they placed the rest of the stakes and secured the tent with ropes, T'Prynn explained her reasons in a calm, matter-of-fact tone. "Had I surrendered to the Starfleet Security personnel who were waiting to escort me from Kren'than, I would have faced an immediate court-martial. The outcome of such a proceeding is not in doubt: I would be convicted.

"Mental illness is the only plausible defense I can present to explain why I tampered with my own Starfleet medical record and abused my security clearance to do so. However, even if a court-martial accepts such an argument and spares me the indignity of incarceration, I will still be made to accept a dishonorable discharge from Starfleet."

She finished securing the tent and moved it into place beneath its broad rock roof. Pivoting to face Pennington, she added, "Regardless of whether my conviction leads to prison or to a discharge, the premature termination of my Starfleet commission will render wasted my decades of acquired skills and experience. If, on the other hand, I can redeem myself through some meritorious action prior to my surrender, I might yet be able to salvage my career."

"I see," Pennington said. "You're looking for leverage."

She arched one elegant eyebrow. "Exactly."

"Nice to see you still think it's all about you," he said. "At least you're consistent." He pulled open the tent flap and ducked inside. "Now, if you don't bloody mind, I'm going to sleep. Wake me when the suns go down."

6

February 20, 2267

Cervantes Quinn hung upside down in his ship's cargo bay and reminded himself pain was his friend.

All the muscles in his torso burned with the effort of folding himself up toward his knees, which were hooked over a horizontal beam he'd installed a year earlier, during the *Rocinante*'s refit by Starfleet Intelligence. He kept his feet tucked under a second beam, which braced him securely while he fought toward his goal of a hundred inverted sit-ups that morning.

Ninety-three, he counted in his head, determined not to stop short. Resisting the pull of the ship's artificial gravity, he relaxed slowly from the tuck and eased back to the starting position rather than let himself fall. With his arms crossed over his chest, he pushed himself into another crunch. *Ninety-four . . .*

Sweat dripped from his buzz-cut head and bare upper body. Despite the thick carpet of hair on his chest and midriff, he could see the outline of his abdominal muscles. He had shed nearly twenty kilograms of weight in the past year, most of it excess body fat. His face had angles again, and for the first time in more than two decades he had only one chin. The only details that differentiated him from his younger self were his receding hairline, gray stubble, and ever-creased forehead.

Ninety-five . . .

Bridy Mac descended the metal ladder from the ship's main compartment. Though she was still an active Starfleet officer, she dressed in civilian clothes because of her undercover status with SI. Her sable hair was tied back in a simple ponytail, as it often was. She walked down the aisle between the stacks of cargo containers, which were secured in place against the outer bulkheads, and stopped a couple of meters from Quinn as he relaxed out of a crunch.

He smiled at her. "Mornin'." He folded himself upward. *Ninety-six . . .*

"Good morning. Almost done?"

Grunting with exertion, he said, "Almost." Down and up again without delay. *Ninety-seven . . .*

She folded her arms and eyed the packed-to-capacity cargo bay with a wry smile. "How much of this is tannot ore?"

" 'Bout three-quarters," Quinn said, dropping from his tuck. One deep breath, then up. *Ninety-eight . . .*

"In other words, enough to level a small city."

Without pausing his routine, he asked with a grin, "Got one in mind?" *Ninety-nine . . .*

"Just making conversation."

She sat on top of a crate. Quinn noticed the small data slate in her hand.

He finished his last sit-up, grabbed hold of a chain dangling beside him, unhooked his feet, and swung himself down to the floor. His legs felt wobbly and uncertain, so he sank into a squat, leaned forward, planted his fists on the deck, and did some push-ups.

The dull gray deck plate under him smelled of the ammonia he'd used to swab it the day before, and it vibrated with the infrasonic pulse of the ship's impulse drive.

He looked up at Bridy Mac as he started his regimen of a hundred slow reps on his knuckles, and asked, "New orders?"

"How'd you guess?"

"It's the only time you ever come down here." He paused and rolled onto his side. "So what is it this time?"

"Another recon."

"Pirates, lobster-heads, or monsters?"

Lobster-heads was Quinn's epithet du jour for the Klingons, and he'd referred to the Shedai as monsters ever since his return from their obliterated homeworld, Jinoteur.

"Monsters," Bridy Mac said. She handed him the data slate. "It's a new lead from the scientists on Vanguard."

Quinn studied the classified communiqué and frowned. "If these coordinates are right, we'll be pokin' around in the lobster-heads' backyard on this one. This is what, maybe ten light-years from their border?"

"Three," Bridy Mac said. "The Klingons annexed FGC 62-24–Gamma last month. They call it Gr'oth now."

Shaking his head, Quinn said, "That's just great." He reached the end of the terse command directive on the data slate. "Is this all your SI pixel-pushers sent? What about advance intel on the third planet?"

"There is none. That's why they're sending us."

"Lovely." He gave the data slate back to her. "Hand me that towel, will ya?"

She grabbed a soft cotton towel from atop the cargo container behind her and tossed it to him. He caught it, mopped the sweat from his face, and draped it around his neck as he stood up. "Did you put in the new coordinates yet?"

"I decided to give you the honor," she said with an insincere half smile.

Quinn headed for the ladder. "In other words, you still can't figure out how to run my custom nav computer."

"Let's just say I'm not used to working with something so primitive," she retorted, following him across the cargo deck.

"Primitive? It's cutting edge!"

"I was talking about you."

"Okay, that was just cold."

He climbed the ladder and strode across the main deck toward the cockpit. *I wonder what Tim would say if he could see this ol' ship today,* Quinn mused, remembering his months of bizarre drunken adventures with reporter Tim Pennington. Back then the *Rocinante* had resembled nothing so much as a flying bar; now there wasn't a drop of alcohol anywhere on board. *I bet*

Tim wouldn't even recognize ol' Rosie like this. Or me, for that matter.

Bridy Mac had never asked Quinn about his former traveling companion and partner in misadventure, and he hadn't volunteered any information about Tim—or any other facet of his past—in all the months he had worked with her. He made no secret of his being more than mildly smitten with Bridy, but even though she was a right pretty bit of eye candy to have aboard on a long haul, the truth was that he missed his friend.

Who'm I kidding? He smiled. *I just liked taking his money when we played poker. Poor guy couldn't bluff for shit.*

He stepped into the cockpit, dropped into the pilot's seat, and punched in the new coordinates. "Ready to set sail," he said as Bridy Mac eased herself into the copilot's seat. "Give the word, m'lady, and our next jaunt—"

"Just go already."

Quinn engaged the warp drive. "Yes, ma'am."

7

Reyes awoke to an ear-splitting screech that sounded like a diamond-tipped saw chewing through steel.

His eyes snapped open as he flinched from the clamor. Rolling over on his hard metal bunk, he realized the unholy racket was coming from the corridor outside the brig. He sat up and looked through his cell's force field.

The door to the corridor slid open, and two Klingon soldiers backed into the brig. They were dragging something. Each warrior held a long pole with a hydraulic grasping apparatus affixed to the end. Trapped in the prisoner-control devices was a struggling Tholian.

Clad in a full-body environment suit of shimmering bronze Tholian silk, the shrieking prisoner thrashed and flailed wildly, fighting to break the Klingons' grip. Pushing the crystalline arthropod from behind were three more Klingon troops; two prodded the creature forward while one labored to control the Tholian's whipping, scorpionlike tail.

The entire group—prisoner and captors alike—stumbled awkwardly from side to side, slammed against bulkheads, and lurched forward and backward and diagonally. If not for the skull-piercing din, Reyes might have found the spectacle funny. At the very least, he respected the tenacity necessary to capture a Tholian alive.

He got up, stood at his cell's force field, and watched the Klingons herd the screeching Tholian. They pulled the creature off balance until it toppled forward, then they shoved it into the cell opposite Reyes's and released it. The soldier closest to the control panel for the other cell activated its force field.

The Tholian charged the Klingons. It struck the invisible barrier, which flared bright white and crackled with shocking energies as it repelled the attack. Undaunted, the Tholian charged again. There was another flash of light and a sharp electric buzzing, and the creature was thrown against the far wall of its cell.

After a moment, the Tholian fumbled to its feet but seemed to have no further intention of challenging its cell's unseen barrier. Scuttling slowly around the tiny space, it appeared to resign itself to its captivity.

Looking worn out, the five Klingons grumbled low curses as they left the brig. None of them spared so much as a glance in Reyes's direction. The door slid shut behind them.

Reyes stood at the front of his cell and said nothing while he watched the Klingons' newest guest explore its confinement. The creature made a number of low scratching and clicking sounds as it probed the ceiling and bulkheads.

Then it took note of Reyes and turned to face him, but said nothing. The two regarded each other for several seconds.

Breaking the silence, the Tholian said through its pressure suit's vocoder, "I am Ezthene." The translated voice had an unmistakably masculine quality.

"Diego Reyes. What're you in for?"

At first, Ezthene seemed perplexed by the question. Then he said, "I was captured while trying to reach Vanguard."

Reyes immediately took a keener interest in the conversation. "Why were you going to Vanguard?"

Ezthene hesitated before answering. "I was a high-ranking member of the political castemoot on Tholia. After our vessel *Lanz't Tholis* returned from Jinoteur, the Ruling Conclave issued an edict calling for the escalation of military force in the Shedai Sector. I . . . *dissented*."

"Mind if I ask why?"

Ezthene made some curious gestures with his forelimbs as

he spoke. "I had met with a member of *Lanz't Tholis*'s crew, a weapons officer named Nezrene. She convinced me there was more to be gained by cooperating with the Federation than by opposing it. Together, we petitioned the Ruling Conclave and asked it to sanction the diplomatic pursuit of a truce. They refused."

Nodding, Reyes said, "And they held a grudge."

"To put it politely, yes," Ezthene said.

"The impression one gets of your society from the outside looking in is that it doesn't much care for iconoclasts."

"True. Nonetheless, we exist." With an expansive motion of his forelimbs, Ezthene continued. "Suspecting we would be in danger after provoking the Ruling Conclave, Nezrene and I decided to seek asylum on Vanguard. To improve our chances, we split up and took separate, mutually unknown routes. I can only hope she was not captured as I was—or suffered a worser fate."

"Well, if she makes it to Vanguard, she'll be okay." Reyes thought about the difficulty the Klingons must have gone through to capture Ezthene and the expense they had likely incurred by hiring mercenaries to capture Reyes himself; he suspected the two abductions were related. "Do you happen to know why the Klingons want you alive?"

"Not yet," Ezthene said. "I was hoping you could explain that, Commodore."

Reyes lifted his brow in surprise upon being addressed by his former rank. "You know who I am?"

"Yes," the Tholian replied. "You became quite well known after the Gamma Tauri IV massacre."

"Did you hear I got court-martialed and convicted?"

Ezthene made a few soft clicking sounds his vocoder didn't translate. Then he said, "I was unaware of that."

"Don't worry about it," Reyes said. "But I'm not called *commodore* anymore. I was stripped of my rank when I got convicted."

Bending its lower limbs to simulate a bow, Ezthene said, "I meant no offense."

"None taken."

"How, then, shall I address you?"

"*Diego* is fine."

Peering across the dimly lit brig with eyes that glowed with the golden fire of molten ore, Ezthene asked, "So, Diego, do you know why the Klingons have taken us?"

Reyes saw no point in lying. "Nope."

"We should consider some of the possibilities," Ezthene said. "Perhaps they wish to interrogate us for intelligence to use against our peoples."

"I've been here for three days," Reyes said. "So far, no one's asked me a goddamned thing."

Ezthene ruminated quietly for a few seconds. "There were rumors the Klingons had placed a bounty on your life."

"It wasn't a rumor," Reyes said. "But if that's all this was, they could've killed me weeks ago. And whoever grabbed me handed me over in a hibernation pod. If they plan to put me on trial back on Qo'noS, why thaw me out before I get there?"

"Excellent queries," Ezthene said. "In any event, their vendetta against you would still not explain my presence."

"Also true," Reyes said. "Unless you ticked them off. Did you ever insult some random Klingon's mother?"

"Not that I am aware of."

Reyes frowned with boredom. "So much for that theory."

"Is it possible," Ezthene asked, "we are being held for ransom?"

"Maybe you are," Reyes replied. "But me? Not a chance."

"Why do you think that?"

Unable to help himself, Reyes let out a grim chortle. He wondered whether Ezthene could appreciate his gallows humor as he replied with a taut smile, "Haven't you heard? I'm dead."

8

Days of hiking through the mountains had left Pennington tasting nothing but dust and dried-fruit rations. After a long night's march over broken ground, he was glad to have the intimidating peaks of the L-langon mountain range behind him.

He and T'Prynn reached Toth'Sen, a settlement just beyond the southern end of the Khomir Pass, shortly after dawn. The small agrarian village glowed like burning gold in the light of early morning. Like most cities and towns on Vulcan, it had been built around a rare oasis of fresh water and green vegetation. Its main roads radiated from its center and were linked at regular intervals by circular boulevards.

"I need to procure supplies for our journey," T'Prynn said. She stopped in front of a small meditation temple. "Wait for me here until I return. Do not speak to anyone. Is that clear?"

Too tired to argue, Pennington said, "Crystal."

Without further explanation, T'Prynn vanished down a street toward the village's center.

Pennington took off his pack and set it against the temple wall. He planted his hands on his lower back and stretched until he felt a few vertebrae release their tension with satisfying pops. His entire back ached, from his shoulder blades to his pelvis—a consequence of spending three days sleeping on a thin bedroll stretched over rocky soil.

Flexing his fingers, he found dehydration had left his skin

feeling brittle and tight. He fished his last canteen of water from his pack and drained half of what was left in it.

There was no shade where he was standing, so he picked up his pack and moved around the corner, beyond the suns' reach. He sat down on the dusty ground and leaned against the over-filled pack.

And he waited.

It hadn't occurred to him to ask T'Prynn how long she would be gone. He silently berated himself for not being more curious.

Spindrifts the color of nutmeg flew low to the ground.

Nevasa burned brighter as it ascended by slow degrees.

From somewhere in the heart of the village, a lonely melody of flute music, as soft as a breath and as light as air, rippled through the town's deep reservoir of silence.

Toth'Sen began to stir. Then all at once it was awake.

Pedestrians cast wary glances at Pennington as they passed by. He began to feel self-conscious and exposed. *Maybe I should find someplace less visible to wait,* he thought. Then he remembered T'Prynn had instructed him to stay at the temple.

Nearly two hours passed without any sign of T'Prynn, and he began to fear she had, in fact, ditched him. *That'd be just brilliant,* he brooded. *Alone and broke on Vulcan.* He smiled as he thought, *Might not be a bad start for a novel.*

He had started to nod off when T'Prynn finally returned. She was almost silhouetted against the pale red sky. He squinted up at her. She had traded her large pack for a small canvas overnight bag, which was slung over her shoulder. He asked, "Where's your gear?"

"I exchanged it to facilitate the creation of new travel documents."

Lifting his arm to shield his eyes so he could see her expression better, he said, "You paid someone to forge a new ID for you? I didn't know Vulcans did that sort of thing."

"Not all of this planet's residents are Vulcans," T'Prynn said.

"And I made the documents myself. My payment was merely for access to the necessary materials and equipment."

"Right," Pennington said. Overcoming the stiffness in his legs and back, he got up. "Someone gave you that kind of access in exchange for camping gear?"

"Actually, Mister Pennington, your pack contains the bulk of our outdoor survival equipment. Most of the contents in my pack were relics from the commune at Kren'than, which outside the settlement are rare and considered rather valuable."

"I'll add forgery and theft to your growing list of crimes," Pennington said. "Did you at least get a good price for your loot?"

"Enough to make my documents and buy us passage on a private transport to Ajilon," T'Prynn said. "An offworld merchant whose business here has concluded offered us a ride to the spaceport in Khomir. There we will board our transport and leave Vulcan."

Pennington shook his head. "I know it might seem like a great plan, but I think you're forgetting a few things. A new ID won't be enough to get you off Vulcan. Even though the UFP says its worlds have open borders, the reality—"

"I am aware of my homeworld's stringent regulation of its citizens' movements on and off the planet," T'Prynn said. "My new travel documents will enable me to overcome any impediments to my travel."

"But they'll scan your DNA so they can verify your identity if and when you return," Pennington said. "The moment they do, they'll know who you really are. And that'll be the end of your little holiday."

She regarded him with determined eyes. "It is therefore imperative that you help me prevent Vulcan Security from forcing me to submit to such a scan."

He wondered if she was being deliberately obtuse. "How am I supposed to do that? All Vulcan citizens have to get scanned before leaving the planet."

"Which is why I must become a citizen of a world that exempts its people from such invasions of personal sovereignty."

It took a second for Pennington to realize what she was proposing. "You mean Earth citizenship? But the only way for me to help you become an Earth citizen would be . . ." His voice trailed off as understanding dawned.

"Correct," T'Prynn said, taking him by the hand and leading him inside the meditation temple. "We are getting married."

9

February 22, 2267

A pair of Klingon soldiers led Reyes into a dimly lit briefing room. "Hello, Diego," said Ezthene.

Reyes nodded at the Tholian, who was being shadowed by two Klingon guards of his own. "Morning," Reyes said.

"Sit down," said one of Reyes's guards. Reyes pulled out a chair from the conference table and took a seat.

A week had passed since Ezthene's arrival, but this was the first time Reyes had seen him since their first night of shared captivity. By the next morning, the Klingons had modified a small compartment to provide the kind of superheated high-pressure environment Ezthene needed if he was to remain a long-term prisoner; just as with most other varieties of self-contained environment suits, the Tholian's silk garment could function for only so long before needing to be recharged and replenished.

The same stench that pervaded every other corner of the ship—a musky blend of sweat and unwashed hair, coupled with a pungent odor of spilled alcoholic beverages—had crept into this cabin, as well. Reyes wondered how much of the stink emanated from the ship itself and how much came from its crew.

Captain Kutal entered. "Before we begin, you both should know that while I have been told to treat you as guests, if you make even the slightest gesture I don't like, I will kill you without warning. Do you understand?"

Ezthene said nothing.

Reyes yawned, then said to Kutal, "Just get on with it."

Kutal growled at Reyes, then looked at the two pairs of guards. "Dismissed."

The order provoked wary glances between the four soldiers. They looked to Kutal for confirmation. He tilted his head toward the portal behind him. Moving with bitter resignation, the warriors filed out of the compartment. Kutal locked the door behind them.

"Now it's time for you both to meet your benefactor," he said. He pressed an intercom switch mounted on the tabletop and said, "We're ready."

Another door slid open, and a lone figure strode in. He was a tall, lanky Klingon with a proud bearing. He had thick, curling brows, and his jawline was adorned by a well-groomed beard. The ornate decorations of his robes and sash identified him as a member of the Klingon High Council.

Reyes would have recognized the man even if he'd been garbed in a burlap sack. He uttered the Klingon's name in a hostile whisper: "Gorkon."

Councillor Gorkon gave Reyes a small smile. "You remember me," he said. "How flattering."

Hearing the Klingon's voice brought back a flood of bad memories from Reyes's years as captain of the *U.S.S. Dauntless*. On numerous occasions he had crossed paths with Gorkon, who back then had been the commanding officer of the battle cruiser *I.K.S. Chech'Iw*. More than a few lives had been lost on both sides during those so-called skirmishes.

The councillor nodded at Captain Kutal. "Leave us."

Kutal tensed. "You should not be left unguarded with—"

"I am armed, Kutal," Gorkon said. "If I need you, I will call for you. Now step outside."

Grudgingly, Kutal unlocked the door behind him and left the briefing room. The door hissed shut as Reyes glared at Gorkon and asked, "What is this? Your overdue revenge?"

Gorkon lifted his chin, and his smile took on a smug air.

"Hardly. I prefer to let my enemies self-destruct. Case in point: you. I couldn't have planned anything as spectacular as that which you have brought upon yourself."

Ezthene's voice crackled through his vocoder as he interjected, "Diego's question stands, Councillor."

Arching one eyebrow, Gorkon replied, "On a first-name basis, are you? I must say, Diego, perhaps I misjudged you. You've learned something about diplomacy after all."

"And you've learned to talk too much," Reyes said. "You must've picked that up serving as Chancellor Sturka's lackey."

Gorkon's smile vanished. For a moment there was a flash of anger in his eyes, but then he drew a deep breath, and his ire subsided. "That was the past. I've brought you both here to discuss the future."

"What future is that?" Reyes asked. "The one where I face a kangaroo court on Qo'noS and get my head chopped off for doing my job? Or the one in which all your people starve to death because your government spends too much on its military?"

Curling his hands into fists, Gorkon clenched his jaw for a moment. Reyes took perverse pleasure in testing the limits of the Klingon politician's patience.

Finally, Gorkon said, "The reason I have expended capital and favors to capture the two of you alive is that you have both, through your public statements and actions, demonstrated yourselves to be big-picture thinkers when it comes to the Gonmog Sector." To Ezthene he added, "Your people call it the Shedai Sector." He glanced at Reyes. "The Federation refers to it as the Taurus Reach."

Reyes remained suspicious of Gorkon's agenda. "Okay, but you didn't bring us here just to sing our praises. What do you want from us?"

"I seek your counsel," Gorkon said. "You both have detailed knowledge of what is at stake in the Gonmog Sector, and the lengths to which your governments will go to control it. Because you both have demonstrated a willingness to rebel against the belligerent mind-sets of your peoples, it is my hope you will be willing to talk with me."

Ezthene asked, "What specifically do you wish to discuss?"

"I want to find a way to steer our nations off this road to mutual annihilation," Gorkon said. "The Federation is sending more ships to Vanguard. The Tholian Assembly is conducting reconnaissance of vulnerable worlds in the Gonmog Sector. And my own government is making moves to seize territory that will cut off Vanguard from supplies and reinforcements, as a prelude to its destruction. And we all know why."

He keyed some commands into a terminal on the tabletop in front of him. A holographic image of a complex DNA molecule appeared above the table and rotated slowly. "This amazing little string of genetic information has pushed our peoples to the brink of all-out war. None of our leaders is willing to compromise or surrender. But this is a war none of us can win—it will consume us all and leave nothing behind."

Gorkon turned off the hologram and added, "We three must find a middle path to peace, or else we're all going to die."

10

Quinn nudged the *Rocinante* out of warp speed a few million kilometers from the Class-M planet he and Bridy Mac had been sent to scout. Checking the proximity sensors, he said to Bridy, "Looks like we're all alone out here."

"Good," she said. Her attention was fixed on the readout from the ship's sensors, which were scanning the system and its third planet. "No radio activity on the planet's surface," she said. "I'm reading a lot of metallic debris in orbit."

"Satellites?"

"I think so." She adjusted the settings on her console. "Some of them have nuclear cores, but none of them is active. No signal activity."

Pointing at the planet's two small moons, Quinn asked, "What about those? Any signs of life?"

"Negative," Bridy said. "Airless rockballs."

The impulse engines thrummed as Quinn piloted the *Rocinante* into orbit. "I'll keep clear of the orbital junkyard if you want to take a closer look at the surface."

"Already starting my sweep," she said. "Looks like all but the tropical latitudes are glaciated."

He settled into a steady orbit a few hundred kilometers above the highest satellites. Locking the course into the autopilot, he asked Bridy, "What about life signs?"

"Mostly concentrated in a band around the equator," she said. "The southern coast of the planet's largest land mass has a decent variety of plant forms and a few groupings of humanoids large enough to register on sensors. And it looks like the oceans are teeming, even under the ice sheets."

Quinn reclined his seat. "Maybe I'll do some fishing."

"Stay on task for once, will you?" She tapped more commands into her console. "Based on the distribution of refined metals and residual topographical features, I'd say this planet used to have hundreds of major population centers. It might have supported a population of as many as two billion people."

Despite his efforts to remain aloof, Quinn found himself curious about the planet. "What happened to 'em?"

"No idea," Bridy said. "A war. Maybe a natural disaster or a virus. No way to tell without going down there."

"Never my favorite answer," Quinn said.

Bridy relayed a set of coordinates to Quinn's navigation screen. "Let's start with an aerial recon of the deserted cities. I want to get a sense of how long ago this civilization collapsed. After that we can head for one of the larger settlements on the southern coast."

"Your command is my to-do list," Quinn said.

He plotted a course through the ring of dead satellites and readied the ship for atmospheric entry. The massive orb of the planet filled his cockpit canopy. Seconds later, a pale orange wall of superheated gas formed ahead of the *Rocinante* as it made its swift descent. Turbulence shook the small cargo vessel, and the ship's spaceframe groaned in protest. The planet's curved horizon quickly flattened as Quinn dived toward its surface. His ship shot like an arrow through a gray mountain of clouds, and he leveled the ship's flight.

Glancing at his instruments, he said, "Comin' up on your first point of interest." He pointed to starboard. "That side."

"Can you take us down to two kilometers?"

"Sure." Quinn eased the ship's nose downward, dropping them to a lower altitude within seconds. "How's that?"

"Perfect," Bridy said. "Give me a slow circle of the area."

Quinn guided the *Rocinante* through a shallow banking turn

that took them around a massive urban ruin. The crumbling remains of once-majestic skyscrapers were overgrown with plant life; some structures appeared to have collapsed only recently, cutting wide swaths across the lush vegetation that was reclaiming the former city.

In a hushed voice he said, "Look on my works, ye Mighty, and despair."

Bridy nodded, apparently recognizing the quote from Percy Bysshe Shelley's poem "Ozymandias." With her gaze still fixed on the decaying metropolis, she replied, "Yup." She looked at Quinn with a somber expression. "Let's move on and see what the next site looks like."

"You got it," Quinn said.

Over the next few hours, they saw dozens of former cities, all in various stages of decay: conquered by wilderness they had once displaced, swallowed by seas they had once kept at bay, buried by a desert's inexorable march, or ground into dust by continent-wide sheets of ice nearly two kilometers thick.

"I've seen enough," Bridy Mac said as they cruised over a moonlit coastline dotted with the disintegrating tops of sunken towers. "Set course for the largest humanoid settlement. Rig for silent running and make our altitude ten kilometers."

"On it," Quinn said. He entered the changes into the helm and relied on his instruments to guide him as night fell and made it impossible for him to tell where the sky ended and the sea began. "I take it I'll be doin' the talkin' if we decide to go down and meet the locals?"

"As usual," Bridy said.

One of the reasons she needed him as a partner was to skirt Starfleet's all but sacrosanct Prime Directive, which forbade its officers from making contact with or interfering in the affairs of pre-warp cultures. As a civilian, Quinn wasn't bound by the Prime Directive. To preserve their cover as traveling merchants and prospectors, he was responsible for initiating contact with species that would be off-limits for Bridy, who was still a Starfleet officer, albeit on detached duty.

"Okay, we're in position," Quinn said.

Bridy ran another sensor sweep and studied the accumulated data. "Looks like they've built on the remains of an old city. Livestock, natural fertilizers in the soil, diverse agriculture . . . it's a pretty large farming community. I'm also reading a lot of small sail-powered ships along the coast." She smiled at Quinn. "There's your fishing spot."

"I'll dust off my rod and reel." He folded his hands behind his head, leaned back in his chair until it was almost horizontal, and stared through the canopy at the flickering stars. "We gonna hover up here all night? Or go down and say hello?"

The lithe brunette shut off the sensor apparatus. "Fine, let's go meet the locals. But this time keep the ship ready for a quick liftoff. I don't want a repeat of that mess on Cygnar."

The mere mention of that planet made Quinn wince. He would never forget the ambush with which that world's primitive reptilian natives had greeted him and Bridy several months earlier. "Don't worry," he said, massaging a phantom pain where a dart had pierced his ribs. "Running away's my specialty."

McLellan watched the shadowy details of a gutted city rise to meet the *Rocinante* as Quinn piloted the ship to a landing on a mostly level patch of rubble-strewn ground surrounded by four ancient brick walls with no roof.

The ship hovered over the landing site for a few seconds, extended its landing gear, and made a smooth vertical descent. With a mechanical whine the wingtips folded into their landing configuration, up and inward over the bulky warp nacelles, which together were as massive as the ship they served. Quick spurts from the directional thrusters kicked up dust and vapor beneath the ship, which submerged into the cloud and settled to the ground with a soft tremor of contact. "Nicely done," McLellan said.

"Years of practice," Quinn replied, switching the ship's systems to ready-standby and activating its exterior floodlights. Beyond the walls that surrounded the ship, several humanoid shapes were approaching. "Looks like we drew a crowd."

"Do they have torches and pitchforks?"

"Not that I can see."

She got out of her chair. "Then let's go say hi."

Quinn followed McLellan aft to the gangplank. She pushed a button, and the ramp descended with a whirring of motors and a hiss of hydraulics. Curtains of white vapor billowed downward and spilled to either side of the ramp, blanketing the ground with fog. Quinn walked outside, taking the lead.

Stepping off the ship behind Quinn, McLellan saw him undo the leather safety strap on the holster of his stun pistol. She kept her own compact phaser tucked out of sight under her shirt, in a sheath attached to her belt.

They waited underneath the thick aft section of the *Rocinante*'s main hull, which was shaped like a narrow wedge. The exterior of the ship was a mottled dark gray with pale splotches from years of crude repairs at various alien shipyards. The cockpit was covered by a dark-tinted canopy.

A group of six humanoids clambered through gaps in the walls around the *Rocinante*. The first ones through reached back to assist the others. Once they were all inside the gutted structure, they stepped into the glow of the *Rocinante*'s floodlamps.

The entourage consisted of what looked like four males and two females. Tall and thin, they had slender limbs and six long delicate digits on each hand. Their chins and foreheads were prominent and squarish, their noses were broad, and their large ears protruded horizontally from their heads. All of them wore simple clothing that looked as if it had been made by hand.

At first McLellan thought they were albinos, but as they moved closer she saw they had pale gray complexions. All six of them had long straight hair the color of white gold.

Their most striking feature, however, was the single lidless multifaceted eye that ran the length of each individual's brow, between the nose and forehead.

The female leading the group stepped forward, paying no heed to Quinn, and addressed McLellan. With a subtle forward bow, the female said, "My name is Naya Parzych. I am the cynosure of Leuck Shire. Welcome to the planet Golmira."

Not wanting to give offense by trying to deflect the woman's attention to Quinn, McLellan mimicked the slight bow and replied, "Thank you. My name is Bridget McLellan, and this is my friend and business partner, Cervantes Quinn."

Dipping his chin, Quinn said to Naya, "Ma'am."

McLellan said, "Our species calls itself human."

Clearly picking up on the cue, Naya replied, "We refer to ourselves as Denn." She cast a disapproving look at Quinn's sidearm. "If you've come in search of plunder, I doubt we have anything worth your trouble."

Quinn raised his palms. "No slight intended, ma'am. It's just for self-defense. Doesn't even have a kill setting." His words seemed to calm Naya, so he continued. "You and yours seem pretty calm for folks meeting alien visitors."

The group's other female stepped forward and spoke with quiet contempt. "You're not the first offworlders we've met. Or the second. Or the third."

Naya glared at the younger woman, who backed away half a step. Looking back at Quinn and McLellan, Naya said, "On behalf of my daughter, Ilka, I apologize. However, her frustration with offworlders is one shared by many of our people."

McLellan folded her arms. "May I ask why?"

"Previous visitors to Golmira left when they learned we had no resources worth exploiting," Naya said. "Our carbon fuels and fissionable elements are long since depleted. Some aliens came in search of special crystals but found we had none. Others were looking for worlds to colonize, but with so much of our planet covered in ice, and the rest barely arable, we must not be worth the effort it would take to make us habitable."

Quinn smiled. "Sounds like they just didn't know a good deal when they saw one. I mean, sure, your planet's a bit of a fixer-upper, but to folks who know what they're doin', it's a garden spot waitin' to happen."

Naya frowned. "I don't understand."

McLellan tried to cut her partner off. "Quinn, maybe we—"

"If you folks are willin' to trade with offworlders, I'll tell you who to do business with: the Federation."

Wrinkles creased Naya's high forehead. "The what?"

"The United Federation of Planets," Quinn said. "Hundreds of worlds, dozens of species, all workin' together in peace. They're pretty far from here, but they got ships and people comin' out this way all the time now. I've been dealin' with 'em for years. They're the most honest business partners I've ever had." Shooting an abashed glance at McLellan, he added, "Present company excepted, of course."

With a glare and a smile, McLellan replied, "Of course."

The Denn behind Naya murmured among themselves. She looked over her shoulder at them, then turned back. "I have no reason to doubt your word," she said to Quinn. "But I have to ask, why would a civilization so advanced that it could repair a world in such dire condition as ours want to do so? What do we have that would make such an effort worthwhile?"

It was to McLellan's dismay that Naya's question made Quinn flash a broad grin and reply, "That's an excellent question. Let's all go discuss it over dinner."

It was the strangest farming village that Quinn had ever seen.

The walk from the *Rocinante* to the center of the hamlet was short. Along the way they passed patches of grain that sprouted from the gutted foundations of crumbled buildings. Broken chunks of what looked like steel-reinforced concrete had been used to build everything from low property walls to sturdy small homes.

Half of a lone skyscraper jutted up in the middle of the fallen city. Its upper portion had apparently fallen away, but there was no sign of its debris. Quinn surmised that any usable materials had long since been scavenged. All that remained now was its metal skeleton, denuded of façade and windows, emptied of contents, and festooned with fruit-bearing vines.

Cresting the horizon were the planet's two moons—one full,

the other a waxing crescent. They bathed the pastoral but decidedly post-apocalyptic landscape in a pale blue glow.

Naya, her daughter, and their entourage led Quinn and Bridy inside a squat but solid-looking house of stone and wood. Its main room was appointed with simple wooden furniture, and a small fire crackled in a nook along the far wall. Thick candles flickered brightly from numerous wall sconces, and oil lamps hung from the ceiling, suffusing the room with golden light. The smooth cement floor was the only clue the house had been built atop the foundation of something now gone.

As Bridy and Quinn entered, a handful of other Denn looked in their direction. Ushering the two humans forward, Naya announced to the room, "Please welcome our guests, Bridget and Cervantes, and set the table for them." To her daughter she added, "Please go ask the landgraves to join us." Ilka slipped out the door while Naya led Quinn and Bridy into the dining room.

"Please, sit down," Naya said, motioning the humans toward the closest chairs at the dining table. "My brothers and nephews will bring us food and drinks momentarily."

"Thank you," Bridy said, taking a seat.

Quinn settled into the chair next to hers and nodded at Naya. "Much obliged, ma'am."

Moments later, a procession of young men carrying plates of food and pitchers of beverages entered through a swinging door. From the kitchen behind them wafted the aroma of cooked meat, pungent spices, and something sweet. A bite of woodsmoke also lingered in the air.

In less than a minute, the long table was covered with food, plates, cutlery, and linens. Quinn was impressed. *They might be funny-lookin',* he mused with a wry half smile, *but they lay out a hell of a spread.*

He expected the half-dozen men to sit down and join them, but instead Naya's male kin all retreated back into the kitchen. *So that's how it is here,* Quinn realized. *Good to know.*

After quickly perusing the offerings arrayed before him, Quinn reached toward a bowl of what looked like meat stew.

Under the table, Bridy kicked her heel into his shin. He jerked his hand back to his side and whispered to her, "What?"

Her voice was hushed but sharp. "Do you see *her* reaching for the food?"

At the head of the table, Naya sat with her hands folded in her lap. No drinks had been poured, and no food had been served.

"Sorry," Quinn said, feeling more than a little ashamed of himself. His mother had taught him proper manners when he was a boy, but it had been a long time since he'd actually needed to put them to use.

He heard the front door open. A steady patter of footsteps followed. Ilka had returned with five other women, all of them adults like Naya. Their hair colors ranged from pale copper to silver, but otherwise they looked much the same as their hostess.

Naya stood as the women fanned out on either side of the table, so Bridy and Quinn did the same.

"Bridget, Cervantes—allow me to introduce the landgraves of Leuck Shire: Yan Cova, Adeva Oros, Enora Yova, Decin Rokon, and Urova Pren."

"Hello," Bridy said.

"A pleasure," Quinn added, though he was sure he wouldn't remember any of these ladies' names in about ten seconds.

Gesturing for everyone to sit, Naya said, "Let us eat."

Quinn let all the women serve themselves before he covered his own plate with slices of white meat in a brown gravy, hearty bread, and assorted raw and boiled vegetables. Then he picked up a copper pitcher and filled his ceramic mug with an amber fluid that, when he tasted it, reminded him of sweetened tea.

For most of the meal, the landgraves spoke only to Bridy Mac. They asked her banal questions: How many worlds had she been to? What was the life expectancy of a human female? Did men on Earth know their place as they did on Golmira? For the sake of satisfying his hunger and staying out of trouble, Quinn let Bridy do the talking for the first hour or so.

He was in the middle of enjoying his dessert, which bore an uncanny similarity to his grandmother's pear cobbler, when the topic of conversation finally turned to the Denn and the recent history of their world.

"The collapse was centuries ago," Naya said. "Journals from that time spoke often of instabilities and upheavals, but no one thought the end could happen so quickly."

The landgraves nodded, and Yan said, "Survivors of the collapse spoke of a *tipping point*. Pollution had been warming the air and the seas for centuries before then, but no one did anything about it."

Decin continued the story. "Our polar caps and permafrost melted, and the seas began to rise, destroying many of our coastal cities. Then the change in the ocean's salinity disrupted the deep currents that moved warm water from the equator out to the polar latitudes, and the deep freeze began."

"After countless warnings about how the planet had been warming," Urova said, "it seemed ironic that Golmira should find itself the victim of a new glacial age. Temperatures plunged. The ice walls advanced, and our ancestors used every bit of energy they could burn to keep their cities alive."

"But there was no stopping the ice," said Adeva, picking up the narrative. "Within decades, the carbon fuels and the fissionable elements were used up. The engines stopped, and the cities went dark."

Enora added, "All that remains of the old world is what you see now. We live in its ashes and grow our crops on its grave."

Bridy asked, "Didn't your ancestors explore solar power? Or biofuels? Geothermal taps? Hydroelectrics? Wind turbines?"

The local women nodded. Naya said, "They tried, but by then it was too late. Biofuels require expendable crops, and once the glaciers came we could barely produce enough to subsist. The other options demand resources that our forebears lacked the wisdom to develop in time, and that are now beyond our grasp."

Quinn leaned forward. "Mind if I ask a question?"

Naya nodded. "Please do."

"Do you have much contact with other towns? When we were flyin' in, we noticed y'all have a decent number of boats, and it looks like there are roads between here and some other prov-inces, or shires, or whatever."

"Yes," Naya said. "We trade and share news with other com-munities on a regular basis. Crops that grow well in one place often fare poorly in others, so we all have an incentive to cooper-ate. All of this is done by sea, however. The roads between the shires aren't safe."

Bridy and Quinn glanced at each other. Bridy asked Naya, "Why aren't they safe?"

"The *Goçeba,*" Naya said. "Superstitious nomads. They roam the desert wastes between the coasts and ice walls, and they like to ambush travelers on the roads."

Decin added, "The only time it's safe to travel the roads is during the month of the summer solstice, when the *Goçeba* gather at the Precursor temple in the Hinterlands."

Quinn felt a tingle of anticipation. It was the same sense of excitement he got at the card table whenever he drew a guaran-teed winning hand or learned another player's tell. Feigning non-chalance, he said, "Why do they like the temple?"

Enora replied, "It's always been a magnet for the delusional, even before the collapse."

"Some legends say it houses an artifact that predates the evo-lution of our species," Naya added. "I've never seen it, so I don't even know if the artifact exists, but the *Goçeba* certainly believe it does. And they worship it like fools."

"I'll bet," Quinn said. "But only once per year, in high sum-mer?" The Denn women nodded, so he pressed on. "And you said it's where, exactly?"

"In the Hinterlands," Adeva said. "In the center of a city once known as Doanhain. It was swallowed by the desert ages ago, but the nomads keep the temple uncovered."

Quinn looked at Bridy, who inquired, "Is it far from here?"

Naya seemed unsettled by the question. "Why do you ask?"

"Ancient cultures are important to the Federation," Quinn said. "If it's as old as your legends say, there are thousands of archaeologists who'd love to study it. That alone could be a huge revenue source for your planet."

Yan leaned forward, her expression eager. "Really?"

Admiring the woman's finely honed sense of avarice, Quinn said, "Hell, yeah. But only if it's *really* old. We'd have to go out and run some tests to be sure, but if that temple's the real deal, we could probably get Federation support and snag some major investors to help rebuild your planet."

His proposal inspired several seconds of terse, whispered discussion between the landgraves and their cynosure.

Naya looked up and said, "Would your Federation help control the *Goçeba*?"

He shrugged. "They'd have to if they want to get anything done."

"Very well," Naya said. "The temple is half a day's ride from here. Tomorrow we'll provide you with mounts, provisions, and a map. Until then, please stay here in Tegoresko as our guests."

Bridy replied, "Thank you, Naya. That's very kind of you."

Quinn sipped his tea and felt as if he'd done some good by inviting himself to dinner. Then he realized there was one very important question he'd neglected to ask.

"It's not high summer, is it?"

"No, Cervantes," Naya said. "It is early spring. The *Goçeba* don't convene for many months yet."

He let out a relieved sigh. "Just checkin'."

11

February 23, 2267

Gorkon slammed his hand down on the conference-room table. "I refuse to believe there is no alternative to war!"

Diego Reyes was too exhausted to react to Gorkon's outburst, and from where he was sitting, Ezthene appeared equally unfazed. "I never thought I'd live to see the day when a Klingon would prove to be a political idealist," Reyes said.

"No one denies that averting a full-scale conflict among our peoples will be difficult," Gorkon says. "But it must be done. The Empire and the Federation both predict they will be victorious, but the truth is that our militaries are more evenly matched than either side will admit. Any war between us would become one of attrition, and with the Tholians and the Romulans waiting to strike us both, we would become the architects of our own doom."

Indistinct metallic scratching sounds emanated from inside Ezthene's environment suit of shimmering Tholian silk. His vocoder translated it for Gorkon and Reyes. "War is rarely the most productive response to a crisis. However, it has been one that your people have chosen many times. Why should this change now?"

"I've already said why," Gorkon said.

"What he meant," Reyes cut in, "isn't why but how."

The Klingon politician grunted softly and ruminated for a moment. "Chancellor Sturka must be persuaded there is more to be gained by negotiating with the Federation for access to the secrets of the Gonmog Sector than there is in taking it by force."

"Good luck with that," Reyes said.

Gorkon shot a withering look at Reyes. "Are you implying the Federation would not be willing to exchange information?"

"Why would they? They got to the Taurus Reach ahead of you, and they've paid in blood for the privilege."

"There must be some way to broker a truce," Gorkon said.

Reyes shook his head. Dull pain throbbed in his temples, and his ears and forehead felt hot. He blamed the Klingon food and the overcaffeinated swill they had told him was "a lot like human coffee," but which tasted more like hot bitter syrup. "I don't know," he said, pinching the bridge of his nose and pushing down to try to relieve some of the pressure in his sinus. "You'd have to lay groundwork on both sides. I'm talking about people working behind the scenes to open up lines of communication, head off conflicts before they go public, create a political pressure valve. But that's not gonna happen in a year or even ten years, Gorkon. We're talking about the kind of change that can take a generation."

Gorkon nodded. "All too true. An accord between our peoples might not be possible during our lifetimes." He smiled at Reyes. "Too many people like us are too afraid of change to let it happen. Which makes it imperative we steer the next generation down that path now, before their course becomes set."

A new chorus of tinny shrieks turned attention back toward Ezthene. "You talk of peace in a generation," he said. "But it will take far longer than that for the Tholian Assembly to put aside its hatred. Its grudges are long and deep."

"I suspected as much," Gorkon said. "At best, the Empire might seek a cease-fire with the Assembly."

"Diego was right about you," Ezthene said. "You *are* an idealist. Most curious."

A tight smile betrayed Gorkon's waning patience with his guests. "I could say the same of you," he replied. "You tried to seek asylum on Vanguard for the same reason I brought you both here. You want to find a new way forward, for all of us."

"How noble of you," Ezthene said. "However, did it occur to you that your method was somewhat less benign than ours? After all, this unofficial summit of yours is hardly conducive to producing any kind of lasting agreement among our respective nations. You abducted us and brought us to Klingon space, where you indubitably hold the upper hand."

Reyes added, "He makes a good point. This is hardly what I'd call a meeting of equals, Gorkon."

"Because I brought you to Klingon space against your will?"

"That, and the fact we're not really playing at your level of the game anymore, if we ever were." Reyes nodded at Ezthene. "He's an exiled dissenter, an outcast from his people. If what he's told me is true, they'll try to kill him on sight. And me? For God's sake, Gorkon, I'm a legally dead convicted military criminal. Not exactly a mover and a shaker, if you know what I mean."

Frowning, Gorkon replied, "I am certain I do not."

"Look," Reyes said. "You sit on the Klingon High Council. You've been the chancellor's right-hand man for years now. That puts you in a position to make a difference. Ezthene and I, on the other hand, aren't exactly poised to make much of an impact on *our* governments. So if you're counting on us to bring your vision of the future to life, I think you're in for a hell of a big letdown."

Gorkon reclined, looked at the overhead, and chortled. "Of course," he muttered. "How foolish of me." He stood and planted his fingertips on the tabletop. "Please accept my apologies, gentlemen. I should have communicated my purpose more clearly when we first sat down together. I did not go to the effort and expense of bringing the two of you here so that I could send you back as envoys to your own peoples. You are not here because I believe either of you is positioned to influence the actions of your leaders or your deliberative assemblies."

Feeling his headache getting worse the longer Gorkon talked, Reyes said, "Get to the point, will you?"

A forbidding scowl creased the Klingon's brow as he replied, "You're not here to sway *your* governments. You're here to help me sway *mine*."

12

"I know it's generally considered gauche to make comparisons between one's former and current spouses," Pennington said, "but I have to admit I enjoyed my first honeymoon a lot more than this one."

T'Prynn looked up from her bowl of *plomeek* soup at Tim Pennington. He had not said much during their first day aboard the civilian transport to Ajilon, preferring to sleep off the fatigue from their trek through the L-langon Mountains. Now that he was awake and facing her across their tiny dining-room table, she wondered if rather than requesting a suite with two bunks she ought to have requested separate quarters.

Without betraying her regrets regarding their travel arrangements, she replied, "If you are referring to the chaste nature of our cohabitation, I should think it would have been entirely expected."

"Actually," Pennington replied between bites of his pasta pesto with *goschmol* mushrooms from Tellar, "I was talking about the lack of fun and conversation more than the lack of sex." He speared another forkful of food, lifted it halfway to his mouth, and stopped. "Wait a minute. What do you mean this should have been expected?"

"First, because I swore my marital vows under an assumed name, they are not legally binding. Ergo, you and I are not actually married, and no act of consummation should be expected."

Cracking a rakish smile, Pennington asked, "Not even to maintain appearances?"

"I doubt anyone is observing our activity here in our cabin, Mister Pennington. Such a charade would in all likelihood be of no value to the preservation of our cover story."

"Bloody match made in heaven," he mumbled, then shoveled the forkful of pasta into his mouth.

T'Prynn added, "Also, since you seem to be unaware, I should make it clear my sexual preference is for women."

He stared at T'Prynn as he chewed and swallowed. "Well," he said. "That throws a wrench in things, doesn't it? Thanks for sharing."

The rest of dinner was quiet.

After placing his dishes outside the cabin door for the ship's housekeeping staff to collect, Pennington said, "I'm pretty sure there's a lounge or pub somewhere on this boat, and I mean to find it."

"I have no doubt that your experience as an investigative journalist will serve you well in that endeavor," T'Prynn replied as she sat down in front of the cabin's comm terminal.

Pennington walked away, and the cabin's door slid shut.

Emancipated from her pseudo-husband's inane small talk, T'Prynn powered up the comm and began a methodical survey of the major news feeds available within the Federation. Before her surreptitious departure from Vulcan, she'd had no opportunity to catch herself up on events that had transpired during the year she had been in a coma. The ban on modern technologies inside her native village of Kren'than had prevented her from learning anything notable during her post-coma convalescence, and her need to move quickly and evade detection after fleeing the commune had made such prolonged research impossible until now.

She intially looked for any news related to Starbase 47 during the year of her absence. The first news items returned by the system had been published within two days of her mental collapse. At the top of the list was a story by Tim Pennington that exposed Diego Reyes as the officer responsible for issuing General Order 24 against the independent colony on Gamma Tauri IV. The resulting photon-torpedo barrage by the starships *Endeavour* and

Lovell had reduced the planet to a molten sphere—and claimed more than thirteen thousand lives, including those of a few thousand Klingons.

Next she read a firsthand account—also written by Pennington—of the rescue of the downed scout vessel *U.S.S. Sagittarius* on the planet known as Jinoteur. The story was extremely detailed, especially in its description of the shapeshifting, consciousness-transmitting aliens known as the Shedai.

T'Prynn wondered how Pennington had evaded the Starfleet censor on Vanguard when filing both stories. Then she saw the next series of linked reports. Commodore Reyes had personally facilitated the release of Pennington's stories, bypassing the normal vetting process and transmitting the journalist's content directly to the Federation News Service.

T'Prynn was perplexed as she skimmed through the redacted transcripts of Reyes's court-martial. Why would Reyes compromise Operation Vanguard in such a manner? Even as she read his condemnation of Starfleet's recent shift toward excessive secrecy, she found it difficult to accept his reasoning. Consequently, she was not surprised to read at the end of the transcript that Reyes had been convicted, stripped of his rank, dishonorably discharged from Starfleet service, and sentenced to ten years' incarceration at a penal facility in New Zealand on Earth.

Then she read that Reyes's transport had been destroyed by an unknown attacker while it was en route to Earth. Lost with all hands. Reduced to a cloud of gas and dust.

Diego Reyes was dead. Murdered.

The usual suspects had denied responsibility, of course. Even though the Klingons had placed a bounty on Reyes's life after the Gamma Tauri IV incident, they insisted they had wanted him to stand trial on Qo'noS, not be granted a glorious death in battle. Figures linked with the various Orion smugglers who prowled the sector protested their innocence, claiming they were merely thieves and not murderers—as if making that distinction gave them some claim to the moral high ground. Predictably, the Tholians said nothing at all.

Without access to hard evidence and witnesses, T'Prynn would not be able to form a hypothesis determining who was responsible for the death of her friend and former commanding officer. But between the reports of increased pirate activity in the Taurus Reach and escalating demonstrations of aggression by Klingon forces in that sector, it seemed clear to her that there was a significant breach in Vanguard's operational security.

That is where my service will be of the most value, she decided. *If I am to redeem myself and reclaim my career, those who destroyed the* Nowlan *must be brought to justice . . . and Starfleet's control over the Taurus Reach must be restored.*

In twenty-five days the transport would deliver her and Pennington to Ajilon. She had that long to come up with a plan.

It wasn't much time. But it would be enough.

13

Reyes pulled back the center tine of his fork and let it snap forward, catapulting a live *gagh* worm across his cell.

The wriggling thing sizzled as it struck his cell's force field. It fell to the floor and was still. Tendrils of vapor rose from its lightly browned skin. Reyes leaned forward, picked it up, and bit off a piece. He chewed for a few seconds, then nodded at Ezthene.

"You're right. They do taste better cooked."

"I am pleased my advice proved useful," the Tholian replied from the opposite cell.

Gorkon had adjourned their meeting for a short lunch break. Rather than send Ezthene back to his artificial environment—which entailed a tedious protocol of adjusting the composition of gasses in his insulated cabin, increasing their pressure by a few orders of magnitude, and raising the temperature until the compartment was as hot as a furnace—Gorkon had elected to let Ezthene remain in the brig with Reyes.

One by one, Reyes launched the *gagh* in his bowl at the force field. When he was sure they were all at least medium rare, he scooped them off the deck and back into his bowl.

"Just one drawback to this little plan," he said.

"And that is?"

"Now my cell stinks like fried worms."

Ezthene waved his upper limbs in an "oh, well" gesture he had learned from Reyes. "No plan is perfect," he said.

Through a mouthful of half-masticated worms, Reyes mumbled, "Got that right." Barely cooked *gagh* was better than live *gagh,* but he didn't care for it either way. Forcing himself to swallow the greasy, mushy mess, he reminded himself it was protein and he needed it to keep his strength up. *At least they let me drink clean water,* he thought with some relief. He picked up his cup and took a swig to wash the taste of *gagh* from his mouth.

Poking inside the bowl with his fork to find the next-most-cooked worm, he asked Ezthene, "What do you eat on this ship? I can't imagine the Klingons have a menu packed with all your favorites."

"My species does not consume organic matter as fuel," the quadruped replied. "We process chemicals from our atmosphere to energize our internal functions."

Reyes grinned. "All you need is the air you breathe, eh? Convenient."

"Yes. Quite."

A few minutes later as Reyes swallowed the last of his worms, the door to the brig slid open with a soft hiss. The *Zin'za*'s commanding officer, Captain Kutal, walked in. He was followed by Gorkon, who wore a disgruntled expression.

Unable to resist the urge to needle his captor, Reyes asked, "What's the matter, Gorkon? You look like someone shot your *targ.*"

"Would that they had," Gorkon said. He came to a halt between Reyes and Ezthene. "I had hoped I might be able to muster enough support among my allies to bring you with me to address the chancellor in an open session of the High Council. Unfortunately, my peers are not as willing to hear foreign perspectives as I am—and unwilling to do so at all in that august chamber."

Ezthene replied, "Imagine my disappointment." The dryness of his sarcasm was only magnified by his vocoder.

"It's just as well," Reyes said. "I wouldn't have had a thing to wear."

Gorkon frowned. "This is a more serious setback than either of you appears to grasp."

"No, I grasp it just fine," Reyes said. "I simply don't care." He folded his arms. "What's the problem, anyway? Aren't you Sturka's go-to guy? If you've got his ear, why do you need to go marching us in front of the council? Or could it be that Sturka doesn't want to see us in there, either? Do you need the council's political muscle to get him to cooperate?"

The councillor's frown became a glare aimed squarely at Reyes. "Very astute of you, Diego. You're right. Sturka *is* resistant to granting you an audience. However, even if he were inclined to let you two speak for the record, it would still be necessary to appease a majority of the council to make such a public audience happen."

Ezthene asked, "So where does that leave us?"

"In custody," Reyes said, cutting off Gorkon.

"Unfortunately, yes," Gorkon said. "It will take time for me to lay the requisite political groundwork for this meeting."

Captain Kutal interjected, "Assuming current events don't render it completely impossible."

Reyes's curiosity was aroused. "What current events?"

Gorkon shot a reproachful stare at Kutal, then said to Reyes, "Hostilities between Klingon forces and Starfleet have been escalating in recent weeks. Rumors of war are afoot."

"As always," Reyes said.

Gorkon dipped his chin. "Well put. In any event, I must return to the First City on Qo'noS. Until I am able to return, I need to ask both of you to be patient."

From the other cell Ezthene replied, "We seem to have little alternative."

"Not hard to be patient in the brig," Reyes added.

For a moment Gorkon took on a pensive countenance. "It is rather disingenuous of me to ask for your aid and counsel while treating you like prisoners of war." He faced Ezthene. "I regret that more of the ship cannot be refitted to your environmental needs, but perhaps we could arrange to provide you with some sort of intellectual diversion."

"I would be satisfied with a simple increase in the ambient temperature of my compartment."

Nodding, Gorkon said, "Very well. Captain Kutal, please see to it the adjustment is made. Also, arrange for Mister Reyes to be moved to private quarters at once."

"Yes, Councillor," Kutal said, obedient but also visibly seething at the order. "May I recommend, however, that Mister Reyes be monitored by armed guards at all times?"

Gorkon glowered at Kutal with a mixture of annoyance and contempt. "Yes, *obviously,* Captain." Adopting a calmer tone, he said to Reyes, "Will there be anything else before I depart?"

"I could use something to read."

That drew a thin smile from Gorkon. "I'll see what I can do."

14

March 22, 2267

Pennington stepped out of the shuttle onto the surface of Ajilon Prime and decided the last three weeks with T'Prynn had been the longest year of his life.

He stepped clear of the other passengers exiting the shuttle and set down his duffel. The waters of Tanada Bay sparkled in the morning sunlight. Colorful boats darted across the azure waves. A crisp, cool breeze kissed his face and carried with it the invigorating scent of saltwater.

This might not be a Federation planet yet, but it will be soon, he mused. Between its natural beauty and its position on the Klingon border, he speculated that its application for membership would be fast-tracked through the Federation Council.

Footsteps halted behind him. He knew without looking it was her. "Mister Pennington," said T'Prynn.

Reluctantly, he turned to face her. "Yes, dear?"

"I wish to inform you our honeymoon is now over. And I wanted to thank you for your help."

She offered him her hand. Shaking it, he asked, "That's it, then?" Noting her confused reaction, he let go of her hand and went on. "I mean, sure, you've reached Ajilon. And knowing you, there's probably some devious scheme already in the works. But do you really think you're safer going it alone?"

"Safety was never one of my chief considerations," T'Prynn said, shifting the bag on her shoulder.

He rolled his eyes. "Now you tell me." He shook his head. "Never mind—what's your next move?"

T'Prynn stepped beside him and gazed out at the bay. "Before leaving Vulcan I prepared an additional set of identity papers. I will use them going forward to obscure any link between the ruse that enabled us to leave my homeworld and my actions to come." She threw a sidelong look at Pennington. "Logically, my best chance of preventing someone from linking my two false identities would be to part company with you."

"Well, obviously," he said, keeping his eyes on the water. "I know you probably won't answer me, but I'll ask anyway. What are you hoping to accomplish?"

An uneasy silence lasted for several seconds. Then T'Prynn said, "I plan to conduct a covert operation to gather intelligence against the Orion crime lord Ganz, his Nalori enforcer Zett Nilric, and whatever smugglers or pirates they have been aiding and abetting in the Taurus Reach."

Pennington expressed his doubt with a sideways tilt of his head. "A useful goal," he said. "Though not exactly the kind of high-stakes poker I'd have expected from someone like you. Why spend your time spying on a bunch of thugs?"

"Because I suspect Ganz's organization serves as a cutout for the Klingons in that sector—and that he or someone who works for him had a hand in destroying the *Nowlan* and murdering Diego Reyes."

While Pennington processed that bombshell of information, T'Prynn turned and walked away from him, across the landing field toward the encircling cluster of small buildings that passed for a town on this tenuously settled ball of rock.

"Hold on!" he called to her. He grabbed his duffel and jogged clumsily after her. "You can prove that?"

Over her shoulder, she replied, "Of course not, Mister Pennington. I said only that I *suspect* it. I intend to gather evidence so that I *can* prove it."

"Right," he replied, feeling like a bit of a berk. "You did say that, didn't you? Sorry."

As he fell into step beside her, she glanced at him through narrowed eyes. "Why are you following me?"

"Y'know," the intrigued young Scot said with a shrug, "to help." He omitted the fact that being able to publish a properly sourced story titled "Who Really Killed Diego Reyes?" would likely win him awards and pave his way to a lifetime of prestige. And adoring fans. Preferably young, female fans.

"I thought I had made it clear my best interests would be served by us going our separate ways."

"You did. But the thing is, I'm not so sure. That you're right, I mean. I learned a lot traveling with Quinn. Enough to make myself useful. Good in a pinch, that's me. Handy."

Christ, he fumed. *I'm babbling. I need to keep cool.*

"Would you perhaps have an ulterior motive for coming with me, Mister Pennington? For instance, a desire to chronicle our shared exploits in journalistic or literary form?"

"Well, I, uh . . ." He made half a dozen strange faces while he struggled and failed to conceive some means of evading her question. "Well, if I learn something newsworthy, I'm going to write about it, aren't I? But I'm not a total sod, T'Prynn. I won't publish something that'll do more harm than good."

Behind them, the shuttle's engines whined and split the air. The small craft took off and ascended into the sky on its way back to orbit. When the din of its departure abated, T'Prynn replied, "Who determines the relative harm or benefit of one of your articles?"

"Well, I guess I do."

"I see."

Passing into the warren of narrow streets beyond the landing field, Pennington and T'Prynn cut through a mass of people. There seemed to be bodies moving in all directions at once, like threads being woven into a living tapestry. On either side, tiny shops stood edge to edge, as if huddled for warmth.

"Look, you can trust me," Pennington said, still trying to plead his case. "And right now, it seems to me like you could use every friend you can get."

As they turned a corner, she replied, "The mission I am about to undertake will be time-consuming, tedious, and at times extremely dangerous." She stopped and faced him. "I am grateful to you for helping me escape custody on Vulcan, but the longer you stay with me, the greater your legal jeopardy becomes. I cannot ask any more of you."

"You don't have to ask," Pennington said. "I'm offering."

She made a small bow of her head. "If that is your choice, then I will not refuse your aid."

He sighed and smiled. "You're welcome."

T'Prynn and Pennington lurked in the shadows on the edge of the town. Beyond the cluster of squat structures, many of the more transient visitors to Ajilon had parked their vessels. They were being tended by a small fleet of hovercraft that brought them fuel and expendable supplies and transported their cargo.

"Looks like a bloody smugglers' cove if ever I saw one," Pennington said, eyeing the line of small vessels and the rogues' gallery of seedy individuals who lurked within and around them.

Pulling an illegal scanning device from under her tunic, T'Prynn said, "An astute observation."

"Travel with Quinn long enough and places like this start to look familiar."

"No doubt." She aimed her scanner at the row of ships and adjusted the device's settings. "Most of those vessels have been illegally modified."

Even though they were concealed in the darkness between two buildings, Pennington felt exposed. Vulnerable. "What're you looking for? Are we trying to link one of those ships to Ganz?"

"No, Mister Pennington. We are going to steal one." She wasted no time selecting a ship. "That one," she said, nodding at a teardrop-shaped craft with a protruding pod on the starboard side. "It will suit our needs well. It has been upgraded with a number of improvements that I suspect were acquired via the black market. It has stealth, speed, and superior offensive and defensive capabilities for a vessel its size." Putting away her scanner, she added, "It also has three people aboard. If you wish to dissociate yourself from my plan—"

"I don't," he said. "I'm in."

"Very well." T'Prynn handed him a plasma blaster.

He looked at the weapon in his hand. Its potential excited and terrified him. He swallowed hard and took a deep breath. "Right. What do you need from me?"

She arched one eyebrow. "A distraction."

Dochyiel stood under the bow of his employer's starship and used a Klingon *painstik* to swat another nymock off the power cables attached to the forward landing gear.

"Damned pests," muttered the Efrosian hired gun. He jabbed the *painstik* into the fallen parasite—to make sure it was dead and to vent some of his anger. *This isn't even supposed to be my job,* he brooded. *But the chief engineer is the boss's best friend, so we can't have him doing scut work when there's booze to be guzzled, can we?* The *nymock* let out a pathetic screech as it expired under the electrical torment of the Klingon prod.

As the Efrosian resigned himself to heading aft to check the other landing struts, a commotion from a few ships away caught his attention. It sounded like a cross between drunken singing and someone trying to strangle a small animal.

Lurching and stumbling along the row of ships was a human man. He was young, fair-haired, and relatively handsome for one of his species. In one hand he held an all but empty bottle of something; in the other he brandished a blaster.

Resting his hand on his own sidearm, Dochyiel kept a watchful eye on the weaving loon who was ranting in singsong gibberish. *This ought to be interesting,* he predicted.

"Garble, gribble, brouhaha!" crowed the mad-eyed human. "Did she say why? No! 'Course not! That would've been bloody civil!" He hiccupped, and his cheeks puffed as if an emetic incident was imminent. Then he sucked in a breath and continued his wild screaming. "Not even a *by your leave, guv*! And what'm I s'posed to say?"

The man dropped his bottle and unfastened the belt on his pants, which fell to his knees. He began dancing spastically in a small circle with one arm held high over his head, and the blaster pointed at his own head.

"Itten bitten little ditten . . ."

Dochyiel keyed his comm to the ship. "Zurtmank, Ertobor. I think you need to come see this."

"Copy that," Zurtmank replied. *"On our way."*

"Oaten boaten little dotin'," chanted the human, whose pants were now bunched around his ankles. He appeared to be growing dizzy from spinning in a circle.

Behind Dochyiel, the ship's ramp lowered and his two crewmates hurried out to stand beside him and laugh at the spectacle. "What a mess," Ertobor said between guffaws that made his fin-like Tiburonian ears flap back and forth.

"Nish diddly oat dote, bode oh ska deet dot . . ."

"Go ahead and shoot," Zurtmank shouted at the human, displaying his finely honed Balduk sense of humor.

"Don't miss," Ertobor yelled. In response, the human pointed the blaster at his own genitals, and all three of the smugglers exploded with hysterical laughter.

The human came to an abrupt halt and declared in a grave voice, "G'night, mates."

Dochyiel steeled himself, expecting to see the man blow his head off.

Zurtmank and Ertobor collapsed to the ground, limp and unconscious. Their faces were contorted and each had one shoulder pressed up against his head.

Spinning to face their attacker, Dochyiel beheld the most beautiful Vulcan woman he had ever seen.

In a blur she poked him in the chest with her index finger.

His head spun, and his knees buckled.

As he felt consciousness slip away, he hoped the woman had killed him—because if she hadn't, his boss would . . . and he would make it hurt a *lot* more than this.

* * *

"This is a lovely ship you've stolen," Pennington said as T'Prynn guided the vessel into orbit.

"I am glad you approve," she replied.

He looked around the cockpit and poked at the consoles. "I guess we'll have to recode its transponder," he said. "Before *our* ship gets reported as stolen."

"Correct." Fixing him with a detached stare she added, "One might get the impression you have done this before."

He laughed nervously. "Me? No, no. But Quinn told me stories about his younger days. Taught me a few things."

"I see."

He pointed at the console nearest him. "I could fix the transponder now, if you like."

"Not until we have warped out of orbit."

"Right," he said. An alert beeped and flashed on the bank of displays beside her. Pennington pointed at the blinking light. "What's that?"

"Space-traffic control on Ajilon requesting our flight plan." She checked the navigation computer and short-range sensors. "They have no means of restraining us, and there are no ships close enough to respond that are capable of overtaking us, so we are going to ignore them." She entered a new course into the ship's helm, engaged the vessel's stealth systems, and jumped it to warp speed.

As stretched starlight drifted past outside the cockpit canopy, T'Prynn said, "You may reprogram the transponder now."

"On it," Pennington said, setting to work. After only a few minutes he looked up and said, "Done. I hope you don't mind, but I changed our ship's name to *Skylla*. In Greek mythology, it was one of the immortal horses that pulled Poseidon's chariot."

"If that is your wish, I have no objection."

"Thank you." He finished his task and reclined to watch the stars melt past. "So . . . what's next?"

Staring into the darkness ahead of them, T'Prynn saw only possibilities. "Now we go hunting," she said.

15

"Things have certainly gotten a bit more interesting," Reyes said from the back of the *Zin'za*'s bridge.

A pack of angry Klingons turned aft and glared at him. They seemed decidedly unamused at having their long-awaited siege of Starbase 47 preempted by a nigh-omnipotent race of interstellar meddlers known as the Organians.

Addressing the Federation and the Klingon Empire, an elder of the Organians known as Ayelborne had appeared simultaneously before the leaders of both nations, and on the bridge of every starship and combat-ready installation of both sides in the imminent conflict. He had rendered the weapons and surfaces of all major systems' controls too hot to touch. In essence, he had warned both sides to behave themselves or else lose their toys.

Reyes found it kind of funny.

Naturally, the Klingons didn't.

The executive officer of the *Zin'za,* a hulking thug named Bel-HoQ, stormed across the cramped space of crimson light and murky shadows to tower over Reyes. "This must be some kind of Earther trick," he said with a voice that sounded as if it were made of gravel. "Your kind knows they are going to lose this war, so they asked these *yIntagHpu'* to interfere."

"I'm guessing you weren't the captain of your debate team in school, were you?" Reyes pointed at the image of the equally crippled *U.S.S. Endeavour* and Starbase 47 on the main viewer. "You and your friends were about to get your asses handed to you. If anybody was looking for the ref to stop this fight, it should've been you guys."

BelHoQ bared his teeth in a growling snarl.

Captain Kutal barked, "Enough! BelHoQ, man your station!"

The XO backed away from Reyes, breaking eye contact only once they were several strides apart.

From his post near where Reyes stood, tactical officer Lieutenant Tonar grumbled, "It seems we'll have to wait until another day to take our revenge for Mirdonyae V."

Reyes had no idea what had happened at Mirdonyae V to piss off the Klingons, and he wasn't sure he wanted to know. "So, is that it? Is this why you woke me up and dragged me in here?"

Eyes wide with rage, Kutal snapped, "I brought you here to see your precious station reduced to fire and fragments! So you could bear witness to our moment of victory!"

Mocking the Klingons' fury with an insolent smile, Reyes replied, "How's that working out for you?"

Kutal looked as if he were about to erupt in a profane stream-of-consciousness rant when the communications officer interjected, "Captain?"

"What is it, Kreq?"

"Priority message from High Command, sir."

Quaking with bottled-up rage, Kutal said in a deathly quiet voice, "Put it on-screen, Lieutenant."

Kreq worked at his console for a moment. Then the image on the main viewer changed to an older, gray-maned Klingon standing in front of a black banner decorated with the Empire's trefoil emblem. *"All fleet commanders,"* said the Klingon. *"This is General Garthog. Stand down. Withdraw from Federation space and return to regular patrols. High Command, out."*

The transmission ended, and the screen reverted to the view of Starbase 47 and the *Constitution*-class ship holding position between the station and the *Zin'za*.

Reyes watched Kutal clench his fists and slowly open them. A black cloud of anger followed the captain as he returned to his chair on the bridge's elevated center dais. He sat down. "Lieutenant Kreq, hail the rest of our squadron."

Seconds later Kreq said, "Channel open, Captain."

"All vessels, this is Captain Kutal. We have new orders from the High Command. Stand down. Disengage from attack formation and set course back to the Somraw Anchorage. Kutal, out." He nodded at Kreq, who cut the channel. "Helm, lay in the course and prepare to lead the fleet home."

"Yes, sir," answered the helmsman.

Vanguard and the *Endeavour* vanished from the main viewer as the *Zin'za* and its fleet broke formation and maneuvered away. In less than a minute the Klingon ships had regrouped in a traveling formation and jumped to warp speed, on a heading back to their own space. Reyes was relieved the battle had been averted, but he also felt a renewed sense of despair that he was being carried away from it still in the custody of his enemies.

BelHoQ checked the bridge's duty stations, then made his sotto voce report to the captain, who responded with a curt nod then waved him away.

Reyes was considering asking his guards to take him to the head so he could do something productive when Kutal walked aft to confront him.

"Starfleet and the Federation will blame this travesty on Ayelborne and the Organians," Kutal said. "The Klingon High Command will no doubt do the same." He stepped forward and pressed his nose against Reyes's. "But if I find out your little summit with Gorkon had anything to do with today's debacle, I'll make sure you both suffer and die in disgrace."

"Don't look at me," Reyes said. "I was just happy to have a front-row seat so I could watch Vanguard kick your ass."

Kutal's mouth stretched into a broad, evil grin. Then he said to the guards lurking nearby, "This *petaQ* is stinking up my bridge. Take him back to his quarters."

Brawny soldiers hauled Reyes away. He cooperated, but it made little difference to the Klingon guards, who seemed to like dragging him rather than letting him walk. He wondered how they planned to carry him down the ladder to the next deck.

Then they reached the ladderway and hurled him down through it.

He landed hard on the deck below, enduring most of the impact with his hands, elbows, and chest. Before he had a chance to assess whether he'd suffered any broken bones, his guards had descended the ladder, grabbed him, and resumed portering him to his quarters.

The door to his room hissed open, and the guards hurled him like a meaty bowling ball into the gray-green broom closet with a bunk and toilet that laughingly passed for quarters on this ship. He was grateful to come to a halt against his bunk frame without losing consciousness. The door slid shut, and he heard the gentle thump of magnetic bolts locking him inside.

Home, sweet home, he mused grimly, climbing onto his bunk.

There was something on the unpadded slab other than a threadbare blanket and a thin pillow: a book.

He picked it up. It was thick and heavy, leather-bound and embossed with gold-foil trim. Printed on its cover: *The Complete Works of William Shakespeare*. Beneath the title was a reproduction of the Bard's signature.

Tucked inside the front cover was a note, handwritten on a scrap of parchment. Reyes plucked it out and held it to the light so he could see it better.

"I hope you approve," it read, "though I think these plays were all better in the original Klingon." Then he saw the signature on the note and laughed.

"Best regards, Gorkon."

Interlude

16

May 26, 2267

Jetanien stood alone on a barren mesa in the midst of a yawning plain. Behind him sat his warp-capable diplomatic shuttle, parked and camouflaged.

Soon the sun would set. Another wasted day would draw to a close, and Jetanien would retire for the evening inside his tiny vessel, eat a reheated meal from the cache of provisions he'd brought from Vanguard, and go to sleep wondering where he had gone wrong.

Already days had passed in silence and solitude since his arrival on Nimbus III. The remote planet had seemed like an ideal setting for a clandestine political summit. Unclaimed and all but unpopulated, it was politically neutral and had little in the way of arable soil or exploitable resources. This was a rock for which no one would be willing to fight a war.

Whether that made it a good place in which to broker a lasting peace, or a good place to die in peace, remained to be seen.

Resting one clawed manus over the other in front of him, he watched a hundred shades of crimson bleed up from the horizon. He tapped his chitinous beak in amusement at one of his fleeting thoughts. *Did I really call this "a remote planet"? Aren't all planets remote, when one thinks about it?*

The sky had a thousand hues and was utterly empty. The Chelon diplomat searched it for any sign of the two peers he had invited here to meet him. The limited window of time during which they had agreed to meet had begun two days earlier.

Jetanien had been there at the first appointed hour. The others had not, but that was to be expected. In moments when his pessimism got the better of him, he feared they would never come at all.

Regardless, he was not dismayed or deterred. He would wait as long as was necessary. He was committed.

Listening to the wind and the dry susurrus of sand over stone, he reflected on the countless mistakes he had made in the past two years, the deadly blunders and the sobering gaffes.

I thought I could forge a new interstellar order, he berated himself. *What arrogance! What audacity!*

He pictured the face of Anna Sandesjo, a Klingon spy disguised as a human woman who had finagled herself a position as his senior attaché. His staff had detected her subterfuge fairly soon after her arrival on Vanguard, but Jetanien had overruled the regulations that demanded they report her to Starfleet Intelligence and the base commander.

I thought we could tap her comms, use her to find out what the Klingons really knew. Shame as deep as an ocean welled up inside him. *I gambled with her life—and she died for it.*

One failure after another haunted him. Political missteps, such as letting the trilateral talks with the Klingon Empire and the Tholian Assembly degenerate into a litany of threats, made him question his wisdom. Military miscalculations, such as not doing enough to forge an agreement between Starfleet and the settlers on Gamma Tauri IV, had costs thousands of lives.

My life is a leitmotif of hubris, he brooded.

The rattling of sabers at Mirdonyae V, to rescue the captured Starfleet officer Ming Xiong from Klingon custody, had only pushed the Federation and the Klingon Empire one step closer to war. Liberating Xiong had been absolutely necessary; Jetanien had never doubted it. But an accidental triggering of the mysterious Shedai machinery on that world had led to the planet's premature destruction, and the Klingons were making as much political hay from the tragedy as they could.

War seems inevitable, Jetanien lamented. *Will history say that I was to blame? That my misjudgments paved the way?*

He bowed his head until his chin almost touched the top of his chest carapace. *You narcissistic fool,* he chastised himself. *Millions of lives are on the brink of destruction, and you're fretting over your reputation? You're worrying about your legacy when others are fearing for their lives? How petty you are.*

Looking up, he drank in the majestic, bleak beauty of the planet around him. Barren, utterly desolate, worthless but for its atmosphere, this blighted orb represented his best hope of making his career stand for more than a farce. It was his last chance to create something of enduring, tangible value to the galaxy.

Part of him was unable to believe his plan could work. It seemed too far-fetched. Too optimistic. Too invested in ideals such as peace, trust, and hope.

The sun's edge sank below the horizon. In the sky, fiery streaks of red turned violet and purple. Stars peppered the darkling heavens.

Despondent, Jetanien walked toward his shuttle, prepared to consign another day to the abyss of time.

As he neared the open hatchway of his shuttle-turned-shelter, he heard something behind the cries of the wind, a rising shriek of thrusters underscored by the low thunder of displaced air. He stepped back from his shuttle, arched his back, and looked up into a growing point of light.

A ship was descending toward the mesa.

Jetanien adjusted his pristine white-and-gold raiment and straightened his black fez, making sure its white drape was centered behind his head. Then he held his hat in place as he watched the first of his invited peers arrive.

The small personal transport slowed as it completed its vertical descent and touched down on the mesa, only a few meters from Jetanien's vessel. Its roaring thrusters shook the ground as it settled into its landing, then they went silent as the ship powered down.

Its design was distinctively Klingon in origin.

Jetanien stepped toward it as its side hatch slid open.

Lugok, the Klingon former ambassador to Vanguard, emerged

from the vessel and strode forward to meet him. Taking the Chelon's *manus* in his powerful grip, Lugok said, "Jetanien, you crafty old *petaQ*. I wasn't sure you'd be here."

"I might have said the same of you," Jetanien replied, shaking the Klingon's hand. "But I'm encouraged to see you have not entirely given up on diplomacy."

Releasing his grip and withdrawing his hand, Lugok said with a jagged smile, "Don't go all soft on me, Chelon. I just came to see if D'tran of Romulus actually shows up. After all, the man's ancient, practically a piece of history himself. Who *wouldn't* want to meet him?"

Folding his arms, Jetanien replied, "Regardless of your motive for making the journey, thank you for coming." Gesturing to his shuttle, he added, "I was about to have dinner. If you—"

"I prefer to eat alone," Lugok said.

"Very well." Jetanien turned and went back inside his ship. Until D'tran of Romulus arrived, he would still be only waiting. But now at least he had company.

PART TWO

Night's Black Agents

17

May 29, 2267

Most mornings, Captain Rana Desai's walk from her quarters on Starbase 47 to the main entrance of the Starfleet JAG Corps' complex in the station's core was short and free of distractions. Today it was a gauntlet.

Desai had barely taken one step through the front door when she was set upon by packs of junior officers, all of them pushing data slates at her while calling out hurried requests.

"Captain, I need you to sign this . . ."

"Can you approve this change-of-venue order, sir?"

"Have you ruled on my discovery motion yet, Captain?"

She scribbled her signature, fired off curt answers, and delegated several bits of tedium. Just when she thought she had weathered all the obstacles keeping her from her desk, she was intercepted by one of her senior personnel, Lieutenant Holly Moyer. The willowy redhead, who kept her long straight hair tucked in a regulation bun while on duty, appeared beside Desai. "Good morning, Captain."

"It is so far," Desai said. "Here to ruin it for me?"

Moyer smiled. "If we had time for a game of racquetball, I would be." She handed Desai a data slate. "I finished the background checks on the incoming security personnel."

Skimming the report, Desai asked, "Any red flags?"

"Just one: Petty Officer Third Class Armstrong. Forensic specialist asking for a transfer from the *U.S.S. Orem.* Multiple reprimands for insubordination, and a history of creating public disturbances. I rejected his application."

Desai looked over the top sheet of Moyer's report and nodded. "Fine. Need anything from me?"

"Just sign next to the *X* and I'll bounce his butt to a graveyard shift on some rock where he won't bother anybody."

"Done," said Desai. She etched her autograph onto the transfer orders with the slate's stylus, then handed both items back to Moyer. "Bounce at will, Lieutenant."

Veering away toward her own office, Moyer replied with a smile and a playful salute, "Aye, sir."

The door of Desai's private office was open, and she could see her desk and chair. She nodded at her assistant and was almost inside her pseudo-sanctuary when a man called out to her. "Captain?"

She turned to see another of her senior lawyers, Commander Peter Liverakos, walking toward her. Like everyone else in the JAG complex that morning, the lean man with a salt-and-pepper goatee had a data slate tucked under his arm. Desai resisted the urge to heave a rueful sigh and said, "Yes, Commander?"

"Sorry to bother you, Captain, but the Orion ambassador's been giving an earful to Admiral Weiland about some of our prosecutions of Orion nationals here on the station. The admiral would like to know where we stand on those cases."

Desai rolled her eyes. "They broke the law on Federation soil. If they'd stayed on their own ships, this wouldn't be an issue." She pinched the bridge of her nose and closed her eyes for a moment. "Where did we leave those cases?"

"I've offered their counsels plea bargains. They haven't replied yet. My guess is they're hoping we'll drop the charges."

"And what does Admiral Weiland want us to do?"

"I think his exact words were, *Crucify them,* but I'd have to check the transcript to be sure."

"Revoke the plea deals," Desai said. "If they want mercy, let them give us something we can use. If they don't, Mars can always use a few more ditchdiggers."

"Aye, sir," Liverakos said with a nod and a grin, clearly eager to get to that day's work.

Finally free of distractions and emergent crises, Desai stepped into her office and settled into her chair. Her computer terminal powered up at the touch of a button, and she began looking over that day's official communiqués from the Starfleet JAG office on Earth, as well as daily situation reports from the station's security division. It had been a fairly busy overnight shift.

Her door signal buzzed. "Come," she said.

The door slid open, and her assistant, Ensign Roberta Lenger, entered carrying Desai's breakfast on a tray. She set a mug of steaming-hot coffee on Desai's desk. "Morning, Captain."

Desai picked up her coffee and smiled at the younger woman. "It is now."

Placing a small plate on the desk, Lenger said, "The commissary was out of raspberry pastries. I hope blueberry is okay."

"It's fine," Desai said. "What's my schedule this morning?"

"You have a meeting in twenty minutes with Admiral Nogura, to review an interdiction order for the Omicron Ceti colony."

Desai shook her head. "As if we need the threat of arrest to prevent people from visiting a planet whose star bathes it in Berthold rays."

Lenger shrugged. "You know how looters get."

"I certainly do. Is the docket set for the afternoon?"

"Yes, Captain. The disciplinary hearing for Crewman Sohl starts at fourteen hundred. You'll be presiding over opening statements and the first part of the prosecution's argument."

A sip of black coffee proved a few degrees too hot for Desai's tongue. She swallowed quickly, winced, and said, "Very good. Anything else?"

"The station's chief of security is outside and waiting to see you. And before you ask—no, he doesn't have an appointment."

Desai cast a longing glance at her breakfast, then grimaced. "I need to let my coffee cool anyway. Send him in."

"Yes, sir." Lenger stepped out and motioned the chief of security inside Desai's office.

Haniff Jackson was a man of average height and impressive physique. His red uniform tunic was stretched taut by his biceps and pectorals. He kept his black hair cropped close to his brown head, and he had recently shaved off his goatee, without which he looked younger than his thirty-six years. He strode to Desai's desk and stood at attention before it. "Captain."

"At ease, Lieutenant. Have a seat."

"Thank you, sir." Jackson pulled back one of the guest chairs and settled into it. Only then did Desai notice the red data card tucked into one of his massive palms.

She folded her hands on the desk. "What can I do for you?"

"For the past year, I've been investigating the bombing of the *U.S.S. Malacca,*" he said. "I've been combing the witness statements, the forensic reports, the internal sensor logs, flight-recorder data from the ship, everything." He handed her the data card. "I think I've found a new lead in the case."

"A new lead?" She looked at the card in her hand. "It's been almost a year. I'd think the trail would be cold by now."

"That's what I thought, too," Jackson said. "But with everything else that's happened here since then, we never really gave this case the attention it deserved. So I did some checking. All the logs and physical evidence we collected are still here, and any personnel we thought might be material witnesses have been kept on—no one's transferred off this station without my permission since the bombing."

Sliding the data card into a slot beside her computer, Desai asked, "And what is this new lead?"

"I have witnesses who link certain suspects to an ongoing smuggling operation involving the Orions on the outside and some of our own people here on the station."

Curious, she accessed the information on the card. Just as Jackson had said, he had several confidential but on-the-record statements from witnesses who alleged pockets of corruption were active within Starbase 47. "Has any of this been corroborated?"

"Only on a circumstantial basis," Jackson said. "That's why I need warrants for arrest, search and seizure, and analysis."

She admired his zeal for the job. "Consider them granted. You'll have them all in hard copy by oh-seven hundred tomorrow."

He stood and extended his hand. "Thank you, Captain."

She shook it. "You're welcome, Lieutenant. Good hunting."

Jackson nodded and left the office.

As the door closed, Desai reveled for a moment in the silence and solitude. She took a bite of her pastry and wiped a fleck of frosting from her upper lip.

Then she looked at the framed photo perched on the corner of her desk of a craggy-faced middle-aged man in a moment of serene repose, and she remembered why she felt so alone all the time, no matter how many people accosted her before breakfast.

Diego Reyes, the man she loved, was dead.

Desai put down her pastry and pushed the plate aside.

She wasn't hungry anymore.

Lieutenant Ming Xiong knew his monthly report to the brass was off to a bad start when the station's commanding officer, Rear Admiral Heihachiro Nogura, kicked it off by saying, "Stick to small words, Xiong. I'm in no mood for technobabble today."

"Yes, Admiral," Xiong said, wondering how he was supposed to convey the critical details of his presentation without using any of the terminology he had developed to define them.

Seated next to the admiral, and just as eager to hear Xiong's report on the latest research findings from the Vault—Vanguard's top-secret research lab devoted to the Shedai—was Xiong's civilian supervisor, Dr. Carol Marcus.

Marcus and Nogura were like night and day. She was blond and curvaceous, fair-complexioned with smooth skin. The Asian flag officer was thin and lean. His tanned face was lined with age and the burdens of office, and his brush-cut hair, once black, now was surrendering to waves of gray. Both had blue eyes, though of different shades—hers were sky blue, and his were closer to the deep bluish gray of tempered steel.

Seated side by side in Marcus's office—which had been

Xiong's office before Marcus was placed above him in the chain of command more than a year earlier (a slight that still had Xiong seething with resentment)—the scientist and the admiral each held a fresh cup of hot coffee. The rich aroma of French roast filled the tiny room, reminding Xiong he still hadn't been able to make time to get his first cup of the day.

"Over the past several weeks, my team and I here in the Vault have suspended all other projects to focus on the Mirdonyae Artifact," Xiong said. He used a small remote control to activate a wall monitor, which displayed the visual portion of his briefing. "I'm happy to say we've made a number of interesting discoveries about this amazing object."

An image of the artifact appeared on-screen. It was a twelve-sided polyhedron; each face of it was shaped like a symmetrical pentagon. "At first, we speculated it might be a key for unlocking Shedai technology, because it certainly provides an unprecedented level of access to their systems, but that wasn't enough to explain some of its more bizarre properties."

Xiong called up some comparative diagrams of energy readings from the object. "For instance, it seems to telepathically trigger a fear response in most humanoids who come within a few meters of it. We ruled out infrasonic frequencies as the cause, and then we found it was pumping out beta waves at a level we've never seen before. That's what was provoking the constant sensation of anxiety and sometimes even terror that people reported while working with it. We've contained the phenomenon by bombarding its isolation pod with inverted waves, which cancel out its effects."

He called up his next data screen: a complex chain of particles. "When we got down to the sub-nucleonic level of its surface material, we found the same multiphasic properties we've come to associate with the Shedai avatar, except it's been uniquely polarized to inhibit the passage of high-energy particles from its interior. This might have been accomplished by reorganizing atoms of a superdense transuranic element in a modified dilithium nanomatrix, but so far we haven't been able to look deeply enough to map its structure. Doctor Hofstadter has proposed a new kind of analysis that might help. It's called an icospectrogram, and I'd like to encourage you both to have a look at his proposal and consider prioritizing—"

Nogura said, "Xiong, I don't mean to minimize the fine work you and your team have done, but I'm afraid I need to cut this meeting short. Doctor Marcus led me to believe you had major developments to share. If you would be so kind as to sum up, I promise to read your unabridged report this evening."

"Yes, sir," Xiong said, secretly relieved to skip the more tedious sections of his report. He switched the image on-screen to one that resembled a ball of fire with burning tentacles flailing in all directions. "This is what lies at the center of the Mirdonyae Artifact. It's the source of the beta wave, and the reason the object can access any piece of Shedai technology it contacts. What you're looking at, sir, is a living but currently disembodied Shedai."

Nogura's eyebrows arched upward. "Really?" He got out of his chair and walked to the screen. Staring at it up close, he seemed quietly impressed. "That's *very* interesting." He looked expectantly at Xiong. "Dare I ask what your second major discovery was?"

"My analysis of the artifact's constituent elements and the nature of its fabrication have led me to conclude that, while it was made to interface with Shedai technology, it was *not* made by the Shedai but by *some other power*."

"Prompting the question of who made it," said Marcus.

Furrowing his salt-and-pepper eyebrows as he stared at the image on-screen, Nogura asked, "Could the Tholians have built something like this?"

Xiong shook his head. "I don't think so, sir. The materials are far more sophisticated than anything we've ever seen them create. For that matter, they're more advanced than anything we currently know how to produce."

"So we have no idea who made it," Nogura said.

"Not at the moment, sir," Xiong said.

The admiral frowned. Using a control panel next to the screen, he switched it to a star map of the Taurus Reach. "Your first report about the artifact said the Klingons had brought it to Mirdonyae from someplace else."

"Yes, sir."

"Do we know where this object of yours comes from?"

Xiong replied somewhat abashed, "Not yet, sir, but we're working on it."

"All right." Nogura faced Xiong and clasped his hands behind his back. "It looks like we've got a pretty good handle on the *what* part of this equation, and not so good a grasp on the *who, how,* or *where*. Which brings me to my last question. Do we know *why* this device was made? Was it to trap a Shedai? To control their machines? Or are those merely incidental details?"

Xiong bowed his head, partly out of humility. "Honestly, sir, we can't say yet why or where it was made, or who made it. But I can tell you this: we are all very, very eager to find out."

18

May 30, 2267

The *Skylla* was a dark ghost drifting in the void between the stars, silently haunting the shipping lanes of the Taurus Reach.

Silent from the outside, maybe, Pennington mused. He was barely able to hear himself think. He had learned to live with the constant racket caused by the repairs and upgrades he and T'Prynn had been making to the stolen ship since its hasty departure from Ajilon more than two months earlier.

"Please hand me a coil spanner," T'Prynn said, reaching a hand out of the crawl space toward Pennington.

Pennington poked around in the tool kit they had found in the ship's engineering compartment and once again was grateful for the time he had spent traveling with Quinn. Because the *Rocinante* had required many impromptu repairs, Pennington had needed to get the hang of starship maintenance to prevent Quinn from getting angry enough to blast him out an airlock. He located the coil spanner and passed it up to T'Prynn, who was hard at work making improvements to some crucial system in the belly of the ship. "Here you go."

"Thank you," T'Prynn said. Seconds later, deep thrumming sounds and a series of ponderous thumps resounded throughout the ship, shaking the deck under Pennington's feet.

He poked his head around the edge of the crawl space and said, "Mind if I ask what you're tinkering with?"

"I am recalibrating the governing mechanism for the ship's inertial dampeners," T'Prynn replied. "When combined with some improvements I plan to make in the firmware for the structural integrity field, we should notice a substantial improvement in this vessel's maneuverability at high-impulse speeds."

"Brilliant," he said, quietly impressed.

The day before she had rewired the vessel's shields. In the preceding weeks, she had improved the sensitivity of their scanners, extended the range of their communications, and enhanced the efficiency of the life-support system, ensuring they would have potable water and breathable air indefinitely.

Their lonely vigil in deep space would be limited only by the ship's available provisions, which upon their last inventory had been estimated at roughly an eight-month supply for two people.

T'Prynn shimmied out of the crawl space and handed the coil spanner back to Pennington. "The modifications are completed," she said. "However, we will need to improve its power supply to make certain it remains reliable during periods of stress."

"Right," Pennington said. "We could route power from the unused crew quarters on the port side to the inertial damper."

"An excellent suggestion," T'Prynn said, moving toward the ship's bow. "Will you assist me in setting up the shunt?"

"My pleasure," Pennington said. He picked up the tool kit and followed her. He was keen to see the Vulcan woman's next bit of technical wizardry. Though he'd learned a lot while hopping from planet to planet with Quinn, he felt as if he had learned more in the past two months of assisting T'Prynn on the *Skylla*.

She pointed to the deck of a narrow corridor that crossed the ship's main passageway. "We will need to remove these deck plates to access the power-distribution system."

"On it," Pennington said. He plucked a mini crowbar from the tool kit and started prying up the plates, backing down the corridor as he went.

T'Prynn lowered herself into the meter-deep space, which was filled with parallel rows of plasma conduits buzzing with energy. She opened some access panels and began shutting off selected circuits.

As the last deck plate in the short passage lifted free, Pennington set it aside, tilted up against the bulkhead like the others. Then he worked his way back through the knot of pipes and cables to T'Prynn. "What's next?"

"I need a decoupler to begin this procedure."

He fished out the tool and handed it to her. "Voilà."

"Thank you," she said, and set immediately to work creating a power shunt from the mass of electro-plasmoid spaghetti that was twisted around their feet.

He was content to stand and watch her work. Because she had eschewed his previous attempts at small talk, he refrained from speaking lest he break her concentration at a crucial moment.

It therefore came as a surprise to him when, while in the middle of her work, T'Prynn said, "I require a parametric scanner, and I wish to ask you a question."

He blinked a couple of times, then said, "Go ahead."

"Why did you join Doctor M'Benga when he brought me home to Vulcan?"

There was nothing accusatory in her voice. She had asked the question in a simple, matter-of-fact way, as if it had been an item of mere curiosity for her.

"You've asked me that before," he said.

"Yes, I have," she said. "On Vulcan." She looked up and fixed him with a piercing stare. "I found your first answer less than satisfactory."

Feeling caught, he bowed his head. "Fair enough." He took a moment to muster his courage. "The truth is, I came because of a vid I took of you." She set down her tool as he continued. "It was right after the bombing of the *Malacca* in Vanguard's hangar bay. Remember that?"

Her mien hardened. "I remember it."

"Well, when I heard the blast I came running with my recorder, trying to get a shot of it for the news. And I was panning with this piece of debris tumbling through zero-*g* in the hangar . . . and the next thing I knew, I was looking at you." He looked into her eyes as he added, "And you were crying."

T'Prynn half turned away, her face neutral but her body language telegraphing shame. "I was not well," she said.

"I know," Pennington said. "But the point is, what I saw of you was real—your pain, your sorrow, your rage. And I knew what you were feeling, because I'd been there myself."

T'Prynn nodded. "When your mistress died on the *Bombay*."

"Right," he said. "When I lost Oriana." He cleared his throat. "Anyway, once I'd shared that moment with you . . . I don't know. I guess you became more real to me: a person instead of a villain. On some level, I guess I felt that maybe you were the only person I knew who could really understand the pain I'd felt." He sighed. "The pain I still feel sometimes."

Silence fell between them. T'Prynn composed herself and faced him again. "Can you ever forgive me for the wrongs I have committed against you, Mister Pennington?"

He handed her the parametric scanner.

"I already have," he said. "And you can call me Tim."

19

June 2, 2267

Quinn dismounted slowly from the back of his *mellul,* a large but relatively docile animal native to Golmira and domesticated by the Denn. The huge, long-bodied quadrupeds had the gracile bodies of hunting cats, and their vulturelike faces were topped by feline ears and surrounded by enormous feathered manes. Their broad and taloned paws seemed well-adapted to traversing the sands of the desert north of Leuck Shire.

The light of two moons spilled brightly across the dune ahead of Quinn as he dropped to his belly and crawled up the slope behind Bridy Mac. They both had adopted native garb over the past few weeks after finding it well-suited to the rigors of desert travel and survival, but the cool coarse sand still got into the robes' folds—and into everything else, for that matter.

Bridy stopped at the crest of the dune and retrieved a pair of holographically enhanced binoculars from under her robes. She activated the device and peered through it into the night. "There's our temple," she whispered to Quinn. "Finally."

"You say that like it's my fault this took three months," Quinn replied as he inched to the dune's peak and peered toward the ruins a couple of hundred meters away. "I didn't ask to get socked in by a six-week sandstorm or sidetracked by monsoon season, and I'm also not the one who gave us food poisoning."

Adjusting her field glasses, Bridy said, "No, but you did lead us smack into that caravan of desert nomads back in the foothills last week, didn't you."

He pulled out his own binoculars. "Ain't my fault Naya and her little farmer friends got dog shit for intel. They said the ruins'd be clear till high summer."

"It *is* high summer."

"Well, *now* it is. Besides, if we'd just flown here in ol' Rosie instead of humpin' it over land on these beaked cats, the delays wouldn't have mattered."

She glared at Quinn. "No, but we'd have brought every nomad for twenty klicks down on top of us when they saw the glow from your thrusters landing on their mound of holy rocks." Continuing her recon of the nearby ruins, she added, "We're just lucky we were able to fall back before they saw us." She looked up from behind her binoculars. "Check out the part of the temple visible through that collapsed section, about a third of the way in from the left. Looks like the Denn built a temple around a Conduit."

Quinn followed the lines of the temple's decaying stone façade until he found the area Bridy was talking about. He switched to a higher magnification. A second later, the image came back into focus, and he saw the structure inside the stony shell: bizarre fluid whorls cast from what looked like superbly polished obsidian. The same kind of design and material he had seen in the Shedai city on Jinoteur.

"Jackpot," he said. "Desert kooks, meet your planet's ticking time bomb." He looked at Bridy. "What's our play?"

Bridy squinted as she eyed the temple. "The nomads are all around it, but none of them seems to be going inside it. That's good." She put away her binoculars and took out her tricorder. "First we document the find, take detailed readings to send back to Vanguard, and gather samples for analysis on the *Rocinante*."

"How you gonna do all that from way over here?"

She scowled at him. They both knew the mission called for her to go inside the temple and scan it from within, but he couldn't resist poking fun at her.

"We'll need a distraction," she said. Pointing to the left, she added, "Maybe a small explosion past that big dune to draw them away. While they're poking around in the sand, I'll slip through their camp and into the temple."

"Okay, sure," Quinn said. "I could set that up, no problem. But they ain't gonna fall for the same trick twice. Hell, they might not fall for it once. Say you get inside—what's your exit strategy? You think they'll just let you stroll on out?"

Bridy began crawling backward down the dune. "I just figured you'd do something gallant, like let them chase you."

Shimmying down the slope beside her, he replied, "What in tarnation makes you think I'd do that?"

"Call it a hunch," Bridy said. Once they were safely out of sight they stood up. Bridy walked to her *mellul* and retrieved a small backpack from her saddle. "How long to set up the explosion?"

"Not long," Quinn said. "Fifteen minutes, tops. I . . ." He let his voice trail off as a glint of light from overhead caught his eye. He craned his head back and gazed skyward.

A single star swiftly grew larger, and the air shuddered with the low-frequency roar of fusion engines.

Watching the point of light grow and reveal itself to be a bulky ship on a rapid vertical descent, Quinn remarked, "That don't look good."

"No, it doesn't," said Bridy, who hurried back up the dune.

Quinn crawled as quickly as he was able. By the time he caught up to Bridy and nosed over the sandy peak, a Klingon heavy transport was touching down fewer than fifty yards from the temple—in the midst of the nomads' camp.

He expected the desert-dwellers to flee. Instead they swarmed around the Klingon ship and brandished their swords, spears, and primitive bows.

A massive bulkhead on the ship's ventral hull detached and lowered into a broad ramp. Seconds later a battalion of Klingon soldiers marched down the incline in a *V* formation. Those in the front rank had their disruptors leveled.

Loudspeakers on the outer hull of the transport blared commands at the natives, who hooted and whooped as they charged up the ramp.

The Klingons held their ground and opened fire.

Quinn winced at the blinding crimson flashes of disruptor fire. When he opened his eyes a moment later, he saw the Klingons continuing to advance—stepping on the charred, smoking corpses of the slain Denn in their path.

A second wave of nomads stood paralyzed with indecision. Another barrage of disruptor fire cut down roughly fifty more of them. The surviving Denn nomads fled in a panic, running in all directions as they abandoned their tents and mounts.

Even from more than a hundred meters away, Quinn could smell the sickly perfume of scorched flesh.

Next came the rumble of motors and the clank of rolling treads. Heavy excavation vehicles started to roll slowly down the ramp from the transport ship. A fresh platoon of Klingons carried large containers stenciled with markings in their native script. Flood lamps mounted on the starboard side of the transport snapped on and lit up the entire temple at once.

"So much for Plan A," Quinn said. "Unless you still think a little puff-boom over that dune'll do the trick."

Bridy frowned. "Not a chance. We're lucky their sensors haven't picked us up yet. We should get moving before they do."

Moving on knees and elbows, she backed down the dune until they were out of sight again. Quinn followed her, and they pulled themselves up into the saddles of their *melluls*. As they began the loping, swaying gallop back toward Leuck Shire, Quinn quipped, "It's just as well they showed up now. I always hate when these things are too easy."

The sun was up but still low on the horizon as McLellan and Quinn reached the outskirts of Tegoresko, the nominal capital of Leuck Shire. "We should go the rest of the way on foot," McLellan said. "In case the Klingons are here, too."

"Makes sense," Quinn said.

They guided their *melluls* inside a low, three-walled ruin. McLellan dismounted first, but Quinn was right behind her. He grabbed a pipe that rose up from the concrete foundation and tried to shake it, but it held fast. "This'll do," Quinn said. He tied his mount's reins around the pipe, then did the same for those of McLellan's steed. "Need anything from the packs?"

"No," McLellan said. "Let's travel light. We'll take turns on point every couple of blocks."

Quinn nodded. "Sounds good. I'll go first." He peeked through the doorway and scouted the street. "Clear."

He slipped through the door, and she stayed close behind him. They crossed the boulevard of broken asphalt, whose prominent fissures were choked with weeds.

Darting from one building's corner to the next, McLellan remained alert for any sign the Klingons might be near. Her fifth turn on point, she heard the sound of disruptors echoing in the distance ahead of them. "Great," she muttered.

"Ain't nothin' to panic about," Quinn said as they ducked for cover inside a deep doorway. "Figured this might happen. The ship's camouflaged, it'll be fine."

McLellan regarded her partner with a scornful stare. "You think I'm worried about the ship?"

"I sure as hell would be," Quinn said.

Frustration made her jaw clench. "I'm worried about Naya and her people. If they make the same mistake the nomads did—"

"They won't," Quinn said. "I showed 'em what Klingons look like and told 'em not to piss the lobster-heads off."

The tension in her jaw melted away as her face went slack with disbelief. "You told them about the Klingons?"

"Seemed like a good idea at the time," Quinn said. "And seein' as they're here, I think I made the right call."

"You realize that's potentially a Prime Directive violation," McLellan said.

He rolled his eyes. "I call it bein' a Good Samaritan. Ain't like the Denn don't know about other worlds, or warp flight. I didn't pollute some precious paradise. And if my bit of friendly advice keeps these folks from gettin' their faces shot off, I'll just call that a win, thank you very much."

Much as it pained McLellan to admit it, he was probably right. "Okay, fine," she said, motioning him to move on. "You're up on point."

Quinn checked the street and moved out. He blazed a trail through the rubble beside the streets, using it for cover as they passed near the village's central square.

Minutes later he and McLellan ducked under a slab of shattered cement and waited while a Klingon squad marched past. When the crisp echoes of stomping jackboots receded, McLellan peeked out from under the slab toward the town square.

Naya and her daughter, Ilka, stood at the front of a phalanx of Denn, flanked by the landgraves who had come to dinner with McLellan and Quinn on their first night as Naya's guests.

A goateed Klingon commander stood facing Naya and read aloud from a scroll-like document. McLellan didn't speak much *tlhIngan Hol,* but she understood enough to know he was explaining the new laws under which the Denn would henceforth live as subjects of the Klingon Empire. As was typical for any such proclamation, the penalty for nearly every offense against the Empire, no matter how trivial, was summary execution.

Quinn looked at the Klingon commander and whispered, "Meet the new boss."

"Pretty much." She stole glances in either direction along the street. "Looks clear. If we can make it behind that row of building façades over there, we should have solid cover all the way back to the ship."

He patted her shoulder to let her know he was moving ahead of her on point, then he broke cover and skulked across the road. She stayed with him, moving quickly but also quietly. For several seconds she felt precariously exposed, but then they were off the street and concealed once more in the embrace of Tegoresko's crumbling urban landscape.

It took them more than half an hour to reach the *Rocinante,* but to their mutual relief the scanner-blocking modifications Starfleet Intelligence had installed on the vessel had kept it hidden from the Klingons. As an added precaution, Quinn had moved the ship from its original landing site to one in the heart of the city, inside a roofless building whose windows and street-level access points had been boarded up or bricked in.

After the ship had been secured, the Denn had added a flimsy faux roof to the building. Though the roof wasn't strong enough to support even one man's weight, it looked more than solid enough to thwart a visual scan, either from orbit or from a recon flyover. As long as the Klingons didn't make a hard-target inspection of every abandoned structure in the city, the *Rocinante* would likely be safe for some time.

Quinn slipped through a gap in one boarded-over window arch, stopped, and listened. "Okay," he said. "No one here." He led McLellan inside the building and over a series of rickety plank walkways and ramps that hugged the walls and sloped down to the bottom of its foundation. He jogged to the ship and entered the code to unlock its rear hatch.

The gangway lowered with a dull hiss and a cloud of vapor. "Home, sweet home," Quinn said as the ramp touched the ground.

He and McLellan hurried inside. She went straight to the cockpit and fired up the communications system.

"Can you do me a favor?" she asked. "Check the sensors and see what kind of ship the Klingons have in orbit?"

"On it," Quinn said, powering up the sensor package. He called up the results and grimaced. "It's a D-7 battle cruiser."

"Lovely."

McLellan typed quickly and composed a brief, code-worded report: *Saw sights. Neighbors are here with a big dog. Staying with friends. Would rather see family. Waiting for next song.* She encrypted the message with SI's latest ciphers and sent it in a low-frequency subspace burst transmission to Vanguard.

"There," she said. "Message is away. Now we wait."

Quinn smiled. "I know a few ways to pass the time." Before she could scold him for his shameless flirtations, he held up a deck of cards. "Texas Hold 'Em, no wild cards, no jokers."

She sighed. *At least it'll keep us busy until we get a response from Starfleet.* "Okay," she said, "but no strip bets. We *both* keep our clothes on this time. Especially you."

He frowned but started dealing out cards. "You're no fun."

20

One minute the view outside the *Skylla*'s cockpit was nothing but stars surrounding a dull orange rock of a planet; the next it was dominated by a Klingon bird-of-prey dropping out of warp all but on top of Pennington and T'Prynn's stolen vessel.

"Bloody hell," Pennington said as he scrambled to shut down all of *Skylla*'s nonessential systems. "Where'd they come from?"

T'Prynn was the picture of calm as she stepped into the cockpit and took her seat beside Pennington. She looked at her console. "They appear to be generating a field that returns false sensor data. Their stealth technologies are improving."

As the hum of the ship's onboard systems faded to silence and the console lights dimmed and went out, Pennington eyed the warship cruising away toward the planet and replied, "The Klingons are developing stealth systems?"

"Indeed," T'Prynn said. "They have been working on them for several years. The fact that this ship eluded our long- and short-range sensors suggests it possesses advanced silent-running protocols." The bird-of-prey became a silhouetted speck against the distant planet. "Fortunately, they do not seem to have detected us, which might indicate their new technology restricts their own sensors' range and precision."

Pennington said, "Lucky us."

The only console still active aboard the *Skylla* was T'Prynn's piloting station. She keyed the ship's thrusters and initiated a slow roll and turn. "We will need to take cover behind the nearby moon to ensure we aren't detected by the Klingons when they return from their initial orbit of the planet," she said as the starscape spun outside their canopy.

I guess I should be used to this by now, Pennington mused as T'Prynn guided the *Skylla* toward safety. During the past few weeks, in between rebuilding the ship from the inside out, they had been forced to "go dark" several times to evade various Klingon vessels and, in one case, a Tholian cruiser.

The enemy ships were ostensibly on routine patrols of unclaimed regions of space, through which he and T'Prynn were tracking signal fragments from two private vessels: the *Omari-Ekon,* an Orion merchantman that belonged to notorious crime lord Ganz; and the *Icarion,* an argosy captained by Ganz's chief enforcer, a Nalori by the name of Zett Nilric. Less than a year earlier, both vessels had often been docked at Vanguard. With the change in the station's leadership, however, the two ships had been pressured into plying their illicit trade elsewhere.

Pennington kept an eye on a timer that was counting down when the bird-of-prey would emerge from behind the planet and be in a position to train its sensors on the *Skylla.* "Ten seconds."

"Acknowledged," T'Prynn said. "Engaging impulse drive at ten percent." A slight bump accompanied the increase in speed as the impulse engines kicked in. "That should move us out of range behind the moon before the Klingons—"

T'Prynn's hand shot up from the helm and pressed a master kill switch over her head. The *Skylla* went dark. The engines cut off instantly, and it began a slow roll as it drifted into the moon's shadow. She and Pennington floated up from their seats in the suddenly zero-gravity environment.

Alarmed, he asked, "What? What just happened?"

"There is another vessel behind the moon," T'Prynn said.

She pointed at it. Pennington strained to discern the shape from the shadows, but then it became clear: two cylindrical warp nacelles mounted on struts beneath a saucer-shaped primary hull. It was a *Miranda*-class vessel, the same type of starship on which his lover Oriana had died more than a year earlier.

"Well, hello," he said. "Who's that, I wonder?"

"If recent news reports are accurate, it is most likely the *U.S.S. Buenos Aires*, presently assigned to Vanguard." As the *Skylla* tumbled, they began to lose their view of the Starfleet ship. She craned her neck to study it for a few moments more. "Its running lights are off, and its nacelles are dimmed. It appears to be keeping a low profile, as well. Most likely its crew is tasked with monitoring Klingon patrols in this sector."

"Do you think they saw us?"

"It's difficult to be certain," T'Prynn said. "However, the fact that we were already in low-power mode when we moved behind the moon might work in our favor. If I was quick enough, it is possible they were unable to obtain a sensor lock before we went dark."

The languid tumbling of the *Skylla* momentarily returned the *Buenos Aires* to view outside the cockpit. Pennington noted how much closer it seemed. "Can't they detect us at this range?"

"To passive sensors we should appear as a bit of random space rock or other debris," T'Prynn said. "Only an active sensor sweep would detect our life signs. It is likely they will refrain from running such scans to avoid alerting the bird-of-prey."

Several minutes passed as the *Skylla* rolled slowly through space. The only sound Pennington could hear inside its cockpit was his own shallow breathing. He began to relax when it became clear the Starfleet ship had not powered up.

"Looks like we're in the clear," he said. "Good reflexes on the kill switch, by the way." He turned toward T'Prynn. "Though I have to wonder why we're running scared from a Starfleet ship. I mean, ducking the Klingons I understand. But it's not like Starfleet makes a habit of boarding civilian vessels, not even in the Taurus Reach."

One of T'Prynn's eyebrows twitched upward. Pennington didn't know if he should interpret that microexpression as one of curiosity, irritation, or disdain.

"You might wish to remember our vessel is stolen," T'Prynn said. "Though we've altered its transponder identification, even a routine check would show the *Skylla* to be, at best, an unregistered vessel—and Starfleet does halt and impound such ships within the territories it controls."

He frowned but nodded at the correction. "I guess you have a point," he said.

"Furthermore," she added, "you should keep in mind that I am at present a fugitive from Starfleet military justice, and you are a Federation citizen who has aided and abetted my flight from custody."

"Say no more," Pennington replied.

Looking out at the lazily turning cosmos, he took her meaning perfectly: for now, in the Taurus Reach, everyone was their enemy; no one was their friend.

All they had was each other.

21

"I nailed him," Lieutenant Jackson said. "Right to the wall."

Rana Desai looked up from the muddle of sworn affidavits, warrant applications, and defense-counsel motions littering her desk to see the chief of security leaning in her office's open doorway. "You made an arrest already?"

"Even better," Jackson said, walking into her office and beaming with pride. He held up a data slate. "I got a signed confession out of him."

Desai held up one palm. "Back up: who is he, and to what has he confessed?"

Jackson handed the data slate to Desai. "Petty Officer First Class Dmitri Strout has confessed to willful breaches of this station's operational security in exchange for monetary compensation from a third party." He pointed to one of the guest chairs. "Mind if I . . . ?"

"Take a seat."

Jackson sat down as Desai skimmed through the arrest report and Strout's confession. It was a long file.

She looked up at Jackson. "Care to sum it up for me?"

"Glad to," he said. "We'd received anonymous tips that Strout was accessing data for which he wasn't cleared. He worked in the lower cargo facility, mostly handling munitions. But he was pulling entire cargo manifests, both incoming and outgoing, using his supervisor's access code."

"How did he acquire that?"

Jackson's narrowed gaze telegraphed his doubts. "He claims Chief Langlois was careless and didn't use the voiceprint safeguard, but her access logs show she did. I think it's more likely someone helped him hack her terminal and copy her voiceprint, but I haven't been able to get him to admit it yet."

"I see," Desai said. "Go on."

"Our surveillance operative witnessed Strout accessing the terminal in Langlois's office, copying classified manifests onto a data card, and depositing the card in some kind of a dead drop in one of the unoccupied sections on level sixteen. We recovered the data card and substituted it with one loaded with false information and marked with a tracking tag. So far, however, no one has come to check the dead drop."

Desai chortled softly. "In other words, you got made."

Jackson responded with a taut and long-suffering smile. "Yeah. I guess we did." He shrugged. "Anyway, we conducted a search of his quarters and found evidence Mister Strout has been sending unauthorized transmissions to an Orion merchant vessel known as the *Omari-Ekon.*"

Nodding, Desai said, "I'm familiar with it. Continue."

"We haven't been able to break the encryption on his messages to the *Omari-Ekon,* but we know the cipher he used isn't one of ours. Our liaison from Starfleet Intelligence says the most likely origin for the encryption key was Orion."

Quickly perusing the rest of the information on the data slate, Desai asked, "How many stolen manifests can we positively trace back to Mister Strout?"

"At least a dozen," Jackson said. "Several of the manifests were for ships that got boarded in deep space by pirates within seventy-two hours of his accessing their logs."

So close, Desai thought, *but still so far.*

She put down the data slate. "You've put together some very damning information . . . Petty Officer Strout is inarguably guilty of enabling pirates in this sector to target the most lucrative cargo on the most vulnerable civilian ships. However, after looking over his confession, I notice it contains no mention of anything having to do with the bombing of the *Malacca*. For that matter, none of the evidence you collected links this suspect to that event in any way, shape, or manner."

Jackson looked taken aback. "What are you saying? You won't prosecute him?"

"No, I'm not saying that," Desai said. "I'll run Strout's guts up a flagpole tomorrow at reveille if it makes you happy. There's enough in here to make sure he dies of old age in a penal colony." She leaned forward. "What I'm driving at is you came to me asking for warrants so you could investigate the *Malacca* bombing. But nothing you've brought me today links him directly to that case. Frankly, when you poked your face through my door and declared you'd nailed him, I was hoping for something more . . . relevant."

The security chief sighed. "I understand. And I know it doesn't look like I made any progress on the *Malacca* case. But I'm convinced Strout is only the tip of the iceberg. And if I'm gonna dig any deeper, I need more help."

Intrigued, Desai asked, "Such as . . . ?"

There was a determined look in Jackson's eyes. "I think Starfleet Intelligence could decrypt his messages to the *Omari-Ekon* if someone with enough clout told them to do it. And I'm betting if we could enforce a warrant to review detailed logs of all communication-relay traffic between here and Orion for the past fourteen months, we'd find new clues to the parties behind the *Malacca* bombing."

"How very optimistic of you," Desai said. "Unfortunately, trying to lay claim to that much raw data risks inviting charges of privacy invasion. We'd have to clear a lot of legal hurdles. And the odds are we'd be refused or overturned on appeal."

"Maybe," Jackson said. "But we'll never know until we ask."

Unable to disagree with his reasoning, Desai relented. "All right," she said. "I'll submit a request for the comm logs."

Rising from his chair, Jackson replied, "Who could ask for anything more?" He stopped at the doorway. "I'll bet you one of my furlough days we get the logs."

His challenge made her smile because Jackson had a well-earned reputation on Vanguard: he never lost a bet.

"You're on," she said.

Admiral Nogura stood in his office facing a wall-size map of the Taurus Reach. His attention was focused on one highlighted dot more than a hundred light-years rimward of Vanguard's position. He asked the Starfleet Intelligence liaison, "When did the signal come in?"

"Approximately thirty-nine minutes ago," said Commander Serrosel ch'Nayla, a middle-aged Andorian *chan* who had filled the position formerly occupied by the now-AWOL Lieutenant Commander T'Prynn. "Its arrival was delayed by the lack of subspace radio relays between here and its point of origin."

The admiral threw a quizzical look at the blue-skinned, white-haired humanoid. "I thought we had relays seeded throughout the region."

"We did," said ch'Nayla. "The Klingons and Tholians have made a sport of seeking them out and destroying them."

Nogura felt the muscles in his lean and weathered face tense as he digested that bit of news. "Wonderful." He nodded at the map. "So what do I need to know about this signal?"

"It's from a pair of nonofficial-cover agents. They were sent to a planet the Vault team thought might harbor a Shedai artifact, and the agents found one—a Conduit. But before they could make a detailed analysis of the structure, a Klingon D-7 battle cruiser entered orbit. It's likely the Klingons have established a major presence on the planet's surface."

Noting the proximity of the system in question to the border of the Klingon Empire, Nogura said, "It was only a matter of time. We know they've been looking for the Shedai artifacts. With that one so close to their space, I'm surprised they didn't find it sooner." He turned away from the map. "Did our agents get off the planet safely?"

"No, Admiral," said ch'Nayla. "They've requested a priority extraction by Starfleet."

Pivoting toward the Andorian, Nogura replied, "I suspect that would provoke more problems than it might solve."

"I have to concur." Ch'Nayla keyed in some commands through an interface on the wall. The star map was updated to display the positions of dozens of Klingon military vessels across the Taurus Reach. "Any attempt to extract our agents will only draw attention to them and risk an escalation of hostilities with the Klingons. If the Empire has claimed that world, our presence there could be seen as a breach of the Treaty of Organia."

"Considering the ink isn't even dry on that thing yet, that would be bad." Nogura stroked his chin while he pondered the situation. "Do we know for a fact the Klingons have claimed the planet?"

"Yes. Signal intercepts suggest they have undertaken a campaign to subjugate the local population. Normally, that would not be a matter of immediate concern. However, our two agents on the planet are being sheltered by a local community. If they are discovered, they will almost certainly be tortured and forced to reveal classified information about Operation Vanguard."

Shaking his head slowly, Nogura said, "This mess just keeps getting bigger the longer I look at it." He turned away from ch'Nayla and began pacing in front of the star map. "Even if I'm willing to risk sparking a war with the Klingons, that system's out at the ass end of nothing. It'll take nearly three months to get anybody out there. Can your people hang on that long?"

Ch'Nayla's antennae swiveled as if they were tracking Nogura's back-and-forth ambulations. "I think so," ch'Nayla said. "One of them is a Starfleet officer who has completed a full SERE program. The other is a civilian operative who has on many occasions proved to be . . . resourceful."

"All right," Nogura said. "Here's what I want them to do until we're able to pull them out of the fire. Tell them to inflict as much damage on the Klingons as possible while keeping a low profile. They should focus on sabotage, inciting civil unrest, and, if they're up for it, guerilla warfare."

"An extremely hazardous assignment," ch'Nayla said. "And not exactly one in keeping with their mission parameters."

Nogura folded his hands behind his back. "Sometimes, Commander, we need to go beyond our limits and exceed our own expectations." He stopped and faced the Andorian. "This is one of those times."

"Aye, sir. I will relay your order to the agents." The lanky *chan* walked to Nogura's side and turned his attention to the star map. "Can I at least assure them truthfully that help is en route?"

"Good question," Nogura said. He stepped over to the control interface and called up a deployment grid for all Starfleet vessels currently active in the sector. "Now that we have enough reinforcements to maintain steady patrols in the alpha and beta grids, I think we can free up a few ships." Standing in front of the wall, he pointed at different vessels' labeled icons. "The *Gloucester* and the *Buenos Aires* can hold the line in the choke point between the Tholians and the Klingons. And the *Intrepid* is close enough that I can task it to watch the Klingon border." He folded his arms and tapped one index finger against his upper lip. "If we're going to make a bid for that distant chunk of rock, we'll have to go all in. We'll send the *Defiant,* the *Endeavour,* and the *Akhiel.* That should be enough to make that D-7 bug out of orbit on the double."

Ch'Nayla's eyebrows lifted in surprise, and his antennae twitched. "Are you certain that will be a prudent use of our resources, Admiral? Sending two *Constitution*-class starships and a frigate escort on a mission that far from Vanguard is a major commitment. It will be at least six months before they are able to return to the station."

"I know. But look how much Starfleet has increased its presence in this sector in the past few months. I think we might be in a position to flex our muscles a bit." He stepped closer to the star map and permitted himself a small but devilish smile of anticipation. "The Klingons seem to get a kick out of running our colonists off their planets. Let's see how *they* like running for a change."

22

June 4, 2267

After more than two months cooped up inside the *Skylla,* adrift in deep space, Pennington was certain he had read and re-read every word printed on every surface and scrap of paper aboard the ship. He'd nosed through every document in the ship's databanks. Listened to every audio file. Watched every vid.

He had tried filling the hours, days, and weeks with his own writing, but his thoughts felt unfocused. The harder he tried to shape his recent experiences into a narrative, the greater his mental paralysis became. Words refused to come.

Sitting alone in the cockpit, gazing out at the stars, he let himself drift into an almost hypnotic trance. Enveloped in blissful silence, he let his mind go quiet. What had started out weeks earlier as excruciating boredom had evolved into something new and unexpected: serenity.

The noise and chaos of his old life fell away. He let go of the need to fill every moment with ordered thoughts, pointless conversation, or entertaining distraction. Finally graced with a surfeit of time, he discovered the simple pleasure of merely letting himself *be* . . .

An alert flashed on the cockpit's main console, and its repetitive buzzing sound dragged him back into the bleak reality of the moment.

He turned and shouted down the main corridor, "T'Prynn! One of your gizmos is harshing my mellow!"

A door slid open, and he heard T'Prynn's soft footfalls. As she entered the cockpit and edged past Pennington to take her seat, he noticed she smelled freshly showered, and that she was wearing her hair down.

She silenced the alert and activated the sensor console. After studying the readout for a few seconds, she removed a small transceiver from the console and placed it in her left ear. Listening intently, she turned to Pennington and said, "We have located the *Omari-Ekon*."

"Ganz's ship?" His pulse quickened. "Is it close?"

"Very," T'Prynn said. "However, it is moving away from us. We will need to adjust course to pursue it."

T'Prynn accessed the helm controls and started keying in commands. A low purr from the aft section accompanied a subtle vibration in the deck as the engines engaged. Outside the cockpit, the stars seemed to spiral and slip away as T'Prynn changed the *Skylla*'s heading.

Pennington found himself imagining worst-case scenarios. "If we go and start following Ganz's ship, don't you think he might notice? And maybe take offense?"

"We will maintain a moderate distance from his vessel," T'Prynn said. "Thanks to the improvements you and I have made to this ship, we might be able to shadow the *Omari-Ekon* without coming within range of its sensors."

"Do you think that's likely? That they might not see us?"

"No, I do not. Orion vessels often are better equipped than Federation civilian starships. We must expect their sensors are at least as accurate as our own and act accordingly." She entered more commands into the helm. "I have programmed the autopilot to maintain a constant bearing and range from Ganz's ship. After I adjust our warp signature to match that of the *Omari-Ekon*, we should appear to its sensors as a subspace echo."

"Will that really work?"

"As I lack powers of precognition, I cannot answer your question with absolute certainty. However, I believe this tactic has a greater chance of concealing our presence than would doing nothing."

Pennington smiled at her. "Which is a lot of fancy words for, 'I'm not a fortune teller, but it's worth a try.' You also could have just said, 'I don't know.'"

"I could have, but I did not." Though her face betrayed no hint of emotion, Pennington was certain he had detected an undercurrent of sarcasm in her voice. She ignored his probing stare and turned her chair to work at a different console. "Now that we have a lock on the vessel's position, our next priority will be to access its internal and external communications."

"Intercepting external communications ought to be a snap," Pennington said. "At least, for someone like you, I mean. But how do you plan on listening to their internal comms?"

Engrossed in her work, she answered without turning around. "I will attempt to remotely activate and enable a number of taps that were covertly installed aboard the *Omari-Ekon* during my tenure as Vanguard's liaison to Starfleet Intelligence."

Leaning forward to make sure he'd heard her correctly, he asked, "Did you say *taps*? As in electronic eavesdropping?"

"Correct," T'Prynn said. "Once I bring them online, I should be able to access a number of linked and isolated databanks aboard that ship, as well as monitor its real-time internal transmissions."

Pennington slowly dragged his palm across his stubbled face and ruminated on that new bit of information. "Aren't all Orion vessels legally recognized as foreign soil by the Federation?"

"Yes, they are." The screen in front of her filled with a cascade of raw information. Schematics, strings of alien text, static images, and vid-clips flashed by. "The taps are still in place and fully functional. All checksums are valid, indicating they have not been tampered with."

After a moment of grappling with his conflicting emotions, Pennington asked, "Isn't what you're doing illegal? Or against diplomacy or something? What if you started a war?"

"It is highly unlikely my act of private espionage would constitute an act of war," T'Prynn replied. "Even if the Orion government wished to take such an exaggerated level of umbrage at my violation of the privacy of one of their ships, its forces would not pose a significant military threat."

He rolled his eyes. "I'm not sure that's the benchmark by which we should—"

"In any event, it is irrelevant unless the commander of the *Omari-Ekon* wishes to publicly admit its security was breached. Based on my previous observations of Neera, I would speculate she is far too pragmatic to risk diminishing her public image by admitting to such a failure on her ship."

Now thoroughly confused, Pennington said, "Hang on. I thought the *Omari-Ekon* was Ganz's ship. Who's Neera?"

"She pretends to be Ganz's harem madam and personal mistress. In fact, like many Orion women who wield influence through powerful men, she lets Ganz serve as the public face of her criminal organization while she rules from the shadows."

Pennington nodded. "I suppose you learned that by using these taps?"

"Yes," T'Prynn said.

"Did any of the information you obtained ever lead to an arrest or a conviction of any of Ganz's men?"

She partially turned her head in his direction. "No."

"Why not?"

"As you have duly noted, our placement of the taps was a violation of sovereign Orion territory. Because they were illegally installed, none of the intelligence they provided could ever be legally admissible in a Federation court of law or Starfleet court-martial."

He waved a hand at the screen full of data and snapped, "If you knew none of this could be used for prosecutions, then what the hell was it for?"

Swiveling her chair to face him directly, T'Prynn said in a cool and measured tone, "Security."

23

Shocks of impact traveled through Quinn's gloved fists and up his arms into his shoulders with every punch he landed on the heavy bag. The leather-covered piece of boxing equipment was suspended loosely by a six-strand chain secured in the overhead and anchored by a single chain to the cargo bay's deck.

Feels good just to hit something, he thought as he bobbed and danced around the bag, throwing jabs and crosses as he went.

He'd always thought the hardest part of boxing—aside from not losing his marbles after getting hit—was the footwork. All that back and forth, the sidling dodges, the stutter steps. It was vital for balance and tempo, for power and follow-through, but it just didn't come naturally to Quinn.

A fast combination: two jabs, two body blows, a knee aimed at where a groin should be, a hard right cross.

Backing off a step, he felt off-balance. *Keep the hands up,* he reminded himself. *Keep 'em tight, one in front of the other.*

Stepping in, he launched a roundhouse kick. It hit the bag just below his shoulder height. *Gotta work on my flexibility.* He threw a few body blows and rounded out the combination with a jab as he bobbed and sidestepped left.

Hit after hit, the bag's ball-and-socket joints creaked as the chains twisted and turned.

Sweat dripped from Quinn's forehead and his arms. His T-shirt was soaked with perspiration, and an hour of this wild exertion had left the cargo bay of the *Rocinante* smelling like the inside of an old shoe. His feet ached, and his back hurt. It would have been easy to call it quits.

His rage simmered as he thought of what the Klingons had

been doing to the Denn since they'd arrived on Golmira two days earlier, and he pictured one of the lobster-headed barbarians standing in the heavy bag's place.

A right cross to the head, a left jab to the body, a knee in the ribs, an elbow thrown in for good measure.

The exertion felt good. But not good enough.

Quinn continued his weaving dance around the heavy bag as he heard Bridy descend the ladder from the main deck. He threw a few more solid punches into the bag, then let himself slump against it as she walked over to him. "If you're lookin' to spar, you're about an hour late. I'm wiped."

"We just got new orders from Vanguard," Bridy said.

Between labored breaths he gasped, "And . . . ?"

"They want us to lay low and sabotage the Klingons' equipment until they can send some in some backup."

"When's that gonna be?" He started untying the laces of his right glove with his teeth.

She folded her arms. "In about three months."

He shouted, "Three *months*? Are they kiddin' me?" His right glove came loose, and he shook it off. "The Klingons might wipe out this whole planet in three months!"

"Look, we knew it was risky when we came out here," Bridy said as she watched him untie his other glove. "Even the *Sagittarius* hasn't gone this deep into the Taurus Reach before."

Yanking off the second glove, Quinn snapped, "Are you sure that's all our orders said? Lay low and break stuff?" Bridy rolled her eyes and looked away, but her lips folded in, showing the dimple in her chin, which told Quinn he'd struck a nerve. "There *was* something else, wasn't there?"

After an angry huff, she said, "Admiral Nogura also wants us to incite the Denn to launch a guerilla warfare campaign."

Quinn tossed aside the glove in his hand and pointed at Bridy as he exclaimed, "Now *that's* what I'm talking about!"

"Hang on," Bridy Mac said, holding out a palm in Quinn's direction. "My tactical training is starship-based. I'm not qualified to teach these people how to fight Klingons."

He grabbed his towel off the top of a cargo container and started wiping the sweat from his face. "Who said you'd be the one training 'em?"

"You think you're qualified? What do you know about waging a ground war against Klingon troops?"

"More than you think," Quinn said. He toweled the top of his buzz-cut head dry and draped the towel around his neck. He started walking aft. "Follow me. I want to tell you a story."

Bridy Mac fell in behind Quinn, who found himself dredging up memories he thought he'd put to rest decades earlier. "Once upon a time, I was just a kid like anybody else. Even went to college, if you can believe that."

"Not really," Bridy said, "but go on."

He led her toward the tool locker. "Six months after I got my degree, I married my college sweetheart. Our families said we were too young. We didn't care. Got married on New Year's Eve." He stopped in front of the locker, put his hand on the latch, and let out a grim chortle. "That was thirty years ago."

She watched him open the gray locker door, revealing a host of heavy tools. He tucked a sonic screwdriver in his pants pocket, grabbed a crowbar, and slammed the locker door. He turned and faced Bridy. "Less than five months after we got married, my wife . . . my first wife, Denise, passed away. Xenopolycythemia. By the time we knew she was sick, it was too late to do anything. They diagnosed her in March. She died in May." His eyes misted with tears, and his throat constricted. Talking about it made it hurt as if it had only just happened, and his grief deepened his native Tennessee drawl. "I remember every detail of that day. The color of the sky. The number of vehicles in the hospital parking lot. The sound of her last breath at two-fourteen PM. Everything."

Crowbar in hand, he walked toward the bow of the ship, and Bridy followed him. "I was lost. My whole life was turned to shit. One day I woke up and knew I couldn't draw one more breath on Earth. I didn't want to look at anything familiar ever again." He stopped beside a cargo container and put the crowbar on top of it.

"I'd heard about a mercenary company that was recruiting for jobs outside Federation space. It was good money, and it sounded like a good way to escape. Soon as Denise was in the ground, I signed up and shipped out."

He put his shoulder to the container and with a furious growl pushed it across the deck. For a moment it seemed like Bridy was going to try to help him, but she recoiled before her hands reached the container. It didn't matter. Quinn didn't need the help. He liked moving something he shouldn't, overcoming its resistance. The effort was its own reward.

After the huge heavy box had been pushed against the port bulkhead, he kneeled beside the exposed deck plate and took out the sonic screwdriver. As he began removing bolts, he looked up at Bridy. "You ever dealt with mercenaries?" She shook her head. He shrugged. "Count your blessings. At first I thought it was the greatest thing in the galaxy. It was all rah-rah macho brother-hood. I was learnin' small-unit tactics, how to blow stuff up, fly small starships, the works. For a young man who just wanted to forget his old life, it was an adventure."

Quinn pulled out the last of the bolts from the deck plate, stood, and stepped over to the moved crate. "Fightin' Klingons out in the middle of nowhere felt heroic, even if we were doin' it for a mining company instead of the Federation." He set the bolts on top of the crate and grabbed the crowbar. "But it wasn't always so black and white."

He walked back to the deck plate and pushed the crowbar into the groove along its edge. Straining with the effort of prying it free, he continued. "Sometimes civilians got caught in the cross fire. Other times they were the targets—innocent colonists who made the mistake of pitching tents on a planet that somebody with more money wanted badly enough to kill for."

The deck plate lifted with a scrape. Quinn wedged the crow-bar under the plate, grabbed it, and pushed it over. It clanged onto the deck with a bright clamor, like the pealing of a church bell. Droplets of sweat fell from Quinn's brow.

In the scan-shielded space under the deck plate was a rectangular steel foot locker. "Give me a hand," Quinn said. "Grab a handle."

Bridy and Quinn lifted the weighty box from its hiding place and set it on the deck. Quinn's fingers hovered over the digital keypad as he tried to remember the code to unlock it. "The guys I served with . . . I watched 'em kill women and kids. And I saw 'em do worse things than that. When I tried to report 'em, I got told to mind my own business. The commanders either didn't care or were the ones who gave the orders in the first place."

Staring at the lock, he remembered Denise's birthday and tapped in the eight-digit code: 03262217. The case's magnetic clamps released with loud thunks.

"They wouldn't let me quit. Said I had to finish my hitch. I couldn't just hide in my rack, so I spent my time gettin' drunk, mouthin' off at the brass, and playin' cards." He looked around at his ship. "By the time I got out, I'd won enough to buy ol' Rosie here. But I couldn't forget what I'd seen. The things I'd done. So I spent the rest of my cash on booze, and then I spent twenty-five years tryin' to drown my memories."

He looked up at Bridy and cracked a bittersweet smile. "Didn't work. Now all I got left is this ship."

And one last spark of my self-respect.

Bridy had a soft expression of concern. "I won't lie and say I know what you went through, or how you feel. But nothing we do here can change the past, Quinn. The Denn's fight isn't ours. I understand wanting to help them, but the smartest thing we can do is respect the Prime Directive and stay neutral."

Quinn opened the foot locker. It was packed with assault weapons, power packs, and explosives.

"I ain't in Starfleet." He picked up a rifle. "So fuck the Prime Directive."

June 5, 2267

"These twenty rifles are all I got," Quinn told his first platoon of Denn fighters. "Same goes for the power cells. So we're gonna have to be careful about when we use 'em, and how much. If we play our cards right, we'll scoop up some of the Klingons' weapons off a battlefield. Then we can arm more of your people."

He walked in front of the lanky, shaved-headed militiamen, who were lined up under the starboard wing of the *Rocinante*. Much as Quinn had expected, Naya and the landgraves had granted his request to recruit a score of able-bodied males to wage a guerilla war campaign against the Klingon occupation. Apparently, male Denn outnumbered females by a ratio of four to one, which gave the women elevated social status and made the men seem expendable.

The tallest of the recruits pulled the trigger of his weapon over and over; he frowned when nothing happened. Quinn stopped and placed his hand atop the man's rifle, pointing its muzzle at the ground. "Okay, Stretch, give it a rest. That's why I didn't give you boys the power cells yet."

Raising his voice to address the group, Quinn said, "Never put your finger on a trigger till you're ready to shoot. Never point a weapon at someone you don't mean to kill. These rifles are not toys. Use 'em right, you can kill a Klingon in one shot." He patted a hand on Stretch's chest. "Aim for center of mass. That's the chest and gut. Don't bother tryin' for head shots unless you're sure you can get a direct hit." He held up his rifle to illustrate his next point. "When you carry your rifle, keep your trigger finger outside the guard, on the side, like this. That way if you trip or fall, you won't blow a hole in one of your buddies by mistake."

He took a few more steps down the line and stopped in front of a heavyset, well-muscled recruit. The man seemed like a natural soldier: his rifle was slung over his shoulder, his posture was straight, and his mien was serious. Quinn gave the man an approving nod. "Lookin' good, Bubba."

At the end of the line, Quinn about-faced and paced back the way he'd come. "I won't take you men into battle till I think you're ready. Over the next few months, I'll teach you the basics of what you need to know to survive in the field: marksmanship, first aid, small-unit tactics, camouflage, demolitions. I'll teach you how to disassemble those weapons and put 'em back together in your sleep."

A reed-thin and awkward-looking Denn raised his hand, but Quinn cut him off. "It's a figure of speech, Spaz. You won't actually be asleep." Spaz put down his hand.

"For the rest of your training, you'll be splitting up into four squads. Stretch, Bubba, Spaz, Mudguts: you're squad leaders." The four recruits nodded. Quinn continued. "In the field, we will be outnumbered. We will be outgunned. Stealth and preparation can help us overcome those challenges. But the Klingons also have another major advantage: a starship in orbit. It has sensors that can pinpoint our locations on the ground. That means we will have the element of surprise only once, before our first attack. After that, we need to be creative. I have some ideas, but we'll get to those later. For now, we—"

He was interrupted by the clattering of metal tumbling across the ground behind him. He turned to see that one of the recruits had already disassembled his rifle. Quinn marched over to confront the youth. "Tater! What the hell're you doing?"

"Taking apart my rifle," Tater said.

"I can see that," Quinn snapped, glancing at the dozens of components littering the ground at Tater's feet. "Do you have a plan for putting it back together?"

Tater nodded. "Yes. The reverse of how I took it apart."

Quinn took a step back and gestured at the mess of metal. "Show me." The recruit knelt and swiftly gathered up the pieces. Then, as Quinn watched with growing surprise, the young Denn reassembled the weapon in record time. As Tater fixed the last component into place and locked the weapon back into its safe mode, Quinn said, "Present your weapon for inspection."

Tater—who'd earned his nickname by having a head shaped like a lumpy potato—held out his rifle with both hands. Quinn took it and checked its linkages. Everything looked right. He took a power cell from his jacket pocket and slapped it into place inside the grip. The weapon powered up with a gentle hum. Its main readout displayed its status as READY.

Well, I'll be damned, Quinn thought. "Platoon, it looks like we have a prodigy on our hands." He removed the power cell from Tater's weapon and handed the rifle back to the recruit. "Do we have any more mechanical geniuses in our midst?"

Several of the recruits exchanged wary looks.

Each man in the platoon began taking apart his rifle.

Quinn stared, dumbstruck, as all twenty Denn exhibited a skill he had not yet taught them. Almost in unison, they finished their disassemblies. When they all came to rest kneeling before their discombobulated weapons, Quinn said, "Reassemble." With the same speed and graceful precision, the Denn restored their rifles to working order. Quinn inspected each weapon by inserting the power cell. Every rifle's display read READY.

"Quick learners," he said. "Good. That just saved us a day. If you're this handy with explosives, we might be ready to face the Klingons sooner than I thought."

The Denn recruits beamed with pride.

Then a female voice cut the moment down to size.

"You boys should know what you're really getting into," said Bridy Mac, who was standing at the entrance to the secret tunnel that led to the *Rocinante*'s hiding place. She walked toward the line of recruits, who turned to face her. "This isn't some game you've signed up for."

Quinn bristled at the interruption of his training. "They know that," he said.

"Are you sure?" She addressed the Denn. "The Klingons have conquered hundreds of worlds more advanced than this one. They're one of the most dangerous cultures in this part of the galaxy. The moment you start any kind of war with them, they'll take it out on all your people. They won't care who the fighters are. Men, women, children—they'll execute innocent civilians until you give yourselves up and the attacks stop. If they have to, they'll drive your race to extinction."

Stepping between Bridy and the Denn, Quinn asked, "Is that what they teach you in Starfleet? The best defense is a quick surrender?"

She shouldered past him and continued talking to the Denn. "There won't be any glory in what you're doing," she said. "No rewards, no victory. Only pain and death."

Stretch looked at Quinn. "Permission to speak?"

"Step forward," Quinn said.

The tall recruit stepped out of the line to face Bridy Mac. "Quinn tells us your people are sending ships and soldiers. They will be here in ninety days. He also says if we stand against the Klingons, we will make it easier for your people to help free us. Is that not true?"

Bridy glanced over her shoulder at Quinn. Her expression was one of barely contained anger. Looking back at Stretch, she said, "Yes, our people will be here in about ninety days. And the more distracted the Klingons are, the better. But I still don't think you—"

"Then we will stand and fight," Stretch said. "We think Quinn speaks wisely when he says it is better to die fighting for freedom than to accept life as a slave."

The Denn's declaration seemed to leave Bridy speechless. Quinn gently guided her away from the recruits and spoke to her sotto voce. "Look, I ain't puttin' these boys into a full-scale ground war, okay? If we time this right, we'll be lookin' at maybe a few weeks of harassing the Klingons before the cavalry comes. I'll stick to minin' roads, settin' traps, layin' ambushes. No stand-up fights till the end. You have my word."

"I'm not the one who needs your promises," Bridy said, scowling. She walked up the ramp into the *Rocinante*.

Quinn turned back toward the men whose lives were now in his hands. "All right," he said. "Let's get back to work."

24

July 14, 2267

Kutal felt the wind in his hair as he dashed through the night. Rain pelted against his naked body, washing the blood from his chest and arms. It ran in a steady stream from the tip of his tempered blade, which was still warm from cutting the throats of four thousand foes in one night.

Cresting the hill, he threw back his head and roared with mad laughter. Thunder rolled and lightning flashed, and Kutal lifted his *d'k tahg* in salute to the memory of Kahless and the honor of his own ancestors, who he now was certain would welcome him into the everlasting glory of *Sto-Vo-Kor*.

Then the comm signal squawked and stirred Kutal from the best dream he'd ever had. Bleary and bitterly disappointed, he pushed himself up from his bunk with a low growl. The signal buzzed again from a comm panel. Kutal silenced it with the side of his fist and barked, "What?"

BelHoQ, his first officer, replied, *"Priority signal from Qo'noS, Captain. It is Councillor Gorkon."*

Of course it is, Kutal thought. He exhaled with disgust. "Patch it through to my quarters."

"Ready on your secure channel, Captain."

Kutal switched off the comm and shambled over to a desktop computer screen. As he entered his security code, he wondered what Gorkon wanted this time. More pillows for the Earther? An Orion slave girl to sing the human to sleep with soft lullabies?

Gorkon had insisted Reyes and the Tholian be treated as guests rather than as prisoners, but Kutal had grown weary of kowtowing to the two aliens.

The screen flashed to life with an image of the Klingon trefoil emblem, which was replaced seconds later by the face of Gorkon. *"Captain, I have new orders for you."*

"I am at your command, Councillor."

Gorkon leaned forward and pressed a key on his desktop. *"I am sending you a classified mission briefing,"* he said. Icon for an in-progress data upload appeared along the bottom of Kutal's screen. *"Our forces have secured an intact Shedai Conduit on a planet near the Vodrey Nebula. So far, we have not had any success accessing its systems."*

The data package finished loading. Kutal opened it on an adjacent monitor while continuing his conversation with Gorkon. Reading through the briefing's top-sheet summary, he said, "I've received your mission file. What is the link between this new Conduit and the document you've sent me?"

"That is all our extant research into an artifact we tested on another Conduit in the Mirdonyae system. It gave us unprecedented control over the Shedai technology on that world."

Skipping to the end of the summary, Kutal frowned. "It says the artifact was captured by Starfleet, and that the planet was destroyed shortly afterward."

"True," Gorkon said. *"However, now that we once again have an intact Conduit under our control, it is imperative we resume our research into this new technology."*

Kutal met Gorkon's steely-eyed stare and asked, "Have we acquired another such artifact?"

"No," Gorkon replied. *"To the best of our knowledge, only the one has been found, and it is currently secured aboard the Federation starbase known as Vanguard. If our work is to continue, the artifact must be recovered with all due haste—and without violating the terms of the Organian treaty."*

"Councillor, Vanguard is very well defended, and in recent weeks Starfleet has escalated its presence in the Gonmog Sector.

Short of launching a full-scale assault, how are we to recover the artifact from the station?"

Gorkon responded with a thin, evil smile. *"Ask our esteemed guest, Mister Reyes, to help you. It's about time he learned our hospitality comes with a price. Make sure he understands that if he doesn't cooperate, or if he leads us into a trap, his beloved Rana Desai will suffer a most gruesome violation before her untimely demise."*

That was more like it. Kutal mirrored Gorkon's diabolical expression. "Understood, Councillor. I'll see to it personally."

25

July 14, 2267

Haniff Jackson leaned on the bar in Tom Walker's place and held ice against his bloodied nose. The melting cubes had soaked the napkin in which they were wrapped, and cold water dribbled over his split lips and bruised chin. The proprietor and patrons of the popular Stars Landing watering hole had fled during the raucous fight minutes earlier, leaving Jackson alone at the bar.

The front door opened, and Captain Desai walked in. She warily surveyed the room, which was littered with collapsed tables, splintered chairs, broken glass, and spilled drinks. Wrinkling her nose as she stepped through the wreckage toward Jackson, she said, "What a lovely fragrance you've invented."

"Don't blame me," Jackson said, his voice a bit nasal thanks to his swollen nose. "I wasn't the one resisting arrest."

Desai joined him at the bar and stood on her toes to get a better look at his injuries. "Blood and scars become you," she said with a teasing smile. Looking down the length of the bar, she asked, "What does a lady have to do to get a drink around here?"

"When that lady's a captain, all she has to do is ask." Jackson set down the melting ice, hopped over to the other side of the bar, and spread his arms. "What can I get you?"

She arched an eyebrow. "Club soda with lime, and a good reason for why you called me down here."

"Coming right up," Jackson said. He grabbed a pint glass from a shelf behind the bar and filled it halfway with a scoop of ice. Then he picked up the carbonated-drink nozzle and keyed the button for club soda. Clear liquid shot from the nozzle and fizzed as it filled the glass. He grabbed a lime wedge from a bowl, garnished the drink, and gave it to Desai.

The JAG captain picked up the glass, sipped the drink, and nodded. "Thanks. And my reason for being here?"

He reached for his data slate and pushed it to Desai. "It's all on there."

She picked up the slate. "Does this have anything to do with the Orion I saw your men hauling away in restraints?"

"Good guess," Jackson said. "You should be a detective."

"I *was* a detective," she replied as she reviewed Jackson's report. "It says here you linked Mister Syanok to Petty Officer Strout, your crooked cargo handler."

Jackson nodded. "Comm logs show a sudden flurry of back-and-forth traffic between him and Strout in the hours before the *Malacca* bombing." He reached over the counter and pointed out a detail. "Syanok initiated the exchange with a coded message a few hours after the *Malacca* filed its cargo manifest with the operations center. Shortly after trading these messages with Strout, our buddy Syanok arranged for a last-second shipment to be placed on the *Malacca*."

Desai stared dubiously at Jackson. "And you think that proves what, exactly?"

"Okay, I admit it's not rock-solid proof of anything, but it definitely suggests Syanok could have seen the pre-final manifest for the *Malacca*."

Putting the slate back on the bar, Desai said, "So what? None of this is damning enough to charge him with anything." Tilting her head, she added, "Except for assault and resisting what will probably turn out to be a false arrest."

"Are you serious? You really don't see the link here?"

"I share your suspicions," Desai said. "But it's not enough for a court of law. I need *evidence*. We don't know the content of Strout and Syanok's messages, or that Syanok's piece of cargo was the one that contained the bomb."

Jackson picked up the slate and called up a new forensic report. "Maybe we don't know for certain that his container held the bomb." He handed the slate back to Desai. "But we have the cargo master's log of where each piece of cargo was secured in the *Malacca*'s hold, and we have a ballistic analysis of the explosion that pinpoints its epicenter to within three meters of where Syanok's container was placed. The only other pieces in close proximity were official Starfleet cargo—Pacifican seagrass bound for the Daystrom Institute, and an experimental grain called quintotriticale bound for Earth."

Desai's eyebrows arched up. "Okay," she said. "That's what I mean by *real* evidence. Why didn't you lead with that?"

He shrugged. "Sorry." Leaning forward, he asked, "So, can we at least hold Syanok as a material witness?"

"I'll do more than that," Desai said. "Consider him remanded without bail." She frowned. "But if you're thinking he'll lead you to more arrests, I wouldn't get my hopes up if I were you."

Jackson didn't like the sound of that. "Why not?"

The JAG officer sighed. "Someone intended for Syanok to be treated as a terminal contact. Odds are you won't be able to link him to anyone else, on or off the station, besides Strout."

"What about the money trail?" Jackson pointed at the data slate. "Syanok had to pay for that shipment on the *Malacca*. It's a good bet whatever account he uses to pay his bills is the same one where he gets his money from the people he works for. If we trace that, we take another step up the ladder."

Desai handed back the slate to Jackson. "His accounts are with private banks on Orion."

He understood what she was implying: that Orion financial institutions would never cooperate with Federation-issued subpoenas. It was maddening, but he knew she was right. His hands curled into fists. "We should at least try," he said. "Serve them with warrants. If they refuse to give us his records, so be it. But I won't just give up my best lead."

"All right," Desai said. "Personally, I think it's a waste of time and effort. Getting intel from the Orions is harder than getting laughs from a Vulcan. But if you feel that strongly about it, I'll have my staff draft subpoenas for Syanok's financial records. If we ever get a response, I'll let you know."

"Thanks," Jackson said.

"Don't mention it." She pushed her half-consumed beverage to Jackson. "Thanks for the drink."

"Any time."

Desai walked to the door, but turned back and looked quizzically at Jackson. "Tell me, Lieutenant, how far will you go to close this case?"

"Into the pit of Hell if I have to."

She smiled. "Good." As she stepped out the door, she said over her shoulder, "It'll be nice to have company for a change."

July 15, 2267

Fewer than twenty-four hours after leaving Tom Walker's place on a hopeful note, Rana Desai found herself saddled with the unpleasant task of delivering bad news to Lieutenant Jackson.

She stood near the back of Vanguard's dark security center and waited for her chance to talk to the security chief. Most of the lighting in the center came from flickering images on the scores of video monitors that covered two of its four walls. Each screen switched every few seconds between multiple feeds, from both inside and outside the station. The wall to the right of the door was dominated by a single master viewscreen more than five meters wide and nearly three meters tall.

There were two dozen personnel seated at monitoring stations, which were arranged in a U shape facing the monitors.

Jackson stood on the far side of the U, beneath the main screen. At that moment, it showed an altercation between two groups of civilians near the airlock for a private freighter.

"Get a quick-response team down to the lower docking ring," Jackson said. "Slip Four, on the double."

The officer behind Jackson nodded and quietly relayed the orders to a security team near the scene of the disturbance.

"Load screen five, feed two," Jackson said.

Desai had no idea who had responded to Jackson's order, but almost instantly the image on the main viewer changed to show a man standing at a security door and tapping numbers into its access keypad. "He's been entering numbers for over two minutes," Jackson said. "Either he's got the wrong door, or he's trying to break into that room. Send a team to talk to him. If he leaves before they get there, track him."

Another hushed acknowledgment came from the semicircle of security personnel standing between Jackson and Desai.

Sensing a possible lull in the center's activity, Desai cleared her throat. No one except Jackson turned to look at her. He lifted his chin to greet her. As he walked toward her, he said to one of his people, "Holmgren, take over." A blond human woman stepped forward and took his place under the main screen.

Jackson joined Desai at the back of the room and said in a quiet voice, "What brings you to the cave? Good news, I hope."

Her lips tensed into something of a half smile, half frown. "I'm afraid not," she said, keeping her voice as low as his. "We've hit a brick wall with Syanok."

"Let me guess," Jackson said. "The Orions."

"Exactly." She handed him a data card. "It's all on there, but I can give you the highlights, if you prefer."

He nodded. "Sure. Hit me."

Desai folded her arms. "His comm logs gave us a partial snapshot of his financial holdings. Some were based on Tammeron, a neutral planet that has limited trade agreements with the Federation. They must want to upgrade their trade status, because they gave us everything they had on Syanok. It looks like he used his Tammeron account to make legal transactions. But most of the funds he deposited to that account came from a major private bank on Orion."

"Did the transaction log identify who paid him?"

"It was a corporate entity," Desai said. "Cygnar-Ralon Interstellar Shipping. CRIS for short. His Tammeron account is registered to Syanok Import-Export, but I'm proceeding on the assumption that CRIS is his original Orion business entity."

"Probably a shell company," Jackson said. "Typical cover for a middleman. Moving the money from one bank to another is the perfect laundering method. All we need to do now is find out where his Orion company gets its money."

Deflating a bit, Desai said, "That's the brick wall, Haniff. Technically, there's nothing illegal about Syanok's business arrangements. As I predicted, the Orion government has refused to enforce my subpoena, and his bank has refused to release any private account information. Also, the Orion ambassador to the Federation has lodged a formal protest over our attempt to violate the privacy of one of its citizens."

Jackson shook his head and flashed a wide smile. "They do love overkill, don't they? They can't just say no; they have to make an interstellar incident out of it." His good humor faded quickly, and he slammed a fist into his open palm. "Dammit, Rana! We're so close to the truth on this one, I can taste it. I don't give a damn what the Orions try to feed us. Syanok was involved in the bombing of the *Malacca*. Maybe he didn't know it, or maybe he was just a cutout, but he was *involved* in this conspiracy. I can feel it."

"I believe you," Desai said. "But I can't issue subpoenas based on your gut feeling."

Jackson folded his arms, aping her stance. "What do we have on him so far?"

"Resisting arrest and assaulting a Starfleet security officer," Desai said. "Despite the ballistics report about his shipping container being the epicenter of the blast, we can't charge him with the bombing attack unless we can establish the provenance of the crate and demonstrate a reasonable suspicion that he knew it contained hazardous cargo."

A cold and calculating look fell like a shadow over Jackson's face. "What if we combed through all the local comm traffic during the months before and after the attack, looking for any signal that included the routing information on Syanok's original Orion bank account? We could use that to link him to his conspirators."

"Or we might link him to legitimate business partners conducting legal transactions, and by so doing infringe on the privacy of all parties and violate the Federation Charter." She shook her head. "It's too open-ended, Haniff. Even a first-year law student would see that as a fishing expedition and quash the warrant or throw out the evidence. I won't sanction it."

His jaw muscles tensed with suppressed frustration. "I didn't come this far just to give up," he said. "I'll bet you dinner at Café Romano the Orions are sitting on all the evidence we need to convict Syanok and his coconspirators in the *Malacca* bombing, and tie the whole thing to a third party—probably the Klingons."

Desai knew he wasn't kidding, but she still laughed. "There's no way I'm taking that bet, Haniff, because I know you're right—and I know you never lose."

"Very true," he said. Leaning closer, he whispered with a rakish grin, "Let me buy you dinner, anyway."

The part of Desai's heart that was still mourning Diego Reyes told her to lie and say she had other plans. Her sense of professional decorum told her to decline Jackson's invitation. And her most insecure inner voice protested that Jackson was at least ten years her junior. All good reasons to say no.

"Okay," she said with a coy smile. "It's a date. Pick me up at nineteen hundred."

26

Neera lurked in an alcove concealed by a heavy scarlet curtain and let her man-toy Ganz bask a bit longer in his charade of authority. The Orion figurehead reclined regally behind the desk of his private office aboard the *Omari-Ekon* and listened to a courteous supplication by a dark-haired human named Joshua Kane.

"First, I'd like to make clear I didn't seek out this contract," Kane said. "The client came to me."

Ganz replied in his rock-steady baritone, "I understand." With one huge green hand he pushed a bowl of roasted Argelian cashews across the polished antique wooden desk to his slender visitor. "Have a nut."

Kane bowed his head and scooped up a small handful of nuts from the bowl. "Thank you, sir."

"You're welcome. Continue."

The bearded human closed his fist around the cashews and used his empty hand to punctuate his words with gestures. "They offered a sizable fee for the job—ten million credits." He held up his empty palm and dipped his chin. "I've arranged for them to make the deposit to your anonymous account on Orion."

"That's good," Ganz said. "I trust you'll have no objection to my taking a standard fifteen percent commission?"

Shaking his head, Kane replied, "No, sir. Not at all." He sounded hopeful as he asked, "Does that mean I have your permission to accept the contract, sir?"

"On two conditions," Ganz said. "First, if anything goes

wrong, or if you or someone working with you gets caught, this never comes back to me. My name is never mentioned. Agreed?"

Kane nodded. "Agreed."

"Second," Ganz said, "no killing. Not one body. If I find out there were fatalities, or that innocent people got hurt, I will be very upset. Is that clear?"

"Perfectly, sir. I haven't taken a life yet, and I don't plan to start now. You have my word: no one dies for this job."

Neera pulled aside the scarlet curtain just enough for Ganz to see her give the signal to dismiss his guest.

The barrel-chested Orion man gave no indication of seeing Neera, but then he said to the human, "I'm glad we reach, Mister Kane. Good luck, and safe travels."

"Thank you, Mister Ganz," Kane said. He bowed his head as he backed away from Ganz's desk and held up his closed hand. "Thanks again for the nuts." The door slid open behind him, and he backpedaled out to the corridor.

After the portal hushed closed, Neera emerged from hiding and pressed a key on the wall that locked the door. She strolled toward Ganz's desk and savored his leer as he watched the swaying roll of her supple hips. "Efficiently handled, my love," she said.

"I'm glad you approve."

She circled his desk, dragging one finger along its edge. "We may have a leak that needs to be plugged," she said.

Ganz stared awestruck at her, as if he had lost himself in her eyes. "What kind of leak?"

"The Starfleet JAG office has been asking our government for access to Orion banking records," she said, giving his rolling chair a gentle push back from the desk.

Her hulking beau sat up straighter. "My records?"

"No." She eased herself onto his lap. "Cygnar-Ralon."

His forehead creased, and his brow furrowed. "Zett's company."

"Yes," Neera said. "It is." She had never liked Ganz's chief enforcer—an impeccably tailored and implacably brutal Nalori named Zett Nilric—and welcomed anything that might persuade Ganz to reconsider his seemingly unshakable faith in the man.

"Do they know it's his company?"

Neera whispered in his ear, "I don't think so." She felt the muscles in his arms and neck stiffen.

"That's still not good," Ganz said. "Why are they asking questions about Cygnar-Ralon?"

Stroking her soft palm over Ganz's smooth, jade-hued pate, Neera said, "They've linked it to a suspect in last year's bombing of the Starfleet freighter *Malacca* inside Vanguard."

"I remember the bombing," Ganz said. Suspicious, he continued, "But I didn't order it, and I didn't sanction it. So why would Starfleet have evidence linking it to Zett?"

It was a rhetorical question, but Neera was determined to make Ganz answer it for himself. She planted delicate kisses on the side of his thickly muscled neck and said, "I'm sure you can reason it out, my love."

An angry sigh flared Ganz's wide nostrils. "Because he's been freelancing without permission."

"Which suggests ambition or greed or both." Shifting her amorous attention to the other side of Ganz's neck, Neera added, "No matter which it is, it's not good."

"No, it isn't," Ganz said. He pulled away from Neera. She got up from his lap and let him stand. When he was anxious, he liked to pace. He circled around his desk. "We've spent a great deal of time and a considerable sum of money working on a way to get back into Admiral Nogura's good graces," he said.

"And it's almost within our grasp," Neera said as she slinked seductively into Ganz's chair.

He began pacing in front of his desk. "But all that time, treasure, and blood will have been spent for nothing if Zett implicates us in a terrorist attack on Nogura's starbase." He cast a pointed stare at Neera. "And we need that safe haven, now more than ever."

"I know," she said, easing the chair forward so she could rest her elbows on the desk and fold her hands in front of her. "But before that can happen, I think we need to accept that Zett might now be more of a liability than an asset."

Ganz's countenance was at once sad and grim. He nodded. "I agree." With a plaintive look, he asked, "What should we do?"

Devious schemes coaxed a half smile from Neera, who narrowed her eyes and told her loyal front man, "Let me handle this my way—discreetly."

27

July 30, 2267

"We've been cooped up in this bloody tin can for more than four months," Pennington complained across the mess cabin table. "If I get arrested by Starfleet, will this period of captivity count as time served against my sentence?"

T'Prynn replied without looking up from her soup, "I think clemency on such grounds would be highly unlikely."

Pennington's head drooped, and he couldn't help but turn a weary frown at the bowl of bland seaweed broth T'Prynn had prepared for that morning's meal. The traditional Vulcan dish was the only thing she ever made for breakfast.

He sighed. "Pass the salt, please."

"*Plomeek* soup has a delicate flavor," she said as she handed the shaker to him. "Adding too much salt or other seasoning will mar its subtleties."

"That's what I'm hoping for." He shook enough salt to cover the entire surface of his soup. After stirring it gently into the liquid, he lifted a spoonful into his mouth and swallowed it. Then his face puckered and he winced in revulsion.

T'Prynn's calm was preternatural as asked, "Is there something wrong with your soup?"

He glared at her, stung by the irony as he said, "It's too salty." Even though the statuesque Vulcan woman did not react, he was certain that behind her placid mask of detachment she was laughing at him.

She ate another spoonful of her soup and said nothing.

Pennington stood, picked up his tray, and placed it in the re-clamator. After the panel slid closed, he heard the whirring and clanking of dishes and utensils being washed and organic matter being flushed away for purification and recycling.

"I thought I might spend today counting my nose hairs," he said to his inscrutable companion.

She swallowed another spoonful of soup. "You should use a tricorder. Its results will be more accurate, and it will take less time to compile."

"Maybe," Pennington said. "But can it braid all those tiny lit-tle hairs together?" He pointed at her and exclaimed with a manic gleam of triumph, "I think not!"

Unfazed, she replied, "Even for a human, your behavior is most peculiar. Do you require a medical examination?"

"No, just a change of scenery."

She finished her soup, got up, and carried her tray to the re-clamator. "I advised you before we embarked on this mission that it would be time-consuming and monotonous. You cannot say I misled you as to its nature."

"I never said you did. Doesn't make drifting in the dark any more interesting."

She consigned her tray and dishes to the food slot. As it hummed from behind the bulkhead, she and Pennington walked out of the mess hall to the main corridor. "Perhaps you would prefer—"

An automated alert over the ship's PA system cut her off. *"Signal intercept in progress,"* said the synthetic male voice.

They dashed to the cockpit and scrambled into their seats. Pennington locked in the signal, boosted the gain, and verified they were recording it. T'Prynn fed the signal through the ship's rebuilt main computer and applied her formidable array of code-breaking algorithms.

"Signal's five by five," he said. "Recording confirmed."

"Decryption has begun," she said. "The message was coded with a Klingon cipher." Flipping switches on her console, she added, "Routing the original message to the forward monitor. It will replay from the beginning."

The forward display stuttered, and the picture rolled for a moment before it stabilized. The first image to appear was that of a male Klingon soldier in a dimly lit space. It didn't look like a ship's bridge, so Pennington assumed it was the man's private cabin. He said, *"Kutal to* Ali Baba, *respond."*

T'Prynn quickly explained, "The *Ali Baba* is a private vessel that frequently docks with Ganz's ship. It belongs to a suspected thief named Joshua Kane."

"Good to know," Pennington said.

The other side of the transmission cut in, and the image automatically split-screened on the *Skylla's* display. The second man was a human with dark hair and a fair complexion. His hair was close-cropped, and his beard was neatly trimmed. *"Captain,"* he said to Kutal. *"Right on time."*

Kutal asked, *"Have you been granted permission to accept our contract, Mister Kane?"*

"Yes," Kane said. *"Have the funds been transferred?"*

"The first half has been sent," Kutal said. *"You'll get the rest on final delivery."*

"Very good."

"Do you have any last questions for our expert?"

"No," Kane said. *"I have all the intel I need. Have you selected a rendezvous point?"*

Kutal tapped an interface off-screen. *"I am sending you the coordinates now. Meet us there exactly eighteen days after you finish the assignment."*

"Understood. Coordinates received. Ali Baba *out."*

The signal terminated, and the screen went black.

T'Prynn stared intently at the darkened monitor. Pennington verified there was no more signal to record, and he shut down the intercept system. "Well, we've got their rendezvous coordinates," he said. "Of course, we have no idea what they're talking about." He slumped in his seat. "What a waste of time."

"Quite the contrary," T'Prynn said. "This intercept has yielded a great deal of valuable information."

"Were we listening to the same conversation? How do you figure that was anything but a bust?"

She cast a sly look across the cockpit. "First, we now know the Klingons are using pirates and criminals as cutouts in the Taurus Reach. Second, whatever it is that Mister Kane has been hired to obtain for the Klingons, it entails a final delivery at a location whose coordinates we now possess. And third, the Klingon captain has let slip a critical piece of top-secret intelligence."

Pennington shook his head. "He did? When? What intel?"

T'Prynn tapped a key and replayed the intercepted transmission. She paused the playback just after Kutal asked, *"Do you have any last questions for our expert?"*

"Computer," T'Prynn said. "Enhance twenty-four to thirty-six, and track forty-five left. Magnify and brighten midtones."

Part of the frozen image was highlighted and enlarged. It was just a muddy-dark slice of the background until the image enhancers kicked in.

Then a familiar face appeared in profile, reflected in a mirror, and Pennington understood immediately.

T'Prynn arched one eyebrow. "Diego Reyes is alive."

28

Jackson felt like a fly accepting an invitation to a spider's web as he walked to the office of Vanguard's liaison to Starfleet Intelligence. In all the years Jackson had served as a security officer, he had never before been summoned by SI.

He stopped outside the door of an unmarked command office on Level Ten. The corridor appeared to be empty in either direction. As he went to press the visitor's signal, the door slid open. Cool air escaped from inside, along with the muted sounds of comm chatter and working computers.

From inside a pleasant voice said, "Come in."

Holding up his head, Jackson put aside his apprehension and strolled inside. A wide partition stood between the door and the rest of the room. He stepped around it. His eyes widened as he surveyed the expansive space on the other side.

In the center of the room, Commander ch'Nayla stood on a low circular dais that was brightly lit from directly overhead. He was surrounded by a 270-degree arc of high-tech consoles mounted atop black pedestals.

Subdued, cool blue lighting spilled across the walls. Huge viewscreens were suspended from the ceiling in an arc that matched that of ch'Nayla's bank of consoles. Displayed on the screens were vids of all kinds, ranging from news reports and official government briefings to surveillance footage and what looked like intercepted foreign military transmissions.

Through the gap in the consoles, Jackson saw that ch'Nayla

had his back to him. Taking a step forward, the security chief said, "You asked to see me?"

The tall Andorian *chan* tapped some keys on his console, turned, and smiled at Jackson. "I did." He picked up a data slate and stepped down from the dais.

Jackson walked over to meet him. "Quite a setup you've got here," he said, nodding at the screens.

"I requested some upgrades to the intelligence center after I transferred to this post," ch'Nayla said. "My predecessor's work environment was a bit spartan for my taste."

Recalling the dim, high-gravity sauna that T'Prynn had used for an office, Jackson nodded. "Yeah, I know what you mean." Switching gears, he asked, "So, what can I do for you, sir?"

"Actually, I asked you here so that I might do something for you." Ch'Nayla handed him the data slate. "I'm sure it will not surprise you to learn I try to stay current on all open investigations by the JAG office and the security division."

"I'd be surprised if you didn't," Jackson said. He skimmed the contents of the data slate as ch'Nayla continued.

"In recent weeks, I've noted several warrants and subpoenas related to certain notable Orion citizens," the Andorian said. "I've also been apprised of your difficulties in obtaining sensitive intelligence from the Orion financial sector."

"*Difficulties,*" Jackson said, echoing ch'Nayla. "That's a nice way to say *utter failure*. I'll have to remember that."

"Perhaps not. The obstacles to that investigation might now be removed." He nodded toward the dais. "Join me." As they walked to the bank of consoles, ch'Nayla continued. "One of my normally taciturn sources on the Orion homeworld has suddenly become loquacious about a private shell corporation—one that figures prominently in Captain Desai's reports."

Jackson felt a tingle of excitement. "How loquacious?"

"Very," ch'Nayla said.

They stepped into the center of the consoles, and ch'Nayla picked up a yellow data card and inserted it into a slot. The screen directly ahead of them changed to display multiple frames of information, including static images, financial spreadsheets, communication logs, and more.

"We have detailed transaction records that show the Cygnar-Ralon corporate entity belongs to a Nalori national known as Zett Nilric," ch'Nayla said. "Though he has never been charged with a criminal offense, his dossier suggests he is a former professional assassin for the Nalori government who now works as an enforcer for the Orion crime boss Ganz."

Pointing at one of the frames of business data, Jackson asked, "Can we enlarge that window, please?" Ch'Nayla magnified it so it filled the right half of the screen. Jackson felt his pulse speed up as he eyed the log of account activity. "The dates on those large cash deposits," he said. "They bracket the date of the attack on the *Malacca*. Can we trace the source of those funds?"

"I already have," ch'Nayla said. "They came from an account on Qo'noS that's been linked to Klingon Imperial Intelligence."

My God, Jackson marveled. *This is it. The proof that ties the bombing to a criminal organization and the Klingons.* He began to wonder what other cases might have ties to Zett Nilric. "Can we analyze the dates on the other transfers and see if they also bracket criminal events from other open cases?"

"Once again I've anticipated your needs," ch'Nayla said. "I have cross-checked these dates with events on file and found what I believe to be seven notable concurrences. Three pertain to major heists on non-Federation planets. Two seem to be linked to acts of deep-space piracy against vessels recently departed from Vanguard. And the final two suggest a link between Mister Nilric and two prominent assassinations of underworld figures believed to have been rivals of Zett's employer, Ganz."

"Wow," Jackson said. "Impressive work."

"Thank you." Ch'Naylah began closing the data frames. "I regret only that my discoveries can't be of more use to you and Captain Desai."

"What're you talking about? There's enough there to let me impound Zett's ship and cavity-search him till he's inside out."

"Unfortunately, there isn't," ch'Nayla said. "Most of this

intelligence was obtained through extralegal methods, and some of it has no clear provenance whatsoever. Almost all of it will be deemed inadmissible regardless of whether it is presented in a civilian court or a court-martial."

Jackson balled his fists and growled at this latest aggravation. "Dammit! How many bullets can that bastard dodge?"

Removing the yellow data card from the console, ch'Nayla replied, "I share your anger at seeing justice obstructed." He handed the data card to Jackson. "Though this information cannot be used to convict Mister Nilric, it's my hope you can use it to disrupt his efforts in the future."

Accepting the card, Jackson blinked in surprise. "You're giving me this intel?"

"I've declassified it for you and Captain Desai, because it is clearly relevant to your respective assignments. I've also briefed Admiral Nogura on my findings."

That news put a smile on Jackson's face. "Thank you. I didn't mean to sound so shocked. It's just that T'Prynn was never very good at sharing intel with other departments."

The middle-aged *chan*'s antennae swiveled in Jackson's direction as he returned the younger man's smile. "I am not T'Prynn," he said.

Eight weeks of not enough sleep and too much caffeine had left Dr. Carol Marcus feeling frazzled and unfocused. Ever since the *Endeavour* had returned bearing Ming Xiong and the Mirdonyae Artifact, she and the scores of scientists in the Vault had been working double and even triple shifts to help Xiong unlock the mysterious object's eldritch secrets.

As she downed the tepid dregs of her fourth cup of coffee for the day, she speculated that her entire department was likely functioning only by the grace of a potent mix of adrenaline and insatiable scientific curiosity.

The reports piled on her desk were too much to face. Stacks of data slates and computer cards threatened to topple over at any moment. When she thought of how hard she had worked to keep her personal work space tidy and organized, the current state of her office felt like a defeat, a surrender to chaos.

It looked like this a year ago, she remembered. *Back when I took it over from Xiong.* At the time she had prejudged Xiong's competence based on the muddled condition of his office; now she admitted to herself that she had been too harsh on him. *This job could make a basket case out of just about anybody.*

Despite the mountains of ostensibly dead-end data their work produced, she and the other researchers had made remarkable discoveries by mining the ancient treasures entrusted to them.

The Taurus Meta-Genome was a complex string of genetic information that, when unraveled, yielded a cornucopia of raw data. Different parts of it had been seeded into seemingly basic life-forms throughout the Taurus Reach, spurring Starfleet to engage in what amounted to an interstellar scavenger hunt.

When coupled with an energy waveform known as the Jinoteur Pattern, the Meta-Genome data was like a key that unlocked one mystery of the universe after another: flawless tissue regeneration, complex matter-energy conversions, and even the first clues to bridging distant points of space-time. Starfleet had documented only part of the waveform's total pattern, however. Its only known source had been the Jinoteur system, which had been violently destroyed more than a year earlier by a space-time implosion that blinked the system out of existence.

Both the genome and the pattern owed their genesis to a mysterious and dangerous species known as the Shedai. Hundreds of millennia earlier, they had been the rulers of this region of the galaxy. Their civilization had collapsed aeons ago, but the Shedai themselves apparently had lived on, hibernating and hiding, only to awaken when Starfleet began unlocking the secrets of their long-dormant technology.

And now there was the Mirdonyae Artifact—the greatest enigma of them all. It promised to unlock many of the most elusive Shedai mysteries, but Xiong and his colleagues insisted it was not a creation of the Shedai. Alas, after more than eight weeks of subjecting it to every test they could imagine, they seemed no closer than before to explaining who had made it, what it was made of, or where it had come from.

Marcus's black coffee was now completely cold. She drank it anyway. The next series of reports were all from Dr. Wolowitz in the materials-analysis group, which promised an afternoon of dry reading.

She picked up a data slate and prepared herself for another long struggle against boredom.

Then she heard shouting coming from the lab outside.

It grew louder as she dropped the slate and scrambled to her door, which slid open ahead of her. As it did, she heard one voice, loud and clear, barking panicked orders.

"Shut it down!" yelled Xiong, who ran from station to station around the central enclosure of transparent aluminum barriers. "Cut all power! Everyone stop, stop, STOP!"

The other scientists reacted with a flurry of frightened scrambling as they fought to deactivate every console and process. All the blinking readouts on the various panels went dark, and the lab's normal undertone of energized components pitched downward in a mellisonant hum before fading to silence.

Marcus stormed across the lab and confronted Xiong. "What the hell are you doing? What's going on?"

He was still trying to catch his breath. "Had to pull the plug," he said between gasps. "Before it was too late."

"Too late for what? I need details, Ming."

Xiong nodded and composed himself. "Sorry," he said. "Let me try to bring one system back online so I can show you what I found." He led Marcus to the nearest console and nodded for the Vulcan man standing there to step aside. Marcus watched as Xiong took care to reboot the console in an offline diagnostic mode. While he worked, she noticed his face was pale and his forehead heavy with sweat.

She placed a hand on Xiong's shoulder. "Try to calm down, Ming. Take a breath and tell me what happened."

He fished a data card from his pocket and inserted it into a slot on the console. "This morning I started analyzing all the tests we've run on the artifact over the last two months. I cross-referenced all the inputs and results with the latest long-range scans of planets we've pinged with the artifact while looking for Shedai Conduits."

The console loaded the data card, and its display changed to show an interactive star map. "This is what we found." He tapped the icon for one of the star systems. What appeared was an image of fiery debris scattered in space. "Every time we've used the artifact to ping a planet that turned out to harbor a Shedai Conduit, *the planet has exploded.*"

Eyes wide, Marcus parroted, "Exploded?"

"Complete geothermal self-destruction," Xiong said. "Over the past two months, we've destroyed eleven planets without even knowing it. And if I hadn't shut down today's experiment, we'd have raised the toll to an even dozen."

Marcus covered her mouth with one hand, as if she could hold back the horror that welled up inside her. "Oh, my God," she muttered. She looked up at the artifact, which was locked inside the experiment chamber. "What *is* that thing?"

Xiong shrugged. "Right now, my best guess is it's some kind of doomsday weapon for attacking the Shedai's interstellar network of Conduits." He stared at the crystalline dodecahedron. "If I know Admiral Nogura, his next question'll be: Can it be used as a weapon against the Shedai?"

She looked at Xiong. "Can it?"

"I don't know," he said. "All I can tell you is we have to be a lot more careful from now on—because that thing's Armageddon waiting to happen."

29

July 30, 2267

Haniff Jackson lunged for the ball as it bounced hard less than a foot behind the short line. He swung his racquet as he dived, but caught nothing but air.

The ball struck the floor a second time and ricocheted off the back wall. Jackson slammed to the deck with a pained grunt.

His opponent gave the racquet tied to her wrist a fast twirl and flashed a cocky grin in his direction. "Thirteen–six," Desai said. "Are you sure you've played racquetball before?"

"Yes," Jackson said. His entire body was drenched in sweat. Beads of perspiration fell from the tip of his nose as he pushed himself up from the floor.

Desai scooped up the ball from the floor and walked back toward the court's service zone. As she passed Jackson, she asked in a sweetly mocking tone, "Do you need a time-out?"

"I'm fine," he said. Flexing his arms to push through the pain of his abraded elbows, he added, "Serve when ready." He rolled his head in a circle to release the tension in his neck, then settled into his stance for another rally.

The petite JAG officer faced the front wall and lifted her racquet. With her left hand she released the ball and let it bounce once. As it returned to its drop-height and seemed to hang for the tiniest fraction of a second, Desai swung in a blur and swatted it. The sharp pop of contact was still echoing off the walls as the ball returned on an almost straight-line trajectory—and hit Jackson in the face.

A red flash filled his vision. When it cleared, he was lying on his back, looking up at Desai. "Time-out," he said.

"Are you all right?" she asked, wincing with embarrassment as she knelt beside him. "I didn't think I hit it that hard . . ."

"It's fine," Jackson said. "I was planning on getting my nose flattened, anyway." Lolling his head toward Desai, he added, "Now that I have your undivided attention, have you given any more thought to that intel we got from ch'Nayla?"

She nodded. "I have. And I'm sorry to say I think he's right. Most of it is completely inadmissible."

Sitting up slowly, Jackson grimaced with discomfort and disappointment. "I guess that means we can't even use it to issue warrants to look for evidence that *isn't* tainted."

"Afraid not," she said. "You and ch'Nayla can use it as a guide to update the station's security protocols, but as far as using it for evidence, it's worthless."

He pulled his hand across his upper lip and wiped away a trickle of blood running from his nose. "Great. Just great." As he got back on his feet, he let Desai hold his arm and offer him a bit of support. "Thanks," he said.

"Any time." She waved her racquet at the front wall. "Ready? That last serve's a mulligan."

Jackson shook his head. "No, thanks. You cleaned my clock in the first game, and you're two aces from handing me my hat in this one." He pulled off his protective eyewear. "I can tell when I'm beat."

Desai followed him as he walked off the court. "Don't talk like that. I know you're upset about the *Malacca* investigation, but that's just how things go sometimes."

"I'm not in the habit of accepting mass murder, arson, and terrorism as an example of 'Just how things go,'" he said, pushing open the door of the court. He turned and passed other courts on his way to the men's locker room. "Fifty-two people died in that attack. On my watch. And while we spend our time worrying about rules of evidence, they spend their time finding new ways to rob our ships and kill our people."

It was hard for Desai to keep pace with Jackson, whose stride was much longer than hers, but she was doing her best. "Haniff, don't you think I want to see Zett and his accomplices put away for life? The rules piss me off, too, but in the end they work in our favor by making our cases as strong as they can be." She caught his arm before he entered the locker room and made him turn to face her. "I promise you, I won't stop until I see him convicted in a fair and open trial."

"How?" Jackson replied. "Nothing we get on this guy ever sticks. Short of him giving you a full, unsolicited confession, how do you plan on bringing him to trial?"

She folded her arms and looked away. "I don't know." Meeting his accusatory glare, she added, "But unlike some people, I won't quit before the game's over."

The challenge implicit in her remark made him smile. "You really want to earn those last two points, eh?"

"No," she said, jabbing him playfully with her racquet. "I want *you* to *make* me earn them."

He admired her spirit. "All right," he said, waving her back toward the court. "Let's go finish this." She led the way, and he put his eyewear back on. "You know, if you took cheap shots like that at the bad guys, we might've put a few more of them in jail." When she frowned at him, he added, "Just sayin'."

She opened the door to the court and waved him inside. "And if your hands were as quick as your mouth, that ball might not have hit you in the face."

"Touché." He set himself into a ready stance on the right half of the court while Desai strolled confidently back to the service zone. He called out, "Before you serve . . . ?" She turned back, and he continued. "I just want to say I'm sorry for going all negative on you. This case just has me feeling like I've been hitting my head against a brick wall for months, know what I mean? To be so close and watch it slip away makes me crazy sometimes." He shook his head. "All I've wanted to do for the past year was bring the people behind the bombing to justice. Is that really so much to ask?"

Desai offered him a bittersweet smile. "I wish I knew what to tell you. On some level I believe in karma. If Zett was the one who bombed the *Malacca,* or part of a conspiracy to make it happen, then I like to think he'll get what's coming to him, either in this life or the next." Walking back toward Jackson, she continued, "There's an old saying: 'The arc of the universe bends toward justice.' You need to have faith in that, Haniff." She stopped in front of him. "Our duty is to serve the truth first, and we do that by obeying the law. Leave justice to the universe."

Then she reached up, grabbed his shirt collar with one hand, and pulled him down into a long, torrid kiss. When she released him, he was short of breath, and he felt dizzy from the sudden rush of blood away from his brain. She gave him a playful shove. "Now get your head back in the game, Lieutenant."

He blinked and tried to focus on something other than Desai's derriere as she strutted back to the service zone.

She lifted her racquet, called out, "Thirteen serving six," and dropped the ball. He saw it bounce once. He heard her racquet make contact.

A red streak caromed off the front wall. A shallow bounce several meters to his left made him lunge and flail to make a backhand return shot. His racquet sliced at empty air.

He landed on his face.

"Fourteen–six," Desai said with a triumphant grin.

"I hate this game," Jackson said.

July 31, 2267

A chirping comm woke Rana Desai from a deep sleep. She opened her eyes to near-total darkness inside her quarters and hoped she had merely dreamed the beeping tone that announced an incoming message. Listening to the soft background hum of the station's ventilation system, she was almost ready to close her eyes and let herself drift back to sleep when the alert sounded again. It was a triple tone, which indicated a priority signal.

Desai stifled a groan and pushed aside her bed covers. She picked up her soft cotton bathrobe from the floor and wrapped it around her naked body as she got up. Tying shut her robe, she padded out of her bedroom to the main room of her quarters and slipped into the chair behind her desk.

She silenced the comm alert before it could shrill again, then activated her desktop monitor. As she rubbed the sleep from her eyes, a familiar face appeared on-screen.

It was T'Prynn. *"Hello, Captain,"* the Vulcan woman said. *"I apologize if I woke you."*

Shock put an edge on Desai's whispered reply. "T'Prynn? What are you . . . ? What's this about?"

"It is urgent that I speak privately with you," said T'Prynn, whose surroundings were nondescript but resembled a ship. *"However, given my current status, a face-to-face discussion seemed imprudent."*

In no mood to be manipulated by the former intelligence officer, Desai said, "You're facing charges ranging from tampering with Starfleet medical records to going AWOL. The only conversation I'm willing to have with you is the one in which you surrender yourself to Starfleet."

"I think you should make an exception in this case," T'Prynn said. *"The reason I am contacting you is that I am offering to trade intelligence."*

"Then you've contacted the wrong person," Desai said. "You should be talking to your successor, Commander ch'Nayla." With mocking sweetness, she asked, "Should I transfer you?"

Unfazed by Desai's challenges, T'Prynn said, *"I have proof the Klingon military is conspiring with criminal elements associated with the Orion known as Ganz and his entourage aboard the* Omari-Ekon. *I would be willing to trade my evidence for certain pieces of information regarding Starfleet's current activities aboard Vanguard."*

"Tempting," Desai said. "Surrender yourself and we can talk about it in detail for as long as you'd like."

"The Klingons appear to have solicited the services of a

suspected master thief," T'Prynn said. *"This is unusual behavior for the Klingons, who as a rule take whatever they want by brute force. Their actions in this case suggest either they lack the strength to take what they want, or they wish to conceal the fact they are the ones who have taken it."* She arched one eyebrow. *"What I wish to know is this: What might be of such great value and dire risk to the Klingons that they would resort to hiring criminals to acquire it on their behalf?"*

Desai replied, "Those are all very interesting questions. I'm sure Admiral Nogura and Commander ch'Nayla will be willing to give them all due consideration when they interview you in the brig here on Vanguard."

T'Prynn remained the picture of calm. *"I understand your reticence to trust me or to share classified operational data. That's why I am prepared to offer you a valuable item of intelligence up front, as a demonstration of my good faith."*

"Why can't you understand this, T'Prynn? You're a fugitive from Starfleet military justice. Until you turn yourself in, nothing you say will be compelling enough for me to treat you as anything other than a suspect. Are you listening to me? Until you surrender, it won't matter what you tell me."

"Diego Reyes is alive and in Klingon custody."

Desai recoiled from the screen. "You're lying."

"I assure you, Captain, I am not."

Shaking her head in furious denial, Desai said, "You have a long track record as a liar, T'Prynn. You tell people what they want to hear, you manipulate them, blackmail them—"

"I am guilty of those offenses," T'Prynn said. *"And one day soon I will stand and answer for them in a Starfleet court. But what I have told you is true: Diego Reyes is alive. I have proof of it, recorded less than forty-eight hours ago, and I can tell you on what vessel he is being held."*

"Tell me now," Desai said, even as she felt the wound of her months-old grief being torn open by T'Prynn's news.

"First I require information. The only location in the Taurus Reach where the Klingons would be reluctant to attempt a sei-

zure by force is Vanguard. What is currently aboard the station for which they would be willing to engage the services of a professional thief?"

Desai's inner skeptic told her not to trust T'Prynn. "No," she said. "I won't be tricked, not like this." Her anger flared. "You know what Diego meant to me. I won't let you use those feelings to make me give you what you want."

"Captain—"

Before the Vulcan could say another word, Desai terminated the transmission. The monitor went dark with a soft click. She pressed a button on her desk and opened an audio channel to the operations center. "Desai to ops."

Lieutenant Commander Yael Dohan, the station's gamma-shift officer of the watch, replied, *"Ops, this is Dohan. Go ahead, Captain."*

"Commander, I need a trace on the source of the priority message I just received in my quarters."

"Yes, ma'am. Hang on a second." Over the line, Desai heard people working and sharing reports in muffled conversations. A moment later Dohan was back on the line. She sounded confused. *"Captain, I think you must be mistaken. The comm logs show no incoming messages to your quarters since yesterday at fourteen thirty-three hours."*

Desai thumped the side of her fist on her desktop and mumbled under her breath, "Damn you, T'Prynn."

Dohan asked, *"Do you want us to check the logs again, Captain?"*

"No, Commander. That'll be all. Thank you."

"You're welcome, ma'am. Good night."

The channel clicked closed, and Desai sat at her desk and fumed in the dark. Then she noticed Haniff standing in her bedroom doorway, the muscles of his nude body well defined by the light spilling from her desktop monitor.

He asked in a groggy voice, "Something wrong?"

"No," Desai lied. "Go back to bed."

He nodded, turned, scratched the back of his neck, and

plodded back into the bedroom. Desai turned off her computer monitor, looked toward the bedroom, and sighed. If T'Prynn was lying, then she was even more cruel than Desai had ever thought. But if she was telling the truth . . .

Then this is certainly going to make things a bit more interesting, Desai brooded.

Pennington shook his head and fought to rein in his temper as T'Prynn shut down the comm terminal. "How could Desai be so stubborn? You practically gave her everything, and she still wouldn't listen to you."

"She has good reason to doubt my veracity," T'Prynn said. "An assessment with which I expect you could sympathize."

The Vulcan woman seemed completely untroubled by the harsh rebuff she'd just received from Captain Desai, and Pennington didn't understand why. "Okay, so if the goal was to win her trust, why not just give her the coordinates for Kane's rendezvous with the Klingons and let Starfleet sort it out?"

T'Prynn got up from her seat. "Because we do not yet know what the purpose of that meeting is." She walked aft, and Pennington followed her down the dark and silent corridor.

"What difference does it make?" he asked.

She answered over her shoulder, "If Kane's transaction with the Klingons turns out to be innocuous, exposing it will be of little or no expiatory value to me." The door to the ship's only shower room opened ahead of her, and she continued inside with Pennington close behind her. "Furthermore, tipping off Starfleet to that meeting before we establish its parties' intentions would prematurely alert Ganz and his retainers to the breach in their internal communications by Starfleet Intelligence."

He turned his back as T'Prynn began undressing. Though she had shown no sense of self-consciousness about disrobing in front of him during their months alone in space, he nonetheless felt discomfited each time it happened. He asked, "So what do we do now?"

Out of the corner of his eye he noticed T'Prynn setting her

folded garments inside a cubby hole above the changing bench. "We will proceed to the rendezvous coordinates and establish a surveillance position."

"More low-energy, run-silent-run-dark, then?"

"Correct. Radio silence and a minimal energy signature will be essential to avoiding detection while we await the arrival of Mister Kane and his Klingon clients." Nude, she stepped into the shower and turned on the water. "Be patient. I suspect that whatever Kane is up to will be revealed soon enough."

30

August 1, 2267

In the hubbub of Vanguard's security center, a system-failure alert came and went so quickly on one of the junior officers' boards that Haniff Jackson almost didn't notice it. "Seklir," he said to the young Vulcan man. "Report."

Seklir keyed in commands, eyed the data on his monitor, and replied, "Power failure in tube four of the main turbolift hub. The cause appears to be an overloaded plasma conduit, which has caused a fire condition on Cargo Deck B."

"On screen three, please," Jackson said.

The image appeared in one frame of the master situation monitor. Flames leaped from cracks in a bulkhead, and smoke billowed from a slagged plasma conduit, filling the corridor.

Jackson asked, "Are fire-control teams responding?"

"Affirmative," Seklir said. "The deck officer reports the fire is contained. Sections one-ninety through one-ninety-eight of Cargo Deck B have been evacuated and sealed off until fire teams arrive."

The security chief nodded. Closing off sections threatened by fire was standard procedure. It limited the supply of oxygen to the blaze and curtailed its ability to spread.

Then he realized the fire was directly above the classified laboratory known to its resident scientists as the Vault. "Seklir, deploy additional security teams to Cargo Deck A, in sections one-ninety through one-ninety-eight."

"Aye, sir," Seklir said.

As the Vulcan ensign relayed Jackson's order to the deck officer on the lowest occupied level of the station, the image from Cargo Deck B went dark on the master display screen.

"What just happened?" demanded Jackson.

Seklir worked at his terminal for a moment. "The fire has spread into the security node at juncture CB/one-ninety-two." He looked up at Jackson. "We have lost surveillance video and internal sensors on Cargo Decks A and B."

Jackson had a feeling something bad was about to happen. *And this day started off so well,* he thought. He turned and snapped to his deputy, "Signal ops to sound Yellow Alert."

Heihachiro Nogura smiled at his yeoman as she set a tray bearing his lunch on his desk. "Thank you, Ensign."

"You're welcome, Admiral," said Ensign Toby Greenfield. The diminutive brown-haired young woman asked, "Is there anything else I can get for you, sir?"

"No," said Nogura. "But I'd like to move the meeting with the department heads back to sixteen thirty hours."

Greenfield nodded. "I'll let them know, sir."

Nogura nodded his acknowledgment, and Greenfield left. The admiral picked up a spoon and began enjoying his chicken noodle soup.

The Yellow Alert klaxon whooped once, and the comm signal on his desk buzzed. Spoon still in hand, he reached over and opened the channel. "What's going on?"

"Admiral," replied executive officer Commander Jon Cooper, *"we're receiving an emergency report from Doctor Marcus."*

"Details," Nogura demanded.

"She says toxic gas is flooding the Vault. Security informs me the fumes might be a byproduct of a plasma fire on Cargo Deck B."

Pushing aside his lunch, Nogura said, "Evacuate the Vault."

"Yes, sir. Engineering is deploying a hazmat unit."

"Belay that," Nogura said, wary of sending personnel who

lacked the proper security clearances into the classified lab. "Contain the situation and seal the lab until Doctor Marcus's team is able to initiate its own recovery protocols."

"Aye, sir," Cooper replied. *"Evacuating the Vault now."*

Blue fog gave every light source in the lab a pale halo as Carol Marcus fought for breath and waved her people toward the Vault's exit. "Move it, people!" she shouted.

Hot, hacking coughs wracked her chest with pain. Fumes stung her eyes, which watered and blurred her vision. Through her hazy veil of sight she struggled to identify and account for all her people. They stampeded past her, toward the bright-white tube tunnel that led back to the nondescript maintenance office they used as their cover address within the station.

She spotted Ming Xiong easily—he was the only person not running for his life. He stood at the exit, shouting to those who couldn't see to guide them to the door. "Gek! Tarcoh! This way, c'mon!"

Dr. Tarcoh, a middle-aged Deltan theoretical physicist, collapsed a few meters shy of the door. Marcus staggered out of the line of escaping personnel and labored to help the tall but seemingly fragile man to his feet. She supported his weight as they stumbled the rest of the way to the exit.

As she passed Xiong, she asked him in a hoarse voice, "Is that everyone?"

"I think so," he said, slipping under Tarcoh's other arm so he could help Marcus carry the man out.

They exited the brightly lit tunnel into office CA/194–6. The twenty-odd scientists who had left the lab ahead of them had packed the office beyond capacity and spilled out its open door into the corridor beyond. A Starfleet security officer was at the door, waving the scientists out of the office. "Everyone please move into the main corridor," he said. "We need to seal this compartment! Please proceed to the corridor in an orderly manner and wait there for additional instructions." The security officer reached out a hand to help steady Tarcoh. To Marcus and Xiong he said, "There are medical teams on the way. Take him to the junction at section one-ninety-two."

Marcus and Xiong nodded at the security officer, who waved them past, ushering them out the door. In the corridor, the other scientists cleared the center of the passage and stood with their backs to the walls.

Looking back to ask the security officer how soon the medical teams would arrive, she didn't see him anywhere. Then she saw the door to CA/194–6 was closed. For a moment she wondered whether the security officer had sealed the compartment from the inside or from the outside, but there was no time to ask questions. She already had her hands full.

Lieutenant Jackson reached Cargo Deck A and sprinted out of the turbolift. He was several sections away from the Vault because the turbolift shaft closest to the lab had lost power when the fire had started on Cargo Deck B.

His every step echoed off the metal deck plates as he ran through the corridors. He saw people standing outside the lab as he passed the junction for section one-ninety-eight. Many of them were dressed like civilians; he guessed they were the scientists who worked in the Vault. Mingled with them were members of the security detail he had sent down to secure the area. Everyone stood aside and let him pass. He kept running until he saw Dr. Marcus and Lieutenant Xiong kneeling beside a middle-aged man with a bald pate.

"Doctor Marcus!" exclaimed Jackson. "Is everyone all right?"

Marcus waved at Jackson as if signaling him to slow down. "We're fine," she said. "The lab's been evacuated and sealed." Throwing a nervous look back toward the Vault's cover location, she added, "I think one of your men might have locked himself in trying to seal it, though."

Suspicion raised the hackles on Jackson's neck. "One of my men is inside?" He looked at Xiong. "Which one?"

Xiong shrugged. "No idea. Never saw him before."

Jackson started walking toward CA/194–6. He stopped at a wall panel and opened a comm channel to the security center. "Seklir, this is Jackson. Can you confirm which one of our people sealed the Vault after the evacuation?"

"Checking, sir," the Vulcan said. A moment later he added, *"None of our people has reported sealing that compartment."*

"Is anyone in the Vault right now?"

"Internal sensors in that section are still offline, sir."

"Retask some from adja—"

Something shook the station as if an earthquake had struck. Jackson and the others in the corridor were thrown to the deck as the lights went out. When emergency illumination flickered on, Jackson pushed himself back to his feet and opened an emergency-equipment panel. "Seklir, do you copy?"

"Aye, sir. What is happening?"

"Something just blew up inside the Vault," Jackson said, retrieving a pair of goggles and a breathing mask with an air canister. "I'm going in to see what it was. Send everyone you can. I want this deck sealed. Got it?"

"Understood, sir."

Jackson ran back to the door and keyed in his security override code. With an asthmatic hiss the door slid open. Heat and fumes gusted into his face. He put on the goggles and strapped on the breathing mask. As he entered the smoky office, he secured the air canister to his belt and opened its valve.

The concealed door to the lab had been shattered into millions of tiny fragments, which lay scattered both inside and outside the cylindrical tunnel. The passage, normally lit to an almost blinding degree, was dark. Jackson moved with speed but also caution. He drew his phaser as he neared the passage's end.

The transparent doors ahead of him were coated with black soot and dust, rendering them opaque. He wedged his fingers between the two door panels. With a pained grunt he forced them apart. They screeched and scraped in their tracks.

He opened the doors wide enough to squeeze his broad chest

through. As he pushed his way into the lab, he saw a shadowy humanoid figure at its center.

The intruder's build looked masculine to Jackson's eyes. He was dressed in black and wore a balaclava-style hood over his head. His eyes were hidden by wraparound black glasses.

Somehow the man had blasted through the protective shielding in the middle of the lab. He was standing in the experiment chamber, next to the testing platform for the Mirdonyae Artifact—and holding the skull-sized, twelve-sided crystal in one hand while giving Jackson a jaunty wave farewell with the other.

As Jackson belatedly lifted his phaser to fire, the intruder ducked out of sight behind the bank of consoles that surrounded the experiment chamber.

Jackson freed himself from the door and ran into the lab, toward the bank of consoles. When he reached them and looked into the area beyond, he saw that a panel had been pulled from the floor, exposing a half-height sublevel filled with machinery, wiring, circuits, and power conduits.

He pulled his communicator from his belt and flipped it open. It responded with a dysfunctional-sounding "no signal" chirp, and he remembered with frustration that the interior of the Vault was hardened against signal traffic. Only hard-line communications could go in or out of the lab.

Dammit, he raged, tucking his communicator back into place on his hip. He hurdled over the consoles and through the breach in the test area's curtain of transparent aluminum. Scrambling through the gap in the floor, he dropped in a crouch to the cramped sublevel.

The security chief spun in fast ninety-degree turns, searching the black maze of machinery and tubing for the escaping thief. All he saw was darkness.

Take the path of least resistance, he told himself. *If you were trying to make an escape, you'd want to move fast.*

He found the direction that had the fewest obstructions and started moving. He shuffled forward, ducking under low-hanging components and occasionally crawling on his belly.

Then he caught a brief flash of dim light and motion directly ahead of him. He quickened his pace. Moments later he clambered out a small maintenance hatch into what he realized was the turbolift shaft disabled by the plasma fire. A few meters below him was a stalled lift car. On top of it, something was smoldering and giving off acrid smoke.

Jackson climbed down the shaft's emergency ladder. He stepped off the ladder onto the lift car and stomped on the burning debris until its fire was extinguished.

Picking through what was left, he recognized a black balaclava hood and a synthetic-skin prosthetic face mask. Both continued to disintegrate even as he inspected them, leading him to suspect they had been treated with a chemical to catalyze their rapid molecular breakdown. Within minutes, both would likely be completely gone, vanished without a trace.

Just like our thief, he brooded, looking up into the impenetrable darkness of the turbolift shaft.

Nogura stood at the Hub, an octagonal situation table located on the elevated supervisors' deck of Vanguard's operations center, and listened to the latest reports with a mounting sense of dread.

"Looks like he escaped up turbolift shaft four," Jackson said over the comm. *"I found the remnants of a disguise on top of a stalled lift car, but no sign of the artifact or the intruder."*

As the operations staff routed the starbase's interior schematics to the Hub, the tall, curly-haired XO organized them in response to Nogura's demands for information. "Cooper," Nogura said. "How many ways out of that shaft are there?"

"Dozens," Cooper said, highlighting all the access points. "And that's not even counting the normal exit points on each deck—that's just crawl spaces and emergency hatches." He tapped some live vid feeds and with a fingertip dragged them across the Hub's interactive surface. "We're monitoring all the main exits from that shaft, and I've got security and engineering working to put eyes on all the other points, but it's a lot of ground to cover."

Feeling his blood pressure rise ever so slightly, Nogura

studied the map and ruminated aloud, "If I were looking to slip out of that turbolift shaft without being noticed, where would be the best place to do it?" He traced the station diagram with his index finger and noted all the parts of the station with which it intersected. Then he stopped near the center of the station's massive primary hull assembly. "Cooper, have security lock down the main hangar deck. Search everyone. Verify their identification. Check every bag and every short-term locker."

Nogura turned away from the Hub and watched the vid feed from the Vault, whose internal sensors had come back online just in time to show off this spectacular breach of its security.

He frowned and declared for everyone in the ops center to hear, "Ground all docked starships. Shut down all transporter systems. No one gets on or off this station until further notice." He paused then added with grim conviction, "Whoever did this can hide, but they can't run."

31

Sixty-four minutes after imposing the admiral's lockdown on the station, Lieutenant Jackson ushered a man named Joshua Kane into an interrogation room near the security center.

"Have a seat," Jackson told the lean, bearded man.

Kane's face betrayed no hint of concern as he pulled back the lone chair from the gray metal table and sat down. His stare was all but blank as he watched Jackson pace on the other side of the table. He said nothing and remained still.

The door signal buzzed. Jackson said, "Come in."

The door opened. A freshly minted Tellarite ensign from the security division stepped inside the room, handed a data slate to Jackson, and left without speaking a word.

Jackson resumed pacing as he read Kane's dossier from the Starfleet JAG office. "You're a man of many incredible coincidences, aren't you, Mister Kane?" The suspect remained silent. "Do you know what I have here?"

With mock cluelessness, Kane replied, "A data slate?"

"That's right, genius. Know what's written on it?" He waited until Kane shrugged, then continued. "Your life story."

"All of it? Skip to the part where I lose my virginity." He grinned. "Talk about incredible coincidences."

"I'm more interested in your amazing knack for being in the vicinity of major crimes," Jackson said. "According to your file, you just happened to be on eight far-flung planets at the exact time of a spectacular unsolved heist on each world. And if we count your presence here today, that would make nine."

Nakedly feigning surprise, Kane asked, "Has there been a burglary on the station, Lieutenant?" He deflected Jackson's most withering glare with a smug half smile.

"You were on Zeta Aquilae in 2254 when its national armory was broken into. The contents of a warehouse filled with military-grade small arms and starship munitions were stolen. Some of those weapons were later found in the possession of Orion privateers harassing shipping in Sector Four."

Kane lifted one bushy eyebrow. "Sounds like the Orions ought to be your prime suspects on that one."

Still reading from the data slate, Jackson said, "You were in the capital city of Denobula when its national reserve bank was broken into and relieved of nearly three hundred million credits' worth of priceless ancient gemstones. Several pieces from that collection were later used by a Nalori arms dealer to solicit a shipment of antipersonnel mines from the Klingons."

Rolling his eyes as if to suggest that the implications of Jackson's statement should be obvious, Kane said, "Well, the Klingons and the Nalori *are* both fierce rivals of the Federation."

"Let me jog your memory again," Jackson said. "April of 2260. The Midas Casino on Risa. You were staying there as a guest when its art gallery was burgled. Dozens of priceless works, including a pair of ancient Vulcan sculptures, were taken in a flawless overnight heist. You checked out the next day."

"Naturally," said Kane. "You can't expect me to stay in a hotel with such poor security. I didn't feel safe."

For a fleeting moment Jackson wished he could beat the smile off Kane's face. Instead, he inhaled deeply and moved on. "March 2261. You just happened to be in the city of Kefvenek on Beta Rigel at the precise time its—" The door signal buzzed, and Jackson snapped, "What is it?" He looked up as the door opened.

Another civilian walked in—an Orion woman unlike any Jackson had ever seen before. Though she had the dark green skin common to her people, her black hair was cut short. She wore wire-frame glasses and a dark business suit over a crisp white shirt. Her shoes were low-heeled, and instead of the erotically charged atmosphere Jackson had come to expect from Orion women, this one was cold and aloof. She carried a metallic briefcase.

"Lieutenant Jackson," the Orion said as Captain Desai followed her inside the interview room, "My name is Denon Veril. I'm Mister Kane's attorney." She set her briefcase on the table. "I need to confer in private with my client, as per his rights under the First Guarantee of the Federation Charter."

Jackson looked to Desai, who nodded in confirmation and motioned for him to follow her out of the interrogation room. Desai left the room first, and Jackson was close behind her.

As the door hushed closed behind him, he asked in a harsh whisper, "His lawyer? What the hell's going on?"

"Apparently, she 'just happened' to be on the station to negotiate a contract with a mining consortium."

"Sure she did," Jackson said, folding his arms.

"Her story checked out," Desai said.

Jackson shook his head. "Most good alibis do."

The JAG officer continued, "Veril says Kane's lunch companion called her on his behalf after we arrested him. She contacted me and immediately filed a motion demanding we turn over any and all security footage of Café Romano in Stars Landing recorded during the time of the alleged heist."

A grim chortle shook Jackson's chest. "This has setup written all over it."

"I agree, but she insists the footage proves her client is innocent. I had Seklir copy the requested files to a data card for Veril. My guess is she's reviewing it with Kane right now."

The door to the interrogation room slid open. Veril poked her head out. "We're ready to speak with you now," she said.

"After you," Jackson said to Desai.

He let Desai enter the room first then followed her in. They took up a position opposite Veril, who stood behind the still-seated Kane.

"After reviewing your charges against my client and the alleged timeline of events that constitute the crime, and hearing my client's alibi, I am prepared to make the following statement on his behalf.

"Between the hours of twelve ten and twelve thirty-four, when your timeline indicates a series of disturbances and security breaches occurred on Cargo Decks A and B of this facility, my client was with his associate Leskon of Delta Leonis, having lunch in Café Romano, in Stars Landing. Mister Kane and Mister Leskon were both in full public view during a period extending from fifteen minutes before the alleged crime began and ten minutes after it is reported to have ended.

"I can produce at least four witnesses who saw and heard my client and Mister Leskon in the café during that time period, including the establishment's proprietor and chef, Matt Romano.

"Furthermore, I offer as exculpatory evidence the following vid recorded by your own security system during the times in question." Veril opened her briefcase, removed the data card, and walked it over to a wall panel with a display screen.

She inserted the card into a slot and started the playback. An image flickered onto the screen. It clearly showed Kane and another man of an alien humanoid species Jackson didn't recognize. The two sat at a table outside the entrance of the café, a popular dining spot in the mostly civilian residential sector, inside the terrestrial enclosure that occupied the upper half of the station's hollow saucer.

"Note the time stamp," Veril said. "This is fifteen minutes before the first reported disturbance. Both men are in plain sight." She fast-forwarded the playback. "Note that during the entire time of the incident on the cargo decks, neither man leaves the table." She released the fast-forward and the playback continued at normal speed. "The time stamp is now twelve minutes after the cargo decks were declared secure. Both men are still at the table."

Veril ceased the playback, ejected the data card, and plucked it from the wall. She turned to face Desai and Jackson. "Unless you have witnesses or physical evidence linking my client to the crime, I insist you release him immediately. If you wish to charge him despite the absence of evidence against him, I am prepared to post bail and file an appeal to the Starfleet Judge Advocate General on Earth."

Jackson was about to challenge the Orion woman to do her worst when Desai said simply, "Release him."

The security chief turned and said, "What?"

Desai looked at the Orion. "Ms. Veril, you and your client are free to leave. Thank you for your cooperation."

Veril nodded, and Kane flashed his irksome smile. Then he got up and followed his attorney out the door. As the door closed, Jackson pounded the side of his fist on the table. "I can't believe we're just letting him go!"

"We have no case," Desai said. "No evidence, no witnesses, nothing. And you saw that recording. His alibi is airtight."

"And what if he has the artifact?"

Desai crossed her arms. "I'll order the customs group to tear apart his ship and search it bow to stern. But if it comes up clean, we'll have to let him leave."

Jackson was sick with rage as he picked up the data slate from the table. "Eight perfect crimes, eight perfect alibis." He shook his head in disbelief. "And now we're number nine."

Desai sat at the briefing room table with Cooper, ch'Nayla, and Jackson, and avoided Admiral Nogura's steely gaze as he leaned on his fists and harangued them.

"Lieutenant Jackson," Nogura said in a voice that made Desai think of broken glass, "the Vault is supposed to be the most secure facility on the station, is it not?"

Sounding humbled, Jackson replied, "Yes, sir."

"And yet an intruder walked in, defeated all our security protocols, stole the most dangerous alien artifact we've ever seen, and then vanished inside our own station?"

"I wouldn't say he vanished, sir," Jackson said. "He escaped pursuit."

Nogura nodded. "How?"

Commander Cooper spoke up. "Sir? Lieutenant Jackson and I have been analyzing the heist, and we've developed a hypothesis for how the suspect Joshua Kane could've pulled it off. We think he might have used a body double or a holographic stand-in to create his alibi in the café. Then, he could have shipped himself from the café's back room to the cargo deck inside a standard supply crate using the station's automated matériel-transfer network. Once there—"

"Commander," Nogura interrupted, "before you waste twenty minutes of our time on this, do you have any proof?"

Jackson and Cooper volleyed abashed glances. The XO replied, "No, sir."

"Then put it in your report. I'll read it the next time I can't sleep." The admiral turned to glare at the Starfleet Intelligence liaison. "Commander ch'Nayla. Any progress locating the artifact?"

"No, sir," the Andorian said. "All outgoing vessels have been thoroughly inspected, and we are continuing to carry out hard-target searches of all compartments on the station."

"Have we dredged the waste processors?"

"Yes, Admiral," ch'Nayla said. "We found no sign of the artifact or any evidence linked to the crime. However . . ." He nodded to the executive officer. "I have reviewed Commander Cooper and Lieutenant Jackson's report speculating on the crime's particulars, and I was forced to draw one inescapable conclusion. Whoever planned this burglary had detailed knowledge of this station and its various systems, especially its most obscure vulnerabilities."

Nogura said, "You're suggesting it might have been an inside job."

Ch'Nayla replied, "I think it's very likely, sir."

"Draw up a list of all personnel who would have had the requisite knowledge to facilitate the crime, and send it to Lieutenant Jackson and Captain Desai." To Jackson he added, "Once you have the list, investigate all communications by those individuals since the acquisition of the Mirdonyae Artifact. I want to know where they've been and who they've talked to." He looked at Desai. "You'll have to investigate Jackson, since I'm sure his name will be on ch'Nayla's list. . . . No offense, Lieutenant."

Jackson replied, "None taken, sir."

Though she had been summoned to brief Nogura on the state of her failed criminal prosecution of Joshua Kane, Desai now realized she had another, more pressing duty: to prevent an unnecessary witch hunt against her fellow officers. Remembering what T'Prynn had told her the previous night, she now regretted omitting some of the details of the conversation from her report to security about the call. "Admiral," she said, "I don't think we need to investigate the station's senior officer corps. I might know of a more likely source for the intruder's information about the station."

She felt as if she had shrank slightly in her seat as the full weight of the admiral's stare fell upon her. "Explain," he said.

"Early this morning, I filed a report with security about an unauthorized communication I'd received last night from the fugitive T'Prynn. I notified security of her warning about the Klingons having hired a known thief. However, I failed to mention what I had dismissed as an outrageous claim."

The room was quiet with anticipation as she confessed.

"She told me Diego Reyes is alive and in Klingon custody. He knew everything Kane would have needed to break into the Vault and escape with the artifact. Which means if T'Prynn is telling the truth, our former commander isn't dead—he's colluding with the enemy."

32

August 2, 2267

Pennington awoke to faint sounds of comm chatter and fingers working the switches of a computer console. He squinted as he checked the chrono. It was just after 0430 ship's time on the *Skylla*. His limbs felt like lead and his eyes itched as he rolled out of his bunk.

The sounds became more distinct as he groggily walked forward in the main corridor. The deck plates felt like ice under his bare feet. A shiver traveled up his legs to his spine.

Not a night goes by I don't regret not packing slippers, he lamented.

Like the rest of the *Skylla*'s interior, the cockpit was mostly dark. A handful of computer readouts bathed the cramped space in weak ambient light.

T'Prynn sat with her back to the open hatchway. She was working at the communications station. A compact transceiver was tucked inside her left ear. She touched it lightly with her fingertips while she made an adjustment on the control panel in front of her.

As Pennington stepped over the cockpit's threshold, she acknowledged his presence with the slightest turn of her head. Nodding in reply, he eased himself into the copilot's seat. He had learned to keep quiet while T'Prynn monitored signals; her hearing was sensitive to even the softest sounds, and he didn't want to distract her while she was working.

Finally, she returned the console to its standby mode and

removed the transceiver from her ear. "I am sorry if I woke you," she said.

"No worries. Anything good?"

She nodded once. "We intercepted an interesting signal from Vanguard to Starfleet Command. I was able to break the encryption sequence, but most of the message is written in a code with which I am not familiar." She called up a transcript of the intercept. "However, this sequence—'Echo Sierra Bravo, nine, seven, red'—appears to be a legacy code from my tenure as the SI liaison."

Leaning forward, Pennington asked, "What does it mean?"

"It indicates that an extreme security breach has occurred in relation to the principal mission objective."

Pennington rubbed the underside of his stubbled chin. "So either Joshua Kane stole whatever it was the Klingons hired him to get, or Captain Desai reported your tip about Commodore Reyes being alive and with the Klingons."

"Or perhaps both," T'Prynn said.

That made Pennington think for a moment. "You're right," he said. "If Kane is working for the Klingon who's holding Reyes, and if the thing the Klingons wanted stolen was on Vanguard, then Kutal could've forced Reyes to help Kane plan the heist. That would be a *major* breach in Starfleet's security, both on the station and in this entire sector."

"Precisely," T'Prynn said. "A most logical deduction."

He shrugged. "Well, you know us reporters: sometimes we put two and two together."

33

The Vault was a shambles. Dust and debris littered the floor at Ming Xiong's feet.

"Most of the damage was localized here, in the experiment chamber," he said to Admiral Nogura, Dr. Marcus, and Commander ch'Nayla. "The intruder used an ultritium charge to knock out the transparent aluminum barrier." Xiong stood in front of a bank of shattered consoles facing the breach in the safety barrier. "Blowback from that detonation destroyed these master terminals. Until we replace them, the lab's internal network will be offline."

Nogura's countenance was grim as he surveyed the damage. "You said you had good news to report, Lieutenant."

"Yes, sir," Xiong replied. He looked at Marcus. "With your permission, Doctor?"

"By all means," Marcus said. "Proceed."

Xiong nodded and continued. "Although our burglar got away with the artifact, we've confirmed he had no access to the Vault's memory banks. When the evacuation alert was triggered, the computer system secured itself automatically. So at least we still have all our experimental data."

"Small comfort," said ch'Nayla. The Andorian flicked a shard of cracked polymer off a charred console. It bounced across the deck and disappeared through the open floor panel into the sublevel.

"It's more important than you might think," Xiong said. "I

saw what little progress the Klingons made with the artifact, both before and after they put me to work on it. We've learned far more about it than they ever did, or ever could." He looked back at Nogura. "I'd like to show you what my team was working on up until we lost the artifact."

The senior officers and Dr. Marcus pressed in close as Xiong found an intact console and coaxed it back to life. "Even though our scans failed to penetrate its outer surface, we were able to measure other phenomena to develop a virtual model of the artifact's subatomic structure." He activated a display screen, which showed an animated wire frame image of the twelve-sided alien object. "Our simulation was able to predict the artifact's response to new stimuli with near-perfect accuracy. I believe we can continue our research even without the original artifact. At least, on a theoretical level."

"Excellent work, Xiong," said Marcus.

Nogura added, "I'll second that. Well done, Lieutenant."

Ch'Nayla was less enthused. "Commendable as this may be, it falls short of the practical application we were led to expect."

Xiong reflexively shot a narrowed stare at ch'Nayla, but forced himself to remain calm in the presence of superior officers. "True," he said. "And the loss of the artifact means we'll be relying on simulations until further notice, so we won't be able to confirm any of our current hypotheses. However, there is one that's very close to ready for a field test."

He used the console to call up his latest project. "I had the idea that we could modulate a particle beam using the waveform from the Jinoteur Pattern. Our simulations and early tests on the artifact suggest this would create a signal that would not only pierce the object's outer shell but also trigger the release of a pulse attuned to the same frequencies the Shedai use to change their physical states. Depending on the specific segment of the pattern we employ, we might be able to use it as bait or as a means of immobilizing them."

Marcus added, "I've reviewed Xiong's proposal, and I think that if it works, it could have even more significant long-range applications in a variety of sciences, from long-distance subspace communications to tissue-regeneration and beyond. Its possibilities could be effectively endless."

"Sounds promising," Nogura said. "How long will it take to weaponize it?"

Ch'Nayla cut in, "There are serious security concerns that need to be addressed first, Admiral."

Nogura eyed the Andorian. "Such as . . . ?"

"It is not yet clear whether bombarding the artifact with energy beams utilizing the Jinoteur Pattern would risk releasing the Shedai entity currently trapped inside it," ch'Nayla said. "If such an event were to occur aboard a starship or space station, to say nothing of on the surface of an inhabited planet, the potential loss of life could be substantial."

The admiral asked Xiong, "Is that a risk, Lieutenant?"

Uncertainty painted a grimace on Xiong's face. "Hard to say, sir. None of the simulations we've done so far indicates any loss of structural integrity to the artifact. On the other hand, we don't really have a baseline. It might have a limit to how much energy it can channel at once before it loses the ability to contain its Shedai."

Horrified, Marcus interjected, "You're all forgetting something very important. The *entity* inside the artifact is not some abstract concept—it's a sentient life-form. Before we start running tests to see how much raw energy we can flood through that thing, I think we need to figure out whether we'd be causing any harm to the creature inside."

Ch'Nayla regarded Marcus with skepticism. "What do you propose we do then, Doctor? Should we gear our efforts toward releasing the Shedai from its captivity inside the artifact?"

"That might be the humane thing to do," Marcus said.

Nogura's eyes widened. "And the most tactically dangerous. In any event, I don't even want to talk about letting it out until we know who put it in there, how they did it, and why."

Xiong held up his hands and said, "There might be a middle path to consider."

"Let's hear it," Nogura said.

"We know from Lieutenant Theriault's encounter with the Shedai Apostate that not all of the Shedai are necessarily hostile. At this point, we don't really know anything about the identity or intentions of the Shedai trapped inside the Mirdonyae Artifact. While I agree with Commander ch'Nayla that releasing it without proper safeguards would be unwise, I think it might be beneficial, from both a scientific and diplomatic standpoint as well as a humanitarian one, to establish contact with it."

Nodding slowly, ch'Nayla said, "Mister Xiong makes some excellent points. If contact could be established, perhaps the entity itself could answer our questions about the artifact's origins and purpose."

"And talking with it might make it possible to defuse tensions," Marcus said. "So if and when we do release it, it doesn't go on a homicidal rampage."

"Okay," Nogura said. "You've convinced me. Xiong, how long will it take to repair the damage in here?"

"About two weeks." Looking around at the dark and deserted laboratory, Xiong continued, "We can swap out those fragged consoles in a day or two, and replacing the transparent aluminum barrier is another one-day job. The real delays will be fixing and upgrading the security entrance, isolating the ventilation system to keep us from getting smoked out again, and sealing that hatch in turbolift four."

Nogura nodded. "Very good. Get it done. If you hit any snags, let me know and I'll make them vanish."

"Thank you, sir," Xiong said.

The admiral shook Xiong's hand, then said to ch'Nayla, "Walk with me, Commander." The pair exited the lab through the wide-open access passageway, whose far end now was under twenty-four-hour armed guard.

As soon as they were out of earshot, Marcus folded her arms and kept her voice down as she said to Xiong, "Are you out of your mind? *Two weeks* to swap out four state-of-the-art consoles, replace a grade-ten barrier, rebuild an entire bulkhead, and install a new security module? That'll take at least a month."

Xiong smiled at her. "Nope. Two weeks, tops."

"Not without a miracle," Marcus said, clinging to her pessimism.

He laughed softly. "Relax, Doctor. For Starfleet engineers, miracles are just standard operating procedure."

Rana Desai had the best table in Manón's Cabaret to herself.

Seated in the front row and just left of center stage, Desai had a perfect view of every member of the jazz quartet providing that evening's musical entertainment. Their set list since her arrival had consisted of low-key numbers with softly plucked bass lines, smooth wire-brush percussion, and mellow back-and-forth riffs by the piano player and saxophonist.

The dinner crowd's conversation was muted. Most of the club's patrons were civilians, but as always there were a few Starfleet officers in the mix.

Manón's served as the station's de facto officers' club for a number of reasons: it offered better food and drinks; its interior design was more pleasing; its furniture was more comfortable; and its acoustics were superior to those of the actual officers' club, a drab gray box with chairs located in the station's core. Last but not least, the view from Manón's newly opened upstairs open-air terrace, of artfully lit buildings in Stars Landing, was far prettier than the official club's view of hangar bay three.

All Desai could see, however, was the empty seat on the other side of her table.

She sipped from her glass of sparkling water and enjoyed the tingle of carbonation on her tongue. Listening to the quartet spin a slow, melancholy tune, she wondered what she was going to say when her guest arrived. It was bound to be an awkward conversation, and Desai admitted to herself that she was dreading every minute of it.

"Mind a bit of company?"

The question freed Desai from her reverie. She looked over her shoulder to see Dr. Ezekiel Fisher smiling down at her.

The gray-haired octogenarian chief medical officer had been

a steady and quasi-paternal presence in Desai's life since they were told of Diego Reyes's alleged death seven months earlier. She had been grateful for Fisher's support, especially since Reyes had been one of his closest friends, and she knew the old doctor's loss had to have been as deep as her own.

But he wasn't who she was waiting for, and his presence could only complicate an already messed-up situation.

She gestured at the empty chair. "Have a seat."

He planted one palm on the table to steady himself as he eased into the chair opposite hers. "I should have known I'd find you here," he said, then exhaled with relief as he settled into place. "This was the table Diego always reserved for you."

"I remember," Desai said.

A waiter appeared from the steady bustle of activity in the dining room, picked up the bottle of water from its ice bucket beside the table, and filled Fisher's glass.

"Thanks," Fisher said with a nod at the waiter, who bowed his head as he returned the bottle to its icy receptacle.

"I'll be back with your menus in a moment," the waiter said, and he slipped away before Desai could explain that Fisher wasn't actually her intended dinner companion.

Fisher traced the rim of his water glass with the tip of his index finger until it produced a dulcet tone. Then he stopped abruptly. "T'Prynn's news about Diego," he said and shook his head. "I just can't get a handle on it. No sooner do I start getting used to the idea that he's gone . . ."

"I know," Desai said. "Part of me screams, *Don't trust her,* but I really want to believe she's telling the truth."

"We all do," Fisher said.

"Except that if he *is* alive, he probably helped the Klingons break into the Vault," Desai said. "So, which would be better: Diego dying as a patriot, or living as a traitor?"

The doctor's vaguely amused countenance turned enigmatic. "Seems like a false choice to me," he said. "If he is alive and with the Klingons, that doesn't prove he's there willingly. We shouldn't jump to conclusions."

Desai considered the common sense in what Fisher had said. "You're right," she admitted. "I'm assuming facts not in evidence. I should know better."

"There you go," Fisher said. "Now ask yourself: If Diego's alive but being held against his will by the Klingons, is that a truth you could live with?"

"Absolutely," Desai said. Then her spark of optimism was snuffed by her doubts. "But it's still a risk, Zeke. If I start believing that and find out T'Prynn lied to me, I'd be crushed to find out I'd been clinging to a false hope."

Fisher cracked a restrained smile. "A long time ago, a wise man once said, 'There is never anything false about hope.' It was true then, and it's true now. Don't give up on hope—it's the one thing no one else can take away from you."

She lifted her water glass to toast him. "Well said."

He picked up his glass and clinked it against hers with the deft touch of a surgeon. "Thank you." Looking around, he added, "What happened to our waiter? I'm starving."

"Um, Zeke . . . ?" She waited until he looked at her. "I . . . uh . . ."

Before she could put her thoughts into words, she heard another voice from behind her shoulder.

"Three for dinner?" Jackson asked. "I thought it was just the two of us."

Fisher looked up at the younger man with an expression of mild surprise, then back at Desai. "Oh. I see." He smiled at Jackson. "My mistake: I seem to be sitting in your chair." He got up just as the waiter returned. Handing the server his water he said, "The gentleman will need a new water glass."

"Very good." The waiter nodded and stepped away again.

Jackson looked back and forth between Fisher and Desai then asked, "What're we talking about?"

With a sly but knowing glance at Desai, Fisher replied, "Whether we dare to hope Diego Reyes is really alive."

"And what's the verdict?" Jackson asked Desai.

"Jury's still out," she said.

As Fisher started to leave, Jackson said, "I'll bet you both dinner here—with drinks, appetizers, and desserts—that he's alive, well, and still on our side."

The wager put a light in Fisher's eyes. "Folks tell me you never lose a bet," he said to the lieutenant.

"That's right," Jackson said.

Fisher shook the man's hand. "That's a bet I'll be happy to lose, son. You're on." Releasing Jackson's hand, he patted the man's shoulder. "Enjoy your dinner."

As Fisher left the club, the waiter returned and set a clean water glass at the table's other place setting. There was no point putting off the inevitable any longer.

Desai motioned to the empty chair. "Have a seat, Haniff. There's something we need to talk about . . ."

34

Pennington's pulse thudded in his temples as he and T'Prynn eavesdropped on transmissions between the Klingon battle cruiser *Zin'za* and Joshua Kane's vessel, the *Ali Baba*.

"Standing by to receive your courier," Kane said. *"Shields are down, and the scattering field has been disabled."*

A guttural male Klingon voice replied, *"Energizing."*

Outside the cockpit, Pennington saw only stars and endless night. The two ships he and T'Prynn had under surveillance were too far away for him to discern with his eyes.

He shifted his weight to keep blood flowing to his fingers; to prevent himself from touching the wrong switch at the wrong moment and giving away their presence to either Kane or the Klingons, Pennington was sitting on his hands.

T'Prynn hovered over the sensor station behind Pennington. "Passive sensors are detecting a transport from the *Zin'za*," she said, her voice calm and neutral. "Signal strength and duration are consistent with a life-form transport."

"Will that data tell us what he gives the courier?"

"Negative," T'Prynn said. "These sensors are not precise enough for us to gauge the exact variance in mass."

A new rough-edged voice said over the comm, *"Tonar to Zin'za. Delivery has been made. Ready to transport."*

The first Klingon voice replied, *"Acknowledged. Stand by. Energizing."*

More data flew across T'Prynn's screen. "Another transport

cycle has begun," she said. "The *Zin'za* is beaming someone or something back from the *Ali Baba*."

Over the comm, Joshua Kane said, *"This fulfills our contract. A pleasure doing business with you, as always.* Ali Baba *out."*

Swiveling her chair toward Pennington, T'Prynn said, "The comm channel has been terminated." She got up and moved forward into the pilot's seat. "Now comes the dangerous part."

"Hang on," Pennington said. "We're sitting within striking distance of a Klingon battle cruiser, hoping it doesn't notice we're not really a piece of space junk, and this isn't even the *dangerous* part? Then why is my colon tied in a knot?"

T'Prynn kept her eyes on the long-range passive sensors and noted the movements of the *Ali Baba* and the *Zin'za*. "Our new imperative is to follow the Klingon cruiser," she said. "We must attempt to determine where it is taking whatever it is Joshua Kane stole from Vanguard."

"How do we know he stole anything? For all we know, based on these intercepts, he could have been delivering beer."

She glanced at him, then resumed studying the sensor readout. "We cannot be absolutely certain," she said. "However, a preponderance of evidence currently in hand suggests this is the case. Logically, the most probable means of obtaining the knowledge we seek is to follow the Klingon vessel."

Pennington rolled his eyes. "More warp-shadow mimicry?"

"For now, yes. However, it will be much more difficult to fool the Klingons' sensors than it was to trick Ganz's. We will need to stay at the very edge of their sensor range, which will put them just outside ours. It will be, as I have heard humans say, a *touch and go* procedure."

"Not a job for the autopilot, then," he said.

"Correct." One of the blips on the sensor screen vanished. "The *Ali Baba* has gone to warp. As soon as the *Zin'za* makes the jump to warp speed, we will plot its course and lay in a long-range pursuit plan."

Watching her work, Pennington felt his latest pang of regret over having volunteered for this quixotic mission. "Say we follow the Klingons all the way to wherever they're going. What then? Do we have a plan? Or are we just a dog chasing a car?" She threw him a bemused look, and he added, "Are we not going to know what to do even if by some miracle we catch up to them?"

"Our objective is to observe, gather verifiable and actionable intelligence, and relay it to Starfleet as soon as possible."

Waving his hands, he replied, "Wait, wait, wait. Are we talking about a *peek from orbit* kind of observation, or is this going to be more of a *run through the Jinoteur shooting gallery* type of observation?"

The second blip disappeared from the sensor display. "The *Zin'za* has gone to warp," T'Prynn said. "Initiating warp core restart." As she powered up the *Skylla*'s main reactor, she added, "Please bring the impulse drive back online."

"Aye, skipper," Pennington said. He flipped switches and was relieved to feel the vibrations from the ship's power plant course through the deck plates under his feet. With any luck, the ship would soon be at least a few degrees warmer than a meat locker, once the life-support system came back to full power.

Casting a sidelong glance at T'Prynn, he said, "You still haven't answered my question. How much heat are we going to take for this little quest of yours?"

She looked almost serene as she entered data into the navigation system. "Ideally, we would remain as distant as possible from our observational targets. We should not attempt to take direct action unless it is absolutely necessary."

He harrumphed with bitter humor. "Who do you think you're kidding? It's *always* bloody *necessary*."

35

Until the deal was done, it was Zett Nilric's job to be the eyes in the darkness, the fair witness to the transaction.

He was alone aboard his argosy, *Icarion*. The modern cargo ship was equipped with the latest state-of-the-art automations, which enabled him to work solo most of the time. It also afforded him the opportunity to travel in a modicum of comfort, which made his current long-term surveillance effort bearable.

Zett had been there for days. He had dropped out of warp a few million kilometers away, then coasted into position on inertia. Thrusters had sufficed to bring his ship to a halt without doing anything to announce his presence.

There was only one seat in *Icarion*'s spacious cockpit. It was located at the forward end of the compartment and centered under the wraparound transparent canopy. Zett cast a tired look at the sensor screen to his left. It showed the Klingon battle cruiser *Zin'za* and Joshua Kane's vessel, the *Ali Baba*, holding station a few thousand kilometers from each other. So far the Klingons appeared to be unaware that Zett was lurking nearby as an observer to the exchange, and there was no sign of any other ship in the area, and no hint of a betrayal.

Good, Zett thought. *It's nice to see the Klingons exhibit a sense of honor once in a while.*

Reclining, he caught his ghost of a reflection on the canopy overhead. Thanks to the darkness of the cockpit, his glossy black skin was all but invisible when mirrored against the backdrop of space. His charcoal-colored suit was nearly as hard to see. Only the pale violet twists of his braided beard bounced back enough light to be visible on the transparent metal overhead, though at first he mistook the spectral image for a smudge on the canopy's exterior.

By now I'm sure Ganz's court is in chaos, he thought, baring a grin of gleaming black teeth. As the Orion crime boss's chief enforcer, it was Zett's job to keep order aboard the *Omari-Ekon* and deal with any delicate problems that might arise during the regular course of business. He didn't like to be away from his employer for too long, though not because he liked Ganz or acted out of any sense of loyalty to him. It had been Zett's experience that Ganz, like many people in positions of power, often placed the blame for serious mishaps on the shoulders of people who were absent and therefore unable to acquit themselves. Zett had seen too many people learn the hard way that *out of sight* didn't always mean *out of mind*—sometimes it meant *out of luck.*

An alert beeped softly on the sensor readout. The Klingons were beaming someone over to the *Ali Baba.*

So far, so good, mused Zett.

He imagined one of the Klingon officers paying Kane his exorbitant fee for executing an all but impossible heist from a secure Starfleet lab on Vanguard. No doubt it would gall the Klingons to pay a thief when their blood burned for combat and conquest. There was a risk they might take out their frustrations on poor Joshua Kane. If the deal went sour, it was Zett's job to cover Kane's escape if possible; if it wasn't, then his orders were to note which ship had been responsible for the betrayal, and leave the rest to Ganz's network of underworld operatives.

Another soft beep turned Zett's head. The *Zin'za* was beaming its courier and prize back from Kane's ship. Moments later the Klingon cruiser powered up its impulse engines and maneuvered away on a rimward heading deeper into the Taurus Reach.

At the same time, the *Ali Baba* engaged its engines and set a course in the opposite direction, back toward the explored region of this hotly contested sector.

Kane's ship was the first to make the jump to warp speed. The Klingons followed suit, and Zett's sensor showed nothing but empty, quiet space.

Another day, another paycheck, Zett thought as he sat forward. He would wait thirty minutes for the Klingons to move out of sensor range before bringing *Icarion*'s warp drive online, then he would set a course similar to that of the *Ali Baba*. If all went well, he would be back on the *Omari-Ekon* in a few weeks.

He was about to restart his impulse drive when a buzzing alert on his console made him stop, watch, and listen.

Turning toward the sensor readout, Zett saw an energy reading from another impulse engine core. It was fewer than ten thousand kilometers away. At first he thought it must be for a very small craft, such as a shuttle, but then he realized certain elements of its power signature were inconsistent with that conclusion. *Must be well masked,* he reasoned. *Which means someone is trying very hard not to be seen.*

The discovery that he was not the only one spying on Kane's meeting with the Klingons made Zett smile. He wondered who else might have a motive for being there, and how they had known where the rendezvous had been scheduled to take place.

He sat back and continued his observation. The other ship took its time restarting its warp drive; whoever was running it was savvy enough to give the Klingons a decent head start. When the other lurker in the darkness finally made the jump to warp speed, it followed a course clearly intended to make it appear to the *Zin'za*'s crew as a mere warp shadow. The maneuver was a classic trick superbly executed, and it was exactly what Zett had expected the other ship to do—because he was about to do the same thing.

Normally, once goods and payment had been exchanged, there was no more need to safeguard the deal. In this case, however, Zett worried that if the mysterious interloper somehow sabotaged the transaction after the fact, the Klingons might decide to seek revenge on the last known parties involved. Zett couldn't take that chance, especially not with a contract this valuable.

More important, he needed to know how the coordinates for Kane's secret meeting with the Klingons had fallen into the wrong hands. Whoever had been out there hadn't followed the *Ali Baba* or the *Zin'za* to the rendezvous; they had to have been waiting for as long as Zett had been, if not longer.

Either someone aboard the *Omari-Ekon* had talked, or the internal security on Ganz's ship had been compromised.

Either way, Zett decided as he brought his warp drive online, *whoever they are, they know too much. And that makes them my problem to sort out.*

Interlude

36

August 24, 2267

A lot of time had passed, and Jetanien and Lugok had run out of interesting things to say to each other.

"These are three months of my life I will never get back, Jetanien," Lugok grumbled over dinner one evening.

Between slurps of his pungent broth, Jetanien replied, "It's not as if you were doing anything that will be missed."

They had taken to eating outside their respective ships, though not necessarily together. The Chelon and the Klingon sat several meters apart, facing each other only indirectly. Both of them were middle-aged and not especially athletic, so the sport of choice atop their shared mesa had become volleying insults.

"I can smell that swill in your mug from here," Lugok said. "What did you say it was called?"

"*N'v'aa,*" Jetanien said. "It's a Rigelian fruit cocktail."

"Stinks like pest repellant."

"Regrettably, it is no such thing. If it were, it would have driven you back into your ship long ago."

The two diplomats went back to eating in black-mooded silence for a while. Jetanien finished his broth and opened a package of pickled *Keesa* beetles. He knew not to offer any to Lugok, who months earlier had made a tremendous fuss about the repugnance of consuming dead food.

As Jetanien savored the acidic tang of the preserved insect crunching between his mandibles, Lugok said apropos of nothing, "He's not coming, you know."

After swallowing his mouthful, Jetanien replied, "He might. Passage out of the Romulan Star Empire is anything but simple."

"Don't be ridiculous," Lugok said. "Three months late? Whoever heard of such a thing? Why are we even here?"

Spearing another beetle with his fork, Jetanien said, "I would not presume to speculate on your motives for remaining. Mine are my own." He paused before pushing the next forkful into his maw. "However, if you find yourself inclined to share something of substance to offset your months of inane bluster—"

"Forget I said it," Lugok cut in.

Dinner dragged on, mute and cheerless.

In truth, Jetanien had speculated at length as to why Lugok continued to bide his time on Nimbus III. For all the man's complaining, he had not once threatened to leave. His repeated demands for Senator D'tran's whereabouts, or his assertions the Romulan statesman would never arrive, did not seem to be sincere declarations of belief. Rather, they appeared to be invitations for Jetanien to reassure Lugok that their patience would be rewarded—if only they waited a while longer.

They concluded their evening meal as the sky turned dark. Jetanien passed the early night hours reading a classic work of Tellarite literature entitled *The Blood Country*. It was far more violent than he had expected, but the writing had been gravid with subtle metaphors and hidden meanings.

Jetanien knew it was time to go to bed each night when Lugok yelled across the gap between their ships, "Give me a good reason not to cut your throat tonight, Chelon."

Every night, Jetanien shouted back his reply, "Because I would slay you in kind, and then there would be no one to greet Senator D'tran when he arrives."

"Sleep well—if you dare," Lugok called out.

"Good night, Lugok."

Each night they turned off the exterior lights of their ships and retired behind unlocked doors to rest themselves for another day spent in idle anticipation.

That night would be different.

A great thunder of engines shocked Jetanien back to consciousness just before sunrise. He scrambled off his sleeping platform with all the haste his heavy, carapace-covered bulk could muster and lumbered outside into the chilly predawn air. Lugok was already out of his ship, staring straight up at the massive vessel descending toward them.

As it neared the mesa, the new ship shifted course and continued past them. A few kilometers from the mesa it hovered over a small hill. Broad doors on its underside opened outward with a great clamor and whine of machinery. Light flooded out of the belly of the long, podlike vessel.

Lugok and Jetanien wandered together toward the mesa's edge, both watching the metallic leviathan hovering nearby, waiting with hope and anxiety to see what would emerge through the enormous starship's ventral doors.

A flurry of loose matter fell from the ship. The dark cascade struck the small hill beneath the ship and spread over it like a fluid. For several seconds the torrent continued, a steady outpouring of solid debris.

As the purging ended, a cold breeze carried the odors of rotting garbage and chemical waste across the mesa.

The big ship closed its cargo bay doors, climbed into the sky, became a shining speck among the stars, and vanished into the night.

Jetanien and Lugok stared at the festering hill of garbage.

The portly Klingon laughed. His guffaws were loud, hoarse, and rich with bitterness. He continued his cynical cachinnation as he returned to his own ship and slammed the door behind him, leaving Jetanien alone at the mesa's edge.

Jetanien found this turn of events to be an apt metaphor for his career.

And on that note, he went back to bed.

PART THREE

One Little Victory

37

September 9, 2267

It was one of the most impressive bits of piloting Pennington had ever seen in person. As soon as T'Prynn guided the *Skylla* out of warp into a system of planets orbiting a yellow main sequence star, she slipped into a close-quarters dance with a large asteroid and set the small ship on its surface without so much as a bump.

"Anchor deployed," she said, turning toward the sensor suite. "I am tracking the *Zin'za*. Monitor the communications between it and the vessel in orbit of the third planet."

Pennington nodded. "Right."

He slipped a small transceiver into his ear and patched it in to the passive subspace antenna. At first the intercepted signal sounded like shrill noise and static. He routed it to T'Prynn's decryption module. Seconds later he was listening to dialogue between deep, gravelly Klingon voices. Engaging the universal translator circuits and the recording unit, he told T'Prynn, "Got something." He routed it to her transceiver before she asked, because he knew she would want to hear it.

Captured in mid-sentence, the first voice said, "*. . . continues on schedule. How soon can the artifact be delivered?*"

"*We will beam it down as soon as we reach orbit. Send final coordinates for transport.*"

"*Acknowledged,* Zin'za. *Transmitting coordinates now.*"

T'Prynn shot an inquiring look at Pennington. He glanced at the data screen, confirmed they were receiving the coordinates being sent to the *Zin'za,* and gave her a thumbs-up.

"They are moving into orbit," T'Prynn said. "Lock in their transport coordinates."

"Already done," Pennington replied. "Now what?"

"We wait," the Vulcan said.

"And after that?"

His question seemed to vex her. "The *Zin'za*'s mission seems to be limited to delivering an artifact to the planet. We will remain on this asteroid until the *Zin'za* completes its business. After it departs, we will wait for the other Klingon vessel to move to the far side of the planet from our position. Then we shall make a precision warp jump into orbit and try to reach the surface before they detect our presence."

"Is the artifact what they stole from Vanguard?"

She narrowed her eyes and stared into space. "Possibly. I recall no mention of an artifact in any of the recent news about the station, so if that was what Joshua Kane procured for the Klingons, it was very likely part of Vanguard's mission to explore the Shedai mystery."

That speculation made Pennington uneasy. "I don't care to think about Klingons playing with Shedai gadgets."

"I share your reservations. The Klingons have been single-minded in their efforts to harness the most destructive aspects of the Shedai's technology. If the artifact is part of that agenda, then it is imperative we relieve them of it."

Pennington concurred with an exaggerated nod. "Absolutely." Then he added, "And if the artifact has bugger all to do with the security breach on Vanguard or the Shedai?"

"That will depend on the *Zin'za*'s next heading," T'Prynn said. "If they set a course back into Klingon space, we will have no choice but to terminate our pursuit. This vessel lacks sufficient stealth technology to cross their border undetected, and it is neither fast enough to outrun a Klingon cruiser nor powerful enough to survive a fight with one."

"So you're saying if the *Zin'za* heads for home, we're going down to check out the artifact."

"Correct."

"And what about Commodore Reyes? Or have you forgotten he's on board the *Zin'za*?"

Before she could answer him, the guttural voices returned to the comm channel. *"Transport complete,"* said the Klingon aboard the Zin'za. *"Excavation team confirms receipt."*

"Acknowledged, Zin'za. *Well done.* Qapla'*!"*

The *Zin'za* officer echoed, *"Qapla'!"*

The channel went quiet, and T'Prynn noted movement on the sensor display. "The *Zin'za* is breaking orbit," she said.

T'Prynn watched to see where the Klingon battle cruiser would go; Pennington didn't know what to hope for.

On the one hand, after spending more than five months trapped in a dark, cold tin can with T'Prynn, he was ready to get out and stretch his legs on a real planet, with real air and real sunshine. On the other hand, a planet occupied by Klingon forces that might be meddling with Shedai artifacts—a practice whose lethal hazards he had witnessed firsthand—was hardly his idea of a vacation spot. The *Skylla* was dim and chilly and stank of antiseptic, but it also had proved to be safe.

"Heading confirmed," T'Prynn said. "The *Zin'za* is on a direct course back to Klingon space. They have just made the jump to warp speed."

In a voice consciously stripped of all enthusiasm, Pennington replied, "Hurray." Then he said a silent prayer for Diego Reyes, who now was being taken beyond their reach.

T'Prynn turned her attention back to the piloting controls. "Anchor retracted," she said, pushing buttons and flipping switches. "Engaging thrusters." The starfield outside the canopy seemed to waver and pitch gently as she guided the *Skylla* away from the asteroid. "Course laid in. As soon as the Klingon cruiser moves behind the planet, we'll make a warp jump into low orbit." She looked at Pennington and added with mild emphasis, "You should fasten your seat's safety restraints. We are likely to encounter intense turbulence."

"Bloody hell," Pennington said as he strapped himself in. "This is like flying with Quinn, except you talk more." The last buckle snapped shut around his waist. "Maybe we should think about this—"

"Engaging warp drive in three . . . two . . . one."

The stars stretched and fused into a blinding flash, which gave way to the surface of a Class-M planet. The *Skylla* shuddered and lurched as it slammed into the upper atmosphere, and T'Prynn fought to maintain control as she nose-dived toward the planet.

Pennington knew he shouldn't ask his next question, but he couldn't help himself. Over the roar of air ramming against the ship and the screaming whine of the engines, he shouted, "What if we don't reach the surface before the Klingons come back around in orbit?"

"They will destroy us with their disruptors," T'Prynn said, as if it were no big deal.

His fingers clenched the straps of his safety harness as he held on for dear life. "All right, then," he hollered back as he watched the ground rush up to meet them. "Carry on."

38

The Klingon convoy announced itself from a few kilometers away with a tower of golden dust that rose from the road behind it.

Quinn lay prone behind a jumbled mass of broken stone, watching through a crack in his rocky cover as the Klingons approached. His squad of Denn recruits crouched on either side of him, their hands closed like vices around the rifles he had given them. After weeks of sniping and hit-and-run attacks, this was going to be their first major assault on the enemy.

"Everyone stay calm and follow my lead," Quinn whispered to the men. "Stretch and his boys are waiting for us to make the first move, but don't worry—they'll be there."

Gesturing as he spoke, he addressed his troops one at a time. "Hopalong, remember to fire a few shots at a time, and check your targets. Don't waste your power cell if you can't hit anything. Slugger, stay behind cover; if you go chargin' into the open without me tellin' you to, I'll shoot you myself. Doc, you got the mortar, so land your shots right in the middle of their formation. Turtle and Spaz, just do what I do and shoot anybody who ain't one of ours. Everybody clear?"

Five upturned thumbs assured him they were ready.

He hunkered down and listened as the Klingons' treaded all-terrain vehicles turned a corner and advanced toward his position. They were right on schedule.

Every week since their arrival, the Klingons had sent their convoy to round up a new batch of laborers and transport them out to the excavated temple. Until the ATVs made their pickup, their only passengers were Klingon soldiers.

Reckon they don't figure it's worth wastin' shuttle fuel to move slaves, Quinn thought.

In the final moments of quiet, every detail seemed hyper-real to Quinn: the uncommon warmth of the early-morning sun, the stillness of the air, the sky's deep shade of blue, a bead of sweat tracing a circuitous route down the side of his face to fall from his jaw to the dusty ground.

Then the convoy rolled squarely into the kill zone, and Quinn's fist closed around the master detonator switch.

Improvised explosive devices on both sides of the street engulfed the four-vehicle convoy in surges of white fire. The ear-splitting thunderclaps of the blasts came a split-second later, followed by the rending of metal as the blast waves shredded the four armored ATVs.

When the initial rush of flames and pitch-black smoke mushroomed up and away, the two ATVs in the center of the convoy had been mangled and knocked onto their sides. Both were on fire. The lead and follow vehicles had been badly damaged: both had lost most of their treads, leaving them immobilized.

Quinn barked, "Doc, hit the lead truck! Squad—now!" He scrambled to one knee, aimed over his protective wall of concrete slabs, and opened fire on the convoy.

His men leaped into action beside him. Just as Quinn had taught him, Doc unleashed a mortar round on the first ATV in the convoy. The plasma charge hissed through the air and slammed through the armored vehicle as if it were made of paper. Half a second later, a detonation inside the ATV scattered its parts and passengers in multiple directions.

Hatches slid open on the two toppled ATVs, and Klingon troops began hurtling up and out, rolling to their feet ready to fight. The passengers in the last ATV also evacuated their vehicle and jumped to cover moments before Stretch's mortar man blew the armored ride to pieces.

The dozen or so Klingons in the street split into two squads and charged at their attackers—one at Stretch's squad, one at Quinn's.

None of the Denn hesitated to shoot. Within moments both groups of Klingons found themselves trapped in the same overlapping fields of fire. A few of them tried to shoot back before they were cut down, but their disruptor blasts caromed harmlessly off the steel and concrete debris that the Denn had chosen for their cover.

The last Klingon dropped to his knees with a smoldering hole in his tunic and metallic sash. He gasped "*PetaQpu'!*" before falling facedown in the dirt.

Quinn shouted, "Cease-fire!"

All at once, the street was silent again. Only the faintest hush of a breeze and the soft crackling of flames disturbed the blissful quiet.

"Check the bodies," Quinn said. "Move in pairs. One man covers, one man searches. If you find a Klingon alive, kill him. Take their weapons, spare power cells, communicators, and sensor devices. We have to be gone from here in two minutes. Move out!"

Across the street, Stretch and his squad fanned out in the same search pattern. Working quickly, they took everything of utility from the dead Klingons, then regrouped at the front of the massacred convoy.

"Good work," Quinn said. "First, turn off the communicators—they can be used to track us." He held up a Klingon communicator and demonstrated the process. When they finished, he continued. "I'll show you how to mask your life signs with their sensor devices later. Now double-quick-time back to base!"

He led them through the ruins, sticking to concealed paths and long stretches of old sewage tunnels that had been dry for ages. Less than an hour later they entered the underground hiding place of the *Rocinante,* where Bridy Mac and the other two squads of Denn guerrillas were waiting. The mood was sub-dued.

"How'd it go?" Bridy asked as Quinn and his men returned.

"We kicked some ass," Quinn said. Nodding at the enemy equipment his men were toting, he added, "Brought back a few prizes." Noting the glum faces that greeted his news, he asked, "Why do y'all look like you came from a funeral?"

Bridy motioned for him to follow her inside the *Rocinante*. "We have an unexpected visitor," she said. "She claims she fol-lowed one of our recon patrols, and I believe her. Which means your boys need to work on their stealth skills."

They stepped onto the main deck of the Mancharan starhop-per. Seated on Quinn's bunk was a Denn woman swathed in the bleached robes of a desert nomad. As soon as the woman saw Quinn and Bridy, she stood and said, "You are the aliens who teach the Shire men to fight the Klingon invaders?"

"Yeah, that's us," Quinn said. "Who are you?"

"I am Lirev, *shahzadi* of the *Goçeba*. My tribe has been en-slaved by the Klingons at the temple."

Quinn rolled his eyes. "Times are tough all over. I'd love to help you folks, really, but I just don't—"

"The Klingons brought something to the temple last night," Lirev cut in. "A gem the size of a skull."

Bridy and Quinn traded doubtful looks, then Quinn said to the female nomad, "They're decorating. So what?"

Lirev's eyes burned with equal measures of fear and fury. "It is not a decoration—it is a vessel of pure evil."

"What makes you so sure?" asked Bridy.

The nomad replied, "Because when the Klingons brought the stone inside the precursor temple, the world trembled in fear."

As he put the facts together, Quinn felt the color bleed from his face. One look at his partner confirmed Bridy had arrived at the same terrifying conclusion: the Klingons had acquired some-thing that enabled them to access the Shedai Conduit hidden in-side the desert temple—and if their past mishaps with Shedai technology were any indication, Golmira was now in imminent danger of being blown up.

Quinn faced Lirev. "If I agree to come check this out, can I trust you and your nomad pals to not try to kill me?"

"I give you my word," she said. "Truce and safe conduct."

"Okay," Quinn said, motioning for Lirev to lead the way. "Let's go have a look."

39

Trudging over one dune after another, Pennington kept his eyes on T'Prynn's back and wished he knew voodoo and had a pin and a doll fashioned in her likeness.

"This is brilliant," he muttered as they lumbered through the shifting sands. "More desert. Our three-day hike on Vulcan wasn't enough for you?"

She answered without looking back. "I did not choose the location to which the Klingons transported their artifact."

"No, of course not," Pennington said. "But you did choose to land the ship plenty far away from it, didn't you?"

T'Prynn reached the peak of the dune they had been climbing and stopped to wait for Pennington, who was lagging behind, a victim of fatigue and heat exhaustion. "It was necessary to set down at a safe distance from the Klingons' ground forces," she said. "Otherwise they would have heard and observed our descent, and we would now be in their custody."

He joined her at the crest of the dune and squinted into the glare of sun reflected off a vista of pale sand. "Maybe," he said. "But sometimes I get the feeling you just like walking in the desert." He met her placid stare. "For the record, I don't."

"I gathered that," she said.

They continued walking east. A gust of hot wind-blown sand scoured Pennington's face. He winced and wrapped a length of fabric from his desert robes around his face and neck, then pulled his goggles down from on top of his head and fixed them into place. "How much farther?" he asked.

Over the howling wind, T'Prynn said, "Approximately twenty-eight-point-four kilometers."

"And how far have we gone?"

"Since leaving the *Skylla,* we have traversed one-point-six kilometers of open desert."

Pennington let out a long, pained groan. "Oh, I hate you."

"If memory serves, you said quite clearly you were looking forward to spending some time outside the ship."

"That was when I thought *outside* would mean grass or trees or water, or something besides sand."

T'Prynn replied, "I see. Your dissatisfaction with our current circumstances stems from your failure to manage your expectations."

He waved his arms in wild exasperation. "Or maybe it stems from having to tromp across a bloody desert!" Pennington waited for T'Prynn's reply, but she said nothing and just kept on walking. Suspecting he was being manipulated, he asked her, "You're just goading me, aren't you?"

"Your reactions do provide a break from the monotony."

"In other words, I entertain you." He shook his head. "Is that all I am to you? A clown?"

"No," T'Prynn said. "You are also a drain on expendable resources and a significant tactical liability."

He fell into step beside her. "That's funny, but who knew Vulcan humor was so cruel?"

"You confuse wit with humor," she replied. "A common mistake among humans."

Scrambling to keep up with the long-legged Vulcan woman, Pennington concluded to his chagrin that he had no comeback that T'Prynn couldn't dismantle with ease. Instead he plodded along behind her, struggling to catch his breath with each step.

Several minutes later T'Prynn said, "If you begin to feel lightheaded, please try to make some sound before you lose consciousness, so I will know to stop and wait for you."

Even silence is no defense, he brooded. He let out a heavy sigh. "Yes, I can tell already," he said. "Your companionship will make this forced desert march just *fly* by."

"You are welcome to turn back and go wait in the ship."

He looked toward the fiery orb that was hammering his head with scorching heat, then glared at T'Prynn. "*Now* you tell me."

40

Quinn slithered on his belly up the slope of the dune. Poking his head over the top he caught sight of the precursor temple rising from the desert.

A Klingon garrison patrolled outside the ruins, cracking the proverbial whip on hundreds of enslaved Denn workers, who were helping the Klingons excavate the site. Men and machines worked side by side, carefully peeling away the artistically carved stone façade to reveal the obsidian, biomechanoid structure entombed within. For the most part the Klingons had focused on exposing the front entrance of the Shedai Conduit; most of the temple's multilevel roof, with its slopes, platforms, and turrets, remained in place though not wholly intact.

That's at least a full company of troops, Quinn observed. Noting a row of prefabricated structures erected alongside the temple, he retrieved a pair of holographically enhanced binoculars from a pocket of his desert robe and surveyed the Klingons' camp compound.

Mess hall, he figured. *Barracks. Latrine. The one with the climate module is probably the CO's office.* Then he spied the only structure that was under guard. *Bingo,* he thought with a smile. *Ammo dump and weapons cache.*

He adjusted the settings on the binoculars and pointed them at the temple's entrance. Filtering out the glare of daylight, he zoomed in on the interior of the ruins, where a Klingon scientist surrounded by high-tech gizmos was conferring with a trio of Klingon officers. True to their reputations, the three soldiers were shouting at the gray-bearded Klingon civilian, who seemed to be making protests the troops didn't want to hear.

In short order the matter seemed to have been decided. The scientist unlocked a protective case and opened its lid. Then he reached inside the container and lifted out a peculiar object.

It was a twelve-sided crystal polyhedron; each of its pentagonal faces had five edges of equal length. The crystal's core pulsed with an intense violet glow. As the scientist lifted it free of its case, the three military men stepped back fearfully.

"Well, I'll be damned," Quinn muttered to himself. "The little one-eyed kook wasn't kiddin'."

The scientist carried the dodecahedron to a pedestal in front of what looked like an altar at the center of the double-arched platform. As the crystal was lowered into a pentagonal indentation on the pedestal, the glossy black surfaces of the Conduit rippled with indigo light, and a deep rumble shook the earth beneath Quinn.

Goddamn, he wondered, *what the hell is that thing?*

Just when Quinn figured his day couldn't get any worse, his gloomy train of thought was derailed by a smug voice that he had hoped never to hear again for as long as he lived.

From behind him, Zett Nilric said, "Hello, Quinn."

Quinn lowered his binoculars and twisted slowly to look down the dune at Zett, who stood holding his disruptor level and ready. The jet-skinned Nalori bastard flashed a grin of coal-black teeth, and even though he was standing in a desert, he was dressed to the nines in a spotless white suit, pale gray shirt, off-white tie, and shoes made from the hide of some ivory-colored reptile.

"Lookin' good, Zett," Quinn said.

Zett shrugged at the compliment. "I do my best." Lowering his chin at Quinn, he added, "Long time no see."

"Not long enough."

"Imagine finding you of all people *here,*" Zett said. "I have to confess, I'm curious what you've been up to all this time. Last I heard, someone mysteriously settled all your debts with Ganz. And just like that"—he pantomimed huffing a feather from his fingertips—"you vanished. Quite a trick."

"Yeah, it's a beauty," Quinn said. "You should try it."

"Oh, I will, soon enough." He widened his grin. "So tell me: What are you doing here, Quinn?"

"Same as always," Quinn lied. "Lookin' out for number one." Nodding over his shoulder toward the temple, he asked, "What about you? Working for the Klingons now?"

"Yes and no," Zett said. "I take their money for the occasional odd job, but that's hardly the same thing as being on their side." A twitch of his thumb changed his disruptor's power setting to maximum. "Of course, I didn't go to the trouble of safeguarding a major heist on Vanguard just to see you screw up the deal by sticking in your nose on this backwater rock." He raised his weapon to eye level. "And killing you won't be business—not like bombing that transport on Vanguard or setting up the hit on Reyes. No, eliminating you will be *my pleasure*."

Quinn was relieved to know this was about nothing more than Zett's psychotic old vendetta. *At least I know my cover's not blown,* Quinn told himself as he got to his feet. *That means Bridy might still be safe.* Standing up halfway down the dune, he said to Zett, "Okay, get it over with."

"I'll shoot you if I have to," Zett said. "But I'd prefer to take my vengeance one cut at a time. And because I'm such a good sport when it comes to murder, I'll even give you a chance to defend yourself." Gesturing with his disruptor, he added, "Drop your sidearm and grab a knife."

It took all of Quinn's self-control not to smile as he unfastened his belt. As he let it and his holster slide to the ground, he recalled the words of Napoleon Bonaparte: "Never interrupt your enemy when he is making a mistake."

He drew his hunting knife from his boot sheath, tucked its flat edge against his forearm, and held it edge-out and ready to draw blood.

Zett holstered his disruptor, drew his curved *yosa* blade, and prowled up the slope toward Quinn. "I'm going to enjoy this," he said with a sneer.

"Not as much as I am," Quinn replied.

The assassin was still a few meters from Quinn when the

smooth slope of the dune behind him heaved upward. As Zett spun toward the hush of spilling sand, more shapes rose from the ground on his flanks. In less than a second he was surrounded by Lirev and four of her nomad clansmen. Each pointed a wide-bladed sword at Zett, whose expression of horror was even more satisfying to Quinn than he'd hoped.

"Meet my insurance policy," Quinn said.

The nomads lunged to attack.

Zett pressed a button on a bracelet around his wrist and vanished in a crimson swirl of energy. Lirev and her people slashed at the transporter beam's afterglow until it faded away.

Rubindium transponder, Quinn realized. *Linked to an automatic transporter recall.* He recognized the setup from one of his first meetings with Starfleet Intelligence. They had been very excited to entrust him with one until he had pointed out the *Rocinante* had no transporter.

Lirev sheathed her sword and approached Quinn, followed by her clansmen. "Did you see the gemstone?"

"Yeah," Quinn said. "I did. It's just like you said. Now I gotta get back to my partner so we can plan our next move."

The nomads murmured among themselves, and then Lirev asked Quinn, "Does this mean you will help us liberate the temple from the invaders?"

"We will, if you'll vow to stop attackin' the Shire people and help us fight the Klingons."

A buzz of protests began to rise from the other nomads until Lirev turned and silenced them with a frown. Then she turned back toward Quinn and said simply, "Agreed. On behalf of the *Goçeba,* you have my word. Peace with the Shires, and alliance against our shared foe."

"All right, then," Quinn said, moving at a quick step back toward their *melluls.* "We've got work to do. Let's ride."

41

The playback from Quinn's holographic binoculars was projected a meter above the deck in the main compartment of the *Rocinante*. McLellan ate her dinner from a scratched metal plate and watched as Quinn enhanced the image to clarify the details he had recorded of the temple's interior.

"I reckon we're talkin' about a hundred and twenty, maybe a hundred and thirty troops," Quinn said as he finished fiddling with the projector's controls. "Looks like they're usin' a virtual perimeter to keep the workers from runnin' off. Nothin' we can't bypass to get in." Pointing at the scientists in the recording, he added, "Only a few of these labcoat guys. Don't think they'll be a problem."

McLellan swallowed a bite of her vegetable wrap—the least disgusting option from their remaining rations—and said, "I think the real problem is your old pal, Zett. Are you sure he said the object in the temple had been stolen from Vanguard?"

"Not in so many words, but that was the gist," Quinn said. "Look, don't worry about Zett. He seems to think I'm here workin' an angle, which means our cover's safe."

"I'm not worried about our cover," McLellan said. "I'm worried about you getting killed by an assassin with a grudge."

Quinn shook his head. "Ain't gonna happen. He got the drop on me once. Now that I know he's here, I'll be ready next time." He motioned toward the holographic projection. "Let's focus on this. We've got less than forty-eight hours before your Starfleet buddies get here. If we want off this rock, we need to do everything we can to put the lobster-heads in a twist."

McLellan shoved the last bite of her wrap into her mouth and studied the projection while she chewed. "Okay," she said at last. "Whatever that glowing thingamajig is, if the Klingons took it from Vanguard, we need to find a way to take it back."

"Hang on," Quinn said. "Smackin' a bees' nest is one thing. Stickin' your hand in to steal the honey is another."

Lifting her hands in mock surrender, McLellan said, "If you want to play it safe, let's talk about lying low till our backup gets here. But if you want to make a difference, we need to find a way to get that gemstone. Because if the Klingons bug out and take it with them, we might never get another shot at it."

He unleashed a disgusted sigh. "Goddammit," he muttered. "Fine. Last I saw, they had it patched into the Conduit through some kind of pedestal. If it's still there in the open, we might be able to draw their forces away with a hit-and-run attack and then slip inside to make the grab."

Backing up the holographic playback, McLellan pointed out the image of the scientists taking the object from a shielded case. "What if they store it in there between experiments?"

Cocking his head and frowning, Quinn said, "Pickin' the lock'll take too long. We'd have to grab the whole case and make a run for it."

"But then the grab's not a one-person job anymore," she said. "And sneaking two people inside increases the risk."

He shrugged and flashed a grin. "You knew the job was dangerous when you took it."

She shook her head. "We need more intel. I have to know whether they leave the stone in place or pack it up."

"So we're talkin' about another recon op," Quinn said. "Gettin' that close to the temple won't be easy unless we ask Lirev's people for help. And this time we'll need to keep a better eye out for Zett."

"Y'know, I lied before," McLellan said. "I am worried about him talking to the Klingons. Whether he knows we're with SI or not, if he gives them a heads-up we're out here, it could mean big trouble."

Quinn nodded. "True, but I don't think that's his game. He's waited a really long time to cap me himself. If he goes and gets the lobster-heads involved, they might get all gung-ho and kill me before he gets a chance to gloat."

"Yes, that would be a shame," McLellan deadpanned.

"Just callin' it like I see it," Quinn said. "Still, no point gettin' sloppy this close to the finish line. We should assume he's workin' with 'em, and that they know I'm here."

McLellan nodded. "Sensible. So how do we play it?"

"The only way I know how," Quinn said. "Head-on."

42

September 10, 2267

Night had fallen, and Pennington and T'Prynn were still walking.

Two moons had risen as the sky dimmed. One had climbed above the horizon shortly after dusk; the second rose as the first stars appeared, and it pursued its sibling in slow degrees across the dome of the sky.

Progress across the desert had been slower than Pennington had expected. On Vulcan the paths had been mostly across the flats, or through rocky passes in the L-langon mountain range. Here he and T'Prynn struggled to find solid footing; each step in the loose sand was followed by random sinking and sliding.

Since leaving the ship, T'Prynn hadn't stopped once—not for food or rest—and Pennington hadn't been able to muster the courage to ask her for a break. Nothing on the horizon ahead of them promised any respite.

As they descended another balance-challenging slope, T'Prynn broke the silence with a softly spoken question.

"Why were you unfaithful to your wife?"

Delivered without provocation or preamble, the question caught Pennington by surprise. For a moment he thought about deflecting her inquiry with a glib remark, but he felt the tug of his conscience and knew he was overdue for a frank personal accounting.

"I wish I could say I had a good reason," he said. "The truth is, it was just the latest in a long series of mistakes I made with Lora, starting with getting married." T'Prynn slowed her pace and sidestepped to allow him to walk beside her as he continued. "I probably never should have married her in the first place. When I started dating her, I stole her from some other bloke, just to see if I could. But as soon as I had her I started sabotaging the relationship. Making passes at her friends. Flirting with girls I'd meet while traveling for work. A couple of those turned into flings."

Casting back through the muddy currents of his memory, he struggled to make sense of his own actions. "On one level, I think I wanted to get caught, to be let off the hook. But I knew how much Lora loved me, how much she trusted me. I told myself I had to hide what I was to keep from hurting her, but the truth is I knew I'd never find anyone else who'd love me the way she did, and I was afraid of losing her."

T'Prynn asked in a nonjudgmental way, "Did you do this because you feared being alone?"

"I don't think so," Pennington said. "I was selfish more than anything else. I wanted the comfort and security of a committed relationship with the excitement of fresh conquests and new romances. Even when I was asking Lora to marry me, part of me was screaming, *Don't do it!* I knew I was getting married for the wrong reasons, but the only other option was to give her up, and I wasn't strong enough to do that."

A cool night breeze tousled his fair hair and pulled a few strands of T'Prynn's raven tresses free of her long ponytail. The desert was eerily quiet except for the hush of the wind.

"Did you ever love your wife?"

The question drew a bittersweet smile from Pennington. "Yes, I did. For a time, at the beginning. Just like I loved all the women I've been with: for a time." The smile left him. "I've always been this way. There's something broken in me. I only ever want what's denied me; if I manage to possess it, I don't want it anymore. I get bored." He felt T'Prynn looking at him, and he turned his head to meet her gaze. "Some part of my psyche confuses love with sexual conquest. I can only stay interested as long as it's a chase."

They crested another dune and began the next careful descent.

T'Prynn asked, "Does this self-knowledge help you control your behavior?"

"I thought it would," Pennington said. "But it doesn't. I just make the same mistakes, over and over. Sometimes I think I'll never really connect with anyone, not like others do. Or if I do, I won't be worthy of it." Throwing another sheepish look at T'Prynn, he added, "I'm a lonely wanker, but when I think of all the stupid things I've done, I guess maybe I deserve to be."

A long silence fell between them. Two moons continued their slow transit of the sky. The wind whispered over the dunes.

Pennington confirmed with a sidelong glance that T'Prynn remained at his side. A question nagged at him, and he had to give it voice.

"Why did you set me up with that fake story about the *Bombay*? Did you know it'd ruin me as a journalist?"

She bowed her head. "I was aware of the potential negative consequences," she said. "At the time I believed such harm was necessary. Because you had a reputation for competence and fairness, being able to discredit a story written by you would discourage other, lesser reporters from pursuing the matter."

"And you think that made it right? Wasn't there some other way you could have persuaded the Council not to go to war?"

She inhaled deeply and looked toward the horizon. "Yes." After glancing in his direction, she added, "I took the easy way out by using you to expedite my task. The Federation Council needed to cast doubt on what was an otherwise incontrovertible fact: that the Tholians ambushed and destroyed a Starfleet vessel without provocation or just cause. It might have been possible to devise other explanations, but they all would have required more time than we had, and they would have entailed a greater number of variables subject to falsification, thereby increasing the risk that our deception would be exposed."

Holding the reins on his anger, Pennington said, "I see."

"I am not telling you this to excuse what I have done," T'Prynn said. "After telling so many falsehoods, however, I feel I owe you the most truthful account of my actions." She bowed her head again. "With a combination of threats and violence, I coerced your friend Cervantes Quinn into planting the false evidence about the *Bombay* that I had prepared for you. And those offenses are in fact the least of my sins."

Halfway up the side of a sand mountain, she stopped, and Pennington halted beside her. She turned to face him. "I have extorted and blackmailed others into my service," she said. "I have inflicted serious harm on unarmed persons. I have condoned acts of sabotage and assault against our enemies that, if they had been exposed, could have led to war. And I have killed."

She looked away as she continued her confession. "For decades I was imbalanced by Sten's *katra*. My logic was impaired, and too many times I let fear or anger guide my actions. When others tried to help me, I obstructed their efforts. That is why I tampered with my Starfleet medical records, to hide my mental illness."

T'Prynn met Pennington's gaze with a cool, unblinking stare. "The tragic irony of my situation is that I face court-martial charges not for my most heinous violations of personal liberty, privacy, or sovereignty; not for my acts of violence or for the life I took; but for the comparatively minor and self-serving crimes of altering my medical file and going AWOL. My greatest transgressions have been all but sanctioned by Starfleet Command."

"So what does all that have to do with us walking through a desert in the middle of the night?"

She resumed climbing the slope with Pennington by her side as she replied, "If our mission here is a success, it might be enough to expiate my recent, minor offenses and redeem my career as a Starfleet officer. But to atone for my true crimes . . ." She frowned and added, "That will be the work of a lifetime."

Pondering his own shameful history, Pennington replied, "Yeah . . . I know what you mean."

43

Quinn fought the urge to look up. With the help of Lirev and her band of free nomads, he had disguised himself as one of the enslaved Denn workers and infiltrated the excavation site at the temple ruins in the desert.

The midday sun felt to Quinn as if it had been focused through a giant magnifying glass and aimed straight at his head, which was hidden by a deep-hooded cowl. He carried a full backpack on his shoulder and kept his eyes on his feet and those of the worker in front of him as they marched inside the temple as a single file of laborers. As he'd expected, the Klingon sentries paid no mind to the slaves trudging past them.

A few meters beyond the main entrance, Quinn spied an open doorway to a dimly lit staircase. He slipped out of line and stole up the narrow flight of steps. Though he took care to tread softly, his feet scraped on the stairs' covering of fine desert sand, and the dry sound echoed off the rough stone walls.

He slowed as he neared the top of the flight and peeked out the next doorway, which opened onto a narrow balcony level overlooking the main chamber of the temple.

Moving in a low crouch, he inched up to the low wall that ringed the balcony level and peeked over it.

Most of the temple's floor and decorative elements had been smashed apart and carted away to reveal the eerily smooth and reflective obsidian surfaces of the Shedai Conduit over which the temple had been built. Only a dozen thick sandstone columns had been left untouched. Looking up, Quinn saw why: the ornately carved octagonal columns were the sole support for the temple's upper levels and its roof.

Perfect targets, he thought with a diabolical smile.

He scuttled to the nearest column. After casting wary glances around the balcony, he opened his bag and removed the first of several compact demolition charges designed for shattering load-bearing supports. He tucked it in the corner where the column met the balcony's low wall.

One down, eleven to go, he mused as he doubled over and jogged to the next column. Though he might never set off these charges, in his experience it never hurt to have options when seeking an exit strategy.

In about ten minutes he had mined nine of the columns and was on the opposite side of the balcony. Below him, workers had been delivering equipment the Klingon scientists had been setting up. On their way out, the Denn slaves pushed carts laden with sand and chunks of broken stone.

As Quinn set the tenth of his charges into place, there came a commotion from the main level. He ducked behind the column and peeked through an opening in the balcony wall. Beneath him, the scientists stood at a portable console while a squad of soldiers ushered out all the workers. There was a great deal of shouting, followed by the familiar slap of a rifle stock being slammed across the back of someone's head. When the last of the soldiers left the chamber, the scientists all faced the glowing artifact, which once more had been placed upon the small pedestal in front of the console.

Quinn snuck to the eleventh column and set his next-to-last charge. Then he heard the terrified shriek of a female voice, and he glanced back through a fissure in the balcony wall to see what was happening underneath him.

A pair of Klingon soldiers dragged in what looked like an adolescent female Denn. Judging from her clothes, Quinn suspected she wasn't one of the nomads but a youth taken from one of the surrounding Shire settlements. She thrashed wildly in the Klingons' grip but couldn't break free. The two hulking brutes slammed her backward onto an obsidian slab beside the glowing artifact and locked her to it while the scientists began entering commands on their jury-rigged interface.

A blood-chilling groan reverberated through the obsidian structure and shook a rain of dust from the ceiling high overhead. A black wall to the left of the scientists began to pulse with deep violet light, revealing symbols in a script that Quinn had never seen before. He reached under his robe, pulled out his borrowed Starfleet tricorder, and began gathering sensor data.

Then he stared in horror as tendrils that looked like living smoke rose from the gleaming black floor around the pedestal and snaked toward the girl on the slab. Her hands were manacled together through a gap in the slab's base, leaving her unable to even turn away from her fate. All she could do was shut her eyes and scream.

Quinn wished he could do the same, but terror compelled him to watch.

The scientists observed the illuminated glyphs on the wall while they made adjustments on their console. They seemed to be working from a checklist. One of them would enter a command, and another would confirm which symbol responded with a momentary increase in brightness.

As they worked, the entity smothering the girl became pale and spectral. Its shape was monstrous: as large as a rhinoceros, it was part lizard and part bug; sinewy limbs ended in clawed extremities; its maw gaped open to reveal swordlike fangs; a stinger-tipped tail whipped hypnotically behind it.

Some kind of organ shot from the ghostly creature's mouth and vanished into the girl's chest. Her screaming ceased. She convulsed, and her eyes snapped open. Then she shriveled like a deflating balloon. Fissures formed in her desiccating skin as her dulled eyes sank into their sockets. Within moments all the color of her body faded to white.

A stentorian roar shook the temple. Quinn and the Klingons below him covered their ears. The force of the cacophony pummeled the husk of the girl's body into dust and bones. Then the clamor ended, leaving only its sonorous echoes to chase one another through the ruins' empty spaces.

On every obsidian wall, glyphs blazed with crimson light—as

did the twelve-sided artifact on the pedestal, from which Quinn felt a sickening aura of fear. He had no idea what that bizarre gem was, but one look at the girl's blanched skeleton was enough to convince him the artifact was too dangerous to leave in the hands of the Klingons—whose scientists were hard at work documenting every sensor reading from their callous living sacrifice.

Quinn switched off and put away his tricorder, planted his final explosive charge, fixed his cowl to cover his face, and stole away down the steps. He resolved to act quickly; there was no time to wait for Starfleet to step in.

Whatever it takes, he vowed, *this ends tonight.*

44

T'Prynn lay prone on hot sand beside Tim Pennington, observing the activity inside the Shedai Conduit, which was partially cloaked by the desert-worn stone edifice of a decaying ruin. The human journalist gazed through a pair of compact holographic binoculars, while T'Prynn looked through a slender field scope borrowed from a rifle in the *Skylla*'s weapons locker.

They were witnessing a gruesome spectacle.

Something either released or produced by a glowing object on a pedestal at the center of the Conduit consumed what T'Prynn presumed to be an adolescent native female. The process appeared to have been initiated and monitored by a team of Klingon scientists inside the temple. When the flurry of light ended, a thunderous booming resonated from within the ruins.

More troubling to T'Prynn was the psychic disturbance that followed it. A concentrated wave of projected fear emanated from the obsidian apparatus, and it seemed to produce anxiety in the Klingons, their native workers, and even in Pennington, who flinched, lowered his binoculars, and ducked behind the dune.

Marshalling her psionic defenses, T'Prynn suppressed her own natural flight reaction and continued her observation.

"Jesus," whispered Pennington. "Did you see that?"

"Yes," T'Prynn said.

He palmed sweat from his face and took a few deep breaths. "What the hell happened in there? What'd they do to that girl?"

"She appears to have been sacrificed to trigger some hidden function of the Shedai Conduit."

Tucking his binoculars back into a belt pouch under his robe, Pennington asked, "Sacrificed to what?"

"I am not certain," T'Prynn admitted. "However, given the circumstances, it is highly likely a Shedai entity of some kind is involved." She peered through her targeting scope again and watched the scientists gather warily around the radiant polyhedron mounted on a pedestal. "The new element in this situation appears to be that luminescent object. I am unaware of anything like it previously being associated with the Shedai."

Pennington nodded. "So you think that's what Kane stole from Vanguard for the Klingons?"

"That is my current working hypothesis," T'Prynn said. "If it is important enough to be of interest to Klingon Imperial Intelligence, then it very likely is of equal or greater interest to the Federation."

"Right," Pennington said. "Now that we've got that sorted, all we need to do is get back to the *Skylla* without getting noticed by the Klingons, and we can signal Starfleet."

He seemed relieved as he began backing down the dune.

"No," T'Prynn said.

Pennington stopped and wore a stunned expression. "Beg your pardon?"

"Whatever that object on the pedestal is," T'Prynn said, "it enables the Klingons to access previously unknown functions of the Conduits. It might also have applications for other aspects of Shedai technology. We must not leave such a dangerous item in Klingon control for any length of time."

Holding up his hands, Pennington replied, "Hang on, love. You said this was just a recon mission."

"I said we would not take direct action unless it was absolutely necessary. In this case, I believe it is."

Under his breath he said, "I bloody knew it."

She continued, "We must acquire that crystal and bring it back to Starfleet."

He shook his head. "There's two of us and a hundred of

them. How are we supposed to take it without getting shot?"

She arched one eyebrow. "Very carefully."

"I meant, what's our plan?"

She avoided Pennington's gaze and looked through her scope at the Klingons' compound. "Most of the details are still taking shape," she said. "But one seems to have been chosen for us. We must wait until dark. But when night falls . . . we strike."

45

Quinn's *mellul* hadn't slowed from a full gallop since he had taken off its blinders back in the desert. He had been forced to clutch the vulture-faced steed's mane and coil the reins around his forearms to keep himself steady while the creature raced back toward Leuck Shire.

That thing back in the temple must've spooked him as bad as it wigged me, Quinn figured.

Thanks to the creature's unflagging speed, it was barely dusk by the time Quinn reined it back to a trot on the outskirts of Tegoresko. The Klingons still had the center of the village under surveillance, which meant Quinn had to take a roundabout path back to the *Rocinante*.

Now that his *mellul* had slowed its pace, and the air was no longer breezing past him, he caught a whiff of the musky odor produced by the animal's exertion. "I was wonderin' what that stink was," he said to the beast while tousling its mane. "Have to hose you down when we get back to the ship."

He tugged the reins to guide the animal around a turn that would lead to a pass sheltered by the piled wreckage of several fallen buildings. Two sets of hands reached out from either side and grabbed his *mellul*'s bridle, halting the creature.

Quinn's hand was already pulling his stun pistol from its holster when he recognized the two Denn women who had stopped his mount. "Naya, Lirev," he said. "What're you doing here?"

Naya replied in an agitated whisper, "He took her, Mister Quinn! He came with the Klingons and took her away!"

Dismounting in a hurry, Quinn looked at Lirev, who seemed a bit calmer. "Took who?"

"Your friend. The one you call Bridy Mac."

The news filled Quinn with a nauseating feeling of dread. "The Klingons have Bridy?"

"No," said Naya, shaking her head frantically. "They helped him, but *he* took her."

Fearing he already knew the answer, Quinn asked, "What do you mean *he*? Who took Bridy?"

Naya looked at Lirev, who answered, "The one you faced on the dunes. The man with midnight skin."

Zett. You sonofabitch.

Again suspecting he knew what bad news was coming, he asked the women, "Do you know where he took her?"

"Back to the desert, with the Klingons," Naya said.

Quinn expected to be so angry he couldn't think straight. Instead, he felt a deathly calm take hold, and he knew exactly what needed to be done.

"Lirev, are your people at the temple good to go?"

"Yes," she said. "They have met up with your fighters and are ready." She lifted one of the Klingon communicators Quinn's men had captured during their recent ambush of the convoy. "When you say it is time, I will use this speaking box to tell our people to attack."

He nodded. "Okay, solid." Turning toward Naya, he said, "Get the landgraves and other females to shelter." To Lirev he added, "Tell the men to wait for my signal to attack."

"What will be the signal?" asked Lirev.

"Trust me," Quinn said. "They'll know it when they see it." He handed Naya the reins of his *mellul* and continued his journey back to the *Rocinante* on foot.

Naya called after him, "Mister Quinn, wait! The man with midnight skin found your ship. He led the Klingons to it."

This just keeps getting better and better. "And . . . ?"

"They left four soldiers there to ambush you," Naya said.

Quinn couldn't help himself. He smiled. "Well, then," he said, "I'd hate to keep 'em waiting."

"Delivered as promised," Zett said as he handed the human woman over to Commander Marqlar, the officer in charge of the Klingon garrison at the desert temple.

Marqlar cupped the woman's face in one large, callused hand. "Skinny and fragile-looking," he said. "And not as young as you'd promised." He looked at one of the scientists standing nearby for confirmation. "Will she suffice?" The scientist nodded, and that seemed to satisfy Marqlar. "Very well. She'll do." He snapped his fingers, and a pair of Klingon warriors dragged her away toward the obsidian altar.

"Can I trust you'll abide by our agreement?" Zett asked.

The barrel-chested officer scowled at Zett. "For now," he said, nearly bowling Zett over with the stench of blood and booze on his breath. "I still want to know what a pair of humans are doing this far from their Federation allies."

"Knowing Quinn, they were looking to cheat someone who's never dealt with their kind before," Zett said.

The commander furrowed his thick eyebrows as he eyed the woman. Like the rest of his garrison, Marqlar looked sand-blasted by his tenure in the desert; tiny granules clung to the coarse hairs of his goatee and seemed to have scoured patches of color from his uniform. Despite his swarthy complexion, his face and hands looked sunburned. He frowned. "Might they be spies?"

"I doubt it," Zett replied as he watched the soldiers force the woman to lie on top of the glossy black slab. "Quinn's never been much of a joiner."

As the woman's wrists were locked together through a gap in the altar's base, Marqlar said, "We'll know for sure once my men capture him and make him unlock his ship's secured systems." He threw a glare at Zett. "Some of the hardware they saw on board was new and highly advanced."

From the altar, the woman called out, "It's also all stolen." She waited for Zett and Marqlar to give her their full attention, and added, "Quinn and I swiped some of it from Vanguard and stripped the rest from a ship docked at Station K-7 about six months ago."

Her declaration made Marqlar smile. "And why are you telling us this?"

"Because there's more hidden on our ship than gadgets," she replied. "Dilithium crystals, tannot ore, laundered credit chips, you name it. Let me go and I'll make you rich men."

Zett held his arms wide and grinned. "I'm *already* a rich man."

"I'm not," Marqlar said. He walked over to stand beside the restrained woman. "But then, not everyone longs for money. And I think you've failed to understand why we've brought you here."

She narrowed her eyes. "Explain it to me."

Marqlar kneeled beside her and dropped his voice to a menacing hush. "Whatever lives inside that artifact at your feet, it responds to blood sacrifice. The more we give it, the more control it grants us over this apparatus."

He caressed her face with his dry, leathery fingertips. "Our first offering was one of the slaves' children. It was a very successful effort, and my research team assures me only one more sacrifice should be necessary for us to take full control of this machine and unlock its secrets."

The Klingon stood and gestured toward the temple's entrance. "Unfortunately, it spooked our workforce. They fled in such terror that it took my men most of the day to round them up." He looked down at the woman. "The last thing I need right now is a slave revolt—not because I couldn't suppress it, but because I can't afford to waste a valuable, finite resource."

Zett stepped beside the woman as he explained, "That's where you come in. You'll make a perfect sacrifice to the Klingons' new toy—just as soon as you've helped me lure Cervantes Quinn to his death."

"You're wasting your time," she said, then shook her head. "Quinn's a selfish coward. He won't come for me."

Zett took a thin synthetic whetstone from a pocket of his white suit jacket and began sharpening his *yosa* blade. The soft scrape of steel against stone drew an icy stare from the woman. He smirked at her.

"You don't know Quinn very well, do you?"

46

Lieutenant Gortog crouched beside the mouth of the tunnel, lying in ambush for the human pilot named Quinn.

The Nalori assassin Zett Nilric—who had helped Gortog's crewmates from the *I.K.S. Rojaq* capture the human woman who had been tending Quinn's vessel until his return—had assured Gortog the tunnel was the only means of access to the insurgents' lair, which was concealed inside a gutted building.

Unwilling to take the killer at his word, Gortog had ordered two of his men to patrol the catwalks that hugged the walls above the battered ship. He also had posted a fourth soldier inside the humans' starship in case Quinn tried to remotely activate its systems and use them against Gortog and his troops. As an added precaution, they'd planted a booby-trap in the ship's impulse drive and concealed a homing beacon behind a bulkhead in its cargo bay.

All that remained was for the human pilot to arrive.

The orders from Commander Marqlar had been clear: Capture the man alive and make him unlock the secured systems on his ship. Fortunately, *alive* did not necessarily mean *unharmed*. Gortog sincerely hoped the human put up a fight.

Breathe slowly, he reminded himself. *Be absolutely still as you await your prey.* He adjusted his grip on his *d'k tahg*. The flat side of the ceremonial dagger's blade was cool against his bare forearm. Though the night air outside the hollow building had begun to cool at sunset, the brick and mortar shell around the humans' ship radiated the heat it had absorbed all day long.

Gortog sniffed and caught the faintest hint of the male human's scent. He was close, but there still was no sound or sign of movement in the tunnel.

Looking up to signal his sentries for reports, he saw no one on the catwalks. And he caught a new scent in the air: fresh blood. *Klingon* blood.

He activated his wrist communicator, lifted it close to his face, and said in a low voice, "Huruq, Kmchok, this is Gortog. Report." Seconds passed without any reply from the men who were supposed to be guarding the roof and walls. Gortog felt his pulse quicken. *Perhaps this human is a worthy foe, after all.*

His eyes darted from one shadow to another, seeking any clue as to the human's position. With his comm unit all but pressed to his lips, he said, "Gortog to Marax. Respond."

There was no answer from the soldier inside the ship.

Gortog turned off his communicator and skulked away from the tunnel entrance. Somehow the human had found another way in.

Moving beside the wall, Gortog circled the ship. There were no lights on inside its cockpit or main compartment. None of its systems had been powered up.

As he neared the aft end of the vessel, he saw Marax's body lying on the boarding ramp.

Then he stepped in a pool of viscous liquid. A heavy drop of something warm splattered onto his shoulder, and he looked up.

Kmchok's lifeless eyes looked down at him through a gap in the catwalk's crooked planks. His throat had been cut.

Tightening his grip on his *d'k tahg*, Gortog trusted his instincts and prowled toward the ship. Regaining control of the vessel was certain to be the human's objective, so if he wasn't already there, he soon would be.

From the far side of the building's ground level came the faint sound of a pebble bouncing across a rocky dirt floor.

Gortog crouched and advanced with silent steps beneath the parked ship. Sheltered in the near-perfect darkness under the vessel, he strained to pierce the shadows beyond the ship. There was no sign of movement. He stalked forward and slipped between the ship's rear landing struts to prevent his enemy from seeing his silhouette in motion.

Searing pain slashed through the tendon behind Gortog's left ankle. Another brutal cut severed the ligaments behind his right knee. His legs buckled as the tip of a blade stabbed into his lower back. He spun as he fell, trying to strike back, but all he could do was flail as he lost his balance and collapsed.

His *d'k tahg* was blocked by another, and a glint of dim light flashed across the temper line of a human-made knife as it cut Gortog's right wrist. Then the knife snapped back and plunged into Gortog's throat. It ripped free, trailing flesh and dripping blood as he landed on his back, unable to move or breathe.

The human male kicked the *d'k tahg* from Gortog's hand. He stood over the fallen Klingon and watched him suffer his death throes. *Maybe the human will end my misery with a mercy stroke,* Gortog hoped.

His enemy turned, walked away, and left him to die.

Quinn stood under his ship and disabled the booby trap the Klingons had clumsily installed in the *Rocinante*'s impulse drive coil. *They're nothing if not predictable,* he mused.

He tossed aside the inert explosive device. It landed on the dirt floor beside the homing beacon he had found behind a bulkhead in the ship's cargo bay.

He shook his head. *Amateurs.*

Walking back up the ramp into the main compartment, he was relieved to get away from the stench of blood that permeated the air outside. In the muggy heat of the late-summer evening, the four dead Klingons—who had not smelled particularly pleasant while alive—had quickly become putrid.

With the push of a button, he closed the ramp behind him. He hurried forward to the cockpit, powered up the ship, and confirmed all systems were operational.

First things first, he reminded himself.

He took the tricorder from his belt and followed the steps Bridy had taught him for uploading its memory core to the ship's computer. When a soft double-beep from the console confirmed that the transfer was done, he began an encrypted burst transmission to Vanguard, sending them all the readings he had taken at the temple ruins in the desert. Though the tricorder had been active for only a short time, it had recorded a massive amount of data.

As the burst transmission continued, Quinn warmed up the ship's impulse engine and sealed off its antimatter fuel pods. *Won't need those where I'm going,* he decided.

A green light flashed on his command console. The burst transmission was complete. *Time to get this show on the road.*

He engaged the antigrav module and the maneuvering thrusters. The *Rocinante* wobbled under him for a moment as it began its vertical liftoff, the engines splitting the air with their high-pitched whine and kicking up roiling clouds of dust from the building's floor. Then the ship's ascent became swift and smooth. The mottled gray starhopper broke through the ramshackle roof, scattering timbers, scrap metal, and a flurry of thatch in all directions. Then it pivoted and raced north toward the temple.

Quinn guided the ship in a low-altitude lightning streak above the Golmira landscape. As he passed over the seashore, he ejected his ship's antimatter pods, which splashed down and sank into the ocean. Then he was back over land, and the sparse vegetation of Leuck Shire gave way to a wind-driven sea of sand. He would reach the desert temple within moments.

The best plan is a simple one, Quinn decided. He called up his tricorder scans of the Klingons' compound outside the temple and set his ship on a collision course with the cluster of buildings that housed the troops' barracks, ammunition depot, and command office. As he locked in the coordinates, he calculated the precise point in his flyover at which he would need to abandon ship in his lone escape pod to make a hard but solid landing on the temple's roof. Then he triggered an audible countdown and patched it through to the pod.

"Eject in twenty seconds," declared the vaguely feminine and utterly mechanical-sounding computer voice.

He dashed out of the cockpit, grabbed his backpack filled with emergency supplies and explosives, and sprinted aft as the *Rocinante* sailed alone on its final flight.

"Eject in ten seconds."

The hatch of the escape pod creaked loudly as Quinn yanked it open and jumped inside. It was about as roomy as a really large coffin, but a lot less comfortable. He slammed the lid shut and primed the ejection sequence.

"Eject in five seconds."

A board dotted with small indicator lights flickered weakly and stuttered into darkness.

"Four . . ."

Quinn bashed it with the side of his fist, and it surged back into service with all lights showing ready.

"Three . . ."

He set his thumb above the master ejection switch. The engines screamed as the ship began its last dive.

"Two . . ."

Remembering all the times this beat-up old rattletrap of a ship had saved his worthless skin, he choked back tears and made a silent apology: *Sorry, old girl.*

"One. Eject."

He pressed the ejection switch. Nothing happened.

Fuck.

Before he could curse the ship for spitefully taking him down with it, the pod lurched and kicked his guts into his throat as it hurtled into free fall.

Through a sliver of a viewport on the side of the pod, Quinn saw the roof of the temple rush up toward him.

He braced himself. This was going to hurt.

It did. The pod smashed hard against the stone rooftop. Quinn bounced around inside the pod like a rag doll.

The shocks of impact ceased, and the feeling of swift downward motion returned. Through the narrow viewport he saw the pod had missed the flat section of the roof and was sliding down one of its sloped portions. *Not good.*

He pulled the hatch-release lever. Small explosive charges blasted the metal door off the pod, which continued to roll erratically down the roof.

With one hand pushing him toward freedom and the other clutching the strap of his backpack, Quinn jumped from the pod. He continued sliding beside the pod, headed toward a very long fall, and flailed to find a grip on the rough stone.

His fingers dug into a deep crack between two slabs, and he hung on with all the strength that existential terror gave him. He looked down and watched the pod tumble over the edge into the night. A few seconds later he heard it make impact.

On the other side of the temple, the *Rocinante* slammed into the Klingons' camp. Then there was nothing to see except a white flash of fire, and nothing to hear but thunder.

T'Prynn held up her phaser and pointed out its controls to Pennington. "This adjusts the power level," she said. "This changes the focus of the beam. And this is the trigger."

Pennington nodded. "Seems simple enough."

She closed her hand around the compact, box-shaped weapon and held it away from her human compatriot. "Do not change any of these settings," she said. "It is currently primed to emit a narrow beam on heavy stun. Hold your fire unless you see a Klingon take aim at me. Is that clear?"

"Absolutely," he said with another curt nod.

Despite harboring some doubts as to Pennington's readiness to wield a potentially deadly weapon, T'Prynn handed him the phaser. "I will attempt to cross the narrowest patch of open ground between here and the Klingon camp. Once I have armed myself, retreat to our rendezvous point and do not engage the enemy. I will enter the temple, attempt to confiscate the artifact, and proceed to our rendezvous coordinates."

"Got it," Pennington said.

Doffing her heavy outer robe, T'Prynn said, "Very well. Take your position at the crest of the dune."

Pennington crawled to the top of the dune and cautiously dug

himself into the soft sand to create a platform for his arms, to
steady his aim. T'Prynn moved up beside him and coiled herself
to spring over the top.

Then her ears detected the sound of a starship's impulse engine shrieking into a power dive. As she turned her head to seek
the source, Pennington did likewise and said in a tense whisper,
"I know those engines! That's Quinn's ship!"

From behind the temple, the *Rocinante* appeared. It arced
over the decaying stone ruins and ejected an emergency pod as it
began a nosedive toward the Klingon's compound.

The pod bounced across the temple's roof and skidded down
a stony slope as its hatch was jettisoned. A humanoid figure tumbled out as the pod slid over the roof's edge.

An alert klaxon blared in the Klingon camp as the Mancharan
starhopper pitched nose-first into the ammo dump.

T'Prynn ducked low behind the dune and pulled Pennington
with her. An incandescent flash lit up the night, and a ground-
shaking explosion made the sandy peaks of the desertscape ripple
like waves in the sea.

A blast wave followed seconds later, pushing a scouring wall
of sand outward from the temple. Pennington and T'Prynn huddled beneath their robes as the manmade sandstorm knocked
them in wild somersaults into a valley between two dunes.

When the din and glare had passed, T'Prynn and Pennington
peeked out from under their robes at each other.

Shaking off her shroud of sand, T'Prynn retained her untroubled mien. "New plan," she said. "We wait and see what Mister
Quinn has in mind."

"Oh, I can tell you right now," Pennington replied, using his
fingers to comb the sand from his hair. "Whatever he's doing, I
guarantee you it's phenomenally stupid."

Stun pistol in hand, Quinn charged into a firefight with the
Klingon squad stationed along the temple's roof.

Dammit, he cursed at himself, *this is really stupid.*

All he had going for him were the element of surprise and the fact that most of the Klingon garrison had been vaporized by his pseudo-kamikaze attack with the *Rocinante*. The golden fireball from the crash was still expanding into the air behind him as he stumbled up the sloped roof and opened fire on the befuddled troops manning a nearby parapet.

By the time the four Klingon soldiers realized they were being shot at, Quinn had dropped three of them. The fourth returned a clumsy off-target shot at Quinn, who twisted to show the man as narrow a profile as possible. Quinn caught the Klingon in the chest and sent him sprawling over the piled bodies of his unconscious comrades.

Quinn reached the peak of the slope he was on and looked out over the rest of the temple's roof. Peaks, towers, and turrets surrounded him. He searched for some way inside the temple and found only one—a wedge-shaped blockhouse with a heavy stone door several dozen meters away, across a flat rooftop terrace below him. As he clambered down toward the terrace, disruptor shots rained down upon him from a high turret.

Another massive explosion from the ground engulfed the side of the temple below the turret. Huge slabs of stone were hurled into the air inside a cloud of pulverized rock fragments. A great cracking noise accompanied the spread of a fissure on the side of the turret's base, which sagged and began to slide away.

Jumping down to the terrace, Quinn saw in the corner of his eye Klingon troops desperately hurling themselves from the turret as it sheared away from the temple and broke apart; they all tumbled to their deaths in a storm of broken stone.

More of the temple's sandstone edifice collapsed, taking with it the center of the terrace. As Quinn struggled to fall back to solid footing, the disintegration of the ancient ruin advanced toward him—and ended as it cut the temple's roof in half, leaving the terrace divided by a broad chasm.

Dust surged into Quinn's nose and mouth. *So much for reaching the door,* he decided.

Through the freshly wrought gap, he heard Klingon troops inside the temple regrouping and preparing to counterattack.

No way down from here, he realized. *I could jump across to the next level with a running start, but it's too far down. I'd break my goddamned legs.*

He couldn't stay put; on the roof he'd either be an easy target once the Klingons got reorganized, or he'd be cut off and unable to help Bridy Mac.

What I need is a stepping-stone.

He heard running footsteps closing in below.

Behind him stood a mostly intact turret. He climbed onto the slope that led to the turret's base and sprinted to it. Taking an explosive charge from his backpack, he made his best guess as to where to place it. *Have to eyeball it.* He jammed it in a nook at the tower's base, armed the trigger, and leaped away.

As a squad of Klingons appeared on the level below him across the chasm, he keyed his remote detonator.

An explosive flash vaporized a sizable wedge of the turret's foundation. Just as Quinn had hoped, it toppled directly over the chasm.

Down below, the Klingons retreated in a panic.

Now the fun part, Quinn mused as he sprang to his feet, ran toward the chasm, and jumped into it.

The turret fell into the gap, smashing through the roof as it made impact. For half a second the tower slowed as it punched through the stony obstacles of floors and walls—and that was the moment Quinn landed on its crumbling surface.

As the rocky structure calved into chunks, Quinn leapfrogged from one to the next, then scrambled forward. Even as his stepping-stone and the floor beneath it dropped away, he bounded off it, rolled past the collapsing section of the floor, and landed on his feet, already drawing his pistol.

Ahead of him, the squad of Klingons stared in disbelief. Then their leader aimed his disruptor at Quinn.

Quinn shot first and took the man down.

The rest of the squad scattered, all of them returning fire on the run. Shots went wild and caromed off the walls, blasting away chunks of rocky shrapnel.

Charging forward and cursing like a berserker, Quinn made the best five shots of his life. As a flurry of light and heat raged past him and tore up the floor at his feet, he felled each of the men shooting at him with one shot apiece. Within seconds, he was the last man standing in the smoke-filled corridor.

Surveying his handiwork, he permitted himself a small, satisfied smile. *Not bad, old man,* he congratulated himself. *This half-assed rescue might turn out okay, after all.*

He felt a surge of confidence as he turned to descend a staircase to the lower levels of the temple. Then he felt something collide with his forehead.

So much for Plan A, he thought, before he sank like a rock into the black pool of oblivion.

47

"Well, that's not good," Pennington said as he saw through his binoculars a pair of Klingon warriors dragging the semiconscious Cervantes Quinn into the main chamber of the temple.

Peering through her targeting scope, T'Prynn replied, "It is an unfortunate turn of events." She turned her head a few degrees and added, "There is movement in the dunes on the far side of the temple."

Shifting his gaze, Pennington watched hundreds of natives in desert garb stand up in droves, emerging from the sand like ghosts born of the desert. Without pause they charged and attacked the Klingon troops defending the ruins.

"I think this is about to get interesting," he said.

T'Prynn put down her scope and took out her phaser. As Pennington lowered his binoculars, T'Prynn said, "This assault by the natives is unlikely to succeed, and certainly not in time to save Mister Quinn. However, it should provide an adequate diversion." She handed him her phaser. "Cover me until I reach the temple. Once I am inside, withdraw and return to the *Skylla*. If I do not return in one day, or if I fail to reach the temple, go back to Vanguard and tell them everything we have learned."

"Are you sure that's—"

Before he finished his gentle protest, T'Prynn was over the dune and running faster than any biped Pennington had ever seen.

Bugger, he fumed, and then took aim at the half-dozen Klingons still standing on this side of the dive-bombed ancient temple, patrolling in the ruddy glow of firelight. T'Prynn had covered most of the distance to the temple before the first of the soldiers noticed her.

The warrior lifted his rifle.

Pennington fired and hit the man in his gut. The shot struck with enough force to knock the Klingon onto his back.

The remaining troops all drew down on Pennington. He kept firing at them, both to hamper their aim and keep them distracted. Disruptor shots streaked toward him and flashed as they strafed his dune. Globs of sand melted into glass flew in all directions and pattered across the slope behind him.

Then one of the Klingons crumpled and dropped out of sight. Half a second later, disruptor shots from the downed warrior's position struck the other four Klingons in quick succession.

With the path cleared, T'Prynn climbed onto an excavation vehicle that had been knocked onto its side and ran up its crane arm, which had smashed through the temple's wall and become stuck there. Seconds later she ducked through the rent in the stone wall and was gone from sight, inside the temple.

Damn, Pennington thought with admiration. *She's good.*

Imagining the danger T'Prynn was facing inside the ruins, Pennington was torn. She had been explicit in her instructions that he should return to the *Skylla*; she was counting on him to be her insurance against failure. But abandoning her felt wrong, and Quinn was his friend—how could he leave him in harm's way?

There's nothing between me and the temple, he realized. *To hell with it, I'm going.* He bolted over the top of the dune and ran toward the ruins. In his head he knew it was a bad idea, but in his heart he knew it was right. His feet felt light as he sprinted across the level sands, and the night air was cool upon his face.

With each step he took the night grew a shade colder. When his breath formed a misty plume ahead of him, he stopped and realized he was shivering. The pale glow of moonlight on the temple's façade dimmed, and a darkness pure and terrible settled upon everything for as far as Pennington could see. Dreading what he would see but unable to stop himself, he looked up.

There was a hole in the sky.

A patch of black blotted out the stars and descended on the temple from directly overhead.

Pennington didn't have to wonder what this horror was.

He had seen it before.

Quinn drifted back toward consciousness aware of two things: the fact that he was being held upright by two people holding his arms, and the tickling sensation of blood tracing a slow path down the middle of his nose, pooling on the tip into a droplet, and falling away.

He opened his eyes to see the droplet land on the tip of a Klingon military officer's boot. Then he lifted his head to see a weathered, goateed face dusted with sand glaring back at him.

"You're still alive," the Klingon officer said.

"That's debatable," Quinn said, wincing at the pain of hearing his own voice inside his throbbing skull.

Breaking eye contact with Quinn, the Klingon said to someone behind him, "He's all yours." Then he stepped away.

"Thank you," said Zett, who stepped forward to take the Klingon's place in front of Quinn. The ebony-skinned Nalori flashed a grin of onyx-black teeth. "Hello again, Quinn." His solid-black eyes made Quinn think of an abyss.

When Quinn said nothing in reply, Zett reached out and with one fingertip gingerly probed the wound on Quinn's forehead. "I hope I didn't cause you any permanent damage," he said. "It would be a shame if one little bump caused you to forget the information Commander Marqlar wants me to extract from that pile of fatty mush you laughably call your brain."

Twisting to speak over his shoulder, Quinn said, "Hey, Marqlar, I'll make a deal with you. I'll tell you whatever you want to know if you'll just kill this guy."

"Tempting," Marqlar said. "If Mister Nilric's methods prove unsuccessful, I will consider it."

Quinn nodded once. "Fair enough."

Zett's cruel smile never wavered. To the soldiers holding Quinn's arms he said, "Turn him around."

The soldiers dragged Quinn about-face to see the glowing artifact on the pedestal—and Bridy Mac bound by her wrists, supine on the altar.

"I'll offer you a choice, Mister Quinn," Zett said. "If you'll tell me what I want to know, I'll kill you quickly and with as little pain as possible before the Klingons sacrifice your beautiful friend to something more horrible than you can possibly imagine."

Fury hardened Quinn's countenance. He didn't need to imagine what was coming; he'd seen it and was sure it would haunt him to his grave.

Leaning in close and dropping his voice to a sinister whisper, Zett continued. "But if you don't cooperate with me, I'm going to glue your eyes open and have these men hold your head still while you watch her die. Then I'm going to kill you with ten thousand slow cuts, so I can savor every last ounce of your pain. Have I made myself clear to you, Mister Quinn?"

"Perfectly," Quinn said. "You're suicidal."

"What makes you think so?"

With perfect calm, Quinn said, "Because you were a dead man the moment you laid hands on her. And you knew it."

"What I know, Mister Quinn, is—"

A disruptor shot struck the neck of the Klingon holding Quinn's right arm. The soldier went limp, let go of Quinn, and fell dead.

Another shot from the balcony killed the soldier holding Quinn's other arm and sent Zett, Marqlar, and the dozen troops and scientists on the main level of the temple running for cover.

Quinn tackled Zett and landed a crushing blow on the Nalori's transporter-recall bracelet, which shattered. Zett elbowed Quinn in the jaw, pushed his way free, and dashed for cover. Quinn stole a disruptor from one dead Klingon, retrieved his backpack from another, then ducked out of the line of fire.

Disruptor shots flew in every direction. Quinn darted to Bridy's side and kneeled next to her. "Don't move," he said.

He put his disruptor's muzzle to the chain of the manacles

binding her to the altar, and he fired. The chain disintegrated. As the cross fire continued around them, he pulled her off the obsidian slab and huddled with her behind it.

"Gutsy plan!" she shouted over the screeching of weapons fire, then ducked as a stray shot passed close overhead.

Gun-shy and bewildered, he yelled back, "What plan?"

Bridy pointed at the glowing gem. "We have to get the artifact before the Klingons beam it out!"

Quinn gestured at the wild crisscross of energy beams. "Be my guest!" He sniped a pair of Klingon officers as they tried to snag the radiant crystal. Whoever was picking off the Klingons from the balcony was keeping Zett and Marqlar pinned down.

"I've got an idea," Quinn said. "If you cover me, I can—"

That was as far as he got before the roof came down and a living nightmare of smoke, shadow, and fear dropped in.

T'Prynn was lining up a shot on the Klingon commander when the roof caved in.

Cascading into the cavernous chamber below, intermingled with smashed slabs of stone and an avalanche of dust, was a dark and chilling presence. As it poured into the temple, the air became cold and sharp with the odor of ozone.

Though she had never before encountered them firsthand, T'Prynn was certain the invading entity was a Shedai.

On the lower level of the temple, Zett Nilric, the Klingon commander, Quinn, and a human woman—who T'Prynn recognized as Bridget McLellan from the *U.S.S. Sagittarius*—all were trying to get to the mysterious artifact on the pedestal.

The Shedai surrounded the object with a dark tentacle of energy, cutting them all off. A second tendril of dark fluid snared the Klingon, then expanded into a black blizzard driven by a foul, cold wind. Within seconds it ripped the burly soldier to pieces, showering the walls with his magenta-hued viscera.

Reaching out with a tentacle that transformed into a dark vortex, the Shedai lifted the artifact high into the air.

The crystal flared with a blinding pulse of light. Beneath it, the pedestal shattered. The glyphs on the walls flickered like high-intensity strobes, and a tremor shot through the temple, splintering the floors and walls with cracks.

The few surviving Klingon soldiers and scientists evacuated the temple. McLellan evaded another falling section of the ceiling. Zett fled down a side passage, and Quinn ran after him. In the center of the mayhem, the Shedai grew larger while filling the air with a sepulchral groaning.

This would seem an opportune time to withdraw, T'Prynn decided. She bolted back to the gap in the wall through which she had entered.

Drawn across the lonely silence of the void by a summons of inchoate pain and rage, the Shedai Wanderer had known that only the *Telinaruul* could be responsible.

She manifested upon yet another former world of the Shedai that had been infested by flickers of life whose ephemerality was matched only by their arrogance. Who were they to defile a Shedai Conduit? To imprison one of the enumerated, one of the *Serrataal,* in this greatest of all abominations, this prison of dimensional folds disguised as a simple crystal?

Look at them flee in terror, the Wanderer gloated as she tore the first of the interlopers asunder. Seeing the simple being's innards liquefied by her wrath filled the Wanderer with pleasure. *They have all earned this retribution a thousandfold.*

The Wanderer took the hated crystal from its interface and turned its vile machinations to her own purposes. She destroyed the pedestal—added ages earlier by another upstart species of *Telinaruul*—and focused her power through the Conduit. With the might of this young world's fiery core yoked to her will, she could at last smash the long-hated abomination and welcome a partner in her quest for justice. Together they would usher in a new era of Shedai sovereignty.

First she needed to purge this Conduit of *Telinaruul.*

Then she would cleanse this poisoned world—and teach these sparks of consciousness to fear their betters.

48

Ragged chunks of the ceiling fell from high above Quinn's head and shattered on the steps ahead of him as he ran up a flight of spiral stairs in pursuit of Zett Nilric.

The ruins quaked. Thunderous sounds reverberated in the temple's walls and echoed through its passageways. A haze of dust rained down on Quinn, who coughed and wheezed. He squinted in pain as fine particles drifted into his eyes, which watered as he struggled to keep Zett in sight.

All Quinn could see of the Nalori thug were his feet, several meters ahead and just shy of the curve of the staircase's inner wall. The rest of Zett was out of sight, sparing the assassin a well-deserved shot in the back.

A massive slab of rock smashed down in front of Quinn, pulverizing three steps into rubble. He stumbled backward and pressed himself against the outer wall as the huge piece of debris rolled past him.

He sprinted forward and almost impaled himself on Zett's knife.

Twisting at the waist, Quinn dodged the stab.

Zett snapped his arm back to wind up for another blow. Quinn raised his arms. The knife jabbed forward.

Quinn swatted the blade aside with his forearm—and a metallic clang of impact as the knife struck the armored bracers concealed beneath the sleeves of Quinn's jacket.

Noting Zett's wide-eyed stare of surprise, Quinn smiled. "I thought we might end up doin' this little dance. Came prepared."

Zett lunged as if hoping to gut Quinn with one stroke. Quinn sidestepped the attack and struck Zett's wrist with a scissoring blow of his armored forearms.

The knife flew from Zett's grasp and tumbled down the stairs behind Quinn, its blade ringing like a chime as it bounced off the stone steps and walls.

As Quinn cocked his arm to pummel Zett, the Nalori's foot snapped forward and hit Quinn in his solar plexus. Pain shot through Quinn's gut as the air left his lungs, and he fell backward. Zett turned and continued his mad dash up the stairs.

Fighting for breath and summoning strength to push through his pain, Quinn forced himself to continue his pursuit.

As he neared the top of the staircase, the tremors plaguing the temple worsened, and the mortar between stones in the walls began to turn to powder. Great fractures split blocks of sandstone with sharp cracking noises.

The staircase let out onto a wide, flat terrace nestled in the temple's roof. Across a small gap, on an adjacent terrace, a Klingon shuttle was powering up to make a hasty retreat.

Zett sprinted toward the shuttle, apparently hoping that with enough of a running start he could leap across the divide to the next terrace, where the Klingon shuttle crewmen were waving for him to hurry.

The assassin came to an abrupt, clumsy halt, pointed, and shouted in *tlhIngan Hol* to the Klingons.

The Klingons stared in confusion for a moment before they realized Zett was pointing behind them, and they turned.

A tall spire toppled over and collapsed onto the Klingons and their shuttle. Tons of rock crushed the small spacecraft into a heap of twisted, sparking metal.

Having nowhere left to run, Zett turned and faced Quinn, who had drawn his borrowed disruptor and aimed it at the sharp-dressed killer. "Lose your weapon," Quinn said. "Two fingers only."

"Don't be stupid about this," Zett said as he lifted his sidearm from its holster using only his thumb and forefinger. "This place is eating itself. You can see that, can't you?"

"Yup." Gesturing with a tilt of his head, Quinn added, "Toss it over the side. Now." Zett threw his disruptor off the roof. Quinn nodded. "Good. Now ditch your knife. The special one you keep under your left arm."

Frowning, the Nalori discarded his *yosa* blade. "There," he said as his last weapon tumbled away into the darkness. "Now what?"

Quinn hurled his disruptor off the roof, then drew his own knife and cast it away into the night. "A fair fight."

Another violent quake rocked the temple, and part of an outer wall collapsed with a roar. From far below, inside the temple, came a nightmarish groaning, as if from Hell itself.

"This is hardly an ideal setting for a duel," Zett said.

Quinn shrugged off his backpack. "Looks okay to me."

He prowled toward Zett, who eased into a fighting stance. The two combatants circled each other.

Zett flashed a predatory grin. "You're going to regret this, Quinn. You forget, I've seen you fight."

"No, you haven't. You've seen me get my ass kicked when I was drunk. You've seen your goons beat me up while holding me at gunpoint." Quinn smirked. "You've *never* seen me *fight*."

They stopped moving. Locked eyes.

Zett charged and launched himself at Quinn. He landed a flying kick to Quinn's chest.

Quinn stumbled backward then steadied himself as Zett charged again, leading this time with his fists.

There was no time to think, only time to react in a brutal dance of motion and collision. Ducks and blocks, strikes and counter-strikes. Hands and feet, knees and elbows.

Crushing blows left Quinn's head swimming with dull echoes of impact. He tasted blood from his own split lips as he felt Zett's nose crack under his fist.

Zett came at Quinn in a frenzy and landed a flurry of hits. Quinn snared the man's arm and twisted it until the wrist broke and the shoulder dislocated.

With his free hand, Zett punched Quinn in the throat. Quinn let go of Zett. They staggered apart, both stunned and bleeding.

"I'll give you credit," Zett said as he steadied himself. "You're better than I thought. But you're still going to lose."

"We'll just see abou—"

Quinn barely saw the spinning kick that nearly knocked off his jaw. A falling sensation preceded a rolling blur of motion. He felt his body strike the roof, kicks and punches slamming against his torso, three of his teeth splintering as they were liberated from his gums. Everything he saw looked purple.

Fighting for balance and solid footing, he eked out one last moment of clear perception—then saw Zett's side kick hit him in the chest. The blow knocked Quinn off his feet. He flew backward and flailed desperately as he rolled over the edge. His hands shot out, looking for purchase.

Just before gravity could lay final claim to Quinn, his left hand seized a small lip in the roof's edge. Despite a lifetime of people telling him never to look down, he did anyway. Far below lay an unwelcoming patch of rocky ground.

Half alive and dangling by his fingertips, he watched Zett step to the roof's edge and loom above him.

"Told you so," Zett gloated.

"Yeah, yeah," Quinn said, his throat tight from the full-body strain of hanging on by one hand. "I know. Fighting was never my strong suit."

The assassin smirked and lifted his foot to stomp on Quinn's fingers. "You *have* a strong suit?"

Zett froze as he saw the detonator in Quinn's right hand.

"Yeah," Quinn said. "Demolitions."

He pressed the trigger.

The charges in Quinn's backpack exploded, engulfing the terrace above him in white-hot fire and high-velocity shrapnel. Searing flames vaporized Zett's suit as bits of metal and stone raked his flesh. The blast wave lifted the assassin into the air and hurled him over its edge.

Fire stung Quinn's fingers as he fought to hang on a few seconds longer, howling in pain the entire time. Turning his face away from the light and heat, he watched Zett's scorched body fall to the ground. The moment of impact was not pretty, but Quinn found it very satisfying.

Above Quinn the blaze abated. He dropped the detonator and reached up to grip the edge with both hands. That was as far as he could get. He was out of strength and too badly hurt to pull his own dead weight back over the edge. *Great plan,* he chided himself. *I get to celebrate for all of ten seconds before I wind up as the stain next to Zett.*

The rock under his hands began to crumble. He half expected to see his life flash before his eyes, but all he could think about was that moment—the grit between his fingers, the pull of gravity, the pain in his head, the lead in his limbs . . .

Two hands locked shut around his wrists.

Bridy Mac was pulling him up to safety.

Her face was red and scrunched with effort as she power-lifted him, starting from a deep squat so she could use her legs and back muscles. As soon as she had his waist above the roof's edge, she let herself fall backward so gravity could work for her instead of against her.

They collapsed together on the blast-scarred terrace.

"Thanks," Quinn said.

"*De nada.*"

A major quake rocked the temple's ruins, and another large section of the ancient structure fell away and sank earthward in a cloud of dust.

"Time to go," Bridy Mac said, climbing off Quinn and pulling him back to his feet. She led the way back to the spiral staircase, and they hurtled down it three steps at a time, bouncing wildly off the walls as they ran.

Several landings short of the bottom, the staircase began to implode. Quinn pulled Bridy back from a collapsing step and out of the staircase onto a landing that wasn't in much better shape.

"That way!" Quinn shouted, pointing down a corridor whose stone floors already were heaving and buckling. He sprinted ahead, leading the way, leaping from one unstable section of disintegrating floor to another.

He was about to make another jump as Bridy grabbed his shirt collar, yanked him backward, and pulled him with her into another spiral staircase that looked as if it was still intact.

Several seconds later they were back at ground level and making a frantic run for the nearest exit.

Then a terrifying voice boomed behind them, its majestic tenor at once monstrous and feminine, its affect as sharp as thunder and as deep as the sea. Worst of all, Quinn heard it in his mind as much as in his ears.

"I know you," it declared, freezing both Quinn and Bridy in mid-stride. **"Both of you."**

They turned and gazed upon the demonic presence towering above them. Violet motes of energy swam in the dark titan's hypnotically shifting form of liquid and shadows. It wore a gruesome horned visage, and murderous hatred burned in its eyes. Trapped inside its form was the crystal artifact.

Quinn had seen this kind of being before. On Jinoteur.

"You were on the First World. You defiled it with your mere presence. For that alone you both deserve to die."

Mustering a weak smile, Quinn said to the creature. "Um, yeah. Well . . . nice catching up with you." Then to Bridy Mac he added in a sharp whisper, "Run!"

They sprinted toward open ground.

A tentacle of shimmering black fluid shot past them. It smashed through stone walls and branched into a web of tendrils, blocking their exit.

Dodging and weaving, Quinn and Bridy scrambled toward another exit. More tentacles stabbed at them, transmuting into gleaming blades of obsidian just before the moment of attack. Each black blade sheared with ease through blocks of sandstone.

Quinn dived and rolled clear of two more thrusts while Bridy somersaulted over a near miss.

Then a flurry of disruptor shots peppered the creature. Turning to look for the source of the covering fire, Quinn saw a squad of desert nomads wielding captured Klingon weapons.

Oh, jeez, he thought. *They don't know what they're getting into.* He ran toward them, waving his arms. "Stop!" he shouted. "Run! Fall back!" Bridy was right behind him—and the Shedai was right behind her. All at once the nomads seemed to understand what was happening, and then they were running, too.

The monster doubled in size as it pursued them down the passageway toward one of the temple's secluded interior courtyards. It bashed through walls and load-bearing columns, and it swatted away multiton slabs of rock as if they weighed nothing at all. *It's a goddamned self-propelled demolition machine,* Quinn marveled even as he ran for his life.

At the threshold of the courtyard, the creature had them. Fire and fury blazed in its very essence. Its tentacles reared up and coiled to strike.

Then it shrieked as if in agony, and it contracted in size. Immediately it turned away and charged back inside the temple, hammering through anything and everything in its path. In its wake lay nothing but rubble and dust.

Bridy looked apprehensively up at the crumbling temple ruins surrounding them. "We're trapped," she said.

Quinn turned and looked at her—then he looked past her. As the dust cloud dissipated, his eyes pierced the dark to see a sleek, Nalori-built argosy parked on the other side of the courtyard. "The hell we are," he said with a broad smile. He led Bridy and the nomads toward the ship as he added, "Come with me."

49

T'Prynn emerged from the rapidly imploding temple ruins to see Tim Pennington hurrying toward her—surrounded by more than two dozen armed Starfleet personnel.

At the front of the group was a tall human woman with fair skin and brown hair. She wore a gold tunic whose sleeves bore the stripes of a lieutenant commander, and she carried a type-II phaser. Making eye contact, the woman asked, "Are you T'Prynn?"

"I am."

"Report. Quickly."

T'Prynn halted as she was met by the woman. "To whom am I reporting?"

"Lieutenant Commander Katherine Stano, first officer, *U.S.S. Endeavour.*" Stano nodded to a dark-haired human man who stopped beside her. He wore a blue tunic and held an octagonal crystal device in one hand. "This is Lieutenant Stephen Klisie-wicz, science officer."

"Very well," T'Prynn said. "There is a Shedai inside the temple. It has acquired a crystalline object that appears responsive to Shedai energy waveforms."

A tall, brown-skinned human man with a mustache stepped closer and asked T'Prynn, "Are there any humans inside the temple?"

Stano noted T'Prynn's reluctance to answer with a small measure of exasperation. "This is Lieutenant Paul McGibbon, our deputy chief of security."

T'Prynn nodded. "Yes, a civilian named Cervantes Quinn

and a Starfleet officer from the *Sagittarius* named Bridget McLellan are inside the temple."

"Okay," McGibbon said. "Let's do this." He nodded to his platoon of red-shirted security officers, who fanned out into a skirmish line. As they settled into their battle formation, Klisiewicz activated the eight-sided crystal device in his hand.

Pennington edged forward. His eyes went wide as he saw what was transpiring. He asked Klisiewicz, "What're you doing, mate?"

Grinning like a child with a new toy, Klisiewicz replied, "Using this gadget Ming Xiong built to lure the Shedai out of the temple and here to us."

Horrified, Pennington exclaimed, "Why the bloody hell would you want to do *that*?"

Before anyone could answer the anxious reporter, a hideous shriek rose up from the temple and split the night. Then came the low rumble of destruction and the steady rhythm of impact tremors shaking the sand under T'Prynn's feet.

The Shedai was coming.

With an epic roar, it burst free of the mountain of pulverized rock that once had been a temple.

It swelled as it surged forward, lashing out with tentacles that glowed with millions of motes of energy. Burning in the center of its mass was the twelve-sided crystal object T'Prynn had seen the entity seize from the pedestal inside the now-buried Shedai Conduit.

McGibbon raised his phaser and ordered his men, "Fire!"

Bright blue phaser beams slashed the darkness and struck the Shedai with electric flashes. None of the blasts seemed to cause the creature any harm; if anything, it only grew stronger.

Stano glanced sidelong at Klisiewicz. "Now?"

"Not yet," said the science officer, his thumb hovering above a button in the center of the device in his hands.

The Shedai scuttled on its tentacles and rapidly crossed the open ground separating it from the landing party. It closed to within twenty meters and was sprouting new tendrils with which to strike.

Visibly nervous, Stano asked Klisiewicz, "Now?"

"Wait for it," he said.

The ends of the Shedai's tentacles solidified into obsidian and shaped themselves into massive spearheads.

"Now," said Klisiewicz, pressing his thumb on the button.

The device in his hand pulsed with blue light—and then so did the crystal artifact inside the Shedai's body. A volatile reaction ensued around the crystal polyhedron.

Another horrific shriek emanated from the Shedai. It shrank rapidly and forcibly ejected the artifact from its body. The crystal tumbled like a die over the sands and rolled to a stop a few meters from the landing party. Then the Shedai flew straight up, away from the object, toward orbit.

The XO pulled her communicator from her belt. "Stano to *Endeavour*."

A woman replied over the comm, *"Go ahead, Commander."*

"Captain, Xiong's little gizmo did just what he said it would, but you've got one ticked-off creature heading your way."

"She's already gone," said the *Endeavour*'s commanding officer. *"Broke orbit at full impulse and didn't look back—just like the Klingons."*

"Chalk that up as one little victory," Stano said.

"Let's not celebrate yet. What's your status?"

Stano surveyed the landscape. "We've secured the Mirdonyae Artifact, and the locals seem to have the Klingon garrison under control." From the far side of the ruins, a nondescript small spacecraft lifted off and cruised away toward the horizon. "Any word from our little cousins?"

"Affirmative," Khatami said. *"They say hello, but they really must be going."*

"Acknowledged," Stano said. "Stand by to beam us up. Stano out." She flipped her communicator shut and looked at Klisiewicz. "Go get the artifact and prep it for transport." Then she nodded at McGibbon. "Lieutenant, you know what to do."

McGibbon pointed his phaser at T'Prynn, and his security team surrounded her and Pennington. "Lieutenant Commander T'Prynn," he said. "You are under arrest for multiple violations of the Starfleet Code of Military Justice. Drop any weapons you are carrying, step forward, kneel, and place your hands on top of your head."

T'Prynn slowly set down her disruptor rifle, stepped away from it, and kneeled as she placed her hands on her head.

Another security guard confiscated T'Prynn's phaser from Pennington and prodded him toward her. "You too," the guard said. "On your knees, hands on your head."

"Timothy Pennington," said McGibbon. "You're under arrest for aiding and abetting a fugitive from Starfleet justice."

As the security team closed magnetic restraints around his and T'Prynn's wrists, Pennington looked at her and smiled.

"Ah, yes," he said. "I'd almost forgotten about this part. Our heroes' welcome."

Quinn sat at the helm of his late rival's vessel, the *Icarion,* and admired the way it handled. *Zett was a bastard,* Quinn mused, *but he had great taste in ships.*

Bridy stepped into the cockpit, followed by Noar, the female leader of the squad of nomads she and Quinn had rescued from the collapsing ruins minutes earlier. "Starfleet's on the scene," Bridy said. "They have the ruins under control, and our friend with the tentacles has taken a rain check."

"Nice," Quinn said. "And our *neighbors* in orbit?"

"Bugged out," she replied with a knowing smile. "Which means it's time for us to move on."

"Not quite," Quinn said. "First we'll head back to Tegoresko and make sure our people and Naya's get properly introduced."

Bridy smiled. "Sounds like a plan."

Out of the corner of his eye, Quinn saw Noar fiddling with the switches on one of the auxiliary consoles. "Hey," he said to her. "Don't touch that."

"Why?" the young Denn asked. "What does it do?"

"Don't know yet," Quinn said. "But I'd rather you didn't mess with it before I find out."

Noar threw a confused look around the *Icarion*'s cockpit. "Is this not yours?"

"Well . . ." Quinn shrugged. "It is now."

Accusingly, she asked, "Did you steal it?"

"No, I borrowed it."

"So whose shuttle is this?"

"It's not a shuttle. It's a starship."

"Oh. Whose starship is this?"

"Zett's."

"Who is Zett?"

Quinn chuckled and couldn't help but grin.

"Zett's dead, baby. Zett's dead."

Interlude

Interlude

50

September 12, 2267

Jetanien and Lugok sat on opposite sides of a small portable table, facing each other like bookends. They were finishing dinner. Each had brought his own repast, and they ate together in silence, as they had for weeks on end.

There was nothing left to talk about. All the topics of idle chatter had been exhausted, and the maddeningly consistent weather in this region of Nimbus III wasn't providing much conversational fodder. During the daytime they tried to avoid each other as much as possible, dropping little more than curt nods on those rare occasions when their paths crossed.

Behind Lugok the sun was setting. Its last surge of dying light flared straight up from the horizon, culminating in a peak that for Jetanien evoked the ancient Chelon myth of his world's first mountain, which rose from the sea to stand before the sky. Had he been a superstitious person, he might have seen the moment as an omen of a beginning.

Instead the moment caught him by surprise.

The wind kicked up and blanketed his dinner with dust. A soft but deep thrumming followed. Lugok was staring straight up, so Jetanien did the same.

A ship descended toward the plateau. It was very quiet, and though its design had a vaguely Vulcan quality, it was unfamiliar to Jetanien.

Lugok and Jetanien rose from their seats as the craft extended three squat legs and made a gentle touchdown a few dozen meters from their ships. As it settled onto the ground, the low purr of its engines faded, leaving only the hush of wind and the dry patter of settling rocks and sand.

On the underside of what appeared to be the vessel's bow, a hatch lowered and unfolded with nary a sound. A dim green glow bled from the ship's interior, painting the pale ground before the ramp as it made contact with a low scrape. Jetanien thought for a moment he could smell the fragrance of incense wafting out of the peculiar vessel.

A silhouetted figure in a deep-hooded robe stepped into the ship's doorway and walked down the ramp with a slow, shuffling gait. The dark-gray fabric of the visitor's cloak fluttered in the arid wind outside the ship.

Jetanien and Lugok stepped forward together to meet the newcomer. When he and they were finally close enough to shake hands, the lone figure stopped and drew back the hood of his cloak, revealing the white hair and creased visage of a very elderly Romulan. "Gentlemen," he said in a rasp of a voice.

"Senator D'tran?" asked Jetanien.

The Romulan replied, "Indeed. You must be Ambassador Jetanien." Cocking one snowy eyebrow at the Klingon diplomat, he added, "And this, I presume, is Ambassador Lugok."

Lugok responded with a curt half nod. "Senator." Then he added, "You're late."

D'tran folded his hands at his waist. "I apologize for my tardiness, gentlemen, and I thank you for your remarkable patience. I regret that I was unavoidably detained on Romulus."

"Apology accepted, Senator," said Jetanien. He gestured toward the table he had shared with Lugok. "Your seat awaits you. Will you join us?"

"With pleasure," D'tran said. "We have much to discuss."

PART FOUR

The End of Ourselves

51

September 13, 2267

Reyes paced in front of the banquet room's tall, arched windows and admired the jagged cliffs and snowcapped peaks that glowed in the moonlight outside the Klingon mountain lodge.

He and Ezthene had been beamed down to Ogat from the *I.K.S. Zin'za* more than an hour earlier, accompanied by Councillor Gorkon and a squad of soldiers. Gorkon had left the room without offering any explanation for what was happening, but the six guards had stayed behind. "To keep us company," Reyes had joked to Ezthene while hooking a thumb at the perpetually scowling warriors standing sentry beside the room's exits.

The room had a medieval quality, in Reyes's opinion. Its floor and walls were made from individual blocks of rough-hewn granite, and dominating the center of the rectangular room was a long table fashioned from dark, richly lacquered hardwood. It was surrounded by matching chairs and packed with Klingon delicacies that made Reyes's stomach churn with disgust.

Narrow banners bearing the emblem of the Klingon Empire hung from the high ceiling and were complemented by similar pennants adorning the walls, draped between broad iron sconces holding lit candles.

Ezthene circled the table full of inedible culinary wonders and poked at the various foods with one of his environment-suit-covered forelimbs. His vocoder translated his metallic shrieks and chitterings into the question, "Is it possible this food was intended for us?"

"I doubt it," Reyes said. "They know you don't eat, and by now they ought to know I won't eat anything that fights back when I chew." He gazed up at the sky and tried to pick out which point of light was Sol. The stars were white as bones.

A door at the end of the room opened. Gorkon walked in and said to the six guards, "Get out, and lock the doors."

The warriors slipped out of the room. Reyes heard the dull thuds of heavy beams being lowered and metallic locks being secured. Gorkon lifted his wrist and whispered Klingon words into his sleeve.

Light and energy swirled into existence beside Gorkon, and a bright drone of white sound filled the room. A shape formed inside the whorl of charged particles and coalesced into a large, broad-shouldered Klingon man garbed in ornate robes of office and carrying a heavy rod of metal-banded wood capped with carved bone and tipped with steel.

Reyes's eyes widened. It was Chancellor Sturka.

The leader of the Klingon Empire glowered at Reyes.

Then he glared at Gorkon. "What is the meaning of this?"

"These are the two I wanted you to meet," Gorkon said. "This is Ezthene, formerly a member of the Tholian political caste-moot, and this is Diego Reyes, the former—"

"I know who he is," Sturka growled, nodding at Reyes. Then he looked at Ezthene. "Though I couldn't care less about the bug."

It was obvious to Reyes that Gorkon was struggling to remain calm in the face of his superior's rebuke. "They are well-versed in how their people think and act, and both have also shown a willingness to break with orthodox thinking. Their insights could help us chart a path to peace."

"You mean help *you* chart a path to peace," Sturka said. "I have no need of such an agenda."

Ezthene interjected, "With all respect, Chancellor, you most certainly do. As do the other powers in this quadrant."

Sturka narrowed his eyes at the Tholian. "Really?" Stalking toward Ezthene, he continued in a low voice. "And why should an empire built on the fortunes of war want to sue for peace? Or care for the needs of its future *jeghpu'wI'*?"

"Because your empire has already overextended itself," Ezthene said. "Why risk a full-scale war with the Federation and the Assembly at the same time? You have neither the ships nor the soldiers to prevail in such a conflict. And diverting more resources to expand your fleet will only starve your people."

Pointing angrily, Sturka said, "You have no idea what the Empire can do when it's called to war!"

"On the contrary," Ezthene said. "I am well aware of your empire's martial prowess and its history of aggressive expansion. But I also know that which you refuse to see."

The chancellor asked with hostility masquerading as curiosity, "And that would be . . . ?"

"You risk the wrath of a sleeping giant."

Dismissing the warning with a wave of his hand, Sturka turned his back on Ezthene as he replied, "We don't fear the Shedai."

Ezthene said, "Chancellor, the giant of which I speak is the Federation."

Enraged, Sturka spun and threw a baleful stare at Ezthene. Then he turned his withering gaze on Reyes. "You've been quiet, human. What's *your* opinion?"

Reyes crossed his arms. "Ezthene has a point. Your fleet has the edge in ships and troops, but we're ahead of you in technology. Slavery gives you an economic advantage, but your ban on foreign trade helps us make deals with worlds on your border. When you want to expand, you have to spend blood and treasure; all the Federation has to do is show up and say 'hi.' A few more decades of this and we won't have to fight you; we'll be able to just sit back and starve you out."

Sturka sneered. "The same old propaganda. 'Research and trade.' That's the cowards' answer to everything, isn't it? Talk every problem to death instead of taking action. Apologies and excuses. That's the human way."

"Don't be so sure," Reyes said. "I admit: these days, it's usually true. But if you think my people aren't capable of bloodlust, or of collective genocidal psychosis, then you don't know our history. The human race has come a long way in the last few hundred years, Chancellor, but deep down we're still savages. If you push us hard enough, we will push back."

The chancellor grinned. "I'm counting on it." He walked back to Gorkon and all but pressed his face to that of his longtime adviser. "This is a waste of time, Gorkon. What in the name of Kahless were you thinking? The Federation and the Assembly both send formal ambassadors to Qo'noS—so why am I speaking to these *petaQpu'*?"

"Professional diplomats are little more than parrots for the policies of their leaders," Gorkon said. "Ezthene and Reyes are iconoclasts. They can help us find a new perspective on the future, perhaps a more viable one."

"The only new perspective I want these two to find is one looking up from a grave on Rura Penthe," Sturka said. "There is a reason why the political process adheres to certain rules, Gorkon. A reason why some parties are allowed to speak under the color of authority and others are not." He stepped away from Gorkon, lifted his wrist comm to his face and spoke into it. Lowering his arm, he added, "Our friendship has been long and my debts to you are many, Gorkon, so I will forgive this grievous error in your judgment. But do not conduct any further talks with these *yIntaghpu'*—and don't *ever* summon me again."

A transporter beam enfolded Sturka. He vanished in a spinning flurry of light and sound that faded within seconds to empty air and silence.

Gorkon grimaced and bowed his head. In a weary voice he said to Reyes, "I presume you have some scathing remark with which to deepen my moment of disgrace."

Reyes offered the man a sympathetic half smile. "Your boss is kind of a dick."

The Klingon chuckled. "Yes," he said. "He certainly is."

"So, Gorkon," said Ezthene. "What is to become of me and

Diego now that we've failed to sway your chancellor? Will you condemn us to your aliens' graveyard as Sturka decreed?"

The councillor walked to a window and clasped his hands behind his back as he gazed out at the rugged mountains. "No," he said. "You've both earned better fates than that. Imperial Intelligence will be most upset with me, and Captain Kutal will likely be quite irate, but I plan to let you go."

"A noble gesture," Ezthene said.

Looking over his shoulder, Gorkon replied, "Call it an apology. I honestly thought Sturka would be receptive to a message of change. Now I see that real political progress in the Empire will require nothing less than new leadership."

"Well," Reyes said, "for what it's worth, Gorkon, you'd have my vote."

"Touching," Gorkon said with a bitter smile, "but the Empire is not a democracy."

Reyes rolled his eyes. "No kidding." Tilting his head toward Ezthene, he asked Gorkon, "What now? It's not like Ezthene or I can just go home again. He's an outcast, and I'm supposed to be dead or in jail. If I go back to Starfleet now, they'll put me on trial for consorting with the enemy."

Ezthene asked, "Might I make a suggestion?"

Gorkon and Reyes traded looks that seemed to say "Why not?"

The Klingon nodded at Ezthene. "By all means."

"Diego cannot go to Vanguard, but I can," Ezthene said. "If you wish, Diego, I could deliver messages to your friends and family on your behalf."

Nodding, Reyes said, "I'd appreciate that. Thank you."

"And what of you?" Gorkon asked Reyes. "Where will you go?"

Reyes cracked a devious smile. "Actually . . . I have an idea."

52

A ferric odor of fresh paint lingered in the air as Quinn started removing the adhesive strips from the stencil plate on his new ship's hull. He smiled at his handiwork. *Much better.*

Bridy Mac descended the folding staircase from the ship's center cabin. "Time to go," she said. "I just filed our report with SI and authenticated our new orders."

Picking at a corner of an uncooperative length of tape, Quinn asked, "Where to this time?"

"Another rock with no name," Bridy said.

"Naturally."

It was pretty much what Quinn had expected. With the Klingon occupation of Golmira routed, his old ship's antimatter pods retrieved from the ocean with some help from Starfleet, the planet's natives united in a request for Federation-protectorate status, and the *Endeavour* en route to Vanguard with the recovered artifact, Quinn and Bridy's work here was done. Their best bet of moving on without Klingon interference was to leave while the *Akhiel* and the *Defiant* were still in orbit, acting as a deterrent.

He pointed to a spray can of clear-polymer hull sealant on the ground and asked Bridy, "Can you hand me that?"

"Sure," she said, passing it to Quinn. Watching him work, Bridy wore a look of mild amusement. "Is this what you've been doing all day? Painting the ship?"

"No way I'm flyin' through the galaxy in a ship called *Icarion*," Quinn said. "That ain't no name for a ship. Sounds too much like *carrion*, for one thing."

Circling behind him to check out his work, she asked, "So what's our new ride called? *Rocinante II*?"

"Never," he said, discarding the wad of tape. "For me there'll only ever be one *Rocinante*." He removed the stencil with care to reveal his new ship's new name: *Dulcinea*.

As Quinn sprayed a protective layer of sealant over the fresh golden-orange paint, Bridy asked, "What does it mean?"

He stepped back beside his partner. "It's from an ancient Earth novel called *Don Quixote de la Mancha*." He looked at Bridy. "Dulcinea was a very beautiful woman for whom a slightly crazy old man did a lot of really stupid things."

She smiled and planted a soft kiss on his cheek. "Sounds about right." Then she climbed the steps and boarded the ship.

He followed her aboard. "So, I was thinkin', the captain's quarters on this boat has a double bed and—"

"Just fly the ship."

"Yes, ma'am."

53

November 19, 2267

Admiral Nogura stood like a rock before the river of bodies pouring from the gangway of Docking Bay Two, where the *Endeavour* had only minutes earlier made its hard airlock seal.

Junior officers on leave flooded up the gangway and broke to either side of Nogura as soon as they saw the markings on his uniform and the stern expression on his face.

Then came a break in the sea of faces, and four figures crossed the suddenly empty gangway in a tight cluster. Three were Vanguard personnel. The fourth was in custody.

Leading the group were Commander ch'Nayla and Lieutenant Jackson.

At the rear of the group, Captain Desai escorted the prisoner, Lieutenant Commander T'Prynn. The Vulcan woman was taller than Nogura had expected, even though he'd read her file a dozen times over the past several weeks.

The group emerged onto the main concourse of Vanguard's docking level and stopped in front of Nogura. He looked T'Prynn in the eye. "Have you been fully debriefed?"

"Yes, Admiral," T'Prynn said.

"Good. Your court-martial has been expedited. It starts in two weeks. You have that long to prepare a defense."

The Vulcan woman nodded. "Understood."

Desai said, "Lieutenant Commander T'Prynn has entered a plea of no contest to all charges." Shifting with what seemed like mild embarrassment, she added, "However, after reading her statements, I think there might be . . . mitigating factors."

At once curious and suspicious, Nogura said, "No doubt." He aimed his steely gaze at T'Prynn, who remained unfazed. "I'm sure we'll hear all about it." He nodded to Jackson. "Take her to the best cell in the brig, Lieutenant."

"Aye, sir," Jackson said. He motioned T'Prynn forward and led the manacled Vulcan woman away. A pair of armed security officers waited for them in an open turbolift.

As soon as the lift doors closed behind Jackson, T'Prynn, and their escorts, Nogura looked at Desai. "I'll see you in the morning, Captain." Then he stepped away and said to ch'Nayla as he passed by, "Walk with me."

The middle-aged Andorian *chan* fell into step beside the diminutive admiral and dropped his voice to a whisper. "The artifact is back aboard the station," he said. "It was transferred off disguised as routine cargo and routed back to the Vault, which is once again secure."

"No," corrected Nogura, "you mean it's *finally* secure."

Chastened, ch'Nayla replied, "If you prefer, yes. That distinction aside, Lieutenant Farber assures me the security flaws have been addressed and that the Vault is now the most impregnable compartment on the station."

"Better late than never," Nogura said. "Tell Doctor Marcus I want real-time updates. The moment anything happens with that thing, I want to know about it."

"That makes two of us, sir."

Anxious eyes greeted the artifact's return to the Vault.

Dr. Carol Marcus stood beside Ming Xiong and watched as a robotic arm lowered the glowing dodecahedron onto a new pedestal that was linked into the lab's various systems, several of which had been engineered to emulate some aspect of the Shedai's technology. As before, a palpable aura of fear traveled with the radiant, skull-sized crystal.

"I've been thinking," Xiong said in a confidential tone to Marcus. "Since I was right about using phased harmonics of the

Jinoteur Pattern to trigger the device, I thought maybe we could try feeding it the regenerative sequence discovered by the CMO on the *Sagittarius*. You know, to see if we could replicate the tissue-repair function Doctor Babitz documented."

"One thing at a time, Ming," Marcus cautioned.

On the other side of Marcus, Dr. Gek leaned in close. "I couldn't help but overhear," said the Tellarite. "If we're planning new experiments, I think we ought to focus on the waveform's potential for large-scale molecular rearrangement. Coupled with our existing transporter technology, we could be on the verge of a major breakthrough in patterned replication."

"All in good time," Marcus said.

She hoped that would be the end of the solicitations, but Gek had spoken loudly enough for several other scientists to overhear, and as a result the floodgates were open.

"I'd like to propose that we prioritize high-energy communication applications," said Dr. Koothrappali.

Then the requests began to overlap, and Marcus no longer knew who was talking.

"Can we start with a test of the Meta-Genome's ability to correct gaps in its sequence?"

"We need to know what that crystal's made of!"

"No, we need to communicate with the entity inside it!"

Marcus held up her hands and shouted, "Enough!" When the hubbub subsided, she added, "Let's all start by focusing on something simple." She threw a worried glance at the artifact. "Like not blowing up any more planets by mistake."

54

December 28, 2267

After nineteen days of witness testimony and forensic evidence examination and six days of deliberations, the court-martial board had reached its decision and summoned T'Prynn and her legal counsel back to the courtroom.

She gave no thought to the audience in the gallery of seats behind her, or to the prosecutor at the table parallel to hers. All her attention was on the raised bench at the front of the room, where three empty seats awaited their occupants. Red UFP flags adorned with white stars stood at either end of the bench, in front of which was a single chair whose armrest was equipped with a biometric sensor. Next to the judges' bench was a computer interface that served as the court's recorder and its link to the station's library computer.

T'Prynn dress uniform was stiff and unyielding.

At her side was her defense counsel, Lieutenant Holly Moyer. The redhead whispered to T'Prynn, "I hate this part."

There did not seem to be any need to respond to Moyer's expression of personal anxiety, so T'Prynn remained silent.

A boatswain's whistle announced the arrival of the judges. Admiral Nogura was the first to enter. The trim, gray-haired flag officer was followed by Captain Desai and Captain Atish Khatami of the *Endeavour*.

Khatami was a tall woman with olive skin, raven hair, and exquisite features. For T'Prynn, the opportunity to spend the weeks of the trial clandestinely admiring Khatami's beauty had provided a welcome distraction from the proceedings, whose outcome she had assumed from the beginning was foregone.

The judges stood behind their chairs and waited while a female Rigellian ensign entered the courtroom, walked to the recording computer, and activated it. When the ensign nodded, Nogura pulled back his chair and sat down, and Khatami and Desai did the same. Once they had settled, Nogura picked up a wooden striker and rang an ancient ship's bell atop the bench to call the proceedings to order.

"Lieutenant Commander T'Prynn," Nogura said. "Despite your plea of no contest to the charges brought against you, the number and importance of the mitigating factors you and your counsel have introduced since your arrest on Golmira have made the adjudication of your case somewhat . . . complicated.

"First, as I'm sure you've been informed by counsel, Starfleet's Judge Advocate General has declined to prosecute your civilian companion, Timothy Pennington. While this board might not agree with the JAG's decision, we have taken its leniency toward Mister Pennington into account during our deliberations.

"Second, having reviewed your unexpurgated medical file, including its most recent entries by Doctor Jabilo M'Benga, which detail the nature of the unusual mental affliction from which you suffered for more than five decades, this court agrees with your counsel that you were acting in a state of diminished capacity at the time of the events for which you stand accused.

"Third, because the information you gathered regarding criminal organizations operating in the Taurus Reach has proved to be accurate and strategically useful, and because you risked your safety and your life to aid in the rescue of Starfleet covert operatives on Golmira, this board has given serious consideration to your counsel's petition for leniency."

Nogura frowned, then sighed. "Unfortunately, as heroic and useful as many of your actions over the past year might be, none of them is sufficient to excuse the criminal actions of which you stand accused. It would be a grave threat to discipline if we were simply to expunge your record as a reward for your decision to engage in rogue intelligence activities."

The admiral looked first to Khatami then to Desai, who both responded with grave nods. He looked back at T'Prynn. "This board has reached its unanimous verdict," he said. "Are you ready to hear its decision?"

T'Prynn held her chin up. "I am, Your Honor."

"On the charge and specifications of unlawfully tampering with official Starfleet medical records, this court finds Lieutenant Commander T'Prynn guilty.

"On the charge and specifications of willfully making fraudulent statements under oath, this court finds Lieutenant Commander T'Prynn guilty.

"On the charge and specifications of going absent without leave, this court finds Lieutenant Commander T'Prynn guilty.

"On the charge and specifications of fleeing Starfleet prosecution, this court finds Lieutenant Commander T'Prynn guilty.

"On the charge and specifications of dereliction of duty, this court finds Lieutenant Commander T'Prynn . . . not guilty."

A pall descended on the courtroom. No one spoke for several seconds. The only sounds were muted clicks and beeps from the recording computer.

Folding his hands, Nogura asked, "Do you wish to make any statement before this court issues its sentencing decision?"

T'Prynn remained at attention. "No, Your Honor."

"Very well," he said. "Lieutenant Commander T'Prynn, it is the ruling of this court that you be immediately reduced two grades in rank, to lieutenant, junior grade. Your security clearance is reduced to level two. Two official reprimands will be entered into your official Starfleet record—one for tampering with your medical file, the other for going AWOL.

"Furthermore, you will be placed on disciplinary probation for a period of five years. During this probation, you will be barred from advancing in rank and from any increase in your security clearance. If, during your probation, you incur so much as a reprimand, you will be subject to a summary dishonorable discharge from Starfleet service, as well as imprisonment.

"Do you understand the terms of your sentence, Lieutenant?"

"Yes, sir," T'Prynn replied.

"Do you wish to challenge the verdict or sentence of this court?"

"No, sir."

Nogura picked up his striker. "Then these proceedings are closed, and this court stands adjourned." The admiral tapped the bell, then stood from his chair. Khatami and Desai got up with him, and together the court-martial board exited the courtroom.

Lieutenant Moyer looked thunderstruck. "I can't believe it," she muttered. Grinning, the young redhead turned toward T'Prynn. "We did it! Congratulations!"

"Thank you, sir," T'Prynn said. Facing the empty bench, she realized she had done exactly what she had set out to do.

Now all she had to do was live with it.

55

"I just wanted to congratulate you on staying out of jail," Pennington said as he and T'Prynn strolled along a path through Fontana Meadow in Vanguard's enormous terrestrial enclosure.

"It would be more appropriate to commend my legal counsel," T'Prynn said, missing the gist of his sentiment as Vulcans so often did. "Her labor secured my relatively light sentence."

Pennington sighed. "I simply meant that your plan to work your way back into Starfleet's good graces was a success."

"True. Though I might not have succeeded without your help." With a sidelong look she added, "I am in your debt, Tim."

He reacted with mild surprise. "I think that's the first time I've ever heard you call me by my first name."

She arched an eyebrow. "Indeed."

They passed by a cluster of off-duty Starfleet personnel playing soccer on one of the lawns near the buildings of Stars Landing. Two men, a brawny human and a lanky Vulcan, stutter-stepped around the black-and-white-checkered ball, vying for control until the Vulcan seized possession and broke away on a charge toward his opponents' goal, trailed by the other players.

T'Prynn asked, "So, will you be staying on Vanguard now that Starfleet has dropped its charges against you?"

"For a while. I just signed a lease on a new apartment." Searching the Vulcan woman's face for any hint of what might be going on under its surface, he asked, "And you?"

"My successor, Commander ch'Nayla, has requested I remain on Vanguard under his supervision," she said. "I am not permitted to share any details beyond that."

Pennington nodded. "I understand."

They stopped in front of the meadow's ornate fountain. High above their heads, its towering plume of water dispersed and became a fine mist that bent the enclosure's ersatz daylight into a rainbow. The cool spray kissed Pennington's face as it fell to the ground, drawn by the pull of artificial gravity.

He sensed T'Prynn was hesitating to say something, but he waited for her to find the right words in her own time. After several seconds, she turned halfway toward him. "Tim . . . my superiors would like to know how much of our shared experience from the past year will be appearing in your future published writings."

It was not an unexpected question.

"None of it," he said.

She looked perplexed. "I do not understand. You are not sworn to secrecy, and as a civilian you have the right to speak and publish freely. Why suppress such information now?"

He tucked his hands in his pockets and smiled at her.

"Call it a wedding present."

56

Where did this year go?

That question nagged at Dr. Ezekiel Fisher as he went about his evening routine. In a few days he would turn another page on the calendar and mark the passing of another cycle of time.

And take another step toward death, he brooded.

Morbid thoughts plagued him with increasing frequency now that he was alone on the station.

Diego Reyes was more than a year gone; his service record had listed him as dead until a recent report from T'Prynn upgraded his status to missing in action.

It had been almost as long since Ambassador Jetanien had departed the station on an indefinite leave of absence. Though the Chelon was normally talkative to a fault, he had been adamantly secretive about his destination and his reasons for leaving. Fisher had never been close with Jetanien, but they had shared a bond because of their mutual friendship with Diego.

Most cutting of all was the absence of Fisher's pseudo-protégé and former attending physician, Dr. Jabilo M'Benga. Despite knowing for more than a year that the young doctor had requested a transfer to starship duty, it still had filled Fisher with disappointment when he'd heard M'Benga wouldn't be coming back.

Onward and upward, he reminded himself as he downloaded that day's personal mail to his data slate.

While the handheld device retrieved his electronic correspondence from the station's computers, he sauntered into his kitchen nook and poured hot water from an old-fashioned kettle into a mug he had prepared with a few tablespoons of cocoa mix.

Tendrils of vapor twisted up from the rich, creamy beverage. A soft beep from the data slate confirmed he had new messages waiting to be read.

It was the usual smattering of crap: solicitations to consider starting a private practice on one backwater rock or another; newsletters from various medical journals to which he subscribed, or from associations he had been foolish enough in his youth to join; a reminder that his sixty-fifth high-school reunion was coming up; a letter from some young know-it-all who had found a picayune error in one of Fisher's old journal articles and just had to bray about it, not realizing Fisher himself had publicly corrected that same error a decade ago; and so it went.

Then he saw it, the grain of wheat hidden in the chaff: a new message from Jabilo. Fisher smiled. *Speak of the devil.*

He carried his cocoa to the main room of his quarters, settled onto the sofa, and rested his feet on his coffee table as he started reading the welcome missive.

> Dear Zeke,
>
>   I meant to drop you a line sooner, but the last several months have been jam-packed with vintage Starfleet SNAFUS.
>
>   First, in January they recalled me to Earth from Vulcan because they said they had a starship billet for me. Well, it was the same old Starfleet story: "Hurry up and wait." I hopped a ride back to Earth on a frigate called the *Tremina*, but when I checked in at Starfleet Medical in February, they said the billet was already filled.
>
>   So guess what they did next?
>
>   They sent me back to Vulcan.
>
>   I got the impression I might be there a while, so at the end of March I accepted a medical-research position at the Vulcan Science Academy.
>
>   Don't fall asleep on me, old man. This is where the story gets interesting.

In June the *Enterprise* made a port call on
Vulcan. Around the same time, there was a rash of
homicides inside the Vulcan Academy Hospital. It
was a huge scandal. I'm sure you read all about it on
the newsfeeds.

In July I was asked to ship out with a Vulcan
medical team that was helping the *Enterprise* crew
treat a plague outbreak on the Vulcan colony of
Nisus. I won't bore you with the details of how we
ended up containing the outbreak; you can download
the official report from the Starfleet Medical
database.

The upshot is that between the homicide
investigation and the mission to Nisus, I made a
strong impression on the *Enterprise*'s new CMO,
Leonard McCoy. He made a formal request to
Starfleet Command to have me transferred to the
Enterprise, ASAP.

Naturally, I was then sent back to Vulcan and
told that McCoy's request would be "processed with
all due haste."

That was in August. By October I'd given up all
hope of seeing the inside of the *Enterprise* ever
again.

Skip ahead to mid-November. Some admiral
wakes me up one morning at oh-dark-thirty and tells
me to pack my gear and get on a fast-warp transport
RFN, no questions asked.

Seventy-two hours later, I'm on Coridan. Turns
out Ambassador Sarek of Vulcan had suffered a
cardiac failure while en route to the Babel
Conference. By the time I arrived the matter had
been dealt with, but I guess nearly losing a VIP
during a major diplomatic mission finally convinced
Starfleet Command that having a Vulcan-medicine

specialist on the *Enterprise* might not be such a bad idea, after all.

Talk about fortuitous timing: a little more than two weeks after I joined *Enterprise*'s medical staff, its half-Vulcan first officer, Commander Spock, got himself shot in the chest by a primitive projectile weapon during a landing mission. It was a close call, but he pulled through.

In many respects, Commander Spock is a remarkable individual. And just between us ol' sawbones, I think one of the nurses is hopelessly in love with him. I'd give her some advice if I wasn't having so much fun watching her make a fool of herself.

Anyway, it's time for me to cut this short. We're in some kind of mad hurry to get to Deep Space Station K-7 all of a sudden. If this turns out to be anything interesting, I'll send you an update as soon as I'm able.

And believe it or not, I do miss you and the rest of the team at Vanguard Hospital—but nothing compares with being out here on a starship, seeing the galaxy with my own eyes. Every day proves the old cliché is true: wonders never cease.

Be well, Zeke. I'll keep you in my thoughts.

Your friend,
Jabilo

Fisher set the data slate on the coffee table and exhaled a deep and tired breath. He was happy for Jabilo, but the younger man's *joie de vivre* only made Fisher more aware of how much his own appetite for life was waning with age.

For the hundredth time that day he flirted with the notion of tendering his resignation with immediate effect. After all, wha was holding him on Vanguard? What was there for him to do that some younger surgeon with a security clearance couldn't do better? Why go on bearing the burden of dire secrets?

You know why, you old coot, he admonished himself. *You made a promise.*

He had told Diego he would look after Rana Desai, that he would be a friend to her in Diego's absence. She was the only person on the station who loved Diego more than Fisher did. For her sake he would stifle his complaints and play the part of the stoic. As long as she stayed on the station, so would he.

Lord help us, he mused with bittersweet humor, *the things we do for love's austere and lonely offices.*

57

T'Prynn stood alone on the stage, the fingers of her right hand barely grazing the keys of the piano.

It had been more than an hour since the last of the club's patrons had been shown the door by Manón, its exotically beautiful alien proprietor. Now that the after-hours cleanup was finished, Manón shooed her employees out of the cabaret.

Transfixed by the details of the baby grand piano—the shine of its polished keyboard, the subtle scratches in its lacquered frame, the reflections of the stage lights on its propped-open lid—T'Prynn only half-listened as Manón closed and locked the club's front door. She remained still, gazing at the bars of black and white beneath her hand as she listened to Manón's footsteps echoing in the empty dining room.

"Everyone's out," Manón said. The elegantly dressed woman's coif of multicolored hair was styled in a helix that curved from her left temple to the back of her right shoulder. Looking up at T'Prynn with her emerald-green, almond-shaped eyes, she asked, "Would you like me to bring you some tea?"

"No, thank you. That will not be necessary."

Manón replied, "All right. Turn off the stage lights after you finish. The back door will lock behind you on your way out."

T'Prynn nodded. "I will. Thank you for your hospitality."

"It's my pleasure. Call it a welcome-home gift." At that, the pale-skinned alien woman slipped away and exited to the kitchen, leaving T'Prynn to face the piano in solitude.

She pulled back the bench a few centimeters and sat down. Placed her hands over the keys. Tried to find her way back to a melody, to a starting point.

There was only silence.

Moving with trepidation, she plunked out one flat note. The sound of it was jarring to her ear. For the first time in her life the instrument felt alien to her. Distant. Unknown.

I remember the notes, she assured herself. *I know the songs.* Forcing her hands to work from rote memory, she pressed them into service. She struck all the notes in the right order, but it was a struggle to find the grace in them, to feel the attack in the keys, to hear the sustain in the chords.

The melody had become hollow. Empty.

There was no beauty in the music.

She let her hands fall from the keyboard and rest at her sides. Her mind was quiet, her thoughts calm and ordered.

For fifty-three years the *katra* of her dead fiancé Sten, whom she had slain in the heat of the *kal-if-fee* to escape an arranged marriage, had haunted her mind. He had brought her nothing but pain and madness. His psychic attacks had clouded her logic and inflamed her passions, eroded her control and dulled her conscience. It had taken her total, public collapse to expose her affliction and deliver her into the hands of Dr. M'Benga and the mystics of her childhood home in Kren'than, with whose help she'd finally cast out Sten's malevolent spiritual essence.

Free of Sten's torments she no longer felt any temptation to succumb to base emotions, but she also no longer felt the sweet stirrings of music. Her emotional equilibrium had been purchased at the cost of her only artistic gift.

T'Prynn closed the keyboard cover. Pushed back the bench. Smoothed the front of her red uniform minidress as she stood. Drew a slow, deep breath and let it go.

She thought of all she had sacrificed in the name of duty and self-preservation: her lover, her sanity, her career. If the price of her repentance had to be the loss of her music, she was hardly entitled to protest.

So be it.

Bidding a silent farewell to her muse, T'Prynn turned her back on the piano. Then she stepped off the stage and back into the shadows, where she belonged.

58

December 29, 2267

Abandoning the most boring staff meeting of his life, Admiral Heihachiro Nogura quick-stepped out of his office into Vanguard's operations center. A shrill Yellow Alert klaxon whooped once in the normally hushed circular compartment.

Nogura hurried up the stairs to the supervisors' deck. "Commander Cooper," he called out, announcing his arrival. "Sitrep."

Cooper looked up from the Hub. "Sorry to interrupt your meeting, Admiral, but we've picked up an armed Orion merchantman on approach. Bearing three-eight mark five, range one million kilometers." Dropping his voice as Nogura drew near, Cooper added, "It's Ganz's ship, sir—the *Omari-Ekon*."

"Give him credit for having a pair," Nogura said. "I told him if he ever came back I'd put a hole in his ship, and I meant it. Raise shields, arm and lock all phaser banks, and order *Endeavour* to stand by for rapid deployment, just in case."

"Aye, sir," said Cooper, who turned and swiftly relayed the admiral's commands to a team of junior officers.

On the lower level of the operations center, the station's other senior personnel filed out of Nogura's office. Jackson, Desai, and ch'Nayla followed Nogura up to the supervisors' deck, while chief engineer Isaiah Farber commandeered a science-purposed workstation for his use.

Ambassador Akeylah Karumé—a striking, colorfully attired, ebony-skinned human woman who had temporarily been promoted into Jetanien's role as Vanguard's senior diplomat—

seemed content to remain removed from what was transpiring around her. She walked to an open area of the operations level between the supervisors' deck and the enormous wraparound viewscreen that dominated the high, curving bulkheads.

For the moment, the center viewscreen displayed an image of Ganz's ship, which was cruising directly toward Vanguard.

Nogura was impatient to know what the hell Ganz was doing. "Hail them," he said, and Cooper delegated the task to the senior communications officer, Lieutenant Judy Dunbar.

The curly-haired brunette started to key the command into her console but stopped. "Admiral," she said, "the *Omari-Ekon* is already hailing us." She swiveled her chair to face Nogura. "It's Mister Ganz, sir. He's asking to speak directly with you."

Looking at his senior staff to gauge their responses, he was met by a series of near-identical wide-eyed stares. He frowned. "Put him on-screen."

Buttons were pushed, and one of the center's three massive screens was filled with the dark green face of the locally notorious Orion crime lord, Ganz. He flashed a smile of immaculate white teeth. *"Admiral,"* he said. *"There's no need for you to aim weapons at my ship. Our shields are down, and our weapons are not charged. We come in peace."*

"You shouldn't have come at all," Nogura said. "I warned you what would happen if you brought your traveling crime spree back into my jurisdiction."

Ganz lifted his broad, thick-fingered hands in a gesture of mock surrender. *"Let's not resort to threats when I've gone to the trouble of bringing you a peace offering."*

Intrigued, Nogura lifted one eyebrow. "And what might that be?"

The burly Orion gestured to someone off-screen. He leaned to his right, out of frame, and returned holding up his hand.

Resting in his palm was a perfectly clear, twelve-sided crystal roughly the size of a human skull. It was identical to the Mirdonyae Artifact, except it appeared to be empty.

"I believe you already have one like it," Ganz said. *"But I hear you might be interested in acquiring another."*

Nogura was so livid he could barely move. When he tried to speak, his jaw felt as if it were wired shut with anger. Recovering his composure, he asked in a tense, low voice, "Where did you get that?"

His question broadened Ganz's grin. *"That,"* said the crime boss, *"sounds like an invitation to begin negotiating my ship's return to a semipermanent docking slip on your starbase."*

"The hell it is," Nogura said. "I'm not going to let you dictate terms to me, Mister Ganz. If you want to discuss financial remuneration for your discovery, fine. But if you think that hunk of rock gives you some license to—"

"Oh, for God's sake," grumbled someone on Ganz's ship who shouldered his way into the frame beside the crime lord. The angle of the transmission adjusted to compensate for the new visual subject, and Nogura's iron jaw went slack as he saw who was standing beside Ganz.

Diego Reyes scowled at Nogura and said over the comm, *"He already knows you have standing orders to acquire anything and everything related to the Shedai, and at all costs, so cut the shit and just make a deal with him already."*

Nogura coped with his surprise by mustering a thin, taut smile. "Well," he said to Reyes, "this is certainly going to make things more interesting."

Then he heard Lieutenant Jackson whisper to Captain Desai, "I think you owe me dinner."

59

Ming Xiong lowered the second artifact onto a new octagonal interface pad inside the Vault's central experiment chamber. Even through the gloves of his hazmat suit, he could feel the icy coldness of the crystal polyhedron.

"Stand by to patch in the baryonic array," he said to Dr. Marcus, who was in the chamber with him and also garbed in bright yellow hazmat gear. Their voices sounded flat and mechanical through their suits' external speakers.

She checked the new interface's connections to the lab's consoles and then gave him a thumbs-up. "All set."

He checked the readings on the command console for the second artifact's interface. "Looks good so far," he said. "Let's connect the chroniton gauge."

Though he was trying to stay focused on their checklist of tasks, he felt the weight of two dozen pairs of eyes staring at him and Marcus while they worked. The delivery of the first artifact's empty twin—by a Tholian expatriate named Ezthene traveling on Ganz's ship, no less—had set the lab abuzz with rumor. Xiong was hardly immune to gossip's pull; he was just waiting for the right moment to ask Dr. Marcus what she'd heard.

That moment seemed as opportune as any other.

"Is it true Diego Reyes is on Ganz's ship?" he asked.

Marcus scowled at him from behind a fall of her blond hair. "Keep your voice down," she said. Whispering, she continued, "Yes, it's true."

Xiong echoed her hushed tone. "Then why isn't he back in custody?"

"Apparently, as long as he stays on the *Omari-Ekon*, he's outside Starfleet's jurisdiction." She flipped some switches, and a few more indicators on the interface panel turned green. "What's next on the list?"

"Tachyon scanner," Xiong said. "It should be on bus three." As Marcus verified the connection, he lowered his voice again and asked, "If Ganz's ship is docked here, how can it be out of our jurisdiction?"

"Because the Federation has no extradition treaty with Orion," Marcus replied. "Interstellar law gives Ganz the right to grant Reyes asylum aboard his ship, and that's exactly what he's done. As long as Reyes doesn't set foot on the station, Nogura can't touch him."

Shaking his head, Xiong said, "That's ridiculous."

"It's the law."

"The two aren't mutually exclusive."

Closing the lower half of the pedestal's access panel, Marcus said, "All set here. How's the board?"

"Green lights all the way," Xiong said. "Ready to release the safeties and bring main power online, on your order."

"Let's do it," Marcus said. She stepped around the pedestal to stand beside the young anthropology-and-archaeology officer. "I think we should run a full range of material tests. Since this artifact is empty, we might be able to get a clearer picture of its composition and internal structure."

"Sure," Xiong said as he began connecting the new pedestal to the Vault's primary power grid. "I also want a look at its ambient energy signature. Having an empty artifact will let us make some baseline measurements that might tell us all kinds of things about the Mirdonyae crystal." He sighed. "I just wish we could get Ganz to tell us where he got this thing. Until we find out where these things come from, we're no closer to solving the riddle of who made them or why."

Marcus gave him a comforting pat on the shoulder. "All in good time," she said. "Right now, this new artifact is a gift. Let's appreciate it for what it is instead of cursing it for what it's not."

She threw an encouraging smile Xiong's way. "Besides, sooner or later Ganz will need another favor from Nogura. When that happens, I suspect he'll use the origin of these crystals as a bargaining chip."

Xiong smiled and nodded in agreement. "It wouldn't surprise me in the least." He entered the final sequence of commands for activating the new interface. "Taking the last safety offline now. Main power is up and steady."

"All systems appear nominal," Marcus said. "Let's go ditch these canary suits."

"Roger that," he said, following her to the airlock and radiation-containment portal for the experiment chamber.

A few minutes later they had stowed their hazmat suits in the equipment room. Xiong smoothed his blue uniform tunic while Marcus pulled her white lab coat back on. There was a tiny glint of mania in her eyes as she asked, "Ready to see what our new prize can do?"

"I can hardly wait," Xiong said.

They returned to the main area of the lab and situated themselves behind a transparent safety barrier set back from the experiment chamber. "First," Marcus said, pushing buttons and flipping switches, "let's see if it reacts when we apply power to the Mirdonyae artifact." She turned a dial and fed a stream of charged particles into the original artifact, which pulsed with eldritch light only a few meters from its inert twin.

"Nothing so far," Xiong said.

"All right. Sending power to the second artifact . . ."

For one brief moment the new polyhedron was surrounded by a golden halo, and the first artifact's aura of fear melted away.

Then the Red Alert klaxon wailed, and all Hell broke loose.

60

The first wail of the Red Alert klaxon was still fresh in Nogura's ears as a thunderous jolt knocked him from his chair and left him wearing most of his cup of hot tea.

He was halfway back to his feet and scrambling toward the door to the operations center when another jarring impact dropped him back to the floor.

More concussions rocked the station as he stumbled out his door and waded into the circle of barely restrained panic outside. He shouted to his XO, "Cooper! Report!"

Hanging onto the Hub with both hands as the deck pitched in response to the continuing attack, Cooper yelled back, "We can't get a lock on who's attacking us! All we've got are shield failures and inertial damper over—"

A new alarm cut him off. He flipped switches on the Hub as Nogura ran up the stairs to the supervisor's deck, and looked up as the admiral joined him. "Hull breach," Cooper said. "Main docking bay. We're venting atmosphere!"

"Put it on screen two," Nogura said.

The display on Nogura's left snapped to a view of the interior of Vanguard's main docking bay. An ugly rent had been torn in the thick gray hull, and a storm of loose debris was tumbling through the zero-*g* environment toward the core of the station. Chunks of broken and twisted duranium caromed off the hull of the docked *U.S.S. Buenos Aires*.

Pushing its way through the ragged gap in the hull was an amorphous dark mass. It moved like a fluid and spread through the docking bay like a black bloodstain. Tentacles shimmering with violet motes of energy sprouted from it and lashed out at anything in their path—automated repair robots, manned work-pods, industrial scaffolding mounted on the bay's ceiling.

A Shedai was attacking Vanguard.

The Wanderer felt the abomination's presence. She had followed its sickly emanations across a vast expanse, waiting for the *Telinaruul* to return to normal space-time so she could assess their vulnerability.

A hollow shell in the darkness. Apparently that was all the arrogant little sparks needed to make themselves feel safe. It was a flimsy construct, hardly equal to her fury.

She pierced its tender skin with ease.

Inside she found air surrounding a narrow shaft. Though the signal from the abomination was muffled, it was not silenced. *The* Telinaruul *must not be allowed to tamper with it any longer,* she decided. Forging ahead toward the structure's core, her intention was resolved. *This place must be destroyed.*

Captain Atish Khatami stared in horror at *Endeavour*'s viewscreen as the Shedai intruder smashed a wedge off the primary hull of the *Buenos Aires*.

"McCormack, arm phasers," Khatami said.

Her first officer, Lieutenant Commander Katherine Stano, snapped at the navigator, "Belay that!" To the captain she added, "You can't fire phasers inside a docking bay!"

"I'm not letting that thing on the station without a fight," Khatami replied. "I've got a clear shot, and I'm taking it." Leaning forward from the command chair, she said to Lieutenant McCormack, "Marielise, arm and lock phasers, *now.*"

The strawberry-blonde junior officer threw an apologetic look at Stano and keyed in the commands. "Armed and locked."

"Fire!"

Blue streaks of phaser energy lanced out across Vanguard's docking bay and struck the Shedai several times in its center of mass. The creature slowed for a moment, then crackled with energy and renewed its headlong plunge into the station's core.

"No effect, Captain," reported McCormack.

Khatami swiveled her chair toward her science officer. "Klisiewicz! Any idea how to stop that thing?"

The dark-haired young man looked up from his sensor display and frowned as he shook his head. "None, sir. It's tearing through the station like it's made of paper."

From the aft quarter of the bridge, communications officer Hector Estrada interjected, "Captain! Vanguard control just issued an evacuation order."

"Docking bay doors are opening," reported McCormack.

Facing forward, Khatami said to her helmsman, "Neelakanta, clear all moorings and take us out, full thrusters. If this station goes boom, we don't want to be here when it happens."

A black blade was cutting its way to the heart of the station.

Haniff Jackson had never seen anything like it. The entity moved like liquid and sliced through decks and bulkheads with ease, leaving shredded metal and sparking power conduits in its wake. On every surface it touched, it left a residue that looked like dirty ice and spread like mold. Everything shook violently.

He flipped open his communicator. "Jackson to ops! Evac core sections nine through fifteen on all levels, now!"

"Copy that," replied Commander Cooper. *"Evac in progress."*

Running footsteps announced the arrival of his backup, but he feared it would be too little, too late. "Set phasers to full power, narrow beam," he commanded the five security guards. He lifted his own phaser and aimed at the iridescent surge of dark matter blocking the corridor ahead. "Fire on my mark! Three . . ."

As quickly as the creature had appeared through one bulkhead, it vanished through another, leaving only the empty tunnel it had bored through the station's infrastructure. Wind rushed past Jackson with a great roar, and the escaping air carried tiny bits of debris back the way the entity had come.

He lifted his communicator and said, "Ops, this is Jackson! We're venting atmosphere into the docking bay!"

"Roger that," Cooper said, sounding distracted. *"We're on it. Stay after the intruder."*

"Acknowledged," Jackson said. He waved for the security team to follow him as he charged through a gap in a bulkhead to pursue the invading entity, but he didn't know how they would catch it, considering the rate at which it was moving.

A minute later he realized they had no chance of catching it at all. They reached the end of the creature's tunnel through the core. It opened into the station's central matériel-transfer conduit, an enormous circular shaft that reached from just below the operations center at its apex to just above the main sensor dish at its nadir. Peering cautiously over the edge into the vertiginous abyss, Jackson could barely see the intruder's black mass making its rapid, unchallenged descent.

"Ops, the creature is inside the transfer conduit," he said into his communicator. "And you'd better warn the folks in the Vault to get outta there—because it's coming right at 'em."

"Everyone out!" shouted Carol Marcus, herding her team of scientists toward the Vault's three emergency exits, in a moment that seemed all too familiar. "Move it! On the double, folks!"

Horrendous booms of impact were followed by the shrieks and groans of wrenched metal. Each second it drew closer.

The lab's overhead lights flickered erratically. Red warning lights flashed on every bulkhead, and gratingly nasal alarms split the air. Marcus tried to keep a running head count as her people hurried past her, but with bodies moving in three different directions there was no way she could keep up.

But she only had to be able to count to one.

One person had ignored the evacuation order and was still standing at a command console, feeding in data and activating systems inside the experiment chamber: Ming Xiong.

Marcus forced her way through a cluster of running bodies

then ran to Ming's side and yanked hard on his sleeve. "Do you have a death wish or something?"

He twisted free of her grip. "I'm playing a hunch," he said, never taking his eyes from his work. "Go without me."

She looked around the room at the exits. The rest of her people were out and moving to safety. Only she and Xiong were left in the Vault, which quaked beneath a steady cadence of hammering blows that sounded as if they were right outside.

"At least tell me what you're doing," Marcus pleaded.

"Setting a trap," Xiong said. With a dubious tilt of his head he added, "I hope."

Something struck one of the Vault's outer barriers with a crash of thunder, and an interior metal bulkhead fractured. Panels and monitors on that wall cracked and sprayed sparks across the room. A steady cannonade of impacts followed.

Moving to an adjacent control panel, Marcus shouted over the din, "What can I do to help?"

"No time to explain," he said. "Just do what I say."

She nodded. "Okay, go."

"Patch in the data sequence from Gek's terminal," Xiong said as he dashed to a different panel and continued entering commands. "Then route all power from the first artifact's reserve cell to the new artifact."

Marcus worked as quickly as she could, and Xiong kept moving from one scientist's terminal to another, apparently trying to slave them all to some arcane task.

As she completed her first two instructions, the inner bulkhead began to buckle inward from a steady brute-force assault. Over the cacophony she called to Xiong, "Done!"

"Last step!" he yelled back. "Lower the safety barrier! I'll get set to open the main power relay!"

Despite her every survival instinct telling her not to do as Xiong had asked, Marcus keyed her override code into the Vault's command console and entered the instruction to lower all the transparent safety panels around the two artifacts.

As the monolithic slabs of transparent steel retracted into the deck, Xiong jogged toward the old-style toggle that served as the manual override for the lab's main power relay.

He got halfway to the switch before the Shedai smashed through the wall in a blur of obsidian liquid surrounded by arcing bolts of electricity.

Xiong drew a phaser and aimed at the creature. It spawned a tentacle that swatted the weapon from his hand.

The phaser skittered across the deck and slid past Marcus. She dived after it.

A flurry of slender tendrils lashed out from the Shedai and struck at Xiong like cobras. He dodged one, ducked another, then plucked a length of broken pipe from the floor and parried the monster's third stabbing assault.

Marcus scuttled across the floor. Scooped up the phaser. Fired it on full power at the Shedai.

The shot did no damage, but it seemed to draw most of the creature's attention toward her. It reared up to attack.

Xiong took a short running start and somersaulted over its back. He rolled across the floor.

The creature spun toward him, forgetting Marcus.

Its tentacles coiled and sprang at Xiong.

He closed his hands around the power-relay toggle and pulled. With a loud clack it snapped shut.

Power surged through the lab—and into the empty artifact.

A burst of light overwhelmed Marcus, and in that moment of white blindness she heard the most terrible screech of torment.

Her vision returned, but all she could see was a painfully bright storm of light and fury. The creature flailed wildly as it was pulled toward the empty artifact, which blazed like a miniature sun. The Vault was filled with an unearthly wailing, a cry of terror and agony that Marcus was sure would haunt her nightmares for the rest of her life.

Then there was darkness . . . and silence.

Dust and smoke lingered in the half light.

Marcus wandered toward the open experimental chamber. As

she arrived at its edge, Xiong joined her. They stood together, staring slack-jawed with equal parts wonder and horror.

They now had two identical glowing artifacts.

Two magenta-hued polyhedrons radiating rage and fear.

A whistling alert signaled an incoming comm. *"Doctor Marcus or Lieutenant Xiong, this is Admiral Nogura. What is your status? Is the Vault secure? Please respond."*

Marcus was transfixed by the unearthly glow of the two artifacts. She mumbled to Xiong, "You take it."

With apparent effort, Xiong tore himself away from the twin crystals and pressed a button to open a reply channel. "Admiral, this is Lieutenant Xiong. The Vault is secure."

"What happened down there, Lieutenant?"

There was an unmistakable note of pride in Xiong's voice.

"Admiral . . . we've captured the Shedai intruder."

The Saga of

STAR TREK®
VANGUARD

Will Continue

ACKNOWLEDGMENTS

As ever, my first thanks belong to my wife, Kara, whose hard work and patience made it possible for me to leave my old life of "day job plus writing" so that I might become an honest-to-goodness full-time writer.

Because the *Star Trek: Vanguard* saga began with editor Marco Palmieri, it is only fitting to thank him for letting me help him bring it to life; and because Margaret Clark is the editor who now keeps the saga's flame alive, I am equally grateful to her for her support and guidance.

In *Precipice* I have built once again on the contributions of fellow authors Dayton Ward and Kevin Dilmore, whose book *Open Secrets* set the stage for this tale. Thanks for pushing me to keep up, guys.

A tip o' the hat is also due to the men whose visuals have consistently inspired my vision of this series: Masao Okazaki, the designer of Starbase 47 and the *U.S.S. Sagittarius*; and digital wizard Doug Drexler, who brings great wireframes to life as breathtaking cover art.

Last but not least, I offer my gratitude to two resources that help me keep my continuity straight: http://memory-alpha.org and http://memory-beta.wikia.com.

Until next time, thanks for reading!

ABOUT THE AUTHOR

David Mack is the bestselling author of more than a dozen novels, including *Wildfire, Harbinger, Reap the Whirlwind, Road of Bones, Promises Broken,* and the *Star Trek: Destiny* trilogy: *Gods of Night, Mere Mortals,* and *Lost Souls.* He developed the *Star Trek: Vanguard* series concept with editor Marco Palmieri.

His first work of original fiction is the acclaimed supernatural thriller *The Calling.*

In addition to novels, Mack's writing credits span several media, including television (for episodes of *Star Trek: Deep Space Nine*), film, short fiction, magazines, newspapers, comic books, computer games, radio, and the Internet.

Mack's upcoming novels include a new, expanded edition of *Star Trek Mirror Universe: The Sorrows of Empire*; *Zero Sum Game,* part of the *Star Trek: Typhon Pact* miniseries; and *More Beautiful Than Death*, an adventure based on the 2009 feature film *Star Trek.*

He currently resides in New York City with his wife, Kara.

Visit his official site: www.davidmack.pro